THE BERLIN ENDING

THE
BERLIN
ENDING

A Novel of Discovery
by
HOWARD HUNT

G. P. Putnam's Sons
New York

TO MY BELOVED WIFE, DOROTHY.

Twenty-three years, three months and one day

It is in the political agent's interest to betray all the parties who use him and to work for them all at the same time, so that he may move freely and penetrate everywhere.

—GALTIER-BOISSIÈRE

THE BERLIN ENDING

1

WHEN the shuttle plane from New York reached Washington, a man left the stream of passengers and headed for the Valet Parking phone. He repeated his ticket number to the dispatcher, bought an evening paper and hailed a skycap. Claim check in hand, the skycap said, "What's it look like? Big or small?"

"About a yard square and thin. Sort of black plastic envelope for architect's drawings. My name's on it—Neal Thorpe. Car's a green Thunderbird with District plates. See you at the Eastern exit."

He climbed the stairs slowly, glancing at the headline, the lead stories; then he was outside going down the sloping ramp, where flakes like lazy moths touched the side of his face and melted almost on contact. New York had been dry and cool, but Washington in early spring was treacherous.

Around him people were waiting under the overhang, protected from the light snowfall, the splash of slush from the wheels of circling cars. There were no taxis—a strike was in progress—and only a few limousines, their seats sharply contested by arrivals growing increasingly desperate over the lack of District-bound transportation.

After a while Thorpe stopped his arriving car, waited for it to near the curb and stepped out, newspaper over his head. He surrendered his parking check and tipped the driver, got behind the wheel and looked around. No sign of his skycap. Horns behind

1

prodded him ahead, and he joined the carrousel of vehicles inching four abreast around the airport's frontal zone.

Windshield wipers moved sluggishly under the accumulation of wet snow, blurring his vision. The first circuit around the circular traffic divider took nearly ten minutes and still no skycap. But two large buses had arrived and were embarking passengers, blocking the road. Thorpe let the Thunderbird idle until the buses moved on, slush spraying like dirty plumes from a liner's wake. Glancing back through the thin screen of sleet, he saw that the waiting area was nearly deserted. There was an elderly couple and, a few yards away, a girl. He lingered, hoping the skycap would appear, but no blue uniform was visible. A car pulled to the curb and boarded the waiting couple. That left only the girl.

As he moved on, he drew even with the girl, clearly visible under the overhead lights.

She was wearing a knee-length Afghan herdsman's coat of sheepskin dyed gray and decorated with colored embroidery. She wore white boots, and her cream colored suitcase and cosmetic box looked new and expensive.

But it was her face he studied until forward progress blocked her from sight. Oval, it showed high cheekbones, a snub nose and pale-white skin. Her dark hair was parted at the crown and fell below the shoulders, dividing to frame her face. She was, he thought, somewhere between nineteen and, say, twenty-three. Then he concentrated on the taillights ahead and made another weary circuit that brought him back in five minutes to the waiting skycap.

Thorpe pulled over to the curb and opened the far door. The skycap fitted the drawings behind the front seats, took his tip and disappeared inside the building.

Thorpe drove slowly toward the waiting girl, lowered the window and called, "There's a taxi strike, but I'm going into the District. Be glad to give you a ride."

She seemed to shrink away from him. Then he met her appraising eyes. "Get in," he said. "There won't be any taxis tonight. I'll take you where you want to go."

Hesitating, she glanced around and made up her mind. "Very well. But only as far as you are going."

He pushed open the door on her side, helped lift her baggage onto the rear seat. Closing the door, she brushed a flake of melting snow from her forehead and looked at him. "You are very kind," she said, and now he detected the lightest of accents in her measured speech. "I was waiting for someone, but perhaps the snow. . . ." Her hands spread. "Would the White House be too far?"

"It's on my way," he said as the car gathered speed. "Without trying to be inquisitive—are you actually going to the White House?"

"Oh, no," she said with a tight little smile. "It is just a location I know—a point of reference. From there I will be able to make my way quite well."

"My name is Neal Thorpe," he told her as the car turned onto the parkway, "and I'm grateful for your company. Until just now it's been a lousy day for me."

A motorcycle escort guided the long black Mercedes limousine through Stockholm's afternoon drizzle to the front entrance of the Grand Hotel, where a small crowd of onlookers had been drawn by the motorcycles' sirens. A uniformed officer stepped smartly to the limousine's rear door and opened it. Frock-coated, the hotel manager bowed stiffly to the passenger who got out of the limousine. Impressively tall, the man shook the manager's hand and waved at the welcoming

3

crowd as it parted to permit his entrance. The limousine chauffeur wound the black, red and gold fender flags around their chromium staffs and hooded them.

The visitor moved steadily into the lobby, surrounded by a miniature galaxy of autograph seekers and officialdom. His rugged, slightly scarred face was topped with tousled blond-gray hair. It was a famous face, one that changed with smooth plasticity from sternness to ready smile. Its owner wore a black serge suit, white shirt and white silk tie. On him the semiformal attire seemed out of place, for he looked more the outdoorsman, woodcutter or trawler hand than a visiting dignitary who was the guest of the Swedish government.

At the elevator, he shook off the trailing crowd and turned to the manager who bowed again. "Herr Minister, you will occupy the official suite. Already your bags have been unpacked. Is there anything I may do to make your stay more pleasant? Fruit, sandwiches, perhaps? Herring in sour cream?"

"Liquor?"

"Both snaps and beer, Herr Minister."

"Thank you. And I do not wish to be disturbed. A speech to revise, you understand. For this evening's banquet."

"Of course." He stepped aside as the elevator doors closed on the Grand Hotel's distinguished guest.

The elevator operator was a boy uniformed neatly in military gray, his short blond hair covered by a round box cap. He gazed at the Herr Minister in awe, swallowed and said, "We are all honored to have you here."

The tall man smiled. "Thank you. Sweden was hospitable to me in my time of need and so I am always glad to return."

The boy fished a stiff card from a pocket and thrust

it outward. "May—may I have your autograph, Herr Minister?"

"With pleasure." He asked the boy's name and wrote it out carefully, signed his name and added the date.

The elevator stopped at the fifth floor; the minister walked along the corridor and opened the door to his suite. As he closed the door, his features sagged and he took a deep breath.

A drink was what he needed, he told himself, and opened a fresh bottle of aquavit. Tilting the bottle, he drank from it, coughed and set it down on the table. He undid his tie and placed ice cubes in a crystal glass. Then he poured the colorless liquor over the ice and watched it settle. The arrival preliminaries were done with, he reflected, and he would have three hours to himself, three hours alone—unless that idiot ambassador and his staff intruded with their forced and unwelcome attentions. As he reached for the glass, the telephone rang.

With a grimace he picked up the phone. "Yes?"

"Herr Minister," a heavily accented voice said smoothly. "Uncle Simon sends greetings."

"Uncle—? I can't see you now. Don't be an imbecile."

"We must see you," the voice continued, unperturbed. "Now, Herr Minister. I will knock three times. Please open quickly." The line went dead.

Slowly his hand lowered the receiver, cradled the phone, then grasped the waiting drink. The cold crystal touched his lips, tilted and emptied.

Gasping, he shook himself, eyed the empty glass. There was a time, he remembered, when callers like these had been welcome, but the debt he owed them had long been repaid. Still, as he peered across the room at the window with the harbor view, he knew that he would always have to receive them. Always. As long as he lived.

With a quick motion he hurled the glass at the marble fireplace. The sound of its shattering echoed thinly through the high-ceilinged room.

Below in the lobby a switchboard operator watched a man step from the house phone booth and join his companion, who had waited outside. The one who had called nodded at the other, and they walked shoulder to shoulder toward the elevator. Both men were stockily built, their too-long topcoats flapping around their ankles as they strode across the lobby. They wore dark felt hats whose brims were wider than current fashion, she saw; their black shoes chunky and utilitarian. But they moved with the assurance of men accustomed to power.

She waited until the door closed behind them, saw the ascent begin, then reached under the Ericcson panel. Her fingers found a small toggle switch and pushed it toward her knees. Then she plugged a jack into the call board, rang the room above and heard a quiet response. "They're going up," she whispered, "just as you said they would." She paused. "How did you know?"

"Because," the voice said tiredly, "I know them. And I know him. You remembered to switch?"

"Of course."

"Be careful, Zarah."

"As careful as you," she said sharply.

"I'll be all right. Now don't call me until after he leaves. Tomorrow."

"Tomorrow, then." Her voice rose. "Good-bye, sir."

Then her fingers busied with the glowing call-board. "Opera tickets, madame? I'll connect you with the concierge."

2

IT was Neal Thorpe's midday custom to lunch lightly in his Canal Square office if the weather was poor or he was swamped with work. But on fine days he lunched in the open air and strolled along the towpath of the C & O Canal. Now, three days after his Manhattan trip, spring was in the air, the sun was bright, and he left his drawing board willingly. He drew on a tweed jacket over his cashmere cardigan, nodded at the receptionist and left by the door labeled Dawes-Thorpe Associates

He took the stairway down the inside of the building's hollow square, bought a *Star* at the vending machine and walked down to the canal landing, where the old mule barges were being scraped and painted for the summer trips ahead. At the towpath he turned west, striding easily along, his square shoulders set as though he were beginning one of the endless Vietnam marches he had known in the Combat Engineers. For a while he glimpsed the green buds, the canal's placid surface, watched bicycle riders and joggers taking advantage of the midday break, then found a rustic bench and sat down.

The morning had brought more than its share of problems, Thorpe reflected as he unfolded the paper. Phil Dawes was adamant about abandoning the firm's efforts in the low-cost housing field. Thorpe's designs

7

had been turned down by Intercontinental in New York, and Dawes was anxious to write off the experiment's cost and return all their energies to profitable Georgetown house remodeling. As Phil put it, they would have to hustle to recoup the thirty or forty thousand dollars Thorpe's "fling" in low-cost housing had cost the firm.

From a branch over the towpath a robin glided down to a patch of border grass and cocked his head.

It's hard for me to fault my partner, Thorpe mused. Phil was a successful architect long before I even began studying for my degree. And when I got it, Dawes was the only firm that made me a decent offer; the others were turned off because I was nearly ten years older than the average graduate. Phil treated me well and let me buy in after only a year. Of course, he's over fifty and looking forward to retiring, but he didn't have to let ne become a full partner. He could have kept me as an assistant on straight salary until doomsday. So I owe him. And I can't discard his judgment.

So what do I do?

I can strike out on my own, follow the dream and maybe make out. Or I can wait a few more years until we've got a solid cash reserve and Phil's talking of retirement. That's the sensible course—except for one thing. The low-cost housing is needed now. Now.

Or, he thought, I could head for one of the underdeveloped countries and try to do there what I can't do here. Now there's a thought. Fewer construction union problems, cheaper labor and an abundance of cheap raw materials. The ideal formula.

After all, he mused, I got the idea abroad. It was there I decided to leave the government and study architecture. I'm single, healthy and solvent. Why not do what I want to now? If I wait three or five or seven years, I'll be too involved to ever break away. And I damn well don't want to spend the rest of my life

8

rebuilding old shacks into Federalist mansions for the wealthy.

For a while he considered his alternatives, deciding finally to drop by the AID offices in a day or two on a preliminary reconnaissance of possible countries where the need existed and he had a reasonable chance of success.

That decision made, Thorpe turned to the newspaper and scanned the news. Another skyjacking under way, countercharges of aggression in the Mideast, a street murder last night in the District plus fifteen assorted robberies, one of them ending in a wild street chase and death at an intersection. Pollution in the Potomac River, a court battle over Interstate 66 and so on. All pretty much as expected. He turned a page and noticed that the German Foreign Minister was visiting nonaligned nations, enlisting their support for worldwide disarmament. So far, Klaus Werber had been to Stockholm and Helsinki. From there, Algiers, black Africa, Latin America, Japan and back to Bonn. He shrugged and moved on to a new international monetary crisis reflected in European gold pressure against the dollar. A few more pages, and his eye was caught by a large notice in the Classified Section under Personals. He read it with growing interest.

> Reward for information leading to location of young woman missing since the 7th. Dark hair, 5'7", wearing gray fleece-lined coat, white boots and carrying two white valises. All information treated confidentially. Call EX 3-1000, Room 748.

Three nights ago he had given a ride to a girl fitting that brief description. She was, he supposed, a runaway sought by anxious parents. Or a girl whose family wanted to inform her of a death or other family crisis. With him she had been so uncommunicative that when he let her off across from the White House, he had not even learned her name. Expensively dressed, she was obviously not destitute, not like the multitude of runaway kids who flocked to Georgetown, the Village and Los Angeles. Or, he thought, she had left home after a quarrel and her parents sought her now for reconciliation. Her presence at the airport indicated she came from outside the Washington area, as did her slight accent.

Thorpe remembered she had said she was waiting for someone. That meant Washington had been her destination from wherever it was she had left. Who was the someone who was to have met her at the airport. A fiancé? Her lover? Were her parents trying to prevent an unsatisfactory marriage?

Speculation could be endless, he reminded himself, tore the notice from the paper and pocketed it, then retraced his steps along the towpath to the first public phone.

The telephone number was answered by the Statler Hilton Hotel. He asked for Room 748, and the ringing was interrupted by a man's voice. Thorpe said, "You placed an ad in the paper?"

"Yes. You have information?"

"I may have."

"Good. Excellent. Please come to—"

"Look, I'm not interested in a reward. I can easily tell you what I know over the phone."

A pause at the other end. Then: "It would perhaps be much better if we talked in private, sir. I will be glad to pay the taxi trip."

Thorpe grimaced. He had not eaten lunch, and a taxi along Pennsylvania Avenue this time of day would take at least fifteen minutes each way. "It's not a question of that, but I appreciate the offer. Are you the young lady's father?"

"Ah—rather a friend of her father and mother. If you would only come, sir," the voice said formally. "All of us are most anxious about the young lady. I promise not to delay you. May I have your name, please?"

"Thorpe. With an *e*."

"Well, Mr. Thorpe, will you come now, please?"

"All right." He saw his noonday lunch flying off on beating wings. "I'll start now."

"Hotel Statler Hilton. Room seven four eight."

"In fifteen to twenty minutes."

"Thank you, sir, so much."

As Thorpe hung up, he reflected on the odd word inversion by the man in the hotel room. The accent, too, suggested Germany or Switzerland, but the Swiss were less formal in conversation, more relaxed than Germans, whose protective formality derived from a bitter past.

He walked up to M Street, deposited his paper in a trash bin and waited for a taxi.

When he got out at the hotel, he entered the lobby and angled toward the elevator bank. There was a waiting crowd whose *"Hello. I'm . . ."* lapel cards proclaimed them members of the Ceramic Tile Producers International Association. A brief wait, and Thorpe found himself rising. He punched the seventh floor button and after five stops got out. At 748 he knocked on the door. It opened, and he saw a man about his own age dressed in a dark suit of finished worsted. The man had thinning blond hair and a reddish, nearly invisible mustache. "Mr. Thorpe?"

"Yes."

"Do come in."

As Thorpe entered, he noticed an absence of luggage, as though the room had been hired for the purpose of receiving telephone calls. Its occupant rubbed

11

his hands together and smiled fixedly. "So, Mr. Thorpe, you may have possession of some interesting information? Please be seated. We are deeply relieved to learn that we may be able to locate our missing girl." As Thorpe sat, the man pulled over a chair and looked at him expectantly.

Thorpe said, "May I know who I'm dealing with?"

"But of course, sir. I am Max Bloch, a friend—a close friend of the girl's parents."

"Where are they?"

"Oh, in London. As I was flying here, they asked me to make inquiries. Where was it you encountered—ah—Berthe, please?"

"You know," Thorpe said, "our police can be very helpful in locating missing persons."

"It is so. But because of family position. . . ." His hands spread. "Discretion. You understand?"

Thorpe shrugged. Clearly the man was not giving out any unnecessary information. "You say her name is Berthe?"

The man's gaze sharpened. "She did not give you that name?"

"She didn't give me any name. Now would you mind telling me what this is all about?"

Now the man shrugged. "An argument over her allowance. Her father is quite well-to-do, but he felt Berthe was spending excessively. So—" He smiled again. "You comprehend?"

"I suppose so."

"Now her parents are interested only in finding her. Please—where did you encounter her?"

"First, I'm not sure we're talking about the same girl. You say she flew here from London?"

"By way of Montreal. At least she boarded a BOAC flight to Montreal. There I learned that she had continued on to Washington. By chance were you on her aircraft?"

12

Thorpe shook his head. "I noticed her at the airport. Dulles Airport," he lied.

"And when was that?"

"Three nights ago. There was a taxi strike, and buses were delayed because of snow. I saw a girl wearing a leather coat like the one you described. White boots, too, but she had no luggage with her." The second lie. For some reason he had zero confidence in Max Bloch's honesty.

"No valises?" Bloch frowned.

"Well, they could have been slow arriving. It was a mixed-up night at the airport. I offered her a ride, but she said she'd prefer the bus."

A forced laugh from Bloch. "How like our Berthe—forever suspicious of strangers."

"Well, around here she has a right to be. When did you reach Washington, Mr. Bloch?"

"Yesterday. At once I contacted the newspapers. And you have responded to my inquiry."

"I don't know that I've been very helpful," Thorpe said apologetically. "In fact, I guess I've just taken up your time. All I've done is confirm what you already know."

"Ah, but that is something. Nothing else occurs to you, Mr. Thorpe?"

"Afraid not." He rose and saw Bloch reach for his wallet.

Thorpe shook his head. "I haven't been all that helpful."

"Your taxi fare, at least?"

"Unnecessary."

"Most gracious of you. When we find Berthe, you will hear appreciation from her parents." His eyes gazed blandly at Thorpe. "You are a Washington resident?"

To anyone else Thorpe would have given his business card. Instead he said, "I'm in the phone book.

13

Robert Thorpe." Robert had been his father's name.

"Then, sir, my great appreciation to you for your generous assistance. Certainly you are a gentleman." His accent made the last word sound like "chentelman."

They shook hands, and Thorpe said, "Has anyone else responded to the notice?"

"Unfortunately, no. But we are hopeful."

"You might try the bus dispatchers at the airport," Thorpe suggested. "She was a striking young lady."

"Yes, quite beautiful, no? But headstrong, as are so many of the spoiled young these days." His face mirrored sorrow over the corruption of a generation.

Thorpe walked to the door, turned and said, "You'll be staying here a time, then. On business?"

"In truth, my business was in New York. *Is* there still. But the father is an old friend, and I feel obligated to do what I can for him."

"Very commendable," Thorpe remarked. "Goodbye, Mr. Bloch."

"Good day, sir. Most grateful, believe me."

Thorpe made his way down to the lobby, headed automatically for the taxi exit, remembered his delayed lunch and walked instead toward the coffee shop.

On the way he passed a pay phone and decided to call his office. To the answering secretary he said, "I've been held up by one thing and another, so I'll be a little late getting back."

"Of course, Mr. Thorpe. No calls for you."

"Good." He was replacing the phone when he caught sight of a man hurrying through the lobby toward the taxi exit. The man wore a dark suit and a thin mustache. Intent on his route, Max Bloch collided with a Ceramic Tile conventioneer, nearly knocking down the lady. Barely pausing, Bloch sped toward the exit, and Thorpe decided to follow. Evidently the half-truths he had passed on to Bloch held an impact.

14

There was something very unkosher about the man, Thorpe mused. The unused hotel room; then flights from abroad landed at Dulles, not National, Airport. But he had met the girl at National. That meant she either had come to National from another area airport or had arrived there on a domestic flight, but not from Montreal by BOAC.

Too, Bloch had not provided the girl's last name, her family's name. As Thorpe hurried after him, he was not even sure the girl's name was Berthe as Bloch alleged. Big Berthe, with a slim figure like hers? Impossible. Thorpe saw Bloch enter a Yellow Cab and head down the exit ramp. Taking the next cab in rank, Thorpe said, "Please follow the cab ahead. My friend forgot something."

"Like money?"

"Money it is," Thorpe agreed and sat back.

"If you want, I can pass him and you can flag him down."

"I want to have a little fun with him after he finds out he doesn't have it."

"Anything you say."

"So just follow along, and when he stops, keep going. I'll brace him after a couple of minutes."

Both taxis followed M Street into Georgetown and turned north on Wisconsin. As the cabs moved and halted, Thorpe found himself wondering why he was going through this business. Habit, maybe. He had spent a year at a special school learning, among other things, surveillance. Outgoing himself, he had an instinctive distrust for others whose stories did not quite come off. And Max Bloch was one of those.

So, he thought, what's to lose but a light lunch? On the plus side, I satisfy my curiosity. And I haven't really harmed Bloch's quest. I confirmed seeing the girl in the Washington area, and no one else has. By not mentioning National Airport or the girl's waiting to be met, I haven't done her any damage either. And if she had good reason for disappearing, making things difficult for her is the last thing I'd want to do.

They reached Reservoir Road and turned west past Georgetown University Hospital and the swath of green park beyond. Instead of turning onto Foxhall Road as Thorpe half expected, Bloch's taxi kept going, and now Thorpe was more mystified than ever. Presently the lead cab's brake lights went on, and it began to slow. An abrupt right turn into a broad drive, and Bloch's taxi pulled up in front of an ultramodern building that to Thorpe had always appeared unfinished because of what appeared to be pipe scaffolding standing out from the large glass windows forming the façade.

"Stop here?"

"No. Make a U-turn in the next block and take me back to Georgetown." He saw Bloch pay his driver and walk quickly into the entrance. From a tall flagpole fluttered a flag whose horizontal stripes were black, red and gold, and it marked the embassy in the United States of the Federal Republic of Germany.

3

FASCHING, Rhine wine, Beethoven and the Schwarzwald was close to all that Germany meant to Thorpe. And apparently it was Germany that Bloch hailed from—Germany as his accent first suggested.

16

Well, Thorpe, thought, as he sipped his second vodka martini of the evening, it's not as though Bloch had gone into the Soviet embassy. But why had phone calls to BOAC failed to confirm that Bloch had flown to Washington yesterday from Montreal? And why had the receptionist at the German embassy denied knowing that a man named Bloch had entered the embassy at midday?

The denial to Thorpe suggested that the name Bloch was an alias. Or Bloch had slipped past the receptionist while she was absent from her desk. There was probably a reasonable explanation for these curious events that began with the waiting girl in the herdsman's coat. He would have settled for that theorem but for his distrust—dislike?—of Max Bloch.

Another hypothesis. Scandal was somehow involved, or a series of happenings that would appear scandalous if connected to the girl's family. Bloch had called them well-to-do. They could be much wealthier than that, and wealth brought prominence, newsworthiness. So Bloch had been sent out from London—why London?—to rectify whatever had occurred, nullify its notoriety.

That seemed the more likely prospect.

Bloch's disappearance into the German embassy suggested either that Bloch was a diplomat or that the girl's father was. If so, then that could explain London; her father was at the German embassy in London. Perhaps as ambassador—the family's apparent affluence would be consonant with an ambassadorship. Man makes his fortune in postwar Germany, dabbles in politics and moves on to the prestige of an appointment to the Court of St. James. Why not?

Wealth, influence, the avoidance of personal embarrassment—all these factors were involved.

Plus the girl.

On a pad he sketched her form as he had first

17

noticed it through the slow-falling sleet. Then a close-up of her head. Below them he printed "Study of an Unknown Girl," dating it three days ago.

Not much, but something for the memory book.

He sipped more from his glass and looked out of his apartment window. Already it was dark outside. Buds on the tree branch looked like studs along a lance. Feudal. Germany again.

With a sigh he turned away, realizing that more than the girl was bothering him. There was the unresolved problem of his future. To stay with Dawes meant a steadily mounting income and security. But wasn't that the problem? His life had become too secure. Three years in the Army—two of them in 'Nam—and three years with the Agency, two abroad.

I could have had a good career there, too, he reflected, but I felt things closing in, becoming too circumscribed, too stratified and bureaucratic. I wanted more freedom, so I got out. Then postgraduate studies in architecture when I was too busy relearning how to learn, too busy with my courses to find life unexciting. And after that, when I went to work for Dawes, I was too busy learning the practical side of my trade to have time for much reflection.

Maybe my problem isn't in making decisions but in making too many of them. Is my dissatisfaction valid or is it only restlessness—like the typist who quits her job and reapplies for it two weeks later? I'd hate to think that, but what's the answer?

Finishing his drink, he looked around the living room of his apartment. Stephanie had chosen the furnishings last year, done the decorating. Then she had slipped out of his life. After her had come Mopsy and last winter Lee. Good companions each one, and with Mopsy the relationship had been particularly exhilarating—he hoped it had been for her. But they were practical girls, dabbling at careers until the call of marriage.

I wonder if it's my guileless face? There's something about me that cries out mate material to nearly every girl I see more than a few times. Not that I'm averse to marrying, but after seeing what's happened to so many friends, reading the annual divorce statistics, I want enough love to last.

So, he thought, that makes me the last of the romantics.

His apartment held expensive hi-fi and television components, excellent paintings and a few pieces of representational sculpture. On his travels he had picked up souvenir art objects from Brazilian Indians, from the cholos of Peru. Tutsi spears and a zebra-covered shield. An ivory Kwan Yin from Hong Kong. Nothing exceptional; all routine, uninspired.

His life was routine, that was it. Lacking was uncertainty, excitement. That was why he had followed Max Bloch, why he kept turning the episode over in his mind, examining every facet like a suspicious jeweler. Without the condiment of excitement his life was as tasteless as boiled beef. As unsatisfying to his psychological palate. That explained his restlessness, the growing sense of dissatisfaction.

Maybe packing up and going abroad to start over again isn't the answer.

He remembered the words of a pretty Pan Am stewardess: " 'Round the block or 'round the world, you take your troubles with you."

You'd think the Agency would have provided enough challenge and excitement for anyone. That it didn't wasn't my fault. It was the Agency. Grown old and cautious. Prim. Reliant on technology far more than human beings. No, I can't fault myself for leaving when I did.

19

He thought of the West Coast: San Francisco and L.A., and he grimaced. Five hundred ramblers built from one universal design: doorways and chimneys on the right or left the only options. Swimming pool by special arrangement with the builder.

What he needed was a new Taliesin to throw his talents into. Mexico, maybe. The Pedregal area where builders took advantage of the volcanic rock, building on and in it; scooping free-form pools from the rock itself with no sign of concrete or vinyl liners. Everything conforming to the environment. But how many Pedregals were there in Mexico, much less the world?

He switched on a tape and heard the music without being sufficiently aware of it to identify the tune. It was just a background to his thoughts. He found himself switching on a light the better to examine his sketch of the unknown girl. Did she really come from London, or as her coat suggested, was Afghanistan, Baluchistan, Nepal, the Khyber Pass her point of origin?

He smiled at himself. The last of the romantics.

Leaving the sketch, he refilled his glass. Tomorrow, or if not tomorrow, sometime this week, he would have to think things through; either work wholeheartedly with Phil or try another path.

This time, he thought, I won't rush the decision-making process, hurry the judgment call as my federally employed friends say. If it takes more than the rest of the week, okay, so be it. This time I've got to be sure. At thirty-two it's nonsense to be uncertain of the future.

He picked up the telephone receiver and dialed the Statler Hilton. Three rings in Room 748. Then a thoroughly American voice: "Yeah?"

"Mr. Bloch?"

"Hell, no. I'm Ames. Walt Ames."

"Sorry. Room seven four eight?"

"That's right, why?"

"Mr. Bloch was there at noon."

"I checked in at three. Tough."

"Not really." Thorpe replaced the receiver, thought a moment and called the hotel again. "I've been trying to deliver a package to Mr. Bloch—Mr. Max Bloch in your hotel. He told me he was in room seven four eight but there's a Mr. Ames there now. I wonder if you could help me."

"We'll try, sir. One moment, please."

Silence, but for the sound of riffling pages. Then: "I'm sorry, sir, but no one by that name was registered in the hotel today."

"Then can you tell me who was occupying seven four eight this morning?"

"I'm sorry, sir, but we cannot provide that information."

Short of a court order, he thought, thanked the desk clerk and hung up.

So Bloch's observed exit from the hotel had been a final departure. Bloch, or whatever his true name was. No baggage meant he was staying—or lived—someplace else. Probably paid cash for the room, no other identification needed. And now vanished.

Thorpe telephoned the *Star*'s Classified Section and referred to Bloch's ad. Yes, a Mr. Bloch had placed the notice yesterday, paying for three insertions. No, client addresses were not kept for cash transactions.

Well, he thought hanging up, at least I've been thorough. Bloch, or whatever his name is, has probably been busy out at Dulles. One lie begets, as it deserves, another. I hope he never finds her. I'd hate to think of her with him—even in a place as public as the Statler lobby.

Thorpe consoled himself with the thought that the little he had told Bloch did the girl no disservice, placed her in no danger of discovery. But the trouble

21

is I'd like to find her, see her again. So Bloch and I are stalemated.

Picking up his drink, Thorpe wandered to the window and glanced down at the street. The Georgetown neighborhood was quiet and residential, blocks distant from the Zippie Trail on Wisconsin Avenue; still, after dark the threat of holdups and mugging usually kept the sidewalks deserted. Which was why he was interested in the figure of a lone man strolling across the street, glancing up from time to time toward Thorpe's window.

They were casual glances, Thorpe told himself; too damn casual. What he could see of the watcher was unfamiliar. A short, thin man with undistinguished features. But watching he was.

Backing from the window, Thorpe kept his eyes on the man across the street, felt for the wall switch and turned out the lights. When the man looked up again, he froze, then hurried to a parked car whose door he opened. As he got in, the brief flash of the dome light showed the man's hand reach toward the dash. Not the steering wheel, but the glove compartment side. The car was dark inside, and it came to Thorpe that the watcher was using a radio mike, calling someone. Reporting to his base station or a companion surveillant. The dome light flashed on and off as the watcher left the car. Now he crossed the street, heading toward Thorpe's apartment door.

He must be waiting for me to leave, Thorpe decided. But why?

If he's an officer of the law, he could come up and knock on my door. Only he doesn't behave like a lawman. Too furtive. So he must be—

The telephone rang. Without switching on the light, Thorpe picked up the receiver, said, "Hello?"

"Mr. Thorpe?" A vaguely familiar voice. Female.

"Yes."

"Are you alone?"

"Quite alone. Why?"

"Because I must talk with you. Please don't hang up."

"Go on." Who was she?

"From the airport a few nights ago you gave me a ride into Washington. Do you remember?"

"I remember. Of course. Your name is Berthe?"

A gasp. "Who told you that?"

"A man who called himself Max Bloch. Only I don't think that was his name. I answered an ad in the paper and—"

"When did you talk with . . . this man?"

"Today. About one o'clock. Never mind him. You said you wanted to talk to me. Why?"

"Because you offered and gave me help spontaneously. Perhaps a little thing, but it set you apart. Will you meet me?"

"Gladly. Where?"

He heard the long intake of her breath. "Where we parted the other night. Is that too far?"

"I can be there in fifteen minutes." He remembered the man posted outside his apartment. To avoid him would take additional time. "Make that twenty minutes, Berthe—if that's your name."

"Anna."

"Have you had dinner?"

"Not—not really."

"Then we'll dine together. My car is—" He stopped. "You know the car."

"Twenty minutes," she repeated, and the line went dead.

Heart pounding, Thorpe pulled on his tweed jacket, wishing he had time to change into a business suit, went to the service door and listened. No sound in the rear stairwell. Slowly and quietly he opened the door and went down three flights of stair to the chained alley door. He looked outside before opening the door, saw no one in the alley and opened the door. Quickly he scaled the rear fence and dropped over onto the beginnings of a garden. From there he made his way unobtrusively to the parallel street, got into his car and drove east toward Lafayette Square.

As he sped along, he realized that his reflexes were better than he remembered them, his vision improved. His pulse was beating, adrenalin pumping through his veins.

Whatever had been lacking from his life before —danger, romance—was more than filling the void.

He was alive again.

4

FROM Zestienhoven Airport, the man drove his rented Consul through midday drizzle along the two-lane road toward The Hague. The parallel canal was invisible through the mist, but marked occasionally by the stacks of slowly moving barges. Holland, he mused, was a country of mediocre roads and excellent canals. The canals were everywhere, the arteries of the country; on them, because of them, commerce thrived. And he thought how different this fluvial nation was from his native country, frozen so much of each year; a land of countless lakes and bays, of fjords and endless forest. He remembered its warm, brief summer and the sharp dark cold of wintertime.

Even the winter he preferred to Holland's ambigu-

24

ous climate, the drizzle and pervasive damp, the fog, the cloudy days.

Passing a rain-soaked group of bicyclists, he checked his watch and decided he would arrive on time. Near The Hague he slowed, watching for the Rijksweg intersection, and turned northeast on the Amsterdam highway. A few kilometers more, and he saw a small sign pointing toward the town of Voorschoten, and presently he turned from the highway to head northwest.

It was raining heavily now, and his first landmark was a humpback bridge over a fork in the canal. There would be another bridge over the other fork, he remembered, and when that too was crossed, he turned due west on the Leidseweg. Nearly there, he told himself, reassured to have made the journey almost alone from memory. Even though he had last been there four years ago, he found himself forgetting things from time to time, a sign of aging, he conceded, even though he was only sixty-three.

A felt hat concealed most of his silver-white hair so that his face seemed the face of a much younger man. The skin was nearly without wrinkles, tinted faintly olive under the tan of men who live habitually in the open. His cheekbones were high, the eyes gray and piercing, the nose thin and straight. He was a man who loved skiing and fishing, elk hunting in the forest fastness and long relaxing sessions in a sauna.

His gloved hands gripped the wheel, and he saw a road sign pointing toward Voorschoten's silver factory. At the Hofweg he turned south toward the canal he had just crossed, and there, under barren trees, was the white-walled tile-topped restaurant. Just as he remembered it.

The car sloshed through puddles, arriving finally near the entrance door. Above it was the name Allemansgeest. No doubt about his memory now.

Turning slowly past the entrance, he found a place

to park among half a dozen cars and wondered if one of them had brought his contact there. He looked at his watch and saw that he was early by less than thirty seconds. With a smile he left the car and hurried toward the heavy oaken door, the shelter of the overhang.

The door opened into a vestibule, where he pulled off his raincoat and hat and shook off surplus water. Then he hung them on the coatrack and went through the inner door into the restaurant proper.

There was warmth from a huge fireplace at the far end, its half-round chimney forming part of the corner like the body of a windmill. The walls displayed a profusion of copper pans and Delft-blue plates. Below them dark heavy tables and perhaps a dozen diners.

As he looked around, a man in a brown business suit approached him, menus under one arm. "You have a reservation?" he inquired.

"Herr Smith is expecting me."

"This way, please." Turning, the *maître* led him toward a door, opened it and said, "Herr Smith is waiting for you."

The door closed on a dimly lighted staircase. Climbing it, he felt a sudden sense of danger. Would Smith be at the top, or had their communication been intercepted? If it had, not Smith would be waiting in the private dining room, but death. The thought made him pause and wonder why he had not considered the possibility before. Shaking his head self-critically, he pushed his ring hand into the pocket of his coat. The fingers closed around a knurled butt of a loaded PPK. He slid the safety off and went up the next few steps to the door at the head of the stairs. Without knocking he pushed the door inward and waited.

Inside, standing at a window, back to the door, was a man in a dark, well-tailored suit. At the sound he turned and faced the new arrival. His head was nearly

26

bald and he wore heavy shell-rimmed glasses. His skin was pale, and as he moved forward in greeting, his steps were slow and labored. "Arne," he said in English. "How good of you to come."

They shook hands, commented on the wretched weather and the difficulty of traveling by air in Europe whenever the weather changed. They spread their hands over the warmth of a large brass brazier, and the man spoke again. "You look well, Arne."

"And you—"

"No—I've been not terribly well—don't lie. I was retired, you know, but when I got your message, I showed it to old friends, who asked me to come today."

Arne's face tightened in concern. "If I had known, I—"

"Believe me I was glad to come. Glad of the chance to do a thing or two once more before I die."

His words troubled the white-haired man. "You must not think of death," he said calmly. "When it comes, that is all. What one can hope for is to have accomplished something beforehand."

"As you have."

"Some small things, true. But the big one. . . ." He turned to the small bar covered with white linen and assorted bottles. Seeing that his host had made a drink, he poured aquavit for himself and turned back to the man called Smith. "The room is secure?"

"Checked out at eleven o'clock. Thoroughly. I think we are quite safe. I was not followed."

"Nor was I."

"You were speaking of the big one." Smith sat down tiredly and looked up at his guest.

"I was. Because now, after all these years, I think I have something we could view as definite proof."

"You sent for me rather than pass the information to one of our stations. Why, Arne?"

"Because I do not trust your people any more than

I trust the French, the Germans or the British. Also, your country has, shall we say, an 'investment' in the man's career. A special interest in maintaining his public image."

Smith shrugged. "All that was long ago. In the days when Werber first emerged, to be an anti-Fascist, a 'freedom fighter,' was the only recommendation our military government needed to let him enter politics. And remember, Klaus Werber had been in the anti-Nazi Schutzbund in the early thirties."

"Not necessarily a recommendation," Arne remarked.

"In the rubble of postwar Cologne it distinguished him the way a Victoria Cross does in England. So, apart from having cleared Werber for public office in 1946, my government has no responsibility for his later career, whether good or bad. And millions of people around the world view it as good and Werber a special hero."

"He visits your President, your President visits him. At the UN, in Geneva, in Vienna, in Brussels, your country counts on his friendly offices. In exchange for them, I am quite sure he is given bits of information—perhaps much more than that, for he is a man whom everyone trusts."

"Except yourself."

Arne smiled thinly. "I have not trusted him since 1943."

Smith got out a pipe and lighted it before he trudged over to the door and turned the lock. "I took the liberty of ordering for both of us—to avoid intrusions by the waiter." He gestured at the set table. On it silver dishes were warming over alcohol flames.

They went together to the table, and when they were seated, Smith poured a small amount of red wine into his glass, tasted approvingly and filled his guest's, then his own. "So, here we are on neutral territory, so to speak. In our halfway house—our *yafka*." Their glasses touched. "*Pross.*"

"Long life to us both."

Through their meal reminiscences poured out, bringing each other up to date on all that happened to them since their last meeting four years before. They were sharing thick Dutch coffee and Willem II cigars before either man returned to the purpose of their meeting. Arne said, "I will give you two names. Think of them and tell me if you have heard of them before."

Smith nodded.

"Gleb Kalugin is one. The other is Yakov Gorytsev. Kalugin. Gorytsev."

Slowly, Smith nodded. He dropped ash from his cigar and studied the high beamed ceiling. "Gorytsev," he repeated. "Chief of the Third Department, First Directorate of the KGB. Central Europe and Scandinavia. PNG'd from a variety of countries under an assortment of names."

"Age fifty-eight, brown-black hair. Height five feet seven, weight fourteen stone. And Kalugin?"

"A very senior man. He is associated with, and may by now even head, the Central Bureau for Political Information—the TBPI. The bureau directs all Soviet political action operations and reports not to the KGB, but to a much higher echelon—the Central Committee of the Communist Party of the Soviet Union."

Arne nodded. "Whatever your physical ills, your memory remains excellent. Kalugin is a year older than Gorytsev and perhaps ten pounds lighter. Otherwise, they look much the same, sharing the gross Slav features I so detest."

Smith sipped from a Delft demitasse. "These men are involved with your target?"

"They are. I believe their involvement is of years' standing, but the past is not my concern. I asked you

29

to meet me so I could tell you that some days ago in Stockholm these men were seen together. I was anticipating them, in that I had made preparations to detect and overhear whatever visitors approached our distinguished internationalist in the privacy of his hotel suite." He grimaced. "As you know, I have done the same thing many times before but always with much less success. My friend, within three minutes of Werber's reaching his suite, Gorytsev telephoned him. What he said was, 'Uncle Simon sends greetings.' Werber didn't expect the contact, didn't want it, but Gorytsev insisted he receive the two of them. And he did."

Smith pushed aside his demitasse. "Breaking all the rules in the KGB book. It doesn't seem reasonable, Arne. Why would they make so open a contact?"

"Contempt for the Swedes, perhaps. Because the Swedish Service does not concern itself with the comings and goings of Russian visitors. They used other names, of course, flying in that morning from Zürich. That much I was able to establish. But what *is* important is that these two men traveled a long way to hold a secret meeting with the German Foreign Minister. So something of great importance had to be discussed."

Smith sat forward. Some color had returned to his skin. "You monitored their conversation?"

"The mikes were planted, the recorders turning." He shrugged. "But the Soviets brought with them an audio interruptor. So the three men talked—for nearly fifteen minutes—inside an electrostatic field. My tapes were worthless."

Smith shook his head slowly. "If only the tapes. . . ." His hands spread. "Without that, Arne—"

"You have my word," he said sharply. "More, you have a description of the circumstances—a scenario in effect. That much should be sufficient to warn your State Department, your President."

"I wish it were that simple. Oh, we can verify the whereabouts of Kalugin and Gorytsev on the day Werber was in Stockholm, check travel lists to learn what Russians flew from Zürich to Sweden that morning, but—"

"You must do more than that," his guest insisted. "Much more. From the defector Sovatkin we learned the term 'Agent of Influence,' a concept we had never before considered."

"Well, not entirely," Smith mused. "For years we felt there was something, some human instrumentality beyond agent and *apparatchik*. We inferred it the way astronomers infer the presence of an unseen star—because of the behavior of other finite bodies. Sovatkin confirmed what we suspected, gave a name to the species."

"But how many, to your knowledge, have you found?"

"Not many," Smith admitted. "Not nearly as many as we believe exist." His head went back, and he regarded the white ceiling lined with heavy smoke-brown beams. "Igor Sovatkin defined the Agent of Influence as either a government official so highly placed that he can exercise influence on government policy or an opinion molder so influential as to be capable of altering the attitudes of an entire country. In either case, though his politics may be of the left, he is not—and cannot be known as—a Communist."

"Klaus Werber is the former," Arne said flatly. "Believe me, old friend."

Smith sighed. "I do, and I have believed it for years. But convincing my people was never possible. Accordingly they refused to approach the Secretary of State. One always hears how useful Werber has been in handling delicate international negotiations, working as go-between sub-rosa. In the Congo, in the Mideast, in Europe itself, even within the NATO Interface. The

31

argument is persuasive, Colonel Lakka. Without hard, contrary proof it will continue to prevail."

For a time the room was silent as the smoke that drifted upward from their dying cigars. Finally Arne Lakka spoke. "I have done what I could—all that I could. I have never had the resources available to you and your people. If I had, perhaps I would have been able to gather the sort of proof you require."

Gently, Smith said, "It's not what *I* require, Arne, but what the director and State—"

"I understand." He was withdrawing into himself military fashion, no longer willing to expose himself to rebuff. "There is nothing left to discuss." Then his tone warmed. "Had I known of your illness, I would not have subjected you to so long and tiring a journey."

"Unimportant. You've spent thirty years trying to unravel a set of mysteries. Surely I can spend a day or two on a visit to an old friend."

"As always you are more than courteous."

"But there is another matter, Arne. In fact, it's why we thought you sent for me. The old codes—your transcripts. I have been authorized a large sum to offer you."

"There is no question of money. Nor was there ever."

"Then suppose—just suppose something were to happen to you . . . how could that priceless material be retained for the West and kept from the other side? While you live, I am not concerned with its safekeeping, but alternatively—" His hands opened. "Your life's work, Arne. Shouldn't you arrange for its safeguarding?"

"It is in a safe place. When my time is come, my daughter knows its position."

"Zarah," Smith said thoughtfully. "How could we find her?"

"She will find you—or your friends. Zarah married, your remember, so her name is Engstrom now."

"Where does she live?"

"Zarah lives and works in Stockholm." He smiled. "From time to time. Last week she was employed at the Grand Hotel—as a telephone operator."

Smith chuckled. "For the time being I'll keep that to myself. But you contrasted our resources with yours, Arne. Think what we could do with your transcripts, the old codes; how much we might be able to learn of value even today. With computers—"

"When I broke the codes, I had no computers."

"But you were a genius—a one-man *shifr odtel*. Today's crop of code breakers is a lesser breed. Lacking the genius spark, they rely on spinning tapes and print-out sheets."

"I know." He reached for the cognac bottle and filled their brandy bowls. Lifting his, he said reverently, "Mannerheim."

"Mannerheim," Smith repeated, and they both drank deeply.

Half an hour later, Colonel Arne Lakka, once of the Finnish Military Intelligence, was driving back along a wet and humpbacked road toward Zestienhoven. Much of the earlier mist was gone, and he could make out the surface of the canal below the road, only a few meters away. Disappointment gnawed him like the cancer he feared was killing Smith. He knew he could not blame his American friend. The opportunity to tape Werber *and* the Soviets had been a godsend. Only the Soviets had come prepared, and they had outsmarted him.

Once more he was alone—alone as he had been so much of his life since the winter war with Russia, the half-remembered years with Marshal Mannerheim. Only Zarah. . . .

He stared at the road ahead, saw the bridge arching

33

the canal and heard a shot ring out. Almost in echo a front tire blew apart. It flattened, and the steering wheel tore from his grip as the car veered across the shoulder and started downward. The brakes were useless because the car was overturning, wheels leaving earth as it plunged into the waiting water.

Half-stunned, he hung inverted by his seat belt as with a heavy jolt the roof hit bottom. Through enveloping darkness he heard the surge of water rushing in to fill the submerged car.

5

"TO answer your question," Thorpe said to the girl, "your face reminded me of someone."

"Of whom, please?"

"Ali McGraw."

She laughed, her head drawing gracefully back, showing the fine cords of her neck and throat. "Seriously?"

"Except that your teeth don't need straightening."

She laughed again. "Fortunately all that was accomplished years ago. Much to my pain and embarrassment."

Thorpe smiled. "But worth every pound and shilling. The man who called himself Bloch—he showed no sensitivity for names. Berthe, indeed."

"Worse," she said, "he gave me a poor character. Taken together, quite unforgivable."

The night before he had found her in front of the

White House with her bags and driven down to War-
renton's Red Fox Tavern, where they dined. Her
name, she told him, was Anna Schroeder. Born near
Geneva. Family in manufacturing. Schools in Switzerland and England. Until last week an art student in
London. She had promised to marry a fellow student,
decided not to and left abruptly to avoid unpleasant-
ness. She had telephoned her mother to say that she
was going away, nothing more. Max Bloch? Perhaps
one of her father's many employees sent to bring her
back. She was not on close terms with either of her
parents, her father least of all. She had come to
Washington because one of her classmates, a girl, left
London to study at the Corcoran Gallery. Anna had
planned on moving in with her; but the girl had left
on spring vacation, and there would be no way to find
her for at least a week. Alone, in a strange and foreign
city, Anna had decided to try to reach the helpful man
in the green car, recalled his name and phoned.

After dinner, Thorpe took her to an apartment
house near Washington Circle where clients of the
firm occasionally stayed and returned to his own place
by the same backyard route. By then, as far as he could
tell, surveillance had been lifted.

It was evening now, and he had spent the afternoon
showing her the tourist sights. She loved London, of
course, but Washington was different: new-appearing
white buildings and clean streets. Georgetown was like
a mini-Chelsea. She was, he thought, the most
enthusiastic tourist he had ever entertained. As well as
the prettiest.

So he had not told her about Bloch's trip to the German Embassy. Or the man who had been watching his
apartment.

"I thought we'd dine American style," he suggested.
"No fraudulent French restaurants. Will that be all
right?"

35

"Your instincts are excellent. And tomorrow I'll shop for dresses that won't embarrass you when we go out." Her head tilted. "I seem to be monopolizing you —though I don't mean to—and you have a business to attend to."

"No problem," he assured her. "Architects tend to expand available work, but I like to work as rapidly as I can; get things out of the way. And restoring old houses is pretty much routine. Besides, I've realized I've had my nose too close to the drawing board for far too long. The change is more than welcome." He added the last of the champagne to their glasses. "Here's to the twenty-hour workweek."

"*Santé*," she responded as their glasses touched.

He watched her drink, lips delicately caressing the rim, and wondered how much of what she had told him was the truth. To Thorpe there seemed a number of obvious gaps. For instance, Anna had not mentioned where she spent her first three nights in Washington. And from what he knew of her, she was not the type of girl who would abandon her London school over the end of a love affair. For another thing, he was not convinced she was Swiss as claimed.

There were, in fact, more questions surrounding her than answers. But she *had* sought him out, made him in a sense responsible for her welfare if only for a time. So Thorpe did not want to muddy the relationship with interrogations. All that really mattered was her presence. She was young, European and beautiful, and she was in some sort of difficulty, trouble being perhaps too strong a word. Still, he had not taken her to his apartment because, for all he knew, it was being watched, and he did not want to risk Anna's being seen by the watchers.

But on whose instructions was his place staked out? Bloch seemed the logical sponsor, but Thorpe had not given Bloch his full name. Unfortunately, as he later determined, there were no Robert Thorpes listed in the District phone directory, whereas he, Neal Thorpe, was listed twice. So Bloch could have determined that "Robert" Thorpe was only an alias.

"Deep thoughts, Neal?"

He roused himself. "Not really. Just inventorying the places we might dine. There's a multitude of restaurants in Washington, but only a few good ones. And prices don't always reflect quality."

"Is that not true everywhere? Geneva and London, too."

He finished his champagne and got up. Setting down her glass, the girl rose, and they were face to face, eyes locked. On sudden impulse he drew her to him, kissed her lips briefly and felt her shrink away. In her eyes flashed something close to terror. "I—I'm sorry," he said awkwardly. "I'm not trying to take advantage of you, Anna. I was out of line."

Her face relaxed, and her eyes became remote. "It never happened," she said huskily. "Someday. . . ." Abruptly she turned and walked toward the single bedroom. Thorpe felt his face flush. Fumbling like a schoolboy, he told himself angrily and determined not to give in to impulses again. Then, as he waited, he found himself wondering why she had reacted as she did. I'm no gorilla, he told himself, and she's been kissed before. By her own account she was engaged, and that implies the embraces of a male. In her artistic ambiance it could mean a good deal more. So perhaps Anna was reacting to something else rather than to him as a person. Some subconscious hang-up that his kiss evoked. . . .

"I'm ready," she said, returning with a light-colored raincoat over one arm. Together they walked to the door and down to the parking area where he had left his car. The dark air was cool, and its dampness suggested rain before the night was over. He helped Anna into her raincoat and got behind the wheel.

From there he drove down Wisconsin Avenue and ordered dinner at the Potomack, whose specialty was early American dishes: peanut soup, stuffed oysters, flummery and mulled wine. Anna seemed to enjoy them, and Thorpe assumed she was accustomed to the heavy cuisine of central Europe. She was fascinated, too, by the Colonial costumes of the waiters and waitresses, the antiqued maple tables and the simulated atmosphere of two hundred years ago. With dinner behind them, they crossed through light mist to Blues Alley, where they enjoyed cognac and coffee to the enthusiastic sounds of a Dixieland band. It was after midnight before Thorpe drove her back to her apartment.

In the lobby she gave him her hand, and said, "Another wonderful evening, Neal. Thank you so much."

"Each time I see you—" he began, but one finger pressed his lips.

"In time," she said quietly, "we could easily be something to each other. But for now I do not believe either of us. . . ."

"I haven't asked questions," he said, "because I wanted to give you time to sort things out. Why you're here, what you fled from. . . . I won't invade your privacy."

She smiled briefly, a little sadly, he thought. "I've never been a very successful liar, I'm afraid. And so I'm grateful you haven't asked me for the truth." Her head turned. "I must not expose you to danger."

"Danger? What?"

"Another time, perhaps. For now, all one can do is live one day at a time, no?"

38

"Always a good program. But the possibility of danger to you concerns me."

"Then let us leave it that I was being melodramatic. What could happen to me?"

"I don't know," he told her, "but my apartment has been watched. That much I know."

Her face seemed to freeze. Tightly she said, "You should have told me before."

He shrugged. "My problem, not yours. Only, if there is anything I can do—whatever it is—please believe you can count on me."

"I believe it."

"Good night, Anna. I'll call you tomorrow."

"Good night, Neal."

After he drove back, he parked three blocks from his apartment and walked toward it noticing streetlights haloed by the mist. At the corner he scanned the street in front of his building and saw neither his surveillant nor his car. Even so, Thorpe entered by the service door and walked up the rear stairway to the door that opened into his small kitchen.

As the door closed behind, he switched on the kitchen light and heard a startled exclamation from the living room. There was a rush, the thud of falling furniture, the wrench of his front door opening and the sharp sound of its slamming shut. When Thorpe reacted, he turned and raced down the rear stairs, hoping to meet the intruder as he left the building. But the snub chain cost him precious seconds, and when he burst out of the side alley, running feet were receding half a block away. Swearing, Thorpe went back up to his apartment, locked the kitchen door and turned on his living-room lights. He righted the fallen end table and set about picking up books and papers frm where they had been strewn. For a moment he considered telephoning the police, then realized the intrusion would be written off as just another attempted robbery. As for fingerprints, Thorpe felt reasonably sure the searcher had worn gloves.

But what was he after?

Pouring himself a short glass of cognac, Thorpe glanced around the room, trying to decide. He kept no cash in the apartment, no jewelry, nothing of much value. Then he walked toward his drawing table and realized his sketch of Anna was gone. He sipped brandy and felt his pulse begin to slow. His eyes surveyed the telephone, and he noticed that the note pad was bare. On it he had written the number of Anna's apartment telephone.

Opening the directory, he found the listing and dialed quickly. When her voice answered, he said, "Someone was going through my apartment. . . . No, I don't know who he was. So far as I could tell he took two things—a sketch I drew of you and this telephone number."

He heard the quick intake of her breath. "Oh, NEAL!"

"I'm sorry," he said contritely. "I shouldn't have left them lying around. But I ought to take you to another place. Tonight."

For a long moment, silence. Finally she said, "I told you I was in no danger. But if you like, I'll move out in the morning."

"I'd prefer now. I can be there in a few minutes."

"No—I'd feel awfully foolish leaving like a thief in the night. But if it would make you feel better, I won't open my door—"

"It would. And don't answer the telephone."

"I promise. Then in the morning I'll go somewhere else."

"Good." He swallowed. "I'll come by at eight."

"So early?"

"Sooner the better."

"I understand. And thank you for calling." He thought she was going to hang up, but after a moment she said, "You drew a sketch of me?"

"As I first saw you—standing there at the airport."

Her voice teased. "Do you sketch every stranger you see?"

"Hardly. Now I wish I hadn't. Because it gives Bloch—or whoever's looking for you—a picture they can show around. And having your telephone number is even worse. Look, let me come over now. Let's not take a chance on the morning."

"No," she said firmly. "I'll be ready at eight. Good night, Neal." Her voice seemed softer. "Sleep well."

"Good night, Anna."

Having replaced the receiver, he went to the hall door and opened it, stooped to examine the face of the lock. Around the keyhole were minute hairline scratches that glinted under the corridor light. The spicules of a spring steel pick had made them, and not long ago. Before leaving the apartment again, he would shoot the dead bolt and go out through the kitchen exit. Not that there was anything left to steal.

Reentering the apartment, he locked the door and set the dead bolt, reflecting that he should have taken the precaution earlier in the evening. Because of his sketch and the written phone number, Anna was vulnerable. She had sought him for help, concealment, and unwittingly he had exposed her to the very people she wanted to avoid. In short, by forgetting tradecraft, he had given her away.

He lifted the brandy glass and sipped thoughtfully. Then he opened the directory and found the telephone number of Don Bitler, who had gone through Agency training with him and, as far as Thorpe knew, still worked on European affairs.

Four times the phone rang before a sleepy voice answered.

41

"Neal?" A smothered yawn. "Six months since we lunched and now a midnight call. Don't tell me you're stoned in a bar—that's not your style."

Thorpe grunted. "Will you have lunch with me tomorrow?"

"To— Old friend, are you *sure* you're not stoned in a bar?"

"Positive. How about letting explanations hold until lunch? Can you make it?"

"Sure—I guess so. You want to drive over to McLean?"

"Rather not. Make it the George Town Club. Twelve thirty?"

"Fine." Another yawn. "I gather this isn't just a social urge to see me."

"More than that, Don. See you tomorrow."

"Man, it's already tomorrow." Bitler sighed heavily. "Twelve thirty, you said."

"Right."

Thorpe hung up and finished his brandy, wondering if his decision to consult Don Bitler had been sound. Have to start someplace, he told himself, and I'd feel foolish going to the FBI with the little I have—end up on the Bureau's crackpot list. But Don could have some ideas that wouldn't necessarily involve either him or the Agency. Guidance is what I need right now. Professional help. I should have found it earlier.

As he turned off the lights, he thought again of Anna, alone in her small apartment. Door bolted, he hoped, and not answering the telephone.

In his bedroom he set the alarm for seven, brushed his teeth and turned in. Sleep came while he was reviewing alternate places where Anna could be entirely safe.

Secure until some of this began to make sense.

A little before eight he reached her apartment build-

42

ing through the rush of morning traffic, left his car in the turnaround, engine running, and went to the house phone. He asked for her apartment and heard the phone ring half a dozen times before he gave up and inquired at the desk, thinking she might have gone into the drugstore for breakfast.

"Why, no, sir, Miss Schroeder paid her bill last night and left."

"Last night?" He stared at the elderly clerk. "Did —did she say where she was going?"

"No."

"Or leave a message?"

"I'm afraid not. The other gentleman asked the same question."

"The other? When was that?"

"Half an hour ago."

"I see." He wet his lips. "Did she leave alone?"

"Yes. She asked me to call her a taxi, and I did. Yellow Cab."

Walking back to his car, Thorpe realized that his call had alarmed Anna, moved her to flight ahead of her pursuers. And as he drove down to his office, he was troubled by the stark reality that wherever Anna was, she was alone and friendless, and the responsibility was his.

They had shared a few meals, some promissory words, and now his life was as empty as before she entered it.

He was back, as the saying went, to square one.

6

BY midmorning fog blanketing the Eastern seaboard thinned under the spring sun, and offshore breezes pushed what remained of it eastward into the Atlantic. As the ceiling lifted, airports along the shuttle corridor resumed operation, and a Dassault Mystère 20 took off from Gander Airport in Newfoundland. From Le Bourget the executive jet had flown nonstop to Gander, where its sole passenger got out to stretch his legs and take morning coffee while the jet was fueled and checked for the last leg of the flight. Once beyond the reach of Gander's radar the pilot turned inland, dropped to three thousand feet and took a DF bearing on the lightship off Sandy Hook. On this new heading, he set the automatic co-pilot, lighted a Gaulois and told his co-pilot to keep a sharp lookout for the eastern tip of Long Island. Presently he dozed off and slept an hour and a half until wakened by the co-pilot. Taking over the controls, he dropped another thousand feet in a long westward turn to bring the plane below the Air Defense radar system and guided the jet over Block Island Sound. Turbofans throttled down, flaps and wheels lowered, the pilot eased the Mystère into a smooth landing on a small private airstrip inland from Mecox Bay.

Comte Gilbert Philippe de Rochepin loosened his seat belt even though the pretty stewardess waved a disapproving finger. "My dear," he said as the plane rolled to a stop and the jets decelerated, "much as I

44

dislike admitting it, I was flying aircraft long before you were born."

Rising, she took down his pearl gray homburg and tucked back his belt straps. *"Votre chapeau, mon cher Comte. Nous sommes arrivés."*

"Indeed we have arrived," he agreed, looking out into the sunshine of the New World. "And my thanks to you, Carlotte, for having made the flight so pleasant."

The door opened, and he heard the self-contained stairs lowering to the ground. Leaving his seat, he took up his walking stick and bent over the hand of the stewardess. *"Avec tous mes compliments, mademoiselle,"* he murmured, and Carlotte felt her heart skip a beat. Finally, after hours airborne together, the count had noticed her. Noticed her as a female, a living, breathing person, not just as a convenience of the charter jet. For a brief moment she had the urge to whisper the telephone number of her flat in the Seventeenth Arrondissement; then reason interposed. If he were truly interested, she realized, he could easily obtain her vital data from the aircraft company that employed her. Then his tall figure bent as he went down the aisle, straightening as he passed through the doorway, and she was left with the memory of his steel-gray eyes, his bronzed skin and hawklike profile—that and the hope of another meeting.

From the doorway she watched him stride across the tarmac toward a waiting helicopter, sun lightening the gray of his double-breasted pinstripe suit. The Comte de Rochepin was both famous and wealthy, and she told herself that life as his *petite amie* would be a great improvement over what she now began to view as a drab and burdensome existence. *Si seulement je pouvais,* she sighed and began collecting glasses, plates and the single bottle of Cordon Rouge consumed by the count during their journey. Ashtrays were littered with stubs

45

of the count's cigarettes handsomely monogrammed with a coronet and the initial "R."

She felt a hand bawdily caress her backside and straightened with a little scream to see the grinning face of Jacques, the co-pilot. "*Crétin*, not here!" she exploded.

"Then later, *mon petit chou*." His strong arms turned her into his embrace, and he kissed her pursed lips, mustache tickling her as it always did. "As for now, prepare to ascend again, for we must fly onward to the great metropolis and make our official arrival. This landing did not count, you understand. It never occurred."

"I know," she said curtly. "And tomorrow we make the return flight to Paris."

"Giving you a second opportunity to impress *le comte* with your charms. But before then—tonight, to be precise—I will enjoy them lengthily. After dinner and a cabaret, of course."

The helicopter blades whined in rising pitch, and the craft lifted. For a moment it hung a few meters above the earth, dust billowing outward from the downdraft of its rotors. Then it wheeled and flew above the white Mystère, wind from its passage entering the cabin gustily and lifting Carlotte's short skirts. Looking up, Jacques grimaced, and Carlotte said, "Where does he go now, our nonexistent passenger?"

"Who knows? And it is not our affair to inquire, *hein*? We are not paid to think, but to fly."

"Nevertheless, *cher* Jacques, the count found me sufficiently interesting to converse with me for the entire crossing."

"Converse?" He laughed shortly. "About what? International politics?"

"Why not?" she challenged. "You may think my head is between my legs, but the count—"

46

"*Ce vieux pédéraste?* Once or twice I looked back at the two of you. . . ."

"And saw—what?" she flashed.

"Nothing. I thought at least you could have given our distinguished passenger a hand job." Quickly he avoided her palm, pinched her behind cheerfully and strode up the aisle to his seat at the controls.

"Jacques," said the pilot, "after lift-off we fly north by east to an altitude of five thousand meters and call Kennedy for landing instructions. All must appear as though we came directly from Newfoundland."

"I understand," Jacques said and pressed the door closure button. By the time the cabin was secure he was thinking of the erotic delights in store for him that night with little Carlotte.

From his helicopter seat, De Rochepin looked around at gray-blue sky, then down at greening woods sectored by miles of ribboned highways and their ant-size cars. Again he felt the contempt, the hatred he held toward all Americans. They were a race of braggarts, of crude inhuman technocrats, and he hoped to live long enough to see them buried once and for all. For his entire adult life he had been making his contribution toward that transcendental goal, and if he were not agnostic, he would pray for its realization. Then there would be universal peace and advancement for the common man.

As for himself, De Rochepin was anything but a common man. His lineage was traceable as far back as the fourteenth century, when a certain ancestor was titled and granted substantial lands in Bourgogne south of Avallon. Certain historians had suggested that the first Comte de Rochepin received his patent of nobility in reward for betraying a conspiracy against Louis X. Others viewed the first count as a successful procurer to the court of the Capets. But wherever the

47

truth lay, De Rochepin land and wealth dwindled through war, venery, treachery and *mésalliances* or were squandered at gaming until what remained to the father of the present count was a run-down chateau and a few hundred hectares of mediocre vineyards. For generations De Rochepins had occupied sinecures in military service or the clergy, and the generation of Comte Gilbert Philippe was no different. He himself had begun a military career at St.-Cyr only to be dismissed for sodomy. One sister married a German baron and killed herself before the year was out. His other sister lived out her brief consumptive life in the Convent of Réconfort. Two somewhat younger brothers were respectively an admiral of the Navy and a general of the Air Force. Gilbert Philippe, after dismissal from St.-Cyr, spent a few years at the *université* and took a minor colonial post in Annam, where he acquired an addiction to opium and Indochinese boys. Later in Algiers, Arab girls so opened his soul to the delights of heterosexuality that he married a wealthy Parisian widow, who later died of dysentery and left him ample money to assuage his appetites and indulge an unaccountable taste for leftist politics. In 1936 De Rochepin was elected to the Chamber as a Socialist deputy from Vézelay and quickly allied himself with the enemies of Lebrun. He fought for and welcomed formation of the Front Populaire, contributed money and influence to the Spanish Republicans and offered his services to the Paris agitprop group headed by Josip Broz. In that capacity, De Rochepin publicized Broz as a front-line machine gunner, when in fact the Yugoslav revolutionary's only lead missiles were those set in type. De Rochepin made three brief clandestine visits to Republican lines, interviewing such loyalists as Pireto, Negrín, Nelken and Del Vayo. One night in an opium stupor De Rochepin was siezed by a SIM Purification Squad and nearly shot as an anarchosyndicalist before being saved by García Val. By then the struggle was nearly ended, and De Rochepin returned to France by air rather than through the Pyrenees as did so many of his co-religionists a few months later.

Defeated at the next election, De Rochepin used the period to reexamine his life in terms of Hitler's growing threat. What he had seen in Spain convinced him that the Soviet technique of political clandestinity surpassed the bolder, less veiled methods of the Germans. And as one who had struggled to keep France militarily harmless, De Rochepin foresaw the outcome of any war between Germany and France. So it was that on a social occasion he drew the Soviet ambassador into conversation and some days later received an ill-dressed visitor with a heavy Slavic accent.

From that time on, De Rochepin ceased overt contact with Communist cells, Communist friends, and left-wing Socialists, devoting himself instead to a flourishing career as journalist, international observer and lecturer. So it was that he remained personally unembarrassed by the Soviet-German Friendship Pact in contrast with the open agonies of the Communist Party of France, its deputies, allies, supporters and fellow travelers. Publicly, De Rochepin's posture was admirable: He was a humanist, an impartial, if liberal, journalist and a patriot devoted, in the final analysis, to the welfare of *la patrie*.

During the German occupation Gilbert Philippe de Rochepin went underground, not with his Marxist friends, but with the apolitical FFI. He helped plan the assassination of two Vichy officials before a message from De Gaulle summoned him to London. There, as an aide to the colonel, De Rochepin's show for concentrated work, apparent dedication to France, cosmopolitan associations and views on world politics brought him the offer of a portfolio in Algiers. Soon De Gaulle's titled Minister of Information created a staff drawn from among his former associations, from the underground, and on recommendation of his Soviet contact.

As De Gaulle energized and consolidated the fragmented sentiments of France d'Outre-Mer, Rochepin grew in stature, power and reputation. It was he who was consulted by Allied journalists, De Rochepin who briefed *le général* before his meetings with Roosevelt, Churchill, Stalin, Koenig and Giraud, providing De Gaulle with a fascinating miscellany of information acquired by De Rochepin through channels the Free French leader would hardly have approved.

De Rochepin's attention was caught by a wave of the pilot's hand. His gaze followed the gesture downward as the helicopter slowed and began a spiral descent toward an ocean-front estate whose manor house and gardens seemed copied from Versailles. Treelined roads and stables, a range for trap and skeet, a huge and empty swimming pool centered among fountains and graveled walks. An inlet cove for yachts and sailing craft. Tennis courts, orchards, croquet greens, guest villas and servant quarters. The estate's expanse seemed endless, but De Rochepin who had visited there once before knew that it encompassed no more than a few hundred acres.

From below faces upturned to watch the helicopter land. De Rochepin gripped his walking stick, and his thin lips met in distaste for what lay ahead.

As a child, as a boy, as a student, as the scion of an old and noble family, he had disliked Jews the whole of his life. He could never have been a Trotskyite, for Trotsky was a Jew, and when he was murdered, De Rochepin exulted in Stalin's revenge. Knowing of his anti-Semitism, the Soviets catered to it by never sending him a contact whose origins were even remotely Jewish.

But now, for the second time in his life, De Rochepin had been dispatched on a mission to a Jew. The same Jew, too.

That he was wealthy changed nothing in De Rochepin's view. That the Jew was ostentatious only confirmed his lifelong belief in the essential vulgarity of the Hebrew race. Besides, De Rochepin knew how that wealth had been acquired; in many ways the Jew's rise paralleled his own. But whereas De Rochepin saw himself as a gifted intellectual, he held the financier host-to-be in the utmost of contempt as a mercenary.

Edward Cerf, he was known in America, De Rochepin reflected. But in the France of a generation ago he had been plain Edouard Hirsch and, as a child, bore an even different name. Cerf-Hirsch had a gift for figures, it was true; a facility for assembling varied factors and disparate quantities; a talent for making profitable moves. But none of this, De Rochepin knew, would have brought Cerf-Hirsch to wealth and fame had he not at an early age followed the advice of his immigrant father and cleaved to the faith of Stalin.

So it was that as the skids touched down and the rotors ceased to spin above his head, Gilbert Philippe, seventeenth hereditary Comte de Rochepin, left the cabin and, with a fixed smile on his face, walked over to greet—though not as an equal—a man his heart despised.

"Cher Edouard!"

"Mon très cher Gilbert Philippe!"

The two men embraced, then walked arm in arm toward the manor where a welcoming luncheon had been laid.

Cerf was bald on most of his head, his face round and his skin olive, with an underlay of gray. He was

51

as squat as De Rochepin was slim, as short as the count was tall. His features were porcine, his belly fat. He was, in short, almost the prototype of Streicher's archetypal Jew, of Stalin's Wall Street imperialist.

Luncheon over, he walked with his guest into a large, book-lined library and shut the heavy door. Offering cigars from a deep humidor, he said, "Was it wise, this mode of arrival?"

"It was ordered. So there would be no trace." Delicately, De Rochepin clipped the end from a Havana Upmann and lighted it with a match, rotating the cigar in his fingers to light it evenly.

"When do you depart?"

"Tomorrow."

Cerf swallowed. "By helicopter?"

"Mais non, mon cher hôte. From here by your limousine to Wall Street. Thence by commercial helicopter to the airport. A brief, quick stroll to a certain hangar, and I embark once more for France."

Cerf's eyes showed his relief. "One cannot be too cautious," he observed, bit the end from a cigar and lighted it with a butane flame.

"Caution," said De Rochepin, "is of course the essence of our trade. Nevertheless, when boldness is required, I am entirely confident you will not be found lacking in that great quality."

"Nor have I been," said Cerf defensively, "when courage was required." But the Frenchman's suave challenge disturbed him. Was it possible De Rochepin knew of— No. It was quite inconceivable. Compartmentation would always interdict the transfer of such knowledge. It could never trickle down to De Rochepin, who operated, after all, at the same level as himself.

The Frenchman sat forward. "No implication intended," he said smoothly, "whatever."

Cerf brought over a decanter and two brandy bowls. After pouring a small amount of cognac into each, he handed one to his guest and held the other in the palm of his left hand. Then he seated himself in a chair that faced De Rochepin. "The message I received," he said, "was that you had a matter of urgent importance to discuss. We can do so now or, if you prefer, when you have rested."

"Now," said De Rochepin. "Then later, when we have reflected on its further implications."

Cerf settled back in his chair, aware that the other man would come to the point in his own time, by routes and methods of his own selection. He assumed his face showed no trace of the internal emotion that had gripped him ever since an unexpected courier had brought him word to prepare for De Rochepin's secret arrival. Edward Cerf had served his masters for more than half a century, accomplished miracles in their behalf and received an abundance of rewards. Still, in all that time it was impossible not to have made a mistake. One, he knew, had surfaced. There had been two others, though, and he lived in fear of their discovery. He was old now, old with a heart condition he had never reported for fear he would be supplanted by a younger, healthier man. He feared the generation now entering power within the Soviet Union. His own generation was lingering on, clinging to what power remained, but today's Soviet leader was no longer of the sweaty proletariat; he was educated, a specialist in affairs of the modern world, and inhumanly adept at politics. Such a man, carefully educated, meticulously prepared, would one day head the financial empire created by Cerf with Soviet funds, Soviet contacts and Soviet guidance.

He felt his forehead bead with moisture as he considered the inevitable. What he had to do now was exercise care in all things, provide no excuse for premature replacement by a man of whom the Soviets could say with certain confidence: "He is ours."

He had not liked the manner of De Rochepin's arrival. Cerf did not use helicopters himself, and so he had turned to a comrade for the service he had been ordered to provide. Helicopters made noise; they were easily seen from the ground even in his secluded portion of Long Island. And then the patrician count had emerged, all smiles; in his lapel, arrogantly displayed, the small rosette proclaiming him a Compagnon de la Libération. Cerf eyed it enviously and realized he was still unable to decide whether the French comrade had come as courier or executioner.

Clearing his throat, Cerf said, "You had a pleasant flight?"

"It was tiring. But one complies with one's duty."

"Of course." The banker turned his cigar in his fingers and examined the smooth gray ash. Holding well; a sign of quality. His eyes lifted to the shelves of books, settled on a leather-bound volume that was the count's first literary success: *Vers la Libération*.

In a show of unconcern Cerf let the silence grow between them.

De Rochepin sniffed the bouquet of his cognac and nodded approvingly. Tasting it, he nodded again. "I have not met its equal since my last visit."

"My dear Count, you must permit me to send back a case with you. Or at least a bottle." Cerf diminished the offer when he recalled De Rochepin's mode of departure. A man burdened by a case of cognac could hardly enter an aircraft hanger unobserved.

"Perhaps a bottle," De Rochepin consented. Once more he sipped from the glass, then lowered it to cradle the bowl in his hand. "The urgent matter arises of course from the difficulty our friend the Diplomat

54

finds himself in. You were instructed to take certain steps—"

"Which I did."

"—but which proved unproductive. Unless—" he let smoke drift from his narrow lips—"there have been new developments since I left Paris."

"I am expecting information at any moment."

A slight frown formed on De Rochepin's face. "The fools of the world cherish expectations, *mon cher ami*; their leaders, on the other hand, produce results." He leaned slightly forward, and his eyes held Cerf's. "What I am saying is that this matter is a serious one. Can you say that it has been treated with the seriousness it deserves?"

"Absolutely," Cerf exclaimed. "One of my best men was sent after the girl. But for an unforeseeable incident he would have had her and—"

"Unforeseeable?" drawled the count. "Pardon me, dear friend, but one does not build such a reputation as yours by not foreclosing every possibility." His voice hardened. "I take it, then, that you have no firm intelligence on where the girl is at this moment?"

Cerf swallowed. Almost inaudibly he said, "No. Not at this moment."

De Rochepin regarded him silently. Then he said, "Although neither you nor I are accustomed to asking or being given reasons for what we are required to do, I will tell you that the girl is in a position to destroy not only the Diplomat, but you and me as well."

Cerf opened his mouth to speak, but De Rochepin waved it shut. "You sent *a* man to locate her? Well, send a dozen more. You were not told how to find her or what to do with her once found. I am telling you now. But I am strongly suggesting that she must be silenced. Otherwise. . . ." His eyes followed a spiral of smoke toward the ceiling.

Hoarsely, Cerf said, "The Diplomat—he brought it on himself with his damn drinking, his craziness, his lust for women! Despicable! Insane!"

"Undeniably. But even if he were a babbling basket case he would have to be made whole. Within a few weeks he will become an announced candidate for the Nobel Prize. It is essential that he win, for canonized with that honor, he can become the next Secretary-General of the United Nations. That is the ultimate goal, *mon cher collègue*. And toward this triumph we are both required to strive—even if we both are sacrificed in the doing."

In the silence that followed, Cerf thought he felt his heart pound arhythmically, and he forced his lungs into a deep, calming breath. He should have taken his capsule after eating, *would* have taken it but for the searching eyes of this diabolical visitor. The more he studied De Rochepin's face, the more satanic it appeared to his raw imagination. High skull, widow's peak of hair, angular eyebrows, depthless eyes, hawk nose and cleft, bony chin.

"Your mind is wandering," De Rochepin said curtly. "I did not come all the way from France to tell you how to resolve what is your own affair. Pull yourself together, Edouard. Now."

Slowly Cerf nodded. With an effort he sat forward. "Is the Diplomat under control?"

"To the extent that he can be controlled. He was visited in Stockholm—again at great risk to persons of consequence." De Rochepin's eyes narrowed. "You know who the girl is, of course?"

"I was not told."

"Then I will inform you so that you may comprehend her importance, gain the correct perspective. The missing girl, *mon vieux ami*, is the daughter of his wife. His own stepdaughter."

For a while Edward Cerf said nothing. Then he

reached down to the telephone at his side, punched out a number and, after listening a moment, began to speak.

When he finished, a spasm of pain gripped his chest. Cerf waited until it passed, then gazed at the Comte de Rochepin.

"Excellent," said the Frenchman with a fox's smile. "Let us hope this effort brings results."

From a breast pocket he extracted a thin gold cigarette case engraved with his hereditary coat of arms. Casually he lighted a monogrammed cigarette, inhaled and let smoke drift slowly from his nostrils.

7

THE man called Smith sat in the library of his cavernous apartment and studied the faces of his two visitors. It was midafternoon, but the library was dim behind drawn blinds. After the death of his wife, the departure of his children, Smith had taken this apartment, retreated more and more within its confines as illness sapped his energies, drained his morale with bouts of deep depression. Now in retirement he left it as infrequently as he could, immersed in books that lined the walls, disciplining his mind through classics and plays, thick tomes of history, ethnology and ancient art.

The war had interrupted his placid academic life, plucked him from his professorship at a small New England college and made him an analyst in the OSS.

But less than a year later he was parachuting through a moonless sky in eastern France to join the maquis of the Vosges. For the next six months he was to guide and witness partisan warfare against the German Army in his sector. But the most savage war of all had been the one conducted by the Marxist partisans of the FTP against the maquisards of his nationalist FFI. At length, wounded in a fire fight—he never knew whether by Germans or the FTP—he was smuggled across the Lucelle near Basel. When his wounds healed, he joined the staff of Allen Dulles in Bern and for the first time gained panoramic knowledge of the hidden side of war. As Dulles' chief of operations, he played a role in the Italian surrender, the plot against Hitler's life. And through his office door came men like Arne Lakka and Hildebrand, crystalline figures in contrast with the flotsam of informers, mercenaries, vengeful traitors and double agents hoping for a piece of his action. From all this he had learned not to expect abnormal sacrifice from average men, learned quick appraisal of a man and his motives, learned to take them as they came—not imbue them with qualities he merely hoped they might possess.

He told himself he might have seen Don Bitler's face before—one of the many youngish faces in the darkened auditorium he had addressed so often over the following twenty-odd years. Even old friends were gracious enough to attend his annual half-day lecture on counterespionage, ask questions which he alone could answer. Within the Agency he had built a small efficient staff of reliable, thoughtful men, dividing them into research and operations and sending the latter category on missions whose complexity was as great as their achievements were beneficial.

Yes, he reflected, he might have glimpsed Don Bitler a time or two before. Of his friend Neal Thorpe he was less sure. Sometimes, as he sat late reading, he closed his eyes from the griping pain and saw in memory the classrooms he had taught before the war. Young, well-attired boys filled the seats, attentive faces mirroring hopes and aspirations that few of them had realized. Fade back thirty years, and both his visitors could blend into that long-ago student pattern. Thorpe, he understood was a resignee; Bitler still on active duty, actually only beginning his career.

"You were quite right to raise the issue back at headquarters," he said to Bitler. "And you, Mr. Thorpe, I think we owe you a vote of thanks for being sensible enough to get in touch with Don."

"I'd like to say, sir," said Bitler, "that I consider it a privilege to have this chance to meet you in person."

"I, too," said Thorpe. "As a trainee I knew the legend; I never thought I'd get to meet the man."

A remote smile crossed the lips of their host. "Men often meet under strange circumstances, but few stranger than those behind this meeting. As I said, Mr. Thorpe—"

"Neal, please."

"Yes. All of us are grateful for your initiative. Your concern for the girl, her whereabouts and safety are well taken. I will fill some of the background gaps for you; some simply remain *in vacuo*. Other information I will not supply because, in my judgment, you have no demonstrated need to know. First, the matter of her identity. Her name is Annalise Bauer and she is twenty-three years old. Her mother is named Freda, a lady of Swiss-Austrian stock who is the second wife of the German Foreign Minister. His name is Werber. Klaus Johann Werber."

Thorpe said, "Why would she lie about her name and parentage?"

"Because she may somehow have stumbled across certain closely guarded information concerning her stepfather and realized its possession placed her in considerable peril. That is one interpretation, and there may be others', but my thesis is supported by a case study covering nearly forty years. The study was compiled by my former staff at my instigation, and valuable contributions to it have been made by friendly foreign intelligence services, of which I might cite the French, British, Israeli and Norwegian, as well as certain individuals formerly active in intelligence matters, not excluding high-level Soviet and East German defectors. The cumulative weight of the evidence—if I may so term it—is that for most of his adult life Klaus Werber has been at the service of the Soviet Union."

"But," Thorpe objected, "Werber gained world attention as a leading anti-Communist cold warrior. I even remember charges that he was subsidized by the Agency."

"He was. One element of the Agency believed he was a valuable asset and initiated his covert support. Others of us, less convinced of his bona fides, concurred in order to see what the outcome would be. We also were confident that if we did not subsidize his political aspirations, the Soviet Union would." His hands spread. "The money gave us access to Werber, access we might not otherwise have enjoyed. At the same time I was instrumental in placing an agent within Werber's *cabinet particulier*, giving us an additional window on his contacts and activities. That agent, I regret to say, was identified by the opposition and murdered in cold blood."

"By Werber?" Don Bitler inquired.

"Likely not. Although his external appearance is of radiant health and confidence, self-possession, I read Werber as a man torn from within, guilt-ridden and haunted by the fear of exposure. You recall the challenges he issued to the Soviet occupiers? Through them Werber gained a reputation for bare-chested

60

personal courage. But suppose Werber had prior knowledge that his challenges would be ignored—how much courage is then implied? No, I see a man too uncertain of past and future to risk his present by personal killing. He has a weakness for drink, and his intellect is something well below the genius level. When faced by problems and challenges he cannot himself resolve, Werber's pattern is to drink. And when he is drunk he talks, he babbles. Thus, the Soviets have on their hands a prime asset, but one whose instability gives them continual nightmares." He smiled. "I'm glad I'm not his case officer."

He gazed at a thin line of sunlight where the window blinds did not entirely meet. Bitler lighted a cigarette, and Thorpe a slim cigar. "But to go back to the beginning," Smith continued, "we believe Werber was born in 1912 near Vardal in Norway, and his given name was Ragnar Garstad. Unfortunately during the German occupation, many civil records were destroyed; what remained after the war had been hidden in churches, and their information was much less complete than a civil registry. We know very little about his youth other than that he helped his family with their fishing and woodcutting, had a good physique and did sufficiently well in secondary school to enter the Univeristy of Bergen. There are no records to indicate his graduation and some evidence to indicate that he dropped out after stormy troubles centering on Agrarian Socialist activism. Shifts now the scene to the Vienna of 1934, when Garstad would have been twenty-one or two. That summer Chancellor Dollfuss was murdered by Nazi conspirators, and in August the Viennese Socialists—the Schutzbund—barricaded the streets and for four days engaged in bloody protest fighting. A film recovered from Abwehr files shows one of the Socialist bravos in particular. Although his

61

face is a close approximation of Ragnar Garstad's, a Viennese contemporary identified the man as a native German named Klaus Werber. Of further interest is the fact that nowhere in German records is the birth of Klaus Werber recorded. Werber himself, as you probably know, has let it be understood that he was born in Kiel, illegitimately, and so the birth was unrecorded. Common credence in his illegitimate birth, of course, gave Werber a considerable amount of sympathy among the Germans, a sympathy he used to political advantage. Then, after the 1934 fighting, he apparently went underground, as did many other anti-Nazi Socialists. In 1938 Hitler absorbed Austria into the Third Reich. We infer that Werber spent at least part of the years between 1934 and 1938 in the Soviet Union undergoing some kind of training, either specialized in the sense of intelligence or advanced political instruction. Then in 1941 German Intelligence arrested a band of Norwegian partisans whose mission was the assassination of Vidkun Quisling. Among them was a man whose name was given as Ragnar Garstad, a man who spoke both Norwegian and German with equal fluency. These men were held in a small prison camp to the east of Narvik in the mountains not far from the Swedish frontier. At that period the Germans had thousands of Norwegians behind bars. Daily there were summary trials, exemplary executions, mass reprisal murders. Terror was the weapon of German common usage. But what is unique about the anti-Quisling partisans is that the Soviet Union mounted a combined air-land operation to destroy the German garrison and free the prisoners. Our suspicion is that the Soviets were concerned with only one of those prisoners—Ragnar Garstad alias Klaus Werber. Of eight men, only three survived the arduous winter trip across the mountains into Sweden. And of those three, only one reached Stockholm."

"Werber?" said Neal Thorpe.

"Exactly. And he came not as Garstad but Klaus Werber. From then on, a high percentage of Werber's activities have become highly publicized information. For there he joined with Social Democrat refugees from Austria, Germany, Italy, Norway, Finland, France and Great Britain, to mention just a sampling of his international group. Also in Sweden as a refugee was a man who had fled there by boat with an infant daughter and two foot lockers of Soviet radio intercepts. This man had been the chief of Finland's Military Intelligence decoding unit, and with some help from British Intelligence he continued intercepting Soviet clandestine radio communications. Through some stroke of genius this man achieved a cryptanalytic breakthrough. He broke the Soviet code. And as he applied his new knowledge, he decoded a number of references to an agent the Soviets called the Norseman. These references continued, and their context placed the Norwegian in Stockholm, his milieu that of the Social Democratic refugees. Through surveillance and with the help of other Allied Intelligence officers —myself included—this Finn concluded that the agent called Norseman by the Soviets was Garstad-Werber, and that the Soviets had rescued him because of grandiose plans for the agent's postwar political career."

Pausing, Smith poured a small glass of water and sipped it. The only sound in the thick-walled apartment was that of elevator cables humming down the hall.

"The Finn bore an incandescent hatred for the Soviet Union. Russian soldiers had slaughtered his wife and burned his home to the ground. Even that long ago he had come to realize that Soviet sympathizers were present in every intelligence service, particularly our own, the OSS. For that reason he consistently refused to supply us—or anyone—with the key to the Soviet code. For us his product came in the form of

63

intelligence summaries, which, if passed by chance or by design to the Soviets, would not reveal their intercept origin. Over the years, this particular Soviet code has shown some internal alterations, but its fundamental structure remained unchanged, allowing the Finn to continue his eavesdropping, as it were, and giving us occasional useful glimpses of Soviet Intelligence interests and their reflections on the repetitive struggles for power within the Kremlin."

"Is he still alive?" Bitler asked.

Smith paused before answering. "He survived the war only because he was able to adopt another and distinct identity. That was his shield from assassination, for the Soviets, if they knew of his accomplishments, would make an endless effort to liquidate him and remove his cryptographic materials from our reach. In any case, because of the Finn's previous occupation and his closeness to Marshal Mannerheim, he was a target for liquidation. For years we believed his disguise impenetrable. Then, not many days ago, as he was driving in Holland, a sniper bullet sent his car into a Dutch canal. This latest incident meant either that he had been traced by the Soviets or that I had been surveilled to a meeting with him a short time before. Because my face is well known to the KGB and GRU, inadvertently I may have led them to my friend. The reason for our meeting was this: The Finn witnessed a recent meeting in Stockholm between Werber and two men high in the Soviet Intelligence *apparat*. For him, this contact was final proof of Werber's treachery, the last nail in the coffin of Werber's reputation. The Finn sent for me by indirect means, and so we met in Holland. What he did not know," said Smith with a glance at Thorpe, "was the reason for this unusual contact in Stockholm. From collateral intelligence we believe Werber's stepdaughter came across informa-

64

tion pointing to her mother's husband as an agent of the Soviet Union. We believe she was unable to handle the realization in any direct way, and so she simply fled from a situation that had become intolerable. You, Thorpe, chanced upon her when she came here from New York. The man Bloch who advertised for information was acting either for Werber or for the KGB. The surveillant you reported watching your apartment was not in the employ either of the FBI or the Agency. So, he was under orders either of Bloch or of some Soviet *rezident*. But back to Werber—we infer either that some alteration in his behavior pattern alerted the Soviets to move in on him or that they attached special significance to the sudden departure of his stepdaughter. Let us view the two men as a damage-assessment unit. From him they would want full details of what occurred. With him they would leave a warning to lay off the sauce and comport himself sensibly during his mission of international peace." His lips twisted, and he sipped a little more water. "Peace," he repeated. "What crimes are committed in thy name!"

Bitler ground out his cigarette in an ashtray. "I suppose NSA would be willing to pay almost anything for the Finn's code material."

"Anything."

"But is he alive?" Thorpe asked.

"His body was not recovered," Smith said with a tone of finality. "However, the body of another man was substituted by our Dutch friends, and so the Soviets have no reason to believe the Finn is not dead. Now, to the present and future: Of first importance is the safety of the girl. For humanitarian reasons, of course, but also because we think she holds the key to exposing a man who is capable of doing our country incalculable damage. We expect him to win the Nobel Prize for Peace—again that trigger word. And after that,

65

Werber is to be presented by Germany and a large number of other nations as candidate for the Secretary-Generalship of the United Nations."

Thorpe grunted in disgust.

"I may agree with your appraisal of the UN," Smith told them, "but so long as our government counts it a worthwhile forum, I feel bound to do so, too. For my part I would like to be rid of Werber for less altitudinous reasons. We have a Mutual Security Treaty with Germany, one of whose provisions establishes an exchange of information—intelligence. Even the little we provide the German Foreign Office is passed on to the Soviets. NATO representatives seem to go all limp with Werber, confiding in him and soliciting his counsel. Within what we call the NATO Interface, intelligence known to one ally is available to all. Thus the great vulnerability to slippage, examples of which would fill a not-so-small book. Put briefly, the persona of Klaus Werber is a current danger to the United States. As he ascends in international importance, his menace increases by quantum leaps. Now the reason I have given you this rather lengthy background is to 'put you in the picture,' as our British colleagues delight to say. And as preamble to enlisting the assistance of Mr. Thorpe." His eyes regarded Thorpe immovably. "You are the one American we know with whom Annalise has established what we could call a meaningful relationship. She trusts you because she has reason to trust you. Accordingly, she may turn to you again, even though the reason for her recent departure seems to have been concern for your well-being. The Agency is anxious to protect her from harm. But to do so, she has first to be found. Does she have money?"

"We never discussed it. She didn't ask for any, and I had no reason to think she needed money. She paid her own bill at the apartment house."

"Even so, her departure from Bonn was abrupt, unplanned. With her she probably took no more than what was in her purse. Was she wearing jewelry?"

"A ring that could have been emerald."

"Which she could pawn for cash. However, my hope is she will shortly run out of funds and contact you again. In which case you have got to persuade her to let us help her stay alive, accept the protection we can give."

Sharply Thorpe said, "What else do you think I'd do?"

"Try to protect her yourself." He saw Thorpe shake his head, said, "Thank you for coming, gentlemen," and showed them to the door. He walked slowly and painfully, stopped to gaze at the oil portrait of a woman with ash blond hair. The afternoon light gave life to her lips and eyes, and he half reached to touch her cheek, then realized it was only illusion, that what he saw on cold canvas was a trick of memory.

The man called Smith moved on to his chair and sat in it, remembering that soon he would have to take his pills again. He was a proud man, struggling bitterly and determinedly against impending death. His true name was Alton Regester, but in his adult life no one had ever called him Al. For a while he sat there brooding about Annalise Bauer, Neal Thorpe, and the strangeness of a world that had seen fit to accord too much in fame and honor to the Soviet agent Klaus Werber. Then Alton Regester got up, went to his bedroom and swallowed two capsules with water. He lay down upon his bed, thinking that rest would help recover his strength, perhaps prolong his life until Klaus Werber could be exposed for what he was.

Thorpe drove Don Bitler to his apartment in an Arlington high-rise, accepted an invitation to come up for coffee or a drink. Bitler's place had one bedroom and was sparsely furnished. The windows had ready-made curtains, and the walls were bare but for an African shield set over two crossed spears, a couple of Day-Glo posters and a framed college diploma. Open shelves held expensive audio components, and near the simulated fireplace stood a color television set. While Bitler was making coffee, Thorpe sat down and opened the glass top of the coffee table. In it were half a dozen knives, among them a Malayan kris, a Gurkha kukri and one with a Damascene blade whose haft was inlaid with ivory and looked North African. Thorpe recognized a montagnard dagger and picked it up, wishing he had brought one back from Vietnam. He was holding it when Bitler came back with two coffee cups and said, "Like my collection? It's only a start, but I've always had a thing about knives. These all came from Agency guys."

Thorpe replaced the glass top and set the dagger aside. "No sugar," he said. "Black's fine."

Bitler sat down beside him. "What did you think of Regester's symposium?"

"Impressive."

Bitler shrugged. "I guess when you've told a story long enough, you get to believing it."

"You don't?"

Bitler sipped and set down his cup. "Look, Neal, there's a mountain of information floating around the Agency that's more rumor than truth—if you'd stayed on, you'd have found that out. For example, one of the deputy directors has Martin Bormann as a private hobby; he's convinced Bormann's in Paraguay—or Peru or Ecuador. It was Brazil last time I heard. Take Alton Regester and the staff he created. They had to have a reason to justify their existence, the high GS levels. I know some of the guys on that staff: there's a body of opinion that says Regester is a monomaniac. According to one of the guys, Klaus Werber isn't the only notable on Regester's Agent of Influence list. I've heard it includes a big-time French journalist-politician, a very wealthy U.S.-European banker with obscure origins, and get this—a Cardinal!" He chuckled. "Can you imagine a Prince of the Church taking orders from Moscow and subverting the Pope?"

Thorpe lifted his cup and drank.

Bitler shook his head. "As I size him up, Regester's a great old guy who maybe did a lot in OSS and the Agency's early days, but for the last ten years he's been an anachronism. You know, the kind who sees spies everywhere. His point of view represents the old conspiracy theory. Frankly, I don't buy it, never have."

Thorpe felt uncomfortable. In Regester's apartment Bitler had seemed genuinely impressed by the retired officer; now Don was dismissing Regester as a senile theorist. He glanced sideways at Bitler and saw his host's amused smile.

Thorpe finished his coffee and cleared his throat. "Apart from that, there's still the girl."

Bitler nodded. "Except that I don't know what kind of protection Regester thinks the Agency can provide. We don't operate that kind of service in this country—that's up to the FBI." He looked at Thorpe. "Thinking it over, I guess I should have let you go to the Bureau direct, without involving the Agency or Alton Regester. Maybe that's what you ought to do, Neal."

He stood up. "I'll sleep on it."

"Do that." Bitler went to the door and opened it. "Now we've reopened communications, don't be such a stranger. I'll call you for lunch next week. Maybe you'll have found the girl by then."

"I hope," Thorpe said, realizing that it was only a slim chance that he could.

They shook hands, and Thorpe rode the elevator down to the parking lot. Driving back to Washington,

69

he reviewed all that Regester had said and Bitler's abrupt put-down. Maybe Bitler was right, and Regester was continuing to live in a world of hostile fantasies. But even if you accepted that, he reasoned, how did you dismiss Bloch, the street surveillants, the break-in at his apartment and the girl, whose fear was authentic if he was any judge? Well, Thorpe thought, I can't dismiss them, because they're real, not fantasies of anyone's imagination. He wondered if Bitler's sudden cynical shift of view was justified or whether, like a good bureaucrat, Bitler had surrendered to nonadvocacy of unpopular causes. Either way, the alteration disturbed him.

Thorpe put in an hour at his neglected office, doing some detail work on what would be a Q Street mansion. Then he locked up and went home.

8

SHE had spent part of the day roaming Georgetown, first trading in her fleece-lined Afghan coat for an ankle-length monstrosity of worn brown fur. Next, she bought an ash-blond wig, sandals, dungaree shirt, faded Levis and a seedy Australian bush hat. From an Army surplus store she acquired a fiber suitcase large enough to hold the combined contents of the luggage she had brought from Bonn. Then she returned to the shabby rooming house where she had taken refuge the night before and in the small bathroom carefully bleached her full dark eyebrows.

That done, she tried on the wig and reluctantly cut two inches from the length of her own dark hair. Now the wig fitted, and Annalise Bauer stared at the change. She got into the heavy fur coat and donned the khaki hat. In the cracked mirror her image blended into the semblance of dozens, if not scores, of girls she had studied on her reconnaissance through Georgetown.

As she pulled off coat and hat, she wondered if even Neal would recognize her now. Of more importance, though, was whether she would ever see him again. Transferring the contents of her two bags into the fiber suitcase, she reflected that she had liked his face from the first. Luckily so, because he had been the only means out of her airport dilemma. She liked his uneven nose, his smile, the wrinkles at the corners of his eyes. He was, she realized, older than herself, but by how much she did not know. Much less than middle-aged, and already successful at his profession. His help had been quick and spontaneous, generous and undemanding. She knew he was attracted to her—taking her in his arms proved the point, if it needed proving. Then that Puritan morality for which Americans were both famed and condemned had intervened. And her own unthinking reaction. . . .

She lay back on the iron-frame bed and stared up at the stained plaster ceiling. She was attracted to Neal Thorpe, she realized, even though she knew little of his tastes, his way of life. The apartment he mentioned would hold clues to both, but he had not asked her there. For a moment she wondered if he were married or living with a mistress. Why not? she thought. Almost everything I told him was untrue, even to my name. Why should I expect him not to lie?

Because, the answer came, I had something to hide, and he did not. His face isn't the face of a liar. He looks like the elder brother I always wanted and never

71

had. Friendly, open and helpful without stint. Concerned.

She was not accustomed to men who were both young and serious. The student element was frivolous; the older males were too serious, too bent on conquest. And there were all those others who saw her as a lever to advancement in the society or government of Germany.

Slowly her thoughts turned to her stepfather and her mother. Poor Mama, she mused; so weak, so dependent on Klaus. You never should have married him. Had four years' widowhood been that intolerable? She remembered her mother coming to the school outside Vevey to tell her of the man she had met and had agreed to marry. A widower, she explained, lonely like herself. A fine, strong man who would prove an affectionate father to her only child.

She knew that her mother's money—really her father's—had advanced her new husband's political career. Mayor of Cologne, patron of the Beethoven Society, the Musikverein, the Philharmonic. Tone-deaf Klaus, she thought with irony, with his pale-white skin, fine blond hair and light-blue eyes. German, yet the image of a Dane.

During her last two years in school she had seen little of her stepfather. Then came her debut—held at Bonn's fashionable Redoute Kurhaus through his influence. Dancing with him that night, she had thought he was pressing her possessively close, but she excused it on the grounds of his having to drink a glass with so many of the guests. Even so, she had avoided their being alone together, although Mama chided her for being cold toward Klaus.

The London School of Painting had been the solution, not that she had talent, but it kept her away from home in Bad Godesberg, gave her the first opportunity to live independently and see a little of what lay

72

beyond boarding school walls. Peter had become her companion; poor, talented and ambitious. From him she learned the vagaries of the artistic personality but, though she tried, was unable to return his love. Still, she reveled in the freedom of London, the easy exchanges with her fellow students. Having her own car, she toured the countryside on weekends and furnished an attractive flat while declining repeated invitations to visit Klaus and Mama in their home.

A week ago, she mused, who would have thought I would be in America today? In Washington. And who could have conceived the reason why? Her eyes closed as she heard again the blurted-out confession, felt the damp, fondling hands of Caliban. . . .

I wanted to die, she remembered, opening her eyes to end the nightmare. He never loved Mama, only himself. A cruel self-centered man. And when he realized what he had done, that I would never—she got up shakily to end the thrust of memory, stared at her face in the mirror and blotted moist eyes with a makeup tissue.

Only where do I go from here? she asked herself. The money won't last forever, and I can't approach the embassy—they're looking for me, if what Neal said about the man called Bloch is true.

Only, more than the embassy may be searching.

They'll kill you if you tell, said Klaus with watery eyes. *They'll kill you if they even think you know*, he said and poured himself another drink.

She knew who they were. In London, living in the student ambiance, she had accepted almost automatically the reflexive anti-Americanism of her companions, the pro-Soviet fervor they displayed. But because of Klaus, from him, she learned in a blinding instant that it was not the Americans she ought to fear, but the friends of her stepfather. His lifelong masters.

And she had realized without even brief analysis that

Mama would not believe her. Mama would believe none of it, when any part would break her heart. Whom could I tell if not my own mother? The German police? They would have laughed at me, telephoned my home and suggested lengthy care in a nursing home.

Slowly she picked up the ratty fur coat and fitted the too-large bush hat on her head. I've got to eat sometime, she told herself. I might as well go now, try out my new disguise. If it passes, I can think of another place to go. Los Angeles, perhaps, or Chicago. They can't have people everywhere.

Pulling on the coat, she left the room and went down the narrow staircase to the door that gave out on the busy street.

The air had cleared, and the feel of rain was gone. Near the corner she found herself enveloped in a youthful crowd bound for a nearby sandwich stand. Putting aside her cares, Annalise Bauer let herself be carried along and found herself after a time with a hero sandwich in her hand.

Evening in Rome. Under a pewter sky the frenzied crush of traffic thinned, lowering the level of sound that penetrated the ornate and ancient palace where guests of the Italian state were housed.

From the suite accorded the Foreign Minister of Germany the last visitors of the day departed in a final reprise of bows, embraces and professions of enthusiasm for his self-appointed task. As Klaus Werber saw the last of them out, his face relaxed from the set smile, and he crossed the sitting room, loosening his tie. For a moment his gaze lingered on the cellarette of liquors provided by his hosts, but he moistened dry lips and put aside the inclination. The warning in Stockholm had been specific and direct. Liquor was his enemy and must be avoided at whatever personal cost. Liquor could destroy him, could carry others along in the avalanche of his destruction. For years his preparation had been planned for the brilliant moment that lay now within his reach. Each step programmed. Nothing, *nothing* must prevent its realization. There was to be no more self-indulgence, no further lapse. Henceforth he was to live as a monk, drawing strength and determination from the example of Lenin.

He looked and felt better than when they had seen him in Stockholm. His eyes were clear, his face less puffy, his hands without tremors. Even so, he knew that liver and kidneys had been affected by his lifelong tendency to drink, but he had always rationalized his addiction as caused by what was expected of him, the pressures under which he lived and did his work. Living many lives, he reflected, he had become not one but many men. And whom did he know who could have done what he did successfully? Each facet of his life was polished to perfection.

Almost.

Seating himself, Klaus Werber let his mind drift back to a hot August afternoon in Vienna, the smoke of burning barricades, the crackling fire of pistols, revolvers and machine guns, the fog of cordite smoke like a pall over the streets. He emptied his revolver at a rush of Christian Democrats, dropped back to take shelter in a substreet doorway. As the barricade was overwhelmed, he shrank further into the shadowed space, looking wildly around for a weapon. Nearby was a litter of bricks and cobblestones pried from the street. Snatching up one, he hurled it into the face staring down at him. With a cry the figure pitched forward, almost into his arms, and he saw in horror that he had killed an unarmed boy. Sightless eyes stared into his; blood oozed from the crushed forehead.

With another brick he smashed the door window,

reached to open the lock and fled through the small apartment to the safety of an alley distant from the fighting still going on. There he slumped trembling against the wall and wiped his bloodied hands. The boy, he learned later, had been returning from school to the basement apartment where he lived. And he was made aware that his crime had been observed.

His eyes ranged the room, pausing briefly on the assorted liquor bottles, as he mused that there was not enough liquor in the world to submerge the face of the boy he had killed.

He remembered the chains around his hands and ankles, the bitter cold of the prison barracks, the wind and snow driving through the cracks to cover the flooring like white silt. Body and mind numb, he had heard the first shots through the wind, the louder crash of grenades and mortar shells. Through the darkness he could see the flash of gunfire, the movement of white-clad bodies, some dying as they climbed the stockade fence, others drifting in on parachutes to clear the high barbed wire. He saw his SS captors die in their black uniforms, die half-naked as they ran for their guns. The barracks door burst open, and he shrank away, thinking SS guards had come to finish them off with their Schmeissers. Instead, he saw sheeted soldiers with red stars on their fur-lined caps.

While he and the other prisoners were being freed, the attackers killed the rest of the garrison and set the buildings afire. Before withdrawing, they fed and clothed him, gave him skis and climbing gear. Then their leader took him aside and told him what he was to do.

With the others who had been freed he left the burning camp and skied eastward into the night. By dawn five who had been starved and tortured had dropped behind to freeze in the snow, and only Olaf and Nils were left. They skied to the base of the final

76

Kjolen spine, burned skis for warmth and water and started up the rocky side. Under clear blue sky they climbed through snow-deep cirques into the upper winds, using ropes and picks and pitons to scale the crags toward freedom. Finally, at the top they rested before beginning to descend the cliff's sheer face.

He remembered the forest beyond the valley far below, the tops of pines thrusting upward through the heavy snow. Like a miniature Christmas *crèche*, said Nils, and Olaf smiled, thinking of his own home that Christmas next he might share with wife and child. Young men, both, Nils younger than I, so when he asked to lead the way, I let him, played out the rope with Olaf going next, said I would carry the rations being bigger, and so they started down the scarp, the *chik-chik* of their picks shearing the thin high air. They called for me to follow, and when I peered down, both were hanging on the rope, their red and blistered faces looking up at mine. Waiting for me to come.

Instead, I laid the knife-edge on the rope and sawed it through. From them one endless wail shattering our frozen silence as they hurtled downward to the valley floor. Like dots their bodies were, black flyspecks on a field of purest white. And when my fear and horror and shaking passed, I gulped my snaps and hung their rations on my belt. My coil of rope I dropped below, fixing the end around a frozen stump, then started down, hand over hand. Hours with the wind tearing at me, buffeting the rope as I inched down. Then finally at the bottom, floundering in snow, half drowned in clinging powder as I flopped like a seal toward the forest that was Sweden.

Beyond, a frozen lake, the hut of woodcutters like the one where I was born. They warmed and fed me, let me rest and took me to the railhead at Kiruna.

Then Stockholm and the house I had been told to find. Inside, a man who was expecting me.

Slowly the reverie wore off. Outside the night had come. The lamps in his room were dark, but he made no move to turn them on. Light would glint on the bottles, the mirror reflect the last human face seen by a boy of twelve and two young men.

I am a murderer, he said to himself in the darkness of the room, and his hands tightened on the armrests until their strain brought pain. I am many things, and murderer is one.

Delicately, the telephone bell sounded, intruding on his thoughts. Three times it rang before he rose and went over to answer, knowing in advance that it was no more than a respectful reminder to begin dressing for the banquet at the Quirinale.

9

AT ten o'clock the television program Thorpe had been watching ended, and he left his chair to change the channel. He was consulting the program guide when the doorbell rang. The unexpected sound froze him; then quietly, he crossed the floor and put his ear to the door. Hearing nothing, he moved aside and snapped, "Who is it?"

"Can I come in?"

Anna's soft voice.

Thorpe unlocked the door and saw a bizarre fur-clad figure that he barely recognized. He drew her in, locked the door and turned off the ceiling lights.

"What—" she began, but he put a finger to her lips and moved to the nearest window.

Parting the blind, he looked down at the street, glanced to right and left. Seeing no surveillant, he turned to her. "Did anyone see you come?"

"I—I don't think so." She pulled off the heavy coat. The bush hat and wig came next, and now, except for bleached eyebrows, she was as he had last seen her the night before.

"I've been plenty worried about you," he told her. "When I went to your apartment this morning—"

"Forgive me, but I thought things over and decided I ought to move out before morning."

"I'm glad you did—there was a man asking about you before I arrived." He ran a hand through his hair. "Coffee? A drink?"

"Both. Coffee with a little cognac."

She followed him into the kitchenette and watched him fill a saucepan with water and set it to boil. Then he measured instant coffee into two cups and got out a bottle of Martell. Filling two small crystal glasses, he said, "Where did you go? Where have you been?"

"A rather shabby rooming house—a pad, I believe it's called—not far from here."

"I've never been more glad to see someone—Anna-lise Bauer."

Her eyes opened wide. "How—how did you learn my name?"

"Through friends in government who know something about your family."

Her shoulders seemed to sag. She lifted the glass to her lips and drank, then took a deep breath. "It was not that I wanted to lie to you—but I felt you would be safer if you did not know everything."

"I don't. But the important thing is you're here."

She smiled briefly. "You must be wondering why, and the answer is my room is not a place one would

79

care to spend a great deal of time—alone. To say it another way, Neal, I was more lonely than I think I've ever been. So . . . I came here."

He removed the saucepan and poured water into their cups, adding cognac to both. Then he carried them to the coffee table, watched her drop her sandals and gracefully arrange her Levi-clad legs. As she lifted her cup she said, "Have you lived here long?"

"A year."

Her gaze traveled around the room. "As a bachelor?"

"Most of the time."

"I suppose I should not ask, but—is there one girl you see more than the others?"

"Not really."

"That was the one thing that made me hesitate before coming. I did not want to interrupt a—be responsible for a—perhaps situation is the word. And because I thought your telephone might be overheard, I did not want to call."

"Good thinking," he said. "And from now on you'll be my only guest."

Her eyes lowered. "You said you learned my name from friends in your government. May I ask what?"

"I might as well tell you," he said reluctantly. "I was in Intelligence for a while."

"But you left. Why?"

"You could say I wanted to do my own thing—which turned out to be architecture."

"These—friends of yours. What did they say, Neal?"

"They said you needed protection, that I should call them if you ever got in touch with me."

Her head moved slowly, negatively. "I don't want that."

"They also told me some things about your step-father. They thought you might know a great deal more, and because of that, you know your life is in

80

danger. Do you want to tell me what it is you know?"

"No. Not now, at least."

"But you can't hide forever."

"I do not think I will have to. I believe Klaus will destroy himself—or be destroyed."

Thorpe sipped from his cup, savoring the aromatic scent of coffee blended with cognac. "How much does your mother know?"

"I think she knows nothing. To her Klaus Werber is a great hero. But I could not go on living in his home, as part of his family—and I knew I could never persuade my mother that her husband is not the man she believes him to be." Anna sat forward. "Do you have to tell your friends I came to you?"

"No."

"Then I am asking a great deal, am I not? To protect me when you do not even know why I need protection."

He shook his head. "Your being here means a great deal."

"It is good of you to put it that way. Now I will admit that it was not only loneliness that drove me from my room. I found myself wanting to see you, talk to you, somehow explain what brought me to this country. Now . . . now, I am very glad that I came." Impulsively, she took his hand, held it between hers. "At the airport we were strangers. How strange what chance can do."

"Or fate."

She nodded, leaned forward and kissed his cheek lightly. As though he were her big brother, he thought, and decided that any demonstration of affection was better than none. "I have an extra toothbrush," he told her. "Tomorrow we can collect your other things."

"Are you quite sure you want me to—move in?"

"I wouldn't have it any other way. But don't forget I've been under surveillance and the apartment broken into."

"Then perhaps this is the safest place I could be."

He brought brandy bowls to the coffee table and poured cognac into them, turned on the tape deck and sat so that he could study her face without being obvious. No question, Annalise was the most beautiful, most desirable female he had ever known. All the others were nothing more than pale imitations—even in her dungaree shirt and Levis. Beyond her own unwillingness to seek official protection, there was his own overwhelming desire to keep her with him. As long as he could.

So when their brandy was finished, he got out sheets and a blanket and made a bed for himself on the sofa. Anna watched with amusement, then brought him a pillow from the bedroom.

When the lights were off and the apartment quiet, he lay alone in the darkness, thinking of all that Regester had told him, thinking back to his first glimpse of her at the airport and all that had happened since that night. Gradually his thoughts drifted away and were replaced by welcome sleep.

The telephone rang. Thorpe rose on one elbow, groggily trying to orient himself in time and place. Not in the bedroom, no. In— The telephone rang stridently, and he got up to lift the receiver.

A voice said, "No names, but we were together this afternoon. Do you understand?"

"I understand," Thorpe said, recognizing Regester's voice. He looked down at the table clock. Two fifteen. "Go on."

"I've just been called by some men investigating a murder. They knew you and Bitler had been with me today. And because I don't believe you could have killed him, I wanted you to know Bitler's dead."

"Dead!"

"Shot. They found your prints in his apartment

—particularly on a knife. Can you account for your time since leaving him?"

"Account— I went to the office for an hour, then came here. I've been here since then."

"Any witnesses?"

He swallowed. "Not until ten o'clock."

"No good," Regester said thoughtfully. "Bitler was killed earlier—eight or nine o'clock. A desk clerk saw a man go into the elevator with Bitler about six. You?"

"Yes. But I left after about twenty minutes."

"Clerk didn't see you leave. So because Bitler was a federal officer, the FBI's got the case. They ought to be at your place shortly."

"What should I do?"

"You can be arrested and try to prove you're innocent—or you can try to get away. Of course, that would leave the girl without anyone to turn to."

"She's with me," Thorpe said, and turned to see Anna standing in the bedroom door.

"Then take her with you. Call me if you make it, and I'll try to help. They won't be looking for two people, just one. So that's a plus. Good luck, Neal." The line went dead.

"What—who was that?" she said.

"We've got to get out of here," he said, his mind totally clear. "Get dressed, and we'll go out the back way."

"Why, Neal?"

"A man has been killed—the police are coming for me."

"But you didn't kill anyone."

"I'm the easiest one to hang it on. Now move."

Obediently, she disappeared into the bedroom. while Thorpe pulled on his clothing in the dark. When Anna reappeared, she was dressed in her wig, fur coat, bush hat and sandals. Thorpe got a raincoat from the closet, put it on and parted the living-room blinds.

Outside the street was quiet, empty but for the rows of parked cars. Carefully he closed the blinds and led Anna to the kitchen's service door, where he listened for a moment before opening the door. The telephone rang. Its sound halted him for a moment; then he closed the door on its ringing.

Together they went down the stairs and out the rear door. He offered to help Anna over the wall; but she climbed quickly over, and Thorpe followed. Bending low, they made their way across the garden's turned earth until they reached the alley. As they neared the street, she said, "What are we going to do?"

"Keep going," he said, and pointed to a dark sedan wheeling up the street. From the rear fender extended a radio antenna, and there were two men in the front seat. Turning, Thorpe gathered her into his arms so that her hat hid the outline of his face. The first car was followed by a second traveling equally fast over the deserted street. "I can't ask you to come with me," he said huskily, "and I don't want to leave you. But if we're together, I'll know you're safe."

"I want to be with you," she whispered. "Was the man killed because of me?"

"I don't know why he was killed."

Slowly, lingeringly, she kissed his lips. "We'll go to my room," she told him. "We need a place where we can decide what to do."

He took her arm, and they strolled along the sidewalk to where Thorpe had left his car. Anna directed him to the rooming house, and he pulled up in front of it, engine idling.

"I've been thinking," he said. "They'll be looking for this car, so I think they ought to find it. Go on up, and I'll be back in an hour or so."

She nodded. "Top floor. The door will be un-locked." Her face tightened. "But if you don't come back?"

84

"Call a man named Regester. Alton Regester." He spelled the name for her. "He's the one who called me."

She nodded, got out of the car, and Thorpe saw her go up the short walk to the entrance. After making a U-turn, he drove down Wisconsin, parked under the Freeway and walked back up the hill to his office in the Canal Square building. Before entering he scanned the outside for surveillants, then the inner court.

The corridors were dark. Thorpe unlocked the office door and went in without turning on lights. From his desk he took his passport and a company credit card he seldom used, opened the office safe and extracted twenty-four dollars from the petty cash box. Then he left the office and drove along Pennsylvania Avenue to a bank with electronic service. Using his plastic banking card he withdrew five hundred dollars from his checking account, got back into his car and drove to National Airport. From the radio came flash accounts of Bitler's murder, the search for an architect named Thorpe, who was known to have been with Bitler before he was shot. The newscaster said the FBI had entered the case, although Bitler's CIA employment was not mentioned.

Thorpe turned his car into the parking lot, took a check from the machine and drove under the lifted barrier. At that hour there was a wide choice of parking slots; he chose one in a far corner, turned off the headlights and ignition. The keys he stuck under the floor mat, closed the door without locking it and walked to a public phone booth. Thorpe dialed his apartment number and heard two rings before a male voice answered with a curt, "Yeah?"

"Neal?" he said.

"Who's this?"

"Must have the wrong number," Thorpe muttered and replaced the receiver. The men in the black sedans had taken possession of his apartment. If he had had more time after Regester's warning call, Thorpe thought as he walked away, he would have taken his phone and address book with him. But now the bureau had it, and they would check each entry methodically. Help, refuge, succor from any of his friends had been foreclosed. He knew that he was shut off from what had been his world. He was isolated. Alone.

From the parking lot he walked down to the air-freight hangars, then up to the street level, where he found a waiting bus. On it were a dozen other passengers. He sat among them to avoid being singled out by the driver, and presently the bus pulled away, heading for downtown Washington. From there he boarded a bus that ran to Georgetown, where he got off and walked to Anna's rooming house. Entering unobserved, he went quietly up the stairs and opened the door of her room.

At his entrance she sat up in the narrow bed. "Only me," he said, and locked the door.

"You were away so long. . . ."

"Things to do." He loosened his tie and took off his jacket. In the darkness of the room he could barely make out her form. He hung the coat on a chair and sat on the edge of the bed, elbows on his knees, face in his hands.

In his entire life, Thorpe had never fled danger, and as he thought about it now, he wondered if he should have followed Regester's implied advice. Eventually the FBI would find his car at the airport. They would spend time searching passenger lists for his name, lose more time interviewing ticket agents, showing blowups of his Agency ID photograph to stewardesses of a dozen airlines that flew from Washington. In any case, locating his car at the airport would widen the search for him, deconcentrate it from the Washington area.

For now the important thing was not to be seen on the street and recognized.

Fragments of Agency training were returning to his mind. A half-remembered caution here, alternate courses of action there. "In the morning," he said, "I'll need some things by way of physical disguise. Not far from here there's a fag wig shop, and since we'll be traveling together, you'd better get me some clothes like yours."

Her hand found his, interlaced their fingers. He lowered his lips to her hand. "This isn't the setting I had in mind to disclose it," he said quietly, "but I love you."

She drew him down beside her, cradling his head on her arm. "Everything that has happened is my fault, Neal. Wherever you go, I want to be with you . . . as long as you want me."

For the first time in hours he felt his lips relax into a smile. The touch of her flesh calmed his mind, ridding it of fear and apprehension. For now, at least, he was content. Tomorrow would take care of itself.

One way or another.

10

AS Edward Cerf watched De Rochepin's helicopter rise from the Wall Street heliport, he felt an overwhelming sense of relief. His eyes followed as it turned and spun off to the east, then was lost in low-hanging clouds.

Taking a deep breath, the financier walked up the ramp to his waiting limousine, got into the rear seat and nodded at his chauffeur. With five minutes the limousine drew up before a handsome building whose oak-framed entrance door bore the gilt legend "Cerf & Co."

A uniformed doorman bowed deferentially as he opened the paneled portals to his employer. Preoccupied, Cerf barely nodded in return, then walked slowly through the handsomely decorated office. A conscious effort had been made to avoid the appearance of a commerical institution. Furnishings were authentic American antiques or replicas separated into suites by low walnut railings. Williamsburg colors predominated on the walls and vaulted ceiling. There were authentic oil paintings of the Revolutionary period, a series of vellum holographs and contemporary engravings of Bunker Hill, Boston Common and the staff of General Washington. Intuitively, Cerf had approved the decorator's scheme, for the decor not only distinguished his institution from other private banking houses, but established a prima facie impression of roots that were deep in the American past and tradition.

But he walked on, oblivious of the *mise-en-scène*, and reached his office at the far end of the building. His receptionist rose, said, "Good morning, sir," and helped him out of the light, British-tailored topcoat. Cerf opened his door and closed it, walked to his desk and sat down. The desk was Louis XV by Cressent, and there was a replica of it in the Louvre. The other furnishings—armchairs, commodes, sconces, and tapestries—were all of the same period, some brought from his Paris establishment when Cerf founded the New York office of his banking house. The setting served to remind Cerf of the French portion of his background and subtly suggested to visitors that Cerf's origins were aristocratic—that he was perhaps a temperamental monarchist.

The polished veneer of his desk was bare but for a thin sheaf of papers that included cables, letters and the latest quotations from the world's principal financial markets. And there was a French telephone, ornamented and chased in gold. Cerf adjusted a pincenez and read through the papers, marking those that required an answer with a simple yes or no.

He rang for his confidential secretary, a young male graduate of the Wharton School, and issued a series of buy and sell orders. Then he reviewed the portfolio of the mutual fund that bore his name and gave instructions to the secretary. Cerf was a very private public man who inevitably declined invitations to address financial associations or socialize with other financiers at small and unpublicized luncheon clubs. Accordingly, his secretary routinely sent regrets to all such invitations; this morning he had declined three without even bringing them to Cerf's attention.

When the secretary withdrew, Cerf looked at an ornamental wall clock and saw that he would have to take his medicine in another seven minutes. At eleven o'clock he would descend to the private health room that had been constructed in the basement area not far from the built-in vaults. There he would steam in the sauna for precisely ten minutes before giving himself over to the ministrations of his personal masseur. By twelve he would be dining in his office, today's menu was a medium lamb chop, cottage cheese nested in lettuce and a glass of iced tea artificially sweetened. Despite the rigorous limitations of his caloric intake, Edward Cerf found it nearly impossible to lose weight. He believed that both his father and mother had been diabetics from the symptoms he remembered, rather than from medical diagnosis. For in the little Russian village where he was born there was no medical wisdom beyond that of midwives and wet nurses. Cerf knew that he suffered from some sort of metabolic imbalance, and he related it to incipient diabetes. But he had avoided clinical diagnosis lest his heart condition be uncovered by agents of the Soviet *rezident* to whom Cerf reported.

Alone in his soundproof room, Edward Cerf thought again of Gilbert Philippe de Rochepin and reflected on the total disparity of their origins. Where the count had succeeded to lands and a hereditary title, Cerf had been born Lazar Zamoilov, one of nine children of Reva and Avram Zamoilov in the Ukrainian village of Ludosk. By the time Lazar was six only five siblings survived and what schooling he received came from the rabbi of Ludosk's lone synagogue. Although Avram Zamoilov was nearly illiterate, a talent for conspiracy drew him to the fringes of the People's Will, the underground anti-czarist organization. The Zamoilov farm produced milk, cabbage, corn and other vegetables, and although the family lived in near starvation, there was seldom a surplus to trade or sell. As a boy Lazar was quiet and introspective, hungrily reading every book the rabbi could provide. When he was ten, his mother died of diptheria, followed within a few days by a younger sister and brother. With the formation of the Duma, Avram Zamoilov became openly identified with Bolshevik agitation, abandoned the farm and moved his family to the outskirts of Odessa. There, for the first time, Lazar received some formal schooling and was recruited by his father as an underground courier who carried messages and money from point to point within the great seaport city. It was there that young Lazar first saw ships from countries of which he was only dimly aware. He read the forbidden writings of Marx and Engels to his father, and on one occasion bore a message to a man in hiding from the Cheka whom Lazar was later to recognize as V. I. Lenin.

After the October Revolution and the dissolution of the Mensheviks, Avram became a member of the Constituent Assembly and took his family to Moscow. There, one winter night, Avram received a man to whom he introduced Lazar. The visitor catechized the boy on his knowledge of Marxist doctrine, reviewed a thin dossier and asked Lazar if he would be willing to serve the Soviet Union abroad.

Unhesitatingly, Lazar agreed, and before dawn, he was on board a train bound for Warsaw, equipped with false identity papers and a small amount of money. In Warsaw he exchanged his papers for another set and rode by train to Berlin, where he was given a third and final identity. In Hamburg he boarded a small coastal vessel and arrived at the port of Le Havre as Edouard Hirsch, an Alsatian of French nationality. When he reported to the OGPU in Paris on the rue des Saussaies, the boy from Ludosk was fifteen years old.

Living under the roof of a French Communist family, Edouard acquired French with the same facility that had enabled him to read Russian and Hebrew with a minimum of help.

Twice each year until he graduated from the University of Paris, Edouard Hirsch was visited by an older man to whom he reported his academic progress and from whom he received instructions. Among them were abstention from politics in any form and the cultivation of young Frenchmen whose families were involved in finance. By now his German surname had been changed to its French equivalent of Cerf, and at the depth of the French depression he was sent to Geneva for two years of banking studies. Returning to Paris, Cerf found employment in the family banking house of a university classmate and rose in rank and responsibilities as high as his Jewishness and lack of blood ties to the family would allow. During this period he was also given certain tasks to perform—passing Soviet money through the firm and making clandestine disbursements to men whose names he quickly forgot. After being called to Berlin one weekend, Cerf returned to Paris laden with gold bars and instructions to form a banking institution that would appear entirely legitimate, though its purpose was to facilitate and perform covert transactions for the Soviet Union through its traveling trade representatives. Within a year Cerf et Cie. was a prospering institution, and Edouard received NKVD permission to marry a French-Latvian Jewess whose father was a client of his bank. The young man never knew whether his father-in-law enjoyed ties to the USSR similar to his own, and he never discussed the possibility with the elder man or with his daughter, Noémi. Their first child was still-born, and it was four years before Noémi produced the first of their three children. By then Edouard was involved in Soviet procurement for the forces of Republican Spain. With the fall of the Blum government, its policy of strict neutrality was replaced by the more liberal policies of Daladier, and Cerf found it less difficult to acquire and transport food, clothing and matériel to Spanish Republican ports. To facilitate his work, Cerf purchased a nearly bankrupt shipping line consisting of seven old freighters. One was torpedoed by a Nationalist submarine off Barcelona, another bombed by Italian aircraft near Santander, but five ships remained intact and under Cerf's control for the remainder of the Spanish Civil War. Although troubled by the Hitler-Stalin Non-Aggression Pact, he was persuaded it represented no more than a tactical time gainer for the USSR.

At the outbreak of World War II Cerf's shipping

line was requisitioned by the French government, and within two months the rusted, worn-out vessels were either torpedoed or bombed at their docks. Well before Wehrmacht troops occupied Paris, Cerf had been told to liquidate his holdings in France and transfer them to the British Isles. In London he received a banking charter granted by authorities sympathetic to Cerf's losses and his status as a Jewish refugee. With the exception of a few transatlantic trips Cerf spent the war years in London, where he developed new financial liaisons and learned the English language. He was in regular clandestine contact with a case officer from the KGB's London *rezidentura*, for which he performed valuable services as a penetration of British financial circles, and as paymaster for several agents of the KGB who were refugees and intellectuals.

At the end of the war, Cerf returned to Paris and found the government's Act of Restitution had brought him a considerable financial windfall. As sole surviving stockholder of the confiscated shipping line, Cerf received the equivalent of thirty-two million dollars, representing the estimated postwar replacement value of his requisitioned and sunken ships. He spent a year reestablishing Cerf et Cie., and when that was accomplished his case officer ordered him to found a private bank in New York, using the restitution funds which Cerf had deposited in a Swiss bank. Cerf was given to understand that the United States was not *glavni vrag*—the principal enemy—and so his expert assistance would be required to bolster the growing Soviet effort in the Western Hemisphere.

Over the years Cerf had become aware of the violent fates that met agents who became suspect or deviated from loyalty to Soviet Intelligence. He had known Jean Cremet briefly as a NKVD courier before Cremet was killed in Macao in 1936. Cerf ruminated over the assas-

93

sination of Dmitri Navachine in Paris during the Moscow Trials and was shaken by the murder in Lausanne of Ignace Reiss. He had met Kurt Landau before the Austrian refugee was kidnapped and killed in Spain. And he knew that other exemplary victims were Hans Wissingir, Erwin Wolf, Trotsky's son, Agabekov, Konovalec, Willi Muenzenberg, and of course Trotsky himself. Cerf was not a man of remarkable physical courage, and he had no desire to become a target for KGB Execution Action.

His wife had died in a London air raid, his two daughters were married—one to a United States Senator—and his son, a graduate of Harvard Law, was associated with the same law firm of which Cerf & Co. was a profitable client. Cerf's daughter-in-law, who had already borne him two grandchildren and promised more, was Russian by birth. Educated at the University of Moscow as a linguist, Rimma Naumovna had met Maurice Cerf at a U.S. trade exhibit into which the young man wandered during the course of summer travel through Eastern Europe. When Maurice told his father that Rimma had been working as an interpreter-guide at the exhibit and that they planned to marry, Edward Cerf was shocked and depressed. He knew —but could not tell his son—that interpreter-guides were employees of the KGB, which would never allow her to emigrate from the USSR. He hoped the passage of time would drain his son's determination, but a year later when Maurice began planning to spend his law school summer vacation in Moscow, Cerf realized that something had to be done. So with the assistance of far-removed banking contacts in Bern and Ottawa, Edward Cerf arranged the departure of his future daughter-in-law from the Soviet Union. In Moscow Maurice gave Rimma money to bribe the head of her section for assignment to an international monetary conference in Bern. After a few days working there

94

as interpreter, Rimma failed to appear at the conference and in time was listed by the USSR as a defector. Meanwhile, traveling with a false Canadian passport, she had flown to Montreal, where Maurice was waiting, married him in St. Jovite and entered the United States as the wife of an American citizen. Cosmetic surgery altered her eyes and profile, and her passport name was changed to Irene in unpublicized proceedings in an upstate New York court.

All that had been nine years ago, Cerf reflected and so far no questions concerning the origins of his daughter-in-law had ever been raised. Not even by the KGB *rezident*. Still, he thought, revelation of the fact that he had conspired to effect and conceal the escape of a Soviet citizen—and, worse, a member of the KGB—would be the equivalent of a death sentence. He would certainly be liquidated, and probably Rimma —Irene—as well.

That was one of two lapses from Soviet discipline that weighed on the conscience of Edward Cerf.

The other had occurred more than twenty years before, not long after the French Act of Restitution awarded his unexpected compensation. Early in 1948 Cerf was visited by a man from the Jewish Agency for Palestine. Arms, food and aircraft were desperately needed by the Haganah to defend the new Jewish state. Dov Apelbaum pleaded his cause emotionally, reminding Cerf of the debt all living Jews owed to the survivors of Dachau, Belsen and Auschwitz, and for the first time since childhood, Edward Cerf felt a sense of personal Jewishness, of identification with a cause other than that of the Soviet Union. He remembered how he had been taught to read by Ludosk's kindly rabbi and that he had profited from the war in which six million fellow Jews had perished. Dov Apelbaum remarked the size of Cerf's windfall award and suggested the donation of a tithe to Israel. So it was,

95

uncharacteristically, that Edward Cerf established for Dov Apelbaum a credit of three million dollars in the Union des Banques Suisses after swearing him to secrecy.

At that time the attitude of the Sovet Union toward partition was unclear, nor did Cerf know whether the USSR would support the Marxist Palmach, the Stern Gang or Irgun Zvai Leumi. In taking independent action, Cerf deviated from decades of unquestioning obedience to the whims and policies of the USSR and exposed himself to charges of deviationist cosmopolitanism. Nor had the passage of the years diminished the danger to him occasioned by his contribution to the cause of Israel. Indeed, the massive support later given to the Arab states by the Soviet Union escalated Cerf's original sin into absolute treachery. True, a certain amount of business had come in "across the transom," transactions with Israeli overtones that Cerf inferred were Dov Apelbaum's way of acknowledging that early and crucial contribution. But Cerf would have been far happier had the matter simply remained forgotten. In a calculated effort to avoid any overt connection between himself and Israel, Cerf had never bought so much as a single Israeli bond or a bottle of Israeli wine, contributed to a Jewish charity or attended an Israeli diplomatic reception. He never visited Israel or permitted Irene and Maurice to go. Only when his grandchildren were born had he entered a synagogue, and then reluctantly and at night.

So it was that Edward Cerf was continuously aware that he had committed two capital crimes and that he could expect no mercy from the KGB if what he had done were ever to become known. It was always at the back of his mind and accounted for his apprehension when something unexpected occurred, such as the visit of Gilbert Philippe de Rochepin.

As Edward Cerf reviewed his life, he realized that his only desire was to live out what remained of it as quietly and comfortably as possible. The affair of Werber's stepdaughter was distressing; the visit from Gilbert Philippe nothing less than alarming. And he resented having been placed in an activist role by the New York *rezident*. Still, he had no recourse but to carry out orders even though all that he had been able to accomplish was ineffective, producing nothing. The Bauer girl was still at large, and the attempt to interrogate Thorpe's CIA friend had erupted into a brawl ending in Bitler's death. All that had evolved on the positive side, Cerf mused, were the disappearance and flight of Neal Thorpe, leaving Annalise Bauer alone and friendless in a foreign land.

It was still possible, he thought, that the girl would turn for help to the German embassy. If she did, arrangements had been made to receive—and silence—her. He found anger growing at the character and conduct of Klaus Werber. It was inexplicable that over the years the Soviet Union had reposed in Werber so much trust and confidence, guided him toward such eminence and world renown. The flaws in a man's character did not suddenly show themselves the way an ice field ruptures without warning; there had to be indices of it in his past. Now he, Edward Cerf, was being told to hazard his own position, perhaps sacrifice everything he had worked toward for his entire life, in order to forestall the disaster threatened by an ox-headed drunkard.

At the delicate chime of his wall clock Cerf removed a silver box from his vest pocket, extracted a minute pill, and set it under his tongue. As it slowly dissolved, he thought of De Rochepin flying east across the Atlantic, safe and secure, leaving Cerf to clean up Werber's tainted mess.

That was not his role, he told himself; to be involved

first in an awkward search, then in murder, was entirely inappropriate. Unfortunately, all that his relayed protests to the *rezident* had produced was a menacing visit from De Rochepin. It was apparent that the directorate took the matter very seriously to risk exposing them both, so he did not intend to offer further objections. At one o'clock he was to receive an interim report from the men who were working in the Washington area, and if by then their reports were still negative, he would have to tell them to redouble their efforts. His field of competence was financial, not physical action, and he told himself that this sort of task at his age, after so many years of uncomplaining service, was not his due. He considered his children and their children and wondered what the impact on them would be if, through some egregious action over which he had no control, the truth of his life were exposed.

For a while longer Edward Cerf brooded in the silence of the room. Finally, he rang for his secretary, prepared to dictate memoranda affecting the London and Paris branches of his firm, matters over which he alone could exercise control.

11

IT always amused the Comte de Rochepin to receive correspondence from a Communist front organization addressed with his full name and title. He was not the only hereditary aristocrat who belonged to the World Council of Peace, for example, or the International Federation of Resistance Fighters, but he felt it only appropriate that secretariat workers in Prague and Vienna remain conscious of the social distance between them and him.

In his apartment overlooking Avenue Kléber not far from the Etoile, Gilbert Philippe de Rochepin slit open an envelope with a Prague postmark and the return address of the International Organization of Journalists. Signed by the secretary-general, the letter invited De Rochepin to address a symposium of Latin American journalists at Santiago, Chile, in July. There would be representatives from each of the Latin American countries, Canada, the United States, as well as fraternal journalists from the Soviet Union, Cuba and Algeria. De Rochepin consulted his leather-bound *agenda* and noted the symposium date. As a matter of principle he had been disposed to attend, but the promise of journalists from *Tass* and *Pravda* made the invitation one he felt he could not refuse. It was the Soviets, after all, whom he needed occasionally to remind how faithful an ally he was and how deserving of their confidence and favors he continued to be.

A second letter bore the return address of the International Radio and Television Organization, and it too had been mailed in Prague. This one, unfortunately, did not carry the promise of expense-paid travel and the attentions of complaisant interpreter-guides. Instead, it was a form announcement offering free footage and film clips describing life in the People's Republic of Czechoslovakia. With a frown De Rochepin crumpled the letter and dropped it into a wastebasket. He was surfeited with shots of happy Slovak villagers and folk dancing, female welders and harvesting combines. This sort of propaganda he received regularly, not only from the East, but from the information services of nearly every embassy in Paris. The popularity of his weekly ORTF telecast, however, was based upon his own abilities as *rapporteur*, to a lesser degree the prominence of guests he interviewed. His weekly hour was too short as it was, too limiting of his personality, and De Rochepin had no intention of further curtailing his personal exposure with canned films of little interest to his nationwide audience. His countrymen had a right, after all, to see and hear Gilbert Philippe de Rochepin when they selected his channel each Sunday evening at eight, and he was disinclined to disappoint them.

His mission to Edouard Cerf, he reflected, had been accomplished as ordered: swiftly and securely. The two-way flight he had found tedious, and the chatter of the stewardess annoying. She was obviously inviting more intimate relationship but De Rochepin could not bear the thought of her thick ankles; moreover, he sensed that like much of the French peasantry, Carlotte bathed infrequently.

Opening *Le Monde*, De Rochepin glanced at a summary of new Common Market problems and noticed with interest that the German Foreign Minister had been enthusiastically received in Cairo where he delivered both private and public speeches. The Frenchman felt a sense of satisfaction over his behind-the-scenes role in advancing the career of Klaus Werber. Only once, he remembered, had he met the German, and that was at a reception in Vienna marking the establishment of the International Atomic Energy Agency, whose formation in 1957 De Rochepin had covered for a segment of the Paris-based press. At the time De Rochepin had been unaware of Klaus Werber's true role and mission. Now, because of Werber's penchant for loose talk, De Rochepin hoped the German was unwitting of his.

The votes of the Afro-Arab bloc were essential to Werber's election as UN Secretary-General, De Rochepin knew, and the report from Cairo was an indication that matters were proceeding according to plan.

Through long years of service to the Soviet Union he had admired the rigid discipline it demanded and its capacity to plan for the years ahead. It was too soon to tell if China would equal the USSR in those two characteristics. Successive French governments had never been able to plan more than an hour ahead, while the goals of the United States seemed to vary with each new week. Consistency was the heart of the matter, De Rochepin knew, and unvarying consistency was possible only in an authoritarian state.

When one thought about it, he reflected, the Communist system was not unlike monarchic rule. Absolute monarchs had done well by France until they became corrupt and dissolute, unable to withstand the challenges of the rabble. To rule successfully, one had to follow unswerving principles, refuse to be sidetracked by nonessential considerations. France, he felt certain, could never reassert its once-great role, not so long as the Chamber of Deputies represented so many fragmented and contesting parties. Not so long as premiers were chosen through bargaining, compromise and concession. What was wanting was a strong and intolerant leader—one such as Charles De Gaulle, who, despite De Rochepin's personal aversion to him, had been such a man.

Rising from his desk, he left the newspaper and opened the drapes. Along Avenue Kléber the lightoliers were haloed by unseen mist, the dark acacia trees barely in bud.

It was time to leave for his rendezvous, he reminded himself, closed the window blinds and selected a weatherproof from the closet. He chose a walking stick from the rack beside the entrance, adjusted a homburg and left the elegant surroundings of his apartment. The doorman opened the heavy wrought-iron doors and offered to call a taxi for *M'sieu le Comte*, but De Rochepin declined, alleging an evening constitutional.

From the apartment door he strolled toward the Etoile, where the Arc de Triomphe was bathed in light. As he walked, he found occasions to pause, look around and otherwise check for surveillants, until at the Avenue de Portugais, he turned and sauntered to a small neighborhood café. Entering, he chose a table concealed from the sidewalk by potted firs and ordered a *fine café*. From a passing vendor, he bought the late edition of *France-Soir* and affected interest in the racing news. Presently, he heard a table chair slide out and looked up to see the face of the contact he knew as Marcel, but whose heavy accent marked him as Russian. Briefly they shook hands, expressing pleasure at the apparently chance encounter, and when De Rochepin's *fine café* arrived, he ordered another for Marcel. When the Russian was satisfied they were not being observed or overheard, he said, "Your mission was successful?"

"Quite. In the sense that I carried out my orders. But as for our friend, I cannot say."

"Explain, please."

De Rochepin spread his hands. "He is a passive man, unaccustomed to action of the sort now confronting him. My feeling is that he resents his situation and cooperated only grudgingly." Lifting his demitasse, De Rochepin sipped slowly, observing the frown on Marcel's face. "That is bad," the Russian said.

"Naturally, I impressed upon him the importance, the vital necessity of the undertaking."

The Russian grunted, then stared concentratedly at the table top. At length he said, "Unnecessarily, a man has been killed."

De Rochepin inclined his head. "It was quite unnecessary."

"Better it was the girl," said the Russian, and remained silent while he was served.

"Amateurism," De Rochepin observed. "Even so,

with the flight of her confidant, the girl is friendless and may come into our hands more easily."

The Russian eyed him without emotion. "We do not want her in our hands. We want her liquidated."

"But I thought—" De Rochepin began.

"What you *thought* is of no importance, my dear Count. Those are the instructions. They have the beauty of simplicity. Now, tell me, was your mission conducted in complete security?"

"Complete."

"There is no means by which your visit to the Jew can be verified?"

"None—assuming the pilot of the helicopter is secure."

"His mother is hostage in Karlshorst."

De Rochepin swallowed. "Then there is nothing to connect the two of us."

"Good."

"Do you have further instructions for me?"

"Yes. Forget the trip you made."

"Beyond that?"

"Continue your customary work."

De Rochepin lifted his cup and drained it. "With permission I will accept an invitation to take part in a symposium of the International Organization of Journalists in Chile."

"When?"

"July."

"I have no objection."

De Rochepin said nothing. Purposely he had not asked Marcel's personal permission, but that of their mutual superior, and he resented the Russian's implied ascendancy.

"Anything else?" said Marcel abruptly.

"Nothing."

"Then we will meet in one week at Site Four." Rising, he left the table as, angrily, De Rochepin resumed reading *France-Soir*. Five minutes later he paid for both coffees and left the café by a side exit. From there he strolled back toward his apartment, his anger at the Russian diminishing slowly, replaced by shock at learning the Soviet plan to kill Klaus Werber's stepdaughter. Initially, and until that moment, he had assumed the goal was merely to ensure her silence through persuasion. Still, he reflected, personal feelings had no place in his covert world, and he had been careful not to protest the girl's murder.

In his apartment he changed into pajamas and dressing robe and took from a wall safe an alcohol lamp, a small tin of gum opium and a darkly stained pipe. On a needle he molded a small bead of dark opium, cured it over the lamp flame and placed it bubbling in the pipe bowl. Reclining on his bed, the Comte de Rochepin drew aromatic vapor into his lungs. His dry mouth grew moist, languor infused tense muscles, and he felt an ineffable sense of well-being. He inhaled more deeply, and now sensuous images formed and began swirling through his brain. He was in Annam of forty years ago, hearing the bell music of childlike temple dancers. Soon, he knew, they would attend him in his bed, ministering to him through the long voluptuous night to an illusive dawn. The rank of dancers broke, and one by one they drifted toward him until he could touch and mold the moist olive skin of their sexually ambiguous bodies, feel in return the caress of practiced hands and mouths.

Seeking to return a kiss, De Rochepin's lips parted, and the ivory pipe stem slipped down to the pillow. Enveloped in the intensity of his dream, De Rochepin breathed in short rasping gasps as the flame of the lamp burned low.

Presently the flame died away, and the pungent, sick-sweet fumes of opium blended with the darkness.

104

Neal Thorpe stepped from the humid evening air of Bourbon Street into a phone booth, and while Annalise waited watchfully outside, he dialed long distance and readied quarters to feed into the phone. From Washington they had taken one bus line as far as Richmond, changed there to another that reached Atlanta in the grayness of dawn. From there to Montgomery, and finally New Orleans by way of Mobile. So far none of the newspapers they had seen carried photographs of him to illustrate the story of Bitler's murder and Thorpe's flight. Thorpe, the stories said, was being sought by the FBI for questioning. The low key was deceptive, he knew, and the lack of photographs meaningless. In any case, the wig he wore curled below the nape of his neck, he wore large horn-rimmed glasses bought in a dime store, and for two days he had not shaved. Like Annalise, Thorpe wore Levis, an old Army coat and heavy boots. The disguise altered his appearance so radically that he was sure not even Dawes would recognize him were they to pass on the street.

When the operator responded, Thorpe gave her the telephone number of Alton Regester, dropped quarters into the slot and heard the telephone ring in Regester's apartment.

Finally Thorpe heard Regester say, "Yes?"

Throat dry, Thorpe said, "No names, please. Understand?"

"I understand. I'm glad you called."

"From what I read, things haven't improved."

"No. Nor are they likely to. So I'm glad you got away. Are you a reasonable distance from me?"

"Yes. We've been talking it over, and we've pretty much decided to try to leave the country."

"Not using your own names, of course."

"No."

Regester cleared his throat. "I've had time to do

105

some thinking, too. Do you think you could get to Europe?"

"I don't know. All we can do is try. Where in Europe?"

"Stockholm, preferably. Do you remember the man I described? The one who broke the wartime code?"

"Of course. But you gave the impression he was dead."

"His daughter is in Stockholm—her name is Zarah Engstrom. Try the city phone books and directory; if she's not listed, ask for her at the Grand Hotel. She worked there recently on the switchboard. If you get to her, say you were sent by Smith."

"All right."

"How is your companion?"

Thorpe half turned and glanced at her profile. "She's the only thing keeping me together."

"Good. Quite frankly, her life is more important than yours. How are you for money?"

"Very short."

"I'll try to transfer some to Stockholm. Zarah will know how to reach me, and it wouldn't be safe for either of us if you cabled or phoned."

"I understand."

"In Stockholm you'd be just two more American drifters among thousands. Besides, no one will be looking for you there."

Thorpe grunted. "How do you suggest we get documents to travel on?"

"Buy them—or steal them. You're intelligent; now be ingenious. If I could be of more help, I would."

"I know that." Thorpe hesitated. "You don't think I ought to turn myself in?"

"Not under any circumstances. There's no warrant for you, but although you're not a fugitive, that could change momentarily. If you had a supportable alibi, I'd never have suggested you leave. But because you haven't you're the principal, if not the sole, suspect. To the authorities it looks open-and-shut—except for motive. Believe me, despite what the lawbooks say, the presumption is of guilt, not innocence."

Thorpe felt his body turn cold. "Can't the Agency do something? They know I contacted Don, why we went to see you."

"It's premature to ask for Agency help. In fact, I've already weighed in against it. Exposing what's happened to date might well help you, but it would very likely destroy everything that's falling into place concerning the Diplomat."

Under his breath Thorpe swore.

"Look at it this way," Regester continued. "The enemy think they've hung their murder on you—the one man in America trusted by the girl. That makes them overconfident on two counts and helps our general cause by giving us time we badly need while they continue looking for your companion."

Thorpe took a deep breath. "Considering what's ahead, it seems to me the girl would be safe if she stayed here under some sort of official protection."

"A reasonable thought, but faulty. Suppose the Agency or the Bureau were to . . . harbor her, keep her in protective custody. Then the German Chancellor—or the Foreign Minister of Germany, for that matter—requested her return. How long do you think State, the Bureau, the Agency—or even the President—would hold out against the request?"

"You've made your point."

"We've talked too long as it is. I'll hope to hear you reached Stockholm. Good luck."

The line went dead.

For a few moments Thorpe held the receiver in his hand; then he replaced it and left the booth. Taking Annalise's arm, he said, "Let's find a place where we can talk."

Through crowded streets they threaded their way past strip joints, booze parlors and handsome Creole homes, hearing the blare of old-time jazz contend with the brain-numbing onslaught of hard rock music, seeing pimps and prostitutes of all colors and sexes, aware of grass and horse dealing on street corners, until finally they emerged on Jackson Square with its equestrian statue to the hero of the Battle of New Orleans.

They sat on a bench while Thorpe summarized his telephone conversation. Then, with a sigh, Anna said, "What are we going to do?"

"Get to Stockholm."

"How?"

"We'll have to get driving licenses, birth certificates. With them we can enter Mexico. From there maybe we can get on a freight flight for Europe."

"All that will take money."

He nodded. "Between us we've got about five hundred dollars."

"And we can sell this ring." She drew it from her finger and placed it in his palm. "My stepfather gave me this for a birthday two years ago. I believe it cost perhaps twelve thousand Swiss francs—three thousand dollars. Let us get whatever we can for it. No, I will be glad to be rid of it—and anything else that came from him."

"Save the ring for Mexico," he said, and dropped it into a pocket of her shirt.

Together they walked toward a bar into which was trooping a group of wayfarers dressed much as Thorpe and Anna were. Holding glasses of draft beer, they searched the crowd for faces even vaguely resembling theirs. At the end of the bar a long-haired youth was arguing with a florid-faced bartender. Thorpe edged toward them and listened to what was being said. When he grasped the situation, he said to the bartender, "If you won't trust him, I will." Then

108

to the startled youth he handed two ten-dollar bills and took the frayed billfold the youth had been trying to press on the bartender. "You can get it back tomorrow night, man. Same place, nine o'clock," opened the billfold and saw it contained a driver's license and Social Security card.

"Far out, man." He handed one ten-dollar bill to the bartender, said "Rip off," scornfully, and drained the inch of beer in his glass. Turning to Thorpe he said, "Right on. Hold the leather till tomorrow, like you said." He gave Thorpe the clenched fist sign, murmured, "Peace, brother," and drifted into the crowd.

Annalise said, "That was wonderful."

"It was luck. Want me to try for yours, or—"

She smiled. "I think I would like to try."

Thorpe watched her move off among the packed bodies until Anna stopped beside a girl whose height was the same as hers. Presently he saw money exchanged for a palm-size purse. Anna lingered chatting pleasantly, gestured at Thorpe and came back to him.

"Americans are so sympathetic," she said, and opened the little purse to reveal a driver's license and student ID card issued by Tulane. "With these I can prove my age and we can be married. Isn't that nice?"

"Splendid. Now let's go before they change their minds." He began leading her toward the door.

"Glenda—that's her name and my new one—tried to change mine. She said marriage was a trap, and why didn't we just live together?"

As they reached the noisy sidewalk, Thorpe said, "And what did you say?"

"I made up a story about an inheritance that depended upon my being married." She linked her arm with his and smiled up at him. "Is marriage a trap?"

"Unquestionably."

109

"But you don't object?"

"The survival rate is very high."

At the edge of the Vieux Carré they located a bus that ran to Moisant Field, boarded it and rode in near silence until the bus drew up at the terminal. Inside they consulted the departure board and went to the Eastern counter, where a bored agent prepared Mexican Tourist cards for Glenda Michalski and Theodore F. Gross and sold them tourist-class tickets for Mexico City. To bridge the two hours until boarding time, they went to the coffee shop and ordered a meal that had been long postponed.

After hanging up on Neal Thorpe, Alton Regester opened a drawer in his desk. From it he took a thick unbound manuscript and some sheets of map-sized paper on which he had diagrammed in chronological fashion the clandestine history of Klaus Werber, a French journalist named De Rochepin and an international financier whose name he had printed as Hirsch/Cerf. One largely empty block was captioned "Irene Cerf: daughter-in-law." All he had been able to determine of her antecedents was that under a different name she had married Cerf's son near Montreal shortly after arriving in Canada on a flight from Switzerland. Regester had also noted the disappearance from Bern of a Soviet female interpreter, Rimma Naumovna, whom the Soviets alleged was a defector, but who had never come into the hands of any Western Intelligence Agency. It could be no more than coincidence, but Rimma's disappearance predated the marriage of Irene Cerf by only two days. And the young man she married had visited Moscow the week before, having spent most of the previous summer there.

Was it possible, Regester wondered, that Edward Cerf's daughter-in-law had been Rimma Naumovna,

110

an interpreter in the employ of the KGB? Possible, yes, but he had never been able to obtain a photograph of Irene Cerf to compare with the CIA file photo of Naumovna. Inquiries in New York and Long Island reflected that Irene Cerf shunned publicity, unlike the overwhelming majority of wealthy young matrons in her circle. There was an abundance of photographs of her husband, Maurice, but, again, only a few out-of-date photographs of Edward, who, Regester knew, led a life that could be described as cloistered.

How ironic, he thought, if Rimma had been the bait in a KGB dangle operation and left Europe with the connivance of the KGB. As a member of Edward Cerf's household, she would be in an incomparable position to report on her father-in-law; after his eventual death she could become a valuable agent-in-place, protected by money, social position and the influence of powerful friends, including the Senator who was her brother-in-law. The equivalent had happened before, he mused, but because he could not close the identity gap between Rimma Naumovna and Irene Cerf, his theory remained theory, persuasive as it was.

Regester turned to a fourth sheet captioned: "*The* Cardinal," and on it noted a piece of information culled from a newspaper story concerning certain disputes within the Papal Secretariat of State. Over the years Eugene Cardinal Rossinol had been an advocate of Vatican relations with the Communist bloc, a partisan of clerical activism in Latin America and an enemy of Cardinals Stepinac and Mindzenty. Moreover, Rossinol was the one through whom the Soviet ambassador in Rome arranged the famous papal audience for Khrushchev's son-in-law, Abzhubei, that had done so much to allay worldwide Catholic apprehensions concerning the Soviet Union. One immediate result had been the rise in Communist Party votes in France and Italy, an increase made possible by Catholic voters.

If the Pope himself could receive Nikita's son-in-law, the argument went, then Communism was religiously respectable and no longer anathema. Catholics around the world could vote for Communist candidates without having to worry about excommunication.

As a young priest in Catalonia, Regester recalled, Padre Rossinol had been one of a very few clergy to survive the stranglings and firing squads that had been the fate of so many other nuns and priests who protested the desecration of churches and graves by the forces of Republican Spain. After the fall of Barcelona, Padre Rossinol had made his way across the Pyrenees into France along with thousands of other refugees. He had stayed in their camps ministering to the reawakened spiritual needs of the wretched Spaniards while asserting himself as a temporal link to French Catholic authorities and gaining a measure of fame for his success in obtaining better treatment from French officialdom.

During the war, Monsigneur Rossinol had served with units of the maquis, been captured by the Abwehr and tortured by the SS. Released from a death camp at war's end, the prelate had been called to Rome and given important assignments dealing with Catholic Relief in Europe and Latin America, where he became a visible and articulate spokesman for the church. Finally, under Pope John, Rossinol became a Prince of the Church, assigned first to the Holy Roman Rota, then to the Papal Secretariat of State. His intervention in Italian politics had caused one Italian President to refer to him as "the Cardinal from Moscow." Even so, Cardinal Rossinol's influence within the Vatican continued to increase, and there were ample indications that when the incumbent cardinal died, Rossinol would become Papal Secretary of State, the second most important office within the Holy See, and himself a contender for election as Christ's Vicar on Earth.

112

Rossinol's past and current activities were damaging enough, Regester reflected, but to consider the Vatican in the hands of the Soviet Union would be a disaster equaled only by the ascension of Klaus Werber to the Secretary-Generalship of the United Nations. There were a great many unanswered questions concerning the circumstances under which his life had been spared by the Spanish Purification Squads commanded by officers of the NKVD. It was as valid a question as one that could be posed concerning the survival of a particular Jew in wartime Dachau, where one might conscientiously surmise that something of value had been traded in return for the gift of life. There was little hope, Regester knew, that after so many years he could find survivors from either side who would know about, remember or be willing to testify to how it was that Padre Rossinol avoided death in a Spanish town.

Besides, Regester mused, at my age, I shouldn't be preoccupied with the fate of the world. I've fought the good fight and largely failed; perhaps that's why I keep my charts alone and with no help from the Agency. I'm a dinosaur, a species nearly extinct. Still, what better thing can I do? Play shuffleboard at Hilton Head with a score of other retired colleagues? Teach prep-school English lit?

After folding the four charts, Alton Regester returned them to his desk drawer. Atop them he placed the unbound manuscript and locked the drawer. Then he poured a small amount of cognac into a glass and sat in a comfortable chair, wondering what was in store for Neal and Annalise. He had lied to the FBI about them, dissembled to the agency. Now he could only hope that they would somehow be able to reach Stockholm together and unharmed.

On that the success of what he was now beginning to plan depended.

12

BECAUSE it was off season in Mexico City, Neal was able to find an inexpensive hotel room for Anna and himself on Avenida Guerrero not far from the Alameda. They slept until midafternoon when shops reopened and set out to survey jewelry stores in the hope of finding one that would buy her emerald ring. After the damp heat of New Orleans, the thin, dry air of Mexico City was a refreshing change. From a street vendor they bought straw sombreros, sunglasses from another. Equipped with these additional items of anonymity, they went into Sanborn's and ate steak and eggs at the counter. From there they strolled along Madero and entered the nearest jewelry store. Thorpe produced the emerald ring and asked the clerk if the store was interested in purchasing it.

"No, señor," the clerk replied. "We do not deal in gems whose origin we cannot guarantee." Thorpe and Anna exchanged glances and left.

"At least," Thorpe said as they walked along, "We've got an indication of what to expect."

The next store was interested enough to examine the stone and suggest an offer of two hundred dollars. The third, a smaller house, was willing to offer four hundred, and they left the place dejectedly. Then at the next corner they heard a "*Psst!*" and turned to see the jeweler who had appraised the stone for the second house. He motioned them off Madero and there, out of sight, he said, *"Cuanto*—how much you want for it?"

"A lot more than the two hundred you offered," Thorpe told him.

"Sí, sí, I know," the man said impatiently. "If I buy, it is to do a little business for myself. The store don't pay me nothing. You have it still?"

Annalise nodded.

"How much?"

"Twelve hundred dollars," she said without hesitating.

"Ah, but, señora. . . ." His arms lifted and fell helplessly. "I am a poor man."

"So am I," Thorpe said, "You know what the ring is worth—so do we."

"The mounting is worth nothing—a few pesos, maybe. You keep the mounting." He took a deep breath. "For the stone, ocho cientos—eight hundred. No more."

"Last chance," Thorpe said. "One thousand dollars. With your connections you can double that in a day."

The man's eyes closed as though he were praying to the Virgin of Guadalupe. *"Bueno,"* he said hoarsely. "You take the money in pesos?"

"Of course."

"To get the money, I will get loan for my car." He drew them back to Madero and gestured toward an old Spanish cathedral. "In one hour—at the *puerta.*"

"The door?"

"Sí. That is the word. The door." Turning, he walked quickly away and was lost among oncoming pedestrians.

"That's one thing I've heard about Mexico," Thorpe said as he took Anna's arm and led her back past Sanborn's toward the Palace of Fine Arts. "Everything can be bought, and everything has its price. I think the man is reasonably honest—at least he didn't suggest consummating the sale in a dark alley after midnight.

The portal of the cathedral makes it seem better some-how."

"Becket was murdered in a cathedral," Anna remarked. "How many pesos will that be?"

"We'll take anything over eight thousand."

"And then?"

"Treat ourselves to a good dinner, then tomorrow back to the airport. There must be twenty small airlines that fly from here to Europe. The problem will be finding one that's, first, willing to take us without passports and, second, take us where we want to go."

"As you said, everything has its price."

There was not, it developed the next day, a great deal of airborne trade between Mexico and Scandinavia, and most of that was flown by large international carriers. However, by tipping judiciously, Thorpe located the airport freight office of a Honduran airline that flew meat, coffee and bananas to Stockholm by way of Lisbon. First, the agent said, they should fly to Tegucigalpa, where all flights to Europe began. Once there, final arrangements could be made. Lack of passports made no difference, he went on; their Mexican tourist cards were sufficient to enter Honduras. In Scandinavia, they had only to leave the plane after dark. Europeans were less particular than Americans about who entered and left their countries.

"All right," Thorpe said. "When can we get to Tegucigalpa?"

"This evening." The agent eyed them. "It will be a cargo plane, but empty. Not first-class passage, you understand. No stewardess with French wines, but it is a means of getting there." He left unspoken the thought: In your circumstances.

"How much?"

"A four-hour flight," the agent mused. "For each of you two hundred dollars."

116

Thorpe shook his head. "Since we're flying cargo, two hundred for *both* of us."

"You have no passports. Four hundred."

"You aren't licensed to carry passengers. Two hundred."

The agent extended his hand. "Pay now."

"I'll pay when we leave."

With a shrug the agent said, "Be here at seven."

"Seven o'clock," Thorpe said. "And the price includes what to do when we get there."

"Por Diós! Who would want to stay in Tegucigalpa?"

Leaving the shed, Thorpe said, "Of necessity I'm learning to bargain."

"Brilliantly."

"He'll give fifty to the pilot and keep the rest for himself. Hell, the pilot's probably his cousin."

It was nearly a mile back to the main airport building. They walked slowly, heavy coats over their arms, shielded from the sun by their sombreros and dark glasses, and Thorpe reflected that he was becoming less uncomfortable in their clandestine existence. Until yesterday, he told himself, I wasn't thinking like an agent. I was still thinking mostly as a legal citizen of the world—a straight guy. But if I'm to get us to Stockholm, that has to change. I've got to remember everything I was taught about surviving as an Illegal, living as a wanted alien in enemy country. Before, I always knew I could fall back on the station as a last resort. Now I can't and a station is the last place I could turn for help. Except the Embassy offices of what the Bureau calls their Legal Attachés.

He laughed curtly, and Anna said, "Something amusing?"

"Far from it. Let's get the New York *Times* at the airport and see what it has to say about me today."

By seven o'clock it was dark enough that Thorpe

117

noticed landing lights through the spattered windows of the cargo shed. He paid the freight agent sixteen hundred pesos and added another hundred-peso note after brief argument. The agent opened the far door and led them toward a parked aircraft whose only lights were in the pilot's compartment. It was an old C-46, and its double cargo doors were open. The three of them climbed up a steel ladder to enter, and the agent said, "Wait here."

He moved up the slanting deck, hailed the pilot, and Thorpe heard an animated conversation in Spanish. After a while the pilot got up and peered back at them. "*Bienvenidos*," he called, and returned to his seat.

The agent shook hands with them, said, "Good luck," and climbed down the ladder to the ground. He swung the cargo doors shut, and Thorpe locked them from inside. Dim lights went on, and for the first time Thorpe realized the fuselage was uninsulated. There were no seats as such, just metal benches that pulled down from the side of the fuselage, with round depressions in them. Exploring forward, Thorpe found a pile of cargo matting, dragged some of the felt mats aft and laid a double thickness along the bench seats. He adjusted Anna's seat belt and covered the lower part of her body with the thick felt.

The pilot's door opened, and a voice called, "We go now."

"Okay." Thorpe tightened his seat belt as the left engine exploded into life. The other engine hung a moment, then caught with a deafening roar. He pulled matting over his legs and kissed Anna's cheek as the plane moved sluggishly toward the runway.

Through dirty windows he could see the lights of aircraft landing and taking off, the outline of the airport building. "*Adiós*, Mexico," he said half-aloud, and wondered what would happen tomorrow in Tegucigalpa, where, as the agent had remarked, nobody wanted to stay.

The plane left the bumpy service road and lumbered onto the smooth runway. The pilot ran up the engines while Thorpe reflected that it had been a long time since he had flown in propeller aircraft. Inside the stripped-down fuselage propeller-engine noise made shouting their only way to communicate. Thorpe tore bits of felt from the matting and twisted them into ear-plugs for Anna and himself. From the overhead heating flue he noticed a faint breath of warm air, but Thorpe knew it would not be enough for them if the altitude were high. The airport itself was nearly eight thousand feet, and he hoped the pilot would fly no higher, for at ten thousand, oxygen would be required.

The plane moved forward, half turned and braked while the engine accelerated for takeoff. Then it lurched forward, gathering speed, tail lifting, until it sped along, the airport lights mere blurs flashing past the windows. Smoothly it left the runway, gradually gained altitude and turned southeast for the long flight over southern Mexico, all of Guatemala, and most of Honduras. Looking down through the window, he could make out only a few scattered lights below. In the cargo shed he had studied the route chart and noticed it would take them near Iztaccihuatl, the legendary Sleeping Woman, whose breast rose more than seventeen thousand feet above sea level. The pilot, he hoped, was familiar enough with the mountain's location to avoid crashing into it. The saving factor, he reflected, was the pilot's natural desire to fly without incident to Tegucigalpa, where perhaps a wife or sweetheart waited.

Thorpe shifted on the padded seat to ease a pressure point caused by the bone-handled switchblade he had bought in an airport shop. It was a sharp and

119

sturdy German product, not a tinny imitation pounded out in some Mexican backyard, and his uncertainty over what might lie ahead was what had caused him to acquire it, though without Anna's knowledge.

Around them the air grew colder, whistling through sprung seams and bent fittings, as the plane droned on through the night. The C-46 could have flown the Hump from India to China in the war of which Thorpe's father had been a part. It smelled faintly of a thousand different cargoes: chickens, cattle and horses, the rank odor of crushed mangoes and too-ripe bananas, sugarcane, sisal and fish. Below, the lush green jungle was no more than black velvet laced with tiny veins of silver that he knew were rivers in the moonlight. Soon he felt the weight of Anna's head on his shoulder. He looked at her face and saw her eyes were closed; she was asleep. Drowsily he thought back to the night he had first seen her waiting anxiously in the sleet and how he had wondered who she was and what had brought her there. Now he knew much more about her, and they were together, fugitives for different reasons, on a plane that might come apart over the next mountain ridge.

Gently he tucked more of the heavy matting around her body, settled back and closed his eyes. Before sleep came over him, Thorpe had time to reflect that he was now immersed in a full measure of the excitement he had once felt missing from his life.

13

THE KGB Illegal *rezidentura* in New York was located in a brownstone row house on Manhattan's East Side, within easy walking distance of the United Nations Building. The *rezident*, who never went to the UN Building or to any other official establishment was a tight-faced man a little over six feet in height who had entered the United States in 1957 with his supposed wife under the Hungarian Emergency Refugee Program that followed the bloody Budapest rebellion. In fact, the *rezident* and the radio operator who posed as his wife were Russians by birth, as required by the KGB. They were also Illegals, who operated independently of such accredited Soviet espionage centers as the Washington embassy, the consulates, trade and cultural missions and the Soviet Mission to the United Nations.

The man who posed as Sandor Varga, Hungarian refugee, had been named Yefrem Petrovich Karpov at his birth in Oboyan, north of Kharkov. His radio operator was documented as his wife, Gyula, but she had been born Raisa Ivanovna at Saratov on the Volga River. Before their selection by the KGB, both had been trained in Soviet technical institutes, he in chemistry and she in electronics and radio engineering. Both had served in the Red Army as officers. Gyula's rank in the KGB was major, while Sandor, who operated a secondhand furniture store on the Lower East Side and whose few customers were blacks and

Puerto Ricans, was a lieutenant general in the KGB. Both had been selected for Soviet Intelligence after Army service and intensive background investigations. For three years, each had studied at the Institute of Foreign Languages in Moscow before beginning their training in espionage, a course lasting eighteen months and covering clandestine communications, report writing, industrial and military sabotage, concealment, photography, physical disguise, weapons, agent recruitment and handling and, finally, the history, customs and traditions of the intermediate country that was to serve as their launching point: Hungary.

For five years prior to the Hungarian revolt they lived as man and wife in the Budapest suburb of Kispest, documented as Hungarian citizens and participating in the uneventful life of their community. There they practiced and perfected their secret professions while outwardly becoming Hungarians. This included scheduled radio transmissions to a KGB adviser to the Hungarian AVH, at 60 Andrassy Ut in Budapest, and with the First Department of the First Chief Directorate, KGB, on Moscow's Dzerzhinskovo Square. Microdot or secret writing was used for lengthy communications.

In the process of becoming Hungarians the Vargas reported on their neighbors, on community opinion in Kispest, and permitted themselves to be drawn into a group of Hungarian nationalists with bitterly anti-Soviet views. Within a short time Sandor Varga's inquiries revealed that at least one section of the group was involved in counterrevolutionary activity, and he reported promptly to Dzerzhinskovo Square. Ordered to penetrate the suspect section, Varga did it so thoroughly that he became one of a reception party for a British parachutist, who was arrested a few days later, and through what he had learned, Varga identified two CIA agents who had been trained in West

Germany and dispatched to Hungary as commercial travelers. To avoid suspicion of complicity, Sandor and Gyula Varga were arrested with other members of the Kispest net, but they alone were not executed. Instead, the AVH resettled them near Sopron, where they remained as *stagiaires* until the Budapest uprisings gave them the opportunity of fleeing across the Danube into Austria. There, legal emigration to the United States was readily arranged.

Settling in Manhattan, Varga served for a few months as principal assistant to the Soviet *rezident* who was to become famous as Colonel Abel. With the arrest of Abel, Varga was instructed to break off all contacts for six months, during which period a replacement *rezident* arrived. As the weeks went on, Varga became contemptuous of his superior, for the new man was paranoiacally fearful of detection and arrest. Accordingly, the *rezidentura*'s production dropped, and the First Directorate ordered its chief to return, carefully couching the orders as an invitation lest the *rezident* be tempted to defect. Having no other qualified *rezident* in the Illegals' funnel, the KGB promoted Varga, who, profiting from what had befallen his predecessors, produced an enormous amount of intelligence for the First Directorate and received prompt recognition and promotion. Varga was careful to file all tax, business and Social Security reports and pay his bills promptly even though there was little real income from the secondhand furniture store. Gyula worked even harder than her nominal husband, and her working hours were after dark when radio transmission was enhanced. She needed relatively little sleep, her health was robust, and she received the most onerous orders uncomplainingly. Occasionally, to calm inner tensions, they had sexual relations even though each had a spouse in the Soviet Union. Their intimacy was assumed by the KGB, which knew through long experience that if agents were denied physical release with each other, they would inevitably find partners outside the *rezidentura*, with all the accompanying risks.

Within the Moscow Illegals *Sektor*, Varga was known as Viktor; Gyula as Nell. Their true identities were known to fewer than half a dozen officers in the Special Directorate which was responsible for transmitting funds to them and seeing to the material needs of their hostage mates.

Normal duty tours for Illegals were seven years. Viktor and Nell had completed two such tours, returning on secret leave to the USSR via a Soviet vessel from the port of Vancouver. On his first home leave Viktor fathered a daughter now eight years old, and after his second return his wife bore him a son who was now a little more than a year old. Occasional messages from their loved ones came via microdot, which, when enlarged and read, were carefully burned within the confines of the *referentura*, a secret and secure room constructed by Viktor and Nell under the basement floor. The *referentura* housed their few files, radio schedules, a transmitter and an array of elaborate photographic equipment. Elsewhere, concealed throughout the house, were a variety of secret caches containing emergency money, cryptographic materials, weapons and other special devices and trappings of espionage.

The anonymity of city life insulated the Vargas from more than superficial contact with neighbors and service personnel, who viewed the Vargas as an industrious couple whose uncommunicativeness could be explained by the horrors of fleeing Budapest. Almost of necessity the Vargas belonged to a Hungarian social club in the upper Eighties where they repaired to celebrate Magyar holidays, join in folk dancing and enjoy Tokay wine. There they were known as fervent nationalists and enemies of the Soviets, who had crushed and enslaved their country. To the Vargas no shadow of suspicion attached, and seated in his store sharing a quart of beer with a business neighbor, Sandor Varga would often complain of the blacks and Puerto Ricans who flooded the Lower East Side, aligning himself with majority white opinion in that deteriorating neighborhood. Nevertheless, in his professional role as Viktor, he made anonymous cash contributions to groups of black activists and Puerto Rican separatists lest their movements wither from lack of funds. Agitation, however, was only an ancillary duty, for Viktor's principal responsiblity was directing a series of highly placed agents, one of whom was referred to in radio traffic as the Banker—Edward Cerf.

During the afternoon a cut-out had waited at a pay telephone, where at the scheduled time, the telephone rang and the *svyazna* received from Cerf his still-negative report.

Although on the principle of compartmentation Viktor had never been informed officially that Klaus Werber was an Agent of Influence, his addition was excellent, and so he realized the gravity of the situation.

Eventually, he knew, he would have to answer to the First Directorate for the clumsy operation that had cost Bitler his life, and so he was not disposed to let anything or anyone stand in the way of recovering the missing girl. Like Cerf, he believed the task should have fallen to someone else; but it had not, and he was burdened with it. In the long run he was responsible and would be judged by his superiors on accomplishment alone. They believed that after fifteen years' residence in the United States he should be capable of anything. What he could never make them understand was the increasing difficulty of his work and the hostile circumstances under which he was required to produce. The FBI seemed to be everywhere, the metropolitan police force had more than doubled, and Gyula warned him increasingly that the length of their radio transmissions was making them vulnerable to intercept and locating devices. Viktor knew that a large portion of the CIA's resources were concentrated in and around Southeast Asia. But once the Vietnam War was over he anticipated their reversion to the Soviet target. Just one KGB defector—if he were the right one—could tell the CIA and the FBI enough about "Viktor" to identify him and end his long career. Had it not been for Hayhanen, Viktor reflected, Colonel Abel could still be in business, and so while his professional tendency was to diminish his level of operation, button up as it were, his superiors demanded operational expansion and highly visible results. He remembered that while in Moscow he could have declined this third tour of duty without reflection on his record, but he had found his wife and son such complete strangers that he decided to stay abroad until retirement. Then, with a roomy apartment in Moscow, a dacha on the outskirts and special privileges at Sukhumi and other seaside resorts, he and his family could enjoy the wealth of his salary accrued in escrow rubles over those many years. Now, as he considered his situation, Viktor sensed that returning to the *rezidentura* had been one of the few wrong decisions of his life. It was too late to request recall and risk the future he had promised himself. All he could do was bear down on his agents and hope that through some miracle—some unexpected fall of fortune—he would be able to report success. It was a dilemma, he throught wryly, that could be well captioned by a title from V. I. Lenin: *What Is to Be Done?*

Gyula began clearing dinner dishes from the table and noticed that he had not moved into the living room to turn on their color television. He seemed more preoccupied than usual, she decided, recognizing

126

at the same time the area of his concern. In English, for they never spoke Russian, she said, "More coffee?"

He shook his head. Inside him grew a feeling of despair. He could not even trust this comrade officer with his burden. On his side there was no emotional attachment to her; she was there like the stove and refrigerator to serve him unquestioningly. Still, one could never be sure that Gyula, with her access to code pads and transmitter, was not sending reports on him to the watchful *Spetsialniy*. So he could not unburden himself even to this comrade with whom he had lived so long, whose bed he shared when necessity drove him to it.

His blond hair was developing traces of gray and thinning on top of his head. There were wrinkles at the corners of his mouth and eyes. He was only fifty-three years old, but he found himself yearning for, more than anything else, the boon of retirement. Abruptly he put the thought from his mind lest it grow unmanageable, rose from the table and shoved back his chair.

Gyula finished placing dishes in the automatic washer and, encouraged by his movement, said, "We've been working too hard. Why don't we go to a cinema?"

"Movie," he said wearily. "Don't say 'cinema' in this country. Movie, eh?"

"Of course," she said worriedly. "Still, it's not a bad idea. We can be back here at eleven in plenty of time for my schedule."

When he said nothing, she went to him and took his arm. "Look, I know what's worrying you, but it's going to be all right. I'm sure of it. You've never failed before."

"Comrade Abel never failed," Varga said morosely. "He was betrayed by a crazy fool of an incompetent. That is what concerns me—that by bearing down too hard on the structure, I will crack it. And for what? This affair of the girl should be the task of the Legal Residency. The worst that ever happens to a Legal who's caught is deportation to the motherland. Is that so bad? Our business is too delicate to risk in an insane pursuit. Lucky for all of us the FBI blames Thorpe for killing his CIA friend."

"But why should we believe what the FBI says?" she blurted unthinkingly. "Suppose it's only to deceive?"

Fist clenched, cheeks reddening, Varga faced her. "That kind of thinking is out of place. Don't create fears and hobgoblins around me!"

To divert his mind, she said quickly, "Everything has been done to find the girl except advertise, Comrade General. We could send an anonymous letter to the press saying she is missing. Then it will be in the papers, and people will begin looking for her."

"Fool!" he said contemptuously. "The press will first check with the West German embassy, and the letter will be denied. But if by some chance the report *is* published, it will increase the likelihood that she will seek out the FBI for protection. And it is *not* desired that she be protected. The girl is to be liquidated. Do you understand? *Liquidated!*"

He stood trembling until his fury spent itself. Then he put one palm to his forehead and tried to press away the pain.

"A little brandy, Comrade General?"

"All right."

She hurried off to pour a small glass of brandy and took it to him in the living room, where he was sitting in his favorite chair.

Wordlessly he accepted the glass, sipped some and said, "Please turn on the television. Then select a *movie* from the paper, and we will go to it. Just so long as we can be back in time for your transmission. Eh? How does that sound, my dear?"

128

"Wonderful," she breathed, grateful that his rage over her stupidities had passed.

"The Banker," he muttered. "The Jew with his fine palaces and tailored clothing, his millions in the bank, enjoying luxury like another czar and ignoring my orders. The son of a whore is incapable of accomplishing one simple task. What fools our service has been to support him in this luxurious fashion so many years that he has forgotten his origins, where his duty lies." He felt the headache returning, so he drained the glass. Gyula remained silent through his denunciation, then went to the kitchen where she opened the entertainment section of the *Post* and ran a finger down the listings until she noticed one promising agreeable entertainment. Carefully she checked its rating and found with prim satisfaction that it was for family viewing. A firm moralist, she was appalled by the filmed pornography offered in New York City. Suggestive marquee titles made her cringe inwardly and avert her eyes. Never in her life had she entered an R-rated cinema, and she thought she would rather die than be forced to sit through an X.

So it was that shortly after dark two middle-aged citizens of unremarkable appearance locked their front door—as did other careful residents of New York's East Side—and strolled arm in arm toward Forty-second Street, where the latest Walt Disney film was playing.

14

TEGUCIGALPA was hotter than New Orleans, and even more humid. Neal and Anna caught a few hours' sleep at the Toncontín airport inn, whose rooms provided thin mattresses and an abundance of roaches that were easy prey for the large furry spiders crouching in closets and corners. Late in the morning Thorpe went around to the airline office whose manager's name had been given him in Mexico. The frame building was covered with a patchwork of galvanized tin, plywood and wallboard. Above the door a flaked sign was lettered: "Sud Air, S.A." Inside there was a wooden counter, and behind it a bulky man on a cot, an electric fan playing on his face. He wore a dirty T-shirt, khaki pants and a mustache that drooped from the corners of his mouth.

"Señor López?"

The man stirred.

"*López!*"

Eyes opened, and the man gazed irritably at Thorpe. "Eh? *Qué pasa?*"

"Business," Thorpe said, "*Negocio.*"

"*Qué tipo de—*"

"In English," Thorpe interrupted. "Manuel Carranza sent me."

"Manuel?" The man sat up and scratched the side of his face. "You come from New Orleans?"

Thorpe nodded.

"How is Manuel?"

"A good businessman. He told me you were, too."

"It depends what kind of business." López drank deeply from a clay jar and waddled to the counter. "When you get here?"

"Last night."

"Where you want to go?"

"Stockholm."

"Why?"

"I like the climate there; I don't like it here."

"That's a good reason." He slid over a clipboard and peeled back some sheets. "The blonde *suecas* very good, too. Not cold like the climate."

"I'm traveling with a blonde."

"Passports?"

"Unfortunately, no."

"Travel costs more without passports."

"Not necessarily," Thorpe said. "Not when there's no passenger manifest for a plane that doesn't carry passengers."

López continued examining schedule sheets. Finally, he took a cigar from under the counter, wet the end carefully and struck a match. Exhaling, he said, "How much you pay?"

"Two hundred each."

"Lempiras?"

A lempira was worth only half a dollar. Thorpe shrugged. "Why not?"

"Three hundred each person."

"Two fifty. That's five hundred lempiras for you, *amigo*. When does the flight leave?"

López peered through a window toward a sag-winged Constellation on the sun-baked field. Large bags of coffee were being loaded through its cargo doors. "Maybe this afternoon," he said. "After siesta."

"Maybe?"

"Depends on the meat—if it comes from the

131

matadero. When it comes, we have to fly quick so the meat not spoil."

Thorpe nodded. "How will I know?"

"You come back here two o'clock. With money."

"I'll have the money."

He went outside and stood in the shade watching the Constellation being loaded. There was no forklift, and workmen hefted hundred-pound sacks of coffee from the truck into the aircraft. At the leisurely work pace, Thorpe wondered if even the coffee cargo could be loaded by sundown.

Lounging in the shade of the main airport building were soldiers, some with sidearms, others with rifles. Except for them, airport security looked reasonably lax. Even so, Thorpe was not tempted to leave Toncontín for downtown Tegucigalpa. All that might be gained was a somewhat better meal, but at the risk of being noticed by someone from the embassy. He went back to the inn and unlocked the door of their room, entered and locked the door again. Shower water was running, so Thorpe pulled off his shirt and lay back on his bed. After a while he opened the room's two small windows in the hope of cross ventilation, but no breeze disturbed the room's concentrated heat.

From the bed he stared up at the cracked white-washed ceiling; from one corner a large spider stared back. Thorpe closed his eyes and found himself thinking of Don Bitler, killed by the very forces whose existence he doubted. A tragic, ironic and unnecessary death, he reflected, and wondered again whether he, rather than Bitler, had not been the killer's intended target. In either case, Bitler and he were only intermediate targets; Anna was the one they sought, and it was she, rather than himself, he must protect.

He heard the shower cease, the plastic curtain rustle as Anna stepped out. Opening his eyes, he called, "I'm back."

"I'm so glad. Neal—there's only one towel. Can we share it?"

"We've shared everything else."

"What news do you have?"

"We may be able to fly today. I'm supposed to learn at two. Are you hungry?"

"Ravenous."

"There's not much by way of restaurants."

"I'll eat *anything*."

Presently she appeared at the bathroom doorway in shirt and Levis, hair bound up in a damp towel. "Are the spiders waiting for me?"

"Avidly." Thorpe got up and scooted away the nearest ones. Anna hurried over the cleared area and stepped on her bed to dry her hair. "Tell me about our flight."

"It's a plane," he said. "Like the other one, pretty ancient. Four engines and four propellers. We'll share space with a cargo of coffee and beef."

She smiled. "At least we need not go hungry."

"Not if you can eat green coffee and raw meat."

He tossed her sandals to the bed, and when she sat to put them on, he toweled her hair until she suggested drying it under the sun.

"Just so long as you're not seen. I don't want the *paisanos* to remember anything except a lurid blonde. So try the roof. There's a stairway leading up from the courtyard."

"I promise not to be long."

"We have until two o'clock. That's when I have to check back at Sud Air. We've got bargain rates, by the way: the equivalent of two hundred and fifty dollars for both of us."

She sighed in relief. "I was afraid it was going to take all of our money."

"Speaking of which, I think you'd better carry our surplus."

She stood up, placed her arms on his shoulders and kissed him lightly. "You trust me, then?"

"With my life."

Unlocking the door for her, he gave her the key. Anna jogged around the end of the building, and soon he heard her footsteps above the room.

The restaurant where they lunched catered to airport workmen and mechanics, and Anna's blond tresses aroused audible interest. Rather than risk spicy mestizo food, they stayed with steak and eggs and decided beer would be safer than local water. As they left the restaurant, Thorpe pointed out the Constellation and remarked that all work had ceased. Under the shadow of the wings stevedores and workmen sprawled in their midday siesta, and he noticed that the coffee truck was nearly unloaded. That left the load of meat, which, as López pointed out, had to be transferred promptly.

Beyond the airfield fence there were tall coco palms, scrub pines, banana plants and wild poinciana heavily laden with roadside dust. Still, the sky was clear, the sun had burned away the morning humidity, and they had reason to believe that tomorrow they would be in Stockholm, where a kind of sanctuary awaited. Above, a buzzard circled effortlessly, airborne by warm drafts from the heated earth, and except for the distant drone of a lightplane engine, the lazy stillness was almost unbroken.

"No wonder," Anna said, "so little seems to be accomplished here. A week of this climate and I would lose all ambition."

"It's even worse on the coast—hotter and wetter."

"Then I hope we will never have to go there." She took his arm and they walked slowly back to their room.

Door and windows open, they lay on their beds, shaded at least from the sun's direct rays, but the heat

134

seemed almost tangible in the room, a heavy presence that shortened breath and brought lassitude to their bodies. Presently Thorpe drifted off to sleep and woke with a start to find it was already two o'clock.

Without waking Anna, he locked the door and walked to the Sud Air office. Before opening the door, he scanned the Constellation and saw that the coffee truck had departed. In its place was a large white-sided truck from which laborers were dragging sides of beef. He went in and whistled López awake.

From his cot the Honduran peered at him.

"Two o'clock," Thorpe said, "What about the flight?"

"Depends on the meat."

"It's being loaded."

López sat up and licked his lips. "The money?"

On the counter Thorpe counted out two hundred and fifty dollars. "Five hundred lempiras," he said as López got up to collect. "What happens now?"

The Honduran squinted through the window at the white-sided truck and back to Thorpe. "Just after the *camión* goes away I drive you out. Where is the *compañera?*"

"Resting. Have you talked with the pilot?"

"*Sí.* Everything fixed."

"What's the flight plan?"

"Here to Horta, Lisbon and Stockholm." He went back to his cot. "Why you really want to go there?"

"We've got friends in Stockholm."

"What kind of friends?"

"My girl's brother is there—hiding from the draft."

"Draft?"

"The Army. Any more questions?"

López lay back and studied the ceiling. "What if the police ask me about you?"

"Tell them you sold us illegal passage to Europe. They'll like that."

With a grunt the Honduran closed his eyes.

Thorpe went out of the office and back to the stifling room. Without waking Anna, he moved a chair under the high window and stood on it to look outside. From there he could see the Constellation and its satellite truck.

For a quarter of an hour he watched until it became apparent that the meat cargo was nearly loaded. Then he stepped down, blotted his face with the damp towel and woke Anna. "Time to go," he said gently, and sat holding her until she was fully awake. Having paid for the room when they arrived, they walked together to the Sud Air office and waited in the outside shade until a jeep drove up trailing twin plumes of dust. In it were two men wearing blue shirts, blue trousers and blue uniform caps with silver wings that bore the initials "SA."

"Looks like the crew," Thorpe said. "Or part of it."

The driver glanced at them, tooted the horn, and after a few moments López appeared in the doorway. "*Son ellos*," he said, indicating Thorpe and Anna. Then: "They take you to plane."

"What are their names?" Thorpe asked, getting up.

"Pilot is Andrés. Co-pilot, Felipe."

"Do they speak English?"

"Some. Time to go."

The thin man at the wheel was presumably the pilot, Andrés. His plumper companion got out so Thorpe and Anna could get into the rear seats, then resumed his place beside the driver.

"Hi," Thorpe said.

"Hello," said Anna.

"*Buenos días*," said the Hondurans.

Thorpe looked at Anna. "Some English is right."

The jeep was heading toward the big aircraft, whose cargo doors were now closed. Its gas tanks were being filled from a large red tanker truck. Anna said, "I've never flown in that kind of plane before."

"It was great in its day," Thorpe said, "but that was a long time ago."

"Still good plane," said the pilot. "Carry much cargo very cheap. You going Stockholm?"

"Didn't López tell you?"

"*Sí*. But sometime López get mixed up."

"Stockholm," Thorpe verified. "How many hours?"

"To Horta, maybe seven, eight. Depends on wind."

"Where's the navigator?"

"I'm navigator," said Felipe with a grin. "Also radio man and engineer."

"Radio working?"

"Not too good. But engines fine, okay."

"Well," said Thorpe, "that's what's important."

The jeep braked, and they got out, Anna climbing the nose ladder ahead of Thorpe and when they were in the crew compartment, they felt the day's accumulated heat. Moving aft into the cargo section that was the rest of the plane's interior, they saw that the coffee sacks had been loaded to form a thick covering the length of the fuselage. On them were piled at least a hundred sides of beef, suet turning to tallow in the heat. The combined smell of green coffee and raw beef was disagreeable. Anna's nose wrinkled, but Thorpe said, "It'll be better once we're flying."

"I *hope* so."

There were no bench seats in the aircraft, so Thorpe and Anna settled down on coffee sacks and made themselves comfortable. Thorpe lay back and closed his eyes, feeling sweat drench his shirt, run in rivulets from his forehead, and he was reminded of a hundred rough flights he had made in 'Nam. This time at least, the carcasses around him were animal rather than human.

He heard and felt the vibration of the departing gasoline truck, and then an engine popped into life, joined at intervals by the other three. The fuselage shook heavily until the engines synchronized. Then the Constellation lumbered toward the runway, and Thorpe saw beef sides move and settle. There was only a minimum of cargo tie-downs. If the cargo shifted on landing, he and Anna could be crushed, or the plane forced into a nose dive, killing them all. The Constellation braked while the pilot ran up the engines. Fresh air flooded the compartment, compressing Thorpe's eardrums and telling him the fuselage, like the crew compartment, was pressurized.

There was a pile of old blankets near the forward bulkhead, Thorpe noticed, and hoped this longer flight would be more comfortable than the one from Mexico to Toncontín.

The Constellation rolled ahead, creaking and groaning, accelerating until the tail lifted. He saw palms and jungle flashing past, felt the upward surge of takeoff, and said to Anna, "At least we're airborne." He kissed her forehead and held her in his arms while the plane climbed and the air grew cool.

When the Constellation was over the Caribbean he got up and carried back a half dozen cargo blankets and arranged them into beds. Then, lulled by the steady drone of the engines, he fell asleep.

Later he woke once in the darkness to see wingtips silvered by the moon, red-blue exhaust flames flaring back from beneath the cowlings.

Thorpe fell asleep, and when he woke again, it was because cold steel was pressing against his throat.

Above him, in the gray light of the Atlantic dawn he saw a man's face. The features were Indian, with mustache and black wispy beard. Thick lips parted and the voice hissed. "Dinero. You give me money."

The man's left hand, the one not holding the knife, lifted, and the palm uncurled. "Dinero—or die!"

15

IN a flat above Odengatan an alarm clock rang and Zarah Engstrom stirred, reached drowsily for the bed table and turned the alarm off, lest it wake her small son, Rolf, sleeping in his nearby crib. She sat up, pulled off her thin cotton nightgown and went into the bathroom before turning on a light. She drew a shower cap over her red-gold hair and stepped onto scales before turning on the water. Then, while the air warmed and the mirror misted, she performed a series of exercises designed to keep her abdomen flat and her full breasts firm. Her hips and buttocks were pleasantly contoured, but she sometimes wished her figure more boyish, as the current fashion. Her features were neither fragile nor extraordinarily beautiful, but her face and figure made her an attractive woman who looked less than her thirty years and whom men turned to ogle when they passed her on the street. She did not linger in the shower but soaped her body purposefully and rinsed, for she lived according to a demanding schedule, and there were times other than work mornings allotted to bodily indulgence.

Zarah dried briskly, drew on a woolen robe and went into the kitchenette, where she set water to boiling and took milk, butter and marmalade from the small refrigerator. She made a cup of tea, poured milk into it and ate a sweet roll with butter, thinking that perhaps again this summer she would be able to go to the Costa del Sol and enjoy the deeply penetrating sunshine that come so infrequently to northern Europe. Advance arrangements for Rolf would have to be made with the day care center, but they were only a formality, and so, as she finished breakfast, she half decided to revisit Spain in July or early August. When the wall clock told her it was time to wake her son, she placed a single egg in a pan of cold water and set it over the burner. Then she kissed Rolf awake and carried him into the bathroom. At four he could do more things for himself than most boys his age, and his mother encouraged self-reliance as an always-useful quality. Her widowed father had instilled it in her from her earliest years, and so when the inevitable break with her husband finally came, Zarah found herself welcoming the freedom to live a rational life again.

Dressing, she reflected that she remained as grateful for Rolf as that early morning when he was first brought to suckle at her breast. She brushed her hair, applied lipstick lightly and tied her son's shoelaces.

While he waited, she quickly washed their breakfast dishes, took their coats from a small closet and led him from the flat to the elevator. From the underground garage she drove her Saab to the day care center in Vasaparken and watched Rolf safely into the doorway where he stopped to wave good-bye.

From there Zarah followed light morning traffic to the tall modern buildings of Hötorgscity, the huge shopping complex, where, recently, she had taken employment in a travel bureau. She steered her Saab into the underground garage, parked and rode the escalator to Sergelgatan. After entering the office, she hung her coat in the common closet, then went to her desk. A graduate of Uppsala, Zarah Engstrom spoke Finnish, Swedish, Russian, English, French and a useful amount of Spanish and Italian. Her hands sorted multilingual travel folders to have them ready when the rush of morning clients began, pausing to glance

140

at a Venetian brochure and reflect that she did not really like Italian men. Her attitude toward sex was healthily open, and prurience dismayed her. She expected thoughtfulness and competence of a partner, but she had found that Mediterranean males viewed Scandinavia as one large sexual smörgasbord; for her part Zarah found the same expectant males to be either impotent, unpracticed or intolerably gross. Accordingly she avoided Southern Europeans, preferring men of her own coloring, complexion and tastes.

Soon, perhaps today or tomorrow, she would have to let her employer know that she did not sleep with office mates and tell Nystrom to keep his hands to himself. He would not discharge her, she knew, for she learned easily and had become a valued employee during the short time she worked for him. Besides, in Sweden, as in Germany, there were many more jobs than available employees, and so if Nystrom became difficult, she would simply find another place in Hötorgscity.

Zarah arranged the folders in orderly piles and began inserting schedule changes into her international airlines reference book. After living with her husband in the small port of Söderhamn, she found excitement and satisfaction in the busy life of Stockholm: cafés, exquisite shops, a comfortable heated flat and excellent care for Rolf. And if one wanted to travel, Stockholm was close to almost any place that counted.

She had traveled widely in Europe, visited Africa and Japan and returned through San Francisco, Chicago and New York. The one place she really wanted to visit was much nearer, but her father long ago had warned her about returning to Finland. Yet, from the tales he had told her night after night through her childhood, she knew that it must be a

141

wonderful country, even Lappland in the farthest north. From Stockholm one could fly in an hour to Helsinki, Zarah mused, and she had often been tempted to slip away and hear, for the first time, everyone speaking the language of her birth. Still, she had never done so: because of her father's work, the legacy he would leave to the West.

A bell rang, the porter opened the glass doors, and Zarah Engstrom looked expectantly at the broad plaza where, even this early in the morning, strollers were beginning to window-shop and enter stores.

Perhaps today, she thought, as the first visitor came into Nystrom's Travel Bureau, she would meet someone interesting, a man out of the ordinary . . . someone handsome and stimulating. . . .

High above the Atlantic, two hundred miles west of the Azores, Neal Thorpe felt a trickle of warm blood from the blade at his throat. *"Dinero,"* hissed the man again, and Thorpe wet dry lips.

"Sí," he managed, smelling the stench of the man's body, and slowly lifted his right hand, fingers spread to show they contained nothing. Slowly, steadily, he lowered the hand and fitted it into his trouser pocket. In it were only a few Honduran coins, change from their airport meal. Anna still had their money, and she was asleep. Thorpe wondered why the man had not put the knife to her throat, then realized that, logically, the male could be expected to carry the couple's funds. So the *campesino* had gone directly to the source of funds.

Thorpe's shoulder lifted as he seemed to have difficulty removing his hand from his pocket, and the *campesino* drew back so that his victim could produce the expected *dinero*. The knife left Thorpe's neck, and he saw the exultant grin on the robber's face. Slowly

142

Thorpe's hand came out of the pocket. Clenched in its palm was the switchblade, but in the dimness the robber could not see; what he heard was the snick of the spring locking the blade into place. Instead of cutting Thorpe's throat, he hesitated, and Thorpe's hand whipped a lateral arc, slashing the switchblade across the man's arm. The robber yelped as Thorpe levered aside and kicked the man's face. On his feet, Thorpe stared down at the man who had wanted to rob him; he lay across a coffee sack, arms outstreched, unconscious.

Wakened by the struggle, Anna sat upright and watched Thorpe bending over the fallen man. She saw him pick up the knife and slit the man's shirt sleeve, rip it to the shoulder and cut it off. Next he twisted it into a tourniquet and tied it around the arm above the open wound. Crawling toward him, she said, "What happened?"

"He wanted our money," Thorpe said matter-of-factly, cut the man's leather belt and rolled his body over. He tried binding the man's hands with the belt, but the leather was too wide and too stiff. "See if you can find something," he said, and sat back to wipe his face.

Remembering the nick on his throat, Thorpe cut a section from the man's other sleeve and tied it around his throat, tightly enough to stem the bleeding. He folded the switchblade into his pocket and picked up the other knife. It was a crude field knife, wooden-handled with a sharp steel blade. He tested the edge of his thumb and heard Anna call, "Over here!"

After making his way over chilled beef, Thorpe reached her side. She was pointing to a canvas strap snapped into a ring on the fuselage. Thorpe cut it off and crawled back to where the man was beginning to stir. He bound the hands behind the man's back, secured the belt around his ankles. Then he rolled the body away until it lodged between two sides of beef.

Anna said, "Your *throat*! Neal—"

"It's all right."

Slowly her gaze left the bandage and settled on Thorpe's assailant. "What about him? Shouldn't we tell the pilots?"

"I'm thinking about it."

"Oh. You mean they could have sent him?"

"Possibly. More likely he's a stevedore who either fell asleep in the plane or decided to stow away and see where Honduras' coffee and meat were going. After seeing Tegoose, do you blame him?"

Thorpe got out his switchblade, sprung it open and gave it to her. "I'll consult our peerless pilots."

"Neal—please. . . ."

"I'll be careful." He crawled over cargo until he reached the door of the pilot's cabin. Slowly he turned the handle, expecting the door to be locked, but it was not. Stepping inside, he closed the door behind him. The compartment was dark except for a red dome light, the subdued glow of the instrument panels. The pilot was asleep in his seat; the co-pilot was settled comfortably back, a small pillow behind his head. The controls were on automatic pilot.

Hanging over the back of the co-pilot's seat were a cartridge belt and a holstered Colt .45. Thorpe lifted the automatic from its holster and slid off the safety. "Felipe," he said.

At the sound of his name the co-pilot turned around, stared at the gun and thrust his hands upward.

"Easy," Thorpe said. "You didn't tell me there was another passenger aboard."

"Passenger?" he gulped.

"Suddenly there's three of us." He motioned Felipe up and out of his seat. "Take a look."

Felipe glanced at the sleeping pilot, took a deep

144

breath and preceded Thorpe to where the man lay. Anna knelt beside him, knife in hand.

Thorpe said, "Ever see him before?"

"No. Believe me. I never saw him, never."

Thorpe lifted the Colt. "Any other weapons aboard? Guns? Knives?"

Felipe shook his head.

"All right," Thorpe said. "If you've got a first-aid kit, see what you can do for him. I cut that arm pretty deep."

Felipe swallowed. "What happened?"

"He wanted to rob me. I didn't want to be robbed." Thorpe followed the co-pilot back into the cabin and waited while Felipe dragged out a dusty medical kit. Then they returned to the wounded man. While the co-pilot bandaged the long cut, he alternately cursed the man and interrogated him. The man answered in a choked voice. He was in pain and frightened.

Standing up, the co-pilot said, "He hid himself. When he got cold, he came up to look for serapes and found you. He has no money."

"What's his name?"

Felipe repeated the question in Spanish, then said, "Juan Domínguez. And he is very sorry for what he did."

"So am I."

"What should be done with him?"

"Take him back to Honduras."

Felipe laughed shortly. "We wanted to stay overnight in Lisboa . . . Now, because of him, we will take on fuel at Horta and fly direct to Stockholm." His eyes dropped to the pistol in Thorpe's hand.

"I'll keep it for now," Thorpe told him. "Go back and fly the plane."

After repacking the first-aid kit, the pilot picked it up and went forward. Thorpe took his switchblade from Anna and said, "Try to sleep."

145

She gestured at the windows. "There is too much light. We could sit together, Neal. Perhaps we could talk."

He looked down at the drawn face of Juan Domínguez, tried to think of something to say, realized the Honduran would not understand and crawled back to their blankets. Laying down the pistol, Thorpe arranged himself so that he could see the wounded man.

Lying back beside him, Anna said, "So we will reach Stockholm earlier."

"Much earlier."

Her head turned so that she could watch the horizon where the sun's first rays shot a red-gold line across the dark horizon. "Do you think we will be safe in Sweden?"

"Safer than where we've been. And we'll certainly be more comfortable." He thought of good hotels, hot baths and appetizing food.

"Will you be able to find the person who can help us?"

"I don't think I can—alone. Is German understood in Stockholm?"

She nodded. "Quite well."

"Then I'll have to depend on you." Lying back, he turned his head to look at her. "You know, we've come a long way, but the hardest part is still ahead."

16

FOR Alton Regester it was a working breakfast, although he had camouflaged it as a social occasion. Across the table from him sat a man he had known since 1956, when their professional acquaintance had begun in consequence of Khrushchev's Secret Speech.

Regester's guest was a short, powerfully built middle-aged man whose bullet head was almost entirely bald. Under his left eye was an inch-long scar whose tissue was raised and slightly darker than the rest of his face. He was an Israeli who had worked in the early fifties at Vienna's Documentation Center. Now he was carried on the Department of State's Diplomatic List as a counselor of the Embassy of Israel; in fact he was chief in the United States of Shin Bet, the Israeli Intelligence service, and his name was Dov Apelbaum.

With a smile he said, "I don't imagine you breakfast on bagels and lox every morning, Alton, so I appreciate the special attention."

"Next, you'll suggest I have an ulterior motive in asking you here."

"Absolutely. Don't you?"

Regester nodded. "I thought that even though I'm retired, there were certain matters we might still be able to discuss."

Delicately, Apelbaum licked a trace of sour cream from his index finger. "In fact, because of your retirement, there are probably things we can discuss even more freely than we could before. You have no obligation to prepare a memorandum of conversation—and neither do I." He looked down at his plate and sighed. "Delicious. You have lost none of your skill in determining a man's innermost vulnerability." He belched happily. "Ah, the pleasures of the palate!"

Regester sipped caffeine-free coffee and set down the cup. "The subject is one we never discussed before. But now, in my dotage, I find it of increasing interest —and importance. It concerns Agents of Influence. You, I know, discovered and exposed one in the Cabinet of your own government."

Apelbaum nodded. "That was some years ago."

"Doubtless there were others," Regester went on, "whom you suspected but lacked sufficient proof to expose."

Apelbaum nodded again. "True. And contrary to logic, that *coup* of mine became a blemish on my record. What was it you had in mind, Alton?"

Regester leaned forward. "Have you ever considered Klaus Werber as an Agent of Influence?"

"Yes."

The reply surprised Regester, and his expression showed it, for Dov Apelbaum said, "Nor am I the only one in my organization who so regards him."

Regester laughed shortly. "May I ask what led to your conclusion?"

"Oh, a number of things over the years. Such as Werber's disinterest in welcoming back those Jews who managed to flee Germany in the thirties. His indecisiveness over the Berlin Wall and the future of Berlin itself. The fact that he did nothing to keep German rocket experts out of Egypt and other Arab countries. Werber's behind-the-scenes role in effecting *rapprochement* with the East, beginning with the exchange of small trade delegations. . . ." He shrugged. "Do I need to go on?"

148

"Dov, you never fail to amaze me—and for years I thought *I* was the only laborer in the Werber vineyard."

"Werber's probably going to get the Nobel Prize for Peace," Apelbaum said casually. "I don't know what could be done about that. But"—and his tone changed—"my country would not be happy if Werber were to become UN Secretary-General."

"Seems very much in the cards, doesn't it?"

"As the hand is now being played."

"Precisely my thoughts." Regester refilled their coffee cups from an antique sterling pot.

"But not all of them?"

"No. You'll forgive me if I don't identify my source other than to describe him as a man I've known since the war and in whom I have the utmost confidence. Through him I learned that when Werber was in Stockholm not long ago—"

"On his self-serving, vote-getting trip?"

"The same. Klaus was visited by a pair of Kremlin specialists: Yakov Gorytsev and Gleb Kalugin."

Now Apelbaum showed surprise. "No mistake?"

"They were seen by two witnesses." Regester went on to summarize the episode and when he had finished, Apelbaum said, "Mind if I report this?"

"Right now it may be premature. But the circumstances of the contact—the fact that the contact was even made—would convince me about Werber even if I hadn't believed it before."

For a long time Apelbaum stared at the coffee in his cup. Finally, he shifted his gaze and muttered, "Bad news."

"In one sense, yes. But with identification it seems to me other possibilities open up."

"By all means we ought to discuss them. But before we begin, let me go on record with this conviction: Werber is too much the beloved international figure to be ruined by, for instance, a covert campaign to assassinate his character. He's much larger than life. Accordingly, low-key measures would be insufficient. Even attempting them might be counterproductive if Werber emerged stronger than ever, haloed and enshrined in the hearts of the world."

"Agreed."

"If fortunate, we might be able to arrange one blow. Just one, Alton, but it would have to be imaginative—and mortal."

"Again I agree. Killing the snake, not scotching it." His eyes lifted, and his gaze traveled briefly about the room. "So here we sit and tell sad stories of the death of kings."

"I detect a classical mood," Dov said with a smile. " 'Superfluous branches we lop away that bearing boughs may live.' "

"Excellent allusion."

"Not bad for a Haganah desert rat, if I say so myself. Besides, the quote provides a comforting rationale for a number of things I've done." He sipped more coffee. "Did you know I was involved in the Eichmann snatch?"

"I assumed it," Regester said. "And a nice clean operation it was."

Apelbaum nodded. "A major reason for success was that very few people knew the overall plan. So if you and I enter into an anti-Werber conspiracy, I would hope we could confine knowledge to, say, those present in this room."

"That would be the two of us."

"With perhaps an occasional assist from my wife." He stretched his arms and looked upward. "I haven't been earning my keep this last year, and what I've been doing mostly is pondering the uncongenial prospect of retirement to my plot in the Negev. So one final, worthwhile *coup* would be of wholehearted interest to me—as I gather it is to you." His face sobered. "How much time do you have?"

"Without extensive surgery, perhaps six months. And even if I submit to surgery, it's unlikely I could ever leave the hospital again." Regester shook his head. "So I would far rather depart this world with a sense of accomplishment and not smelling of bedpans."

"I don't want to become maudlin, but I want you to know how profoundly sorry I am. You don't need me to remind you of it, so I'll say no more from now on."

"I understand—and thank you."

"So where should we start?"

Regester went over to his desk, unlocked it and drew out his charts. Selecting two, he opened Werber's on the desk, smoothed it and beckoned to Apelbaum, who pulled up a chair to study the intricate diagrams.

While his guest absorbed information, long memorized by Regester, the retired CIA officer cleared the breakfast table and transferred their dishes to the kitchen. Some time during the day a maid would take care of them, dust the apartment and make up his bed. His life, Regester reflected, was reduced to a few basics: ingestion, digestion, evacuation, medicine, rest and a modicum of diversion. He felt inwardly elated that the Shin Bet chief had so readily fallen in with his plans for extra-official action against Klaus Werber. Apelbaum, he knew, spoke several European languages, as well as excellent Russian, and a linguist would be needed.

He thought about Arne Lakka and wondered where his Finnish friend might be, whether he was even, in fact, alive. And from Lakka his mind moved on to Neal Thorpe and the girl. So far he had heard only once from Thorpe, who was, by now, he hoped, in Mexico. Regester reviewed the counsel he had given and decided that while Thorpe's disappearance must be an

151

annoyance to the Bureau, that was of no importance compared to the safety of Annalise Bauer. What he had done was to provide Annalise with an escort and protector, and that accomplishment outweighed any putative obligation he might have to the FBI.

Leaving the kitchen, Regester returned to his guest who was sitting eyes half-closed in apparently deep thought. Regester sat down at his desk and waited until Apelbaum spoke.

"I admire the way you've used hypothesis as a bridge between facts, but I can't argue against your conclusions." Apelbaum gestured at the diagrams. "Aside from the character of the man himself, I see only two apparent vulnerabilities: his wife and stepdaughter. Is much known of the wife?"

"Very little. A wealthy Swiss widow when Werber married her and still a handsome woman. They live outside Bonn in Bad Godesberg."

"Then perhaps her daughter is the key."

"Certainly from the Soviet point of view. But let me put it this way: The Soviets have no reason to believe anyone except Annalise knows of Werber's involvement, thus their strong effort to find and silence her. For the Soviets, she's the sole obstacle to Werber's and their success. They don't know that others are aware of what Werber is—you and me, for instance."

"And Neal Thorpe."

"Unless Bitler talked before he was killed—and I don't think he did. At least he wasn't tortured. So as I see it, Soviet concern is centered on the girl rather than on a larger circumference. That gives us some space for maneuvering. Now you and I know that any revelation she might make in public could be discredited—if not by Werber alone, then by Soviet allies in the European press. All of which means casting Annalise in a supporting, rather than principal, role."

152

Apelbaum nodded approval. "In fact, we might not even need her services."

"I can foresee that, too. Of course it would be nice to know details of what she learned and how, but I don't feel it's essential. Not if we can do most of the work ourselves."

"It shouldn't take much money," the Shin Bet man observed. "More inspiration than money."

"Money is something I haven't much need for. What I have I'd be more than willing to invest in our undertaking. Regester looked at his guest. "Any ideas?"

"Oh, I think the general category is obvious: a deception operation. For example, convincing Werber's Soviet masters that he's gone over to our side. Setting him up, in other words. Letting him become a disposal problem to the Soviets. In that the girl could be helpful if she were available. Is she?"

"She's left the country."

"Alone?"

"With Thorpe. I recommended they try to reach Europe."

"They won't be looking for her in Europe. Perfect."

"Within a few days I'll know whether they made it."

"Well, the sooner we settle on a plan, the better. But let's make it flexible enough to work without the girl. Right now we have to do some professional thinking, so let's get together again tomorrow and work out an operational draft. If it won't strain your hospitality, I'll come here for breakfast. That will keep my office routine the same and not cause any questions."

"Breakfast it is." Regester's eyes lowered, and his gaze rested briefly on the second chart he had brought out but not yet unfolded. "As long as you're here, Dov, I have a question for you. Do you know a man who goes by the name of Edward Cerf? In France, before the war, he called himself Hirsch. Edouard Hirsch."

"Hirsch? The banker?" Apelbaum nodded reminiscently. "At a time when Israel very much needed help, Hirsch gave me three million dollars for the Haganah. I have nothing against him."

Wordlessly, Regester opened up the chart that bore Cerf's name and passed it across the desk to Apelbaum. "Then I think you ought to have a look at this."

17

DURING the midday working slack, Neal and Anna were able to leave Arlanda Airport unobserved through a cargo gate. An SAS bus took them to the airlines terminal in central Stockholm. There they changed part of their money into kronor, walked along the waterfront and took a room at the Strand Hotel, whose sign they noticed as they left the terminal. Their room was reasonably priced and clean, and after showers they went down to a heavy lunch at a nearby restaurant. Next, they found clothing at a department store and returned to the room to change, Anna into a light tweed pants suit, and Thorpe into flannel slacks, Norse sweater and uncomfortably fitting shoes. Because Regester's promise of funds had been tenuous, Thorpe economized on his shoes, buying a Swedish brand rather than astronomically priced American or British imports, and as they walked down Nybrokajen, he regretted it.

A tourist map of Stockholm guided them to the

Grand Hotel, a short distance from their own. Thorpe took a table at a sidewalk café and watched Anna walk into the front entrance of the Grand.

A porter directed her to the hotel personnel office, where, in German, she identified herself as a distant cousin of Zarah Engstrom, whom she was trying to locate.

"No wonder," sniffed the personnel clerk, a small gray-haired woman. "Your cousin flits from job to job. Why, she worked here barely two weeks!"

"I know," Anna said in a voice expressing disapproval. "Zarah sent me a postcard from the Grand, saying she worked here. And that is really my only clue. I'd be so grateful if you could help me find her."

"Well—we don't usually give out employee information, but since you're her cousin. . . ."

"If I don't find her, I won't have even one friend in Stockholm," Anna said wistfully. "I understand it's not easy here for a single girl."

"It's just terrible," the clerk said with a shake of her head. "And the nasty things they expose in store windows. . . ." Turning, she went to a card file, searched it briefly and brought back a card. "Here, you'd better write this down." She supplied Anna with pencil and a scrap of paper. "There's no address, only a notation she was seeking lodgings. But the telephone number is 63-47-51."

"I have it," Anna said brightly. "Thank you ever so much."

"When you see your cousin, you might remind her that in employing her the Grand expected her to stay, not flit away."

"I'll do just that," Anna promised, inserted the paper into her purse and smiled her way out of the office. She found Neal sipping coffee and produced the telephone number for his inspection.

"Good girl," he said. "Why don't you order some-

155

thing?" and walked off to a telephone kiosk located near the tour boat office. He dialed, deposited a coin and listened to the telephone ring. It rang a dozen times before he gave up and rejoined Anna at their table.

"No luck," he said. "Zarah's probably at work. We'll try again later on."

"She didn't leave an address with the hotel. Perhaps that's not even her phone number."

"Dismal thought," Thorpe said and sipped from his cup. "Even so, I think she'd have to provide some way of being reached in case the hotel needed her for special duty. So let's think positively."

Cars and buses passed them along the quai; glass-topped Delfin tour boats carrying only a few sightseers moved over the Strömmen's murky waters. The sky was clear, the breeze from the water cool; like a March day in Washington, Thorpe reflected and wondered what success the FBI was having in its search for him. Remembering Bitler's death sobered him, and he found himself hoping Don's killer would be found, less to ease his own difficulties than to see justice, for a change, prevail.

Through nearly budless branches he could see the distant gray pylon that was the tallest structure in Scandinavia: the Stockholm Tower with its microwave and radio antennas. He remembered reading about it in an architectural review. A tourist brochure had told him there was a restaurant at the top, viewing terraces and shops. On a pleasanter day he would take Anna to see it, but now he was still tired from the long flight, the tensions of guarding the stevedore who tried to rob him. Aside from the cut on Thorpe's neck, the pilots were the ones most affected. Lisbon was cut from their schedule, and they had to take turns guarding their prisoner on the plane, denying them an evening's relaxation in Stockholm's cabarets.

Anna said, "I thought we agreed on no more long silences."

"Sorry. Won't happen again." He managed a carefree smile.

"Since we have some time to pass before calling Zarah again, I thought I would do something about this frightful wig." She fingered the long, obviously false blond tresses.

"Do what with it?"

"Dispose of it, then have my own hair bleached. Or streaked, if you prefer."

"Streaked—if they can do a good job."

"I noticed a salon in the Grand. Can we afford it?"

"Why not? It's your money we're living on. Maybe I'll consult the barbershop while you're in the salon. The wig I'm wearing makes me look like one of the Three Stooges. Any suggestions?"

She nodded. "Have a partial bleach and a different hairstyling. You look far too American."

"I sort of like the way I looked—B.W.—before the wig."

"So did I. But this is a question of self-preservation."

"You're right." He beckoned over the waiter and paid their small bill. "See you back at the hotel?"

Anna glanced at her wristwatch. "About five. But don't worry if I'm not there exactly at five."

"Why shouldn't I worry?"

"Because I'll probably have to wait for an opening. And the process isn't done in a minute." Rising, she kissed him, then walked away toward the Grand.

Thorpe waited for his change, tipped the waiter and went into the hotel by a side entrance. In the men's room he pulled off his wig, dropped it into a trash container and combed his hair. He found the barbershop under a sign that read "Frisör," entered and found several barbers waiting. "Anyone speak English?" he asked the valet.

157

"Almost everyone, sir," said the valet and showed him an empty chair. To the barber Thorpe explained what he wanted done, adding that he had decided to preserve the mustache that had grown over the several days he had not shaved.

The valet handed him a copy of the Paris *Herald*, and Thorpe glanced at it as the barber adjusted a clean covering around his neck. FUGITIVE BELIEVED IN CANADA read a front-page lead, and Thorpe found himself staring at a photograph of himself. Quickly, he folded the paper and buried it under the sheet. The barber eased back the chair, and Thorpe closed his eyes, feeling his body begin to relax. The photo was reproduced from the ID photograph in CIA security files, and although it was an old one, he knew he could still be recognized from it. Luckily, he thought, there were no current photographs of himself in the apartment, which by now must have been thoroughly ransacked.

As the barber's work began, Thorpe reminded himself that he had been expecting publication of a photograph, and seeing it should have come as no surprise. What shocked him instead, was the *fact* of its publication, the starkness of the story describing him as a fugitive. Neal Thorpe, fugitive from justice, sought in Canada.

At least they haven't begun looking for me in Europe, he reflected. Leaving his car at National Airport had turned out to be good misdirection—unless, of course, the Bureau was doing some misdirecting of its own.

The barber shampooed his hair, razor-cut it, and began applying smoky chemicals. The process took about an hour, and when it was over, Thorpe looked drowsily into the mirror and saw a light-haired mustached stranger. He got out of the chair, casually returned the *Herald* to the valet, paid and tipped the

barber and went out into the corridor. At the newsstand he bought a copy of the *Herald* and rolled it
under his arm to read later in the hotel room. The
lobby clerk told him he had more than an hour to kill,
so he took the stairs down to the sauna, showered,
enjoyed a good pounding massage and steamed in the
sauna cabinet for half an hour. A plunge in the ice-
cold pool revived him, and after a rubdown he left the
Grand Hotel in long, muscular strides.

He unlocked the door of his room and found the
interior dark; Anna was still at the beauty salon. Turning on the lights, he lay down on his bed and began
reading the *Herald* story. In it he was described as the
principal suspect in the murder of a CIA employee.
His car's being found at the airport suggested sudden
flight to avoid prosecution, and an airlike clerk
remembered his photograph as that of a man who had
purchased a ticket to Toronto by way of Cleveland.
Fragments of his biography were supplied, together
with a quote from Phil Dawes, who denied that his
partner could be guilty of the crime. "Besides," Dawes
was quoted as saying, "why would Mr. Thrope want to
kill Mr. Bitler? What possible motive could there be?"

The story continued on a speculative note, hinting
at a homosexual quarrel between the two men, and
emphasized the circumstantial aspect of Thorpe's having been the last person known to have been with
Bitler. An enterprising reporter had dug up a former
enlisted man who had served in Thorpe's company in
Vietnam. "Captain Thorpe was a rough, chicken
——SOB," bartender Frank Makiewicz of Lack-
awanna, New York, was quoted as saying. "He didn't
know when to quit. He tried to get us all killed. Yeah,
I'd have fragged the SOB if I'da thought I could get
away with it."

Thorpe folded the paper and laid it on the night

159

table. Yes, he remembered Private Frank Makiewicz: sad sack, malingerer, who finally got out of 'Nam on a self-inflicted wound. We agreed on one thing, Thorpe mused. I'd have fragged *him* if I had thought I could get away with it.

A knock at the door. Then Anna's voice: "Neal?"

He opened the door, locking it behind her. Gone was the blond wig; gone, too, the straight black hair parted at the crown. In its place was a light tumble of gray-gold hair.

"Do you like it?" she asked hesitantly.

"It's lovely."

"And you—" She reached to touch his head. "Neal, you are more handsome than ever."

"Well, we'll have to come back to Stockholm; they know how to treat strangers."

"Indeed they do. Is it too early to telephone again?"

"Probably." He gestured at the *Herald*, saw her take it up and sit on the bed to read.

When she finished reading, her eyes were moist. "How can they *say* such terrible things about you?"

"Reporters have an intimidating effect on a lot of people. But the important thing is *you're* not mentioned. That's the object of the whole exercise."

"I know," she said doubtfully, "but if it weren't for me. . . ."

He sat down next to her, kissed the nape of her neck. "We've gone over all that before, Anna. And it's not as though I hadn't gotten something out of it."

"What?"

He kissed her again, this time on the lips. "You," he said gently. "You, Annalise Bauer. I'd never have met you in Bonn or Bad Godesberg. You had to come to me."

"I know," she said softly, "but I think always of your friend who was killed by the friends of my stepfather."

"I think of him, too," Thorpe admitted. "But all we

160

can do for Don is keep going, find a way out of all this." He got up and handed her a folder from the desk. "While I'm calling Zarah, choose a restaurant for dinner."

"Very well."

"And lock the door after me."

He took the elevator to the lobby and went to a pay telephone where he dialed the number. He heard the telephone ring three times and was about to hang up when a voice said, *"Ja?"*

"Zarah?"

"Ja."

"I'm an American, so please speak in English."

"An American? What do you want? Who are you?"

"I was told to tell you that I am a friend of Mr. Smith's." At the quick intake of her breath he said, "Mr. Smith, Zarah. A friend of your father's."

"Ja—yes. Where are you?"

"At a pay phone."

"Just a moment, please." Seconds passed before she said, "It will be safer if I call you from another place. What is your number?"

He read the six digits to her, and she repeated them. "Please stay where you are, and I will call. In no more than five minutes."

He left the booth and went slowly to the newsstand, where he bought copies of *Der Spiegel* and *Time*. Going back to the booth, he saw a woman enter it and close the door. With a silent curse, Thorpe sat in a lobby chair and opened *Time*, pretending to read but carefully watching the phone booth.

On the lobby clock the minutes ticked away. Finally, the woman left the booth, and Thorpe went to it, hearing the bell ring when he was still yards away. On the fourth ring he picked up the receiver, said, "Sorry about the delay," and closed the door. "A woman was using the phone."

161

"Do you have a message from Mr. Smith?"

"I'm in trouble, Mrs. Engstrom, for reasons your father would understand. So Mr. Smith sent me to you."

"I see," she said slowly. "Can you identify yourself in any other ways?"

"I can try. First, your father and Smith were together in Holland not long ago. After they met, an attempt was made on your father's life."

"A number of people know that. In particular, the enemy."

"Yes. How about this: Klaus Werber is known in some circles as the Diplomat. His stepdaughter is with me."

"Could you explain?"

"She found out about Werber and the Soviets, so she had to get away. I came across her in Washington, and Mr. Smith asked me to take care of her."

"Tell me this: How did you learn my telephone number?"

"Mr. Smith told me you worked at the Grand Hotel recently. At a time when Werber had two visitors. Soviet visitors. Today the hotel gave your number to my companion."

"Have you been followed?"

"No. In fact, we're in Sweden illegally—false names."

"What shall I call you?"

"Mr. Davidson."

"Very well, Mr. Davidson. Will you and your companion be safe until tomorrow?"

"Yes."

"Good. Because I can do nothing tonight. Tomorrow I can meet you at midday, I have a half an hour off from work. Do you know the Stockholm Tower?"

"I've seen it from a distance."

"On the top level there is an open terrace with a telescope. What will you be wearing?"

"A brown and white sweater with gray slacks and tan shoes. Uh—I have a mustache."

"How tall are you?"

"A little under six feet. Light brown hair."

"Then I will meet you at one o'clock. By the telescope. But do not bring the girl, eh? Come alone."

"One o'clock," he repeated, and hung up.

He took the magazines to the room and handed *Der Spiegel* to Anna. "All the amenities of home." He dropped *Time* on his bed.

"Did you?"

"Yes." He nodded. "We talked. I'm to meet her tomorrow at lunchtime."

"Where?"

"The top of that monster radio tower."

She nodded. "The Kaknästornet. Why there?"

"Zarah doesn't fully trust me—and I don't blame her. Wants to look me over first."

"And while she is doing that, I will be looking her over."

"No—I'm to come alone."

She looked up at him. "Neal, what do you know of her?"

"Only that she's the daughter of the friend of a friend."

"Do you know what she looks like?"

"I wasn't given that information."

"Then, to go there alone—is that not . . . dangerous?"

"If it is, then all the more reason you shouldn't be there." He drew her to her feet. "So if the bar downstairs will serve a coatless alien, we deserve a drink before dinner."

In a room a few blocks from Zarah Engstrom's apartment building sat a man with earphones on his head. It was a room whose blinds were permanently

163

drawn and, except for a small bed and a chair, devoid of conventional furnishings. Set against one wall was a long table that held two Uher tape recorders connected to a VHF receiver. The antenna was a long thin wire scotchtaped to the ceiling and leading to one window. The wire passed over the sill and under the window to the outside of the building.

The man sat silently in the darkness, smoking the last of a cigarette, and when it was finished, he ground out the butt and pulled over a telephone. After dialing, he waited until a voice answered in Russian, and then he said, "The woman received a call. From an American."

"Was she expecting the call?"

"No. I don't think so."

"What did he say?"

"He said he was a friend of Mr. Smith."

"That must be a recognition phrase."

"It sounded that way."

"What then?"

"She went out to another telephone to call him. He gave her this number." The man repeated the number Thorpe had given Zarah.

"That should be helpful."

"Of course it could be only some kiosk."

"I will check its location." For a few moments there was silence. Then the man said, "This is an interesting development. I will report it, and you are to report any further calls to or from the American to me. Without delay."

"I understand. Will you come over to hear the tape?"

"Not unless it is necessary. Do you think it is?"

"No."

"Then good night."

The man replaced the telephone and turned off the tape recorder long enough to set the voice-activated relay. That done, he removed his earphones and stood

164

up. He stretched and walked into the kitchenette, where he took a bottle of St. Eriks Extra ale from the small refrigerator and uncapped it, blinking at the interior light. There was dark bread and sausage on one of the shelves, an egg and a pot of butter. Deciding to eat later, the man poured ale into a glass and carried it back to the lightless room. He propped a pillow at the end of the bed, leaned back and sipped from the glass. The tape recorders were motionless. The only light in the room came from the greenish glow of the VHF receiver dials whose needles were still.

The life of a listening post technician was a lonely one, the man reflected. He had been hopeful his superior would want to listen to the tape and provide him at the same time with a few minutes' companionship to relieve the monotony of sitting day after day in this same room, sealed off from the rest of the world. Perhaps Boris would come tomorrow.

He drank more ale and looked over at the VHF receiver. It was unlikely Zarah Engstrom would receive any other calls for the rest of the night, not if she followed the pattern he had become familiar with over the past several weeks. He wondered who the caller was and what they had discussed on the other telephone. At least, he thought, we can locate the phone he used and have it watched in case the *Amerikinits* is foolish enough to use it again.

18

CARLOTTE BERANGER opened the door of her small apartment, pulled off her beige stewardess cap and angrily hurled it across the room. Half the afternoon she had waited with the flight crew for a charter to Amsterdam only to have it canceled by the client, a Swiss jeweler, who decided to take the Trans European Express at the telephoned urging of his wife, who had seen him crash in a dream. Carlotte cursed the jeweler and his wife, for the cancellation would bring her only half pay for the three-hour wait, rather than flight pay for an entire day.

She unbuttoned her blouse and dropped it to the floor, her short skirt followed, and she kicked off her shoes. It was now after five o'clock, and because she had thought she would be away from Paris, Carlotte had made no dinner plans, and that wretched Jacques had not suggested a last-minute date. That left her alone for an entire evening, something she neither liked nor was accustomed to.

Barefoot, she padded into the small kitchen and took a bottle of vermouth from the cupboard. She rinsed a glass in the sink and filled it from the bottle, drank deeply and wandered into the other room, where she sat on the unmade bed and regarded her disorderly surroundings with distaste.

There was never time enough for anything, she told herself irritably. Even on off hours Le Bourget was more than an hour away by public bus, and charter flights left at unpredictable times. There was a week's washing to do, but she was not in the mood to haul her basket to the neighborhood launderette, put everything in and wait for the laundry to wash, then wait again for it to dry. Worse, at this hour there would probably be queues for washing, as well as drying, and there was nothing more boring on earth than waiting in line. Besides, she had had enough of waiting for one day. Quite enough.

Carlotte drank again and found herself longing for a cigarette. She got up and opened her handbag, rummaged through it and remembered smoking the last cigarette in the captain's car on the return trip from Le Bourget. She opened her bureau drawers and began going through them, one by one. Finally, through a pair of nylon underthings she felt the hardness of metal, remembered what it was and drew out a thin gold cigarette case. With a sigh of relief she opened it and took out one of the monogrammed cigarettes it contained. She lighted and inhaled deeply, then coughed, for the blend of Turkish tobaccos was stronger than the Gauloises Bleues she customarily smoked. Still, she thought, it's better than a trip down to the corner store, and began studying the richly glinting case, engraved with the Comte de Rochepin's coat of arms.

She had come across the cigarette case after the return flight from New York, half-concealed between cushions in the seat used by the count. Her first impulse had been to inform the captain, but momentary reflection suggested two alternatives: Sell the case for whatever she could get or return it to the count in person. Undecided between the two, she had put the case away, and what with flights to Marbella, Zürich and Algiers it had drifted from her mind. Now, filled with dissatisfaction and resentment, she turned

167

the case in her hand and considered what wisdom indicated she should do.

Carlotte had enough money to last until her next payday, so she could not justify selling the case as a matter of desperate need. Besides, places that bought ownerless objects would pay her only a fraction of its value. For all she knew the case might be solid gold —probably was—but some old man with a loupe would swear it was no more than gold-filled and offer her twenty francs. Rather than accept so little, she would keep and use it herself, arousing envy and admiration wherever she brought it out. To certain close friends she could confide that the cigarette case had been given her by the Comte de Rochepin as a token of his regard for her; to others she could intimate that De Rochepin had pressed it on her as a tender gesture following a night of unbridled pleasure.

As Carlotte pondered alternatives, it occurred to her that an evening, perhaps even a night, with the count was not out of the question. She had to concede that De Rochepin had not followed up her veiled suggestions made as they crossed and recrossed the Atlantic, but perhaps he felt himself, if not too old for the chase, then too far above it. Besides, he was a busy man, what with the demands of his television programs and the frequent articles he wrote and published.

Suddenly she was titillated by the thought that she had in her possession something he might want.

Suppose she were to telephone the count, tell him of her discovery and make it appear that she had been away from Paris ever since their parting? If she put it that way, he would have no way of knowing that she knew he had not tried to get in touch with her. The cigarette case was valuable—of that she was convinced. Surely, he was too much of the gentleman to suggest she return the case to him by mail. More likely, he

168

would hint at a rendezvous. He possessed far too much flair, too much *style*, to do anything so gauche.

Carlotte drained her glass, inhaled the aromatic smoke and coughed again. They were certainly strong cigarettes!

Still not entirely decided, she left the bed and pulled the Paris metropolitan telephone directory from its storage under the kitchen sink. De Rochepin, she found listed on Avenue Kléber at a number fashionably near the Etoile. But that was no more than she expected.

Turning down a corner of the page, she looked up at the telephone listing of ORTF, the national radio-television network, and carried the directory back to her bed. The telephone was hidden under a used towel. She lifted it to the bed and dialed ORTF, asking for the Comte de Rochepin's office. Presently a secretary answered. Carlotte gave her name and asked to speak to the count.

"May I inquire the subject, mademoiselle?"

"It concerns a valuable object of the count's. I discovered it and would like to return it."

"Of course, I will see if the count is able to speak with you."

Carlotte's heart beat faster. Would he even remember who she was?

The secretary spoke: "One moment, please. He will take the call."

Then the count's resonant voice. "My dear Carlotte, how good of you to remember me. How and where have you been?"

"I've been very well, *merci*, but I've been away from Paris all this time. It's only now that—"

"I understand—now let me think. Could it be that you found my cigarette case?"

"Yes. I'm very sorry I've been so long in letting you know."

"Please, my dear. Apologize? Hardly. It is I who regret the inconvenience caused you by my forgetfulness. Believe me, *chère* Carlotte, I am overwhelmingly grateful. Another person might have been, well, shall I say, less . . . responsible? But not you, dear child. Oh, it may have some slight intrinsic value, to be sure, but I cherish it for family reasons. You see, it belonged to my father the late Comte de Rochepin." The flow of words broke off, and when De Rochepin spoke again, she realized he had been consulting his *semainier*. "Carlotte, would it be presumptuous of me if I were to suggest our dining together? That is, unless, of course, you have a prior engagement. . . ."

"Well," she said doubtfully, "I've only just returned from Algiers. Perhaps—"

"I will not *permit* you to plead fatigue," he interrupted. "Surely one as young as yourself has little need for sleep."

"But I—" she began to protest, realizing too late that she had acted without considering consequences. Without the hairdresser, a proper dress, a manicure, she could hardly present herself attractively to the count. But, no, having gone this far she could not back off. And postponement might be fatal to her plans. "Very well," she said with a hint of reluctance. "Where shall we meet?"

"My flat, of course. Avenue Kléber, thirty-one. Will eight be convenient? We'll share a *coup*, then dine at, say, the Relais?"

The Relais was not, well, Maxim's, but then she owned nothing appropriate to wear at Maxim's. After tonight, perhaps, all that might be changed. "I'll be happy to join you at eight. *A bientôt.*"

"*Tout à l'heure.*" He rang off suavely, and she felt her heart leap. Hurrying to the kitchen, she poured a full glass of vermouth, reconsidered and poured back half of it, spilling some in the process. Immensely pleased

170

with herself, yet disturbed by her lack of foresight, Carlotte went back to the bed and set the magic telephone on the floor. She drank from her glass and began making a checkoff list of things to be done before eight. Her alarm clock showed a quarter to six, barely two hours off. First a soak in the bathtub, combined with a brisk shampoo. Her short hair took no time at all to dry and she would not attempt to set it. Manicure and pedicure, press the violet dress she had bought in Marbella; eye shadow and a trace of color for her lips, not too much for a man of his *goût exquis*. Then a touch of the tax-free perfume she had bought at Geneva's airport store. . . .

She drank more vermouth, fumbled for the gold case and lighted another monogrammed cigarette. After a few moments she realized she was wasting time, so she turned on bath water. While the tub was filling, she paraded naked around the room, glass in hand, cigarette in her lips, feeling more confident of herself than ever before in her life. The mirror showed her firm, medium-size breasts, her taut abdomen and thighs that were more plump than she would have liked. Still, she thought, *Monsieur le Comte* will like them as well as what is between. The glinting gold caught her eye, and she bent to spill the remaining cigarettes from it. Scooping them up, she placed them in the top drawer of her bureau. The count would never miss them, and she could always turn to her cache when she was short of Bleues. While they lasted, they would be a memorable souvenir.

Carlotte Béranger drained her glass, turned off the tub faucets and tested the water temperature with a toe. Hesitantly she lowered one foot and leg, then the other, squatting finally and took the cigarette from her lips long enough to tap its ash onto the floor. The water rose even with her small pointed nipples. She watched them swell, stimulated by the heat of immersion until the sensation set her teeth on edge. With a sigh, she closed her eyes and forced her body to relax. After a while she groped for a bar of soap and slowly and carefully began to cleanse her body.

It was nearly one o'clock when the Comte de Rochepin brought Carlotte back to his apartment. For him it had been a maddening evening. Five hours of her uninformed comments, her foolish chatter had worn his nerves raw. And in all that time, after all the cocktails, liquor, wine and cognac she had drunk, the girl had never mentioned returning his cigarette case. Had she done so, he would have been able to take her home directly from the Relais, but until he had it safely in his possession, he was condemned to be her prisoner. So there was nothing to do but tender the obligatory invitation for a nightcap.

Ever since De Rochepin noticed the absence of his cigarette case, he had worried over its whereabouts. Initial alarm gave way after a few days to a lower plateau of concern; finally, he encouraged himself to believe his pocket had been picked or that he had left the case on the aircraft, where it had been discovered and appropriated. Earlier, when Carlotte telephoned, he had been tempted to send around for the case, then realized she was probably holding it subtle hostage for a meeting between them. So he had improvised the invitation as a certain means of securing return of the case. She had no way of knowing its significance, its particular importance to him, and so he was careful to avoid arousing either her cupidity or her suspicions by making his concern too obvious. His fear had been that she would show the case around, tell friends she had acquired it on a mysterious flight, and from whom. The police were everywhere; if the special flight came to their ears, they would at least enter it

172

in the dossier he was sure the DST had been maintaining on him for years. At worst they would interrogate Carlotte for details. And so he had played the amiable *boulevardier*, intrigued by her charms and hopeful of her favors.

De Rochepin watched Carlotte clumsily remove the green satin evening cape. To his practiced eye it was not only cheaply made, but the color was atrocious. She let the cape slide onto a chair and began to move about the room, touching objects she had admired earlier in the evening. Obviously the liquor had affected her, and he could only hope fervently that she would not break any of his fine Dresden or Meissen china, drop the Swedish crystal. Unfortunately, he thought, she was not so drunk that he could simply take the cigarette case from her purse where he had glimpsed it during the evening.

"Cognac, my dear? I recommend a touch of very ancient Hine."

Turning, she gazed at him adoringly. "Anything you say, Count."

The expression in her cow eyes made him want to vomit. Turning away, he went to the cellarette and drew out an antique decanter. He lighted an alcohol flame and warmed two brandy bowls, then poured a small amount of cognac into each. He carried them to where Carlotte was seated on a silk-covered sofa and let her take one from his hand, then saw with horror that it almost slipped from her fingers. Recovering the glass, she flashed him a broad smile. "Been drinking too much." She waved a roguish finger at him and motioned him to sit at her side.

Reluctantly De Rochepin complied. Almost at once she leaned her head against his shoulder. "I've never met a man like you before, Count. You're just a complete gentleman."

"Thank you, my dear. And you must call me Gilbert."

"Gilbert," she purred. "Just the perfect name for you. Such a silky sound."

Lifting his brandy bowl, he reached across to touch it against hers. *"Votre santé,"* he said.

She lifted her glass. "To us, eh?" she slurred, then drank.

"Would you care for a cigarette?"

"Ciga—" Her lips drew into a sly smile. "Why, yes, Gilbert."

"Unfortunately I can offer only my own brand. Perhaps you have others you prefer in your bag?"

She licked her lips. "In my bag," she repeated dully. "Where is it?"

"Over there on the table." He started to rise, but she pressed him down and struggled to her feet.

Swaying, she moved unsteadily across the floor, grasped the bag and drew out the gold cigarette case. With a look of triumph she came back to him. "This is yours, Gilbert!"

He nodded. "So it is. And I will be very glad to have it back."

He reached toward it, but she clutched it against her belly. Her face became coquettish. "Reward?"

De Rochepin swallowed. "Of course. Anything within reason." Damned female games! He lowered his arm, hand clenched tautly.

"Let me think. . . ." She gazed upward. "What *would* be an adequate reward?" Her head tilted coyly, invitingly.

De Rochepin forced his arms to remain rigidly at his sides. "You have only to suggest it, my dear," he said tightly.

Holding the cigarette case between thumb and finger, she twirled it tauntingly, just out of reach. "Oh, Gilbert, think creatively," she crooned. "On television

174

you're never at a loss for words." Her full lips parted. "Don't you *like* me? Do you want me to think you asked me to dine only for *this*? That isn't very flattering," she reproved. "After all, I *am* a woman. A *young* woman."

At last he understood. The moment he had dreaded was upon him. Forcing a smile, he dropped to his knees. "I hesitated only out of respect for you, Carlotte—not from lack of desire." Taking her left hand, he brought it to his lips.

"That's much better, Gilbert." Her hand lifted, bringing him to his feet before her. Her eyes were moist, expectant.

Closing his eyes, he steeled himself for the embrace, drew her into his arms and kissed her waiting lips. Carlotte moaned, her tongue touched his, and involuntarily a shudder passed through his frame. Abruptly she pushed away, screeched, *"So that's what you are! Mon Dieu*, I never thought—" She was backing from him, golden case clutched firmly in her hand.

White-faced, he spat, *"Let me have it!"*

His anger halted her. She stared at the case, and her eyes narrowed. "Why's it so important to you? And why was the flight so mysterious? Where did you go in America? Where did that helicopter take you?" The realization of what he was, the humiliation of her situation inflamed her. She shook the cigarette case at him. "Tell me, pederast!"

With his full strength he struck her jaw. The cigarette case flew out of her grasp, and she staggered back. Before she could recover, he kicked her to the floor, threw himself upon her. A blaze of fury blinded him. His hands were around her throat, thumbs pressing her windpipe. Beneath him her body writhed and struggled, gradully grew slack, then still.

His spasm of fury diminished; sanity returned.

The Comte de Rochepin forced his fingers to open, withdraw from the embedded flesh of her neck.

175

He touched the neck artery and knew that she was finally dead. Sitting back on his haunches, he stared at her suffused and mottled face, the fixed, dead eyes, the froth at the corner of her mouth. Little slut! She tried to trick me, judge me. She, no better than a harlot.

He viewed her twisted mouth, the wisps of hair that now lay damply clinging to her forehead, to her cheek, as slowly the normal pace of breathing returned. He mopped his face with a handkerchief and got stiffly to his feet. Leaving Carlotte's body, he turned on a lamp, then searched the floor for the cigarette case. He found it under a chair, one corner badly dented, placed it in a pocket and went to the cellarette. After pouring a glass of cognac, he sipped, found a chair and slumped into it.

Neither doorman nor concierge had seen them return to the apartment. At the Relais he had chosen a shaded corner, where it was not likely he would be recognized. He did not frequent the place, and so the waiters did not know him. His lips drew into a grim smile: It was almost as though he had planned what she herself had provoked him into doing.

One problem, that of the cigarette case, was solved. In its place was an even more serious one; what to do with her body.

His gaze lowered to the noxious violet of her dress, whose length was gathered now around her hips, twisted there by her struggling. Her naked thighs were unattractively rotund.

She was going to do one of two things, he told himself reflectively—blackmail me or expose me. Neither would have been tolerable. What else could I do but kill?

He had never killed before, never faced the dilemma of how to dispose of a body. There was her purse, of

176

course, and the ugly green cape. They, too, would have to go.

He noticed that one of her feet was bare; the missing shoe he found under the sofa fringe and replaced it on her foot. Her flesh was cooling, suggesting the onset of rigor would not be long delayed. Remembering a detective *ciné* that impressed him at the time, De Rochepin got up and went to his bedroom. There he stripped an electric blanket from the bed and carried it back to Carlotte's body. He covered her and plugged the cord into a wall outlet. The dial lighted, and he turned it to maximum heat. Now he had more time to compose himself, apply his intellect to a disagreeable but unavoidable problem.

Through the blanket he could discern the lift of her nose, and he remembered the repelling feel of her lips, her twisting tongue.

She couldn't know, he mused, that her coarseness of itself disgusted me, or that I was unwilling to reveal my impotence. She thought only that I was a pederast, a species she despised. And then she thought of other things.

He opened the sprung cigarette case with difficulty and found it empty. She smoked them all before returning it, he told himself. Cheap to the last.

He drank more cognac and felt it begin to warm him, opened a drawer and took a cigarette from a silver box. Lifting it, he looked at the body again, gazed at it unseeingly as a plan began to materialize.

After a while he drew on a pair of gloves and opened her purse, emptying the contents on a table. He put the few coins and franc notes into his pocket, burned her airlines identification card in an ashtray and replaced the lipstick and inexpensive compact. As he did so, it occurred to him that he had not the least idea where she lived.

177

For a time he reflected that Marcel would know how to dispose of an unwanted body; the Russian would have learned it in his training. But the Comte De Rochepin knew that he could not apply to his Soviet contact for help in a matter such as this. Instead, he would resolve it on his own.

He placed the purse in Carlotte's cape and thrust it under the blanket. Lifting the body, he passed the blanket under it and rolled the body until it was enveloped but for the head.

After drinking the last of his cognac, he opened the rear service door and went quietly down three floors to the courtyard where his Citroën was parked. He unlocked both doors and opened one. Then he went back up the stairs and hoisted Carlotte's body over his shoulder. The strain of carrying her inert weight had him panting as he emerged into the courtyard. Without ceremony he dumped the body onto the passenger seat and closed the door. From behind the wheel he unraveled the blanket far enough to reach the cape, which he fitted around her throat and shoulders. Seat and shoulder straps held her body erect, and now, from outside the car, she would appear to be a sleeping passenger, head relaxed against the seat.

De Rochepin got out of the Citroën and, with one hand on the wheel, began pushing it though the open arch that gave out onto Avenue Kléber. Once beyond the curb he got behind the wheel again and waited until a truck drove past. Its sound cloaked the noise of his starting engine, and he turned east toward the Etoile, driving through thin traffic in the direction of Montmartre.

19

A little before noon Zarah Engstrom left her desk and made her way unhurriedly to the basement level. There she joined a stream of Hötorget shoppers, disappeared briefly into a lavatory and emerged finally on Sveavägen, where she strolled to a bus stop and waited for the first bus that came along.

At the Hotel Anglais she got off, went into the hotel and bought a copy of *Dagens Nyheter*. From there she walked three blocks and boarded a bus that took her along Storgatan as far as Nobel Park. There she selected a bench and unfolded her newspaper, ostensibly reading, but looking carefully for surveillants as she turned the pages. When she was satisfied that she was not being followed, Zarah crossed the park to Strandvägen, where a final bus took her to the base of Kaknästornet.

The indirect route had taken nearly forty-five minutes, leaving Zarah a quarter of an hour to lose herself in the crowds circulating through the upper levels of the tower. She got into line at the ticket window, paid two kronor and entered the base of the tower, where she joined the elevator line. A short wait for an empty car, and she got out at the second stop, the shopping level. Entering a novelty shop, she went casually from counter to counter, finally choosing a grotesque troll doll she thought would amuse Rolf. Taking her change, Zarah glanced at the clock: time to leave for the rendezvous above. She inserted coins

179

in her purse, scanned nearby shoppers and those passing the window and went out into the corridor. Entering the stairway, Zarah went slowly up the stairs and reached the outlook terrace.

The breeze was fresh. She drew a scarf around her hair, knotted it under her chin, then went to the railing and looked down.

There spread out below was Djurgaden Park with its broad meadow. Sheep were browsing, tended by a shepherd and collie dog, and she reflected on the contrast between the quiet rural setting and the teeming city to the west. She could make out bridges and the royal palace, the Norse Museum and Stadshuset tower with its pillared bell canopy. Zarah thought she could even see her apartment building to the northwest. She resumed walking toward the telescope, and as she rounded the corner, there was a man lounging against the nearby railing. He was wearing a Norse sweater of brown-and-white design, gray slacks and dark glasses. Wind lifted the points of his open collar as he read a folded newspaper, and as she neared him, she saw that he wore a slim mustache.

Around the telescope pedestal a group of school children clamored for a schoolmate to stop using it and let someone else take a look. The man's eyes lifted, and he glanced at the children, then Zarah. Dropping her purse, she began to pick it up, but the man knelt and recovered it. "Thank you," she said, "Mr. . . . Davidson?"

Thorpe nodded, and together they moved toward the railing, where they could not be overheard. He said, "Before you get involved any further, I think you ought to read this." He passed her his *Herald*, and she glanced at it long enough to see what must have been an old photograph of him and the caption.

"I will read it, but not now."

"But you should know what I'm charged with."

Zarah shrugged. "Many charges can be made against a man. But all I need to know about you is contained in a communication I received last evening. From your friend, Mr. Smith. Where did you telephone me from?"

"A telephone in the lobby of my hotel."

"Then you must leave that hotel, and do not call me again at my apartment." At his questioning expression she said, "There is a device on my telephone. The people who placed it there will be able to trace your call."

"I understand. What did Smith say?"

"That you were innocent of any crime, and you were protecting a young woman sought by the Soviets."

"Is there any way you can let him know we arrived?"

She nodded. "I have already done so. Is there a message you would like to send?"

"He knows I'll need money. He said he would try to send some."

"Then he will. You must change your lodging today. Do not go directly from the old place to the new. Later tonight we can meet again." Unobtrusively she passed him her office telephone number. "I will be there until six. Call and let me know where you have moved; then I will telephone you about our meeting place."

The children having left the telescope, Zarah drew him toward it, and said, "You and the girl are using false documents?"

"They're authentic, but they're not ours."

"So no one knows you are in Stockholm?"

"Only you—and Mr. Smith." He thought of López and Carranza, of the two flight crews, the stowaway whose knife mark was still visible on his throat. None of them would be able to recognize Annalise Bauer and Neal Thorpe, and they had every reason not to try.

181

From the park below came carrousel music, borne in snatches by the wind.

"Only the three of us—and Annalise," he said.

"Do you want to bring her tonight?"

"You should meet each other in case—well, if something should happen to me."

Zarah glanced at her watch. "I must go back to the office now. Be sure to telephone me before six." Thorpe saw her move away while he readied the telescope. After he had scanned city and environs, he left the mount and walked back to the stairway. Zarah Engstrom was nowhere to be seen.

For a quarter of an hour he toured the tower before taking a bus back to Norrmalmstorg. In a department store he bought an inexpensive dark suit and a pair of ties. Then he returned to the Strand and scanned the lobby for surveillants before taking the elevator to his room. There had been a nondescript woman seated on a sofa apparently waiting for someone. From her vantage point she could view the lobby door, the desk and the elevator. He had been lax in telephoning Zarah from the lobby, he reflected, and so they were faced with the inconvenience of still another move.

He unlocked the door and found Anna reading *Der Spiegel* in the comfort of her bed. Before talking with her, he turned on the shower to cover their voices in case the room was bugged. Then he told her what had happened at his meeting with Zarah Engstrom.

In less than an hour Anna left the hotel by the service exit. Thorpe paid their bill, noticing that the waiting woman was still at her apparent post. He strolled into the bar, ordered a bottle of Pilsner and lingered over it. Leaving money on the bar he went into the men's room and climbed out through the ventilation window into an alley. From there he walked two blocks to a taxi stand and took a cab to the Ringbaren cafeteria, where Annalise was waiting.

182

Streetlights were coming on along Fifth Avenue when Irene Cerf left the beauty salon and turned north on the east side of the street. She was wearing a Bergdorf pants suit of blue-and-white houndstooth. A small blue patent-leather bag swung from one shoulder on a gilt link chain, and her patent-leather boots matched her bag. Noticing thin mist in the air, she unfolded a Hermès scarf and covered the hairstyle just created for her by Gabriel, in whose salon she had received a manicure and pedicure, facial massage and finally the hairstyling. Including tips, the afternoon had cost her husband eighty-four dollars, and it amused Irene to pay capitalist dollars for her personal pleasure and adornment.

Considering her age, which was somewhat older than she allowed her husband to believe, Irene Cerf was an attractive woman. Her face was oval, the skin light olive. Her hips were broader than the smallness of her breasts might suggest, but the overall effect of her figure implied dietary discipline and daily exercise. Plastic surgery had left her features with a slightly Oriental cast, creating a sense of the exotic in her appearance that fascinated men and women in the Cerf's social circle. Although Maurice had not known it, Rimma Naumovna was married when they met, but the KGB's Second Chief Directorate, the VGU, arranged a secret divorce when she was ordered to leave the USSR and marry the Banker's son. Only occasionally did she think of her first—her real—husband, but she suppressed the nostalgia of romance, and now, so many years having gone by, the little that survived of Vasiliy was as disembodied, as intangible, as a shadow on a distant screen.

She waited for a light, crossed the street and walked past the Sherry-Netherland, pausing to examine a floral window display. Then she continued on to the Pierre, where she turned in under the entrance canopy, removed her scarf and walked down the corridor to the second telephone booth. She closed the door, took a dime from her bag and pretended to dial. Then, at precisely six o'clock, the telephone rang. Releasing the cradle lever, she spoke into the telephone mouthpiece. "Yes?"

"How is Aunt Natasha?"

"Aunt Natasha sends greetings," Irene responded, completing the recognition formula.

"We are ready to receive your report," the impersonal voice said. "Proceed."

"I have seen the old man only twice this week. Each time he has seemed preoccupied. Also, he does not appear to be very well. At dinner Tuesday night he ate hardly anything, excused himself early and was driven back to Long Island."

"What did he say to indicate preoccupation?"

"The indication was negative. He talks hardly at all."

"Has he mentioned any names unfamiliar to you?"

"None."

"Should he mention a French name at any time, take careful note of it."

"Of course."

"Do you believe him to be facing business problems?"

"No."

There was an interval of silence. Then: "What are your relations with your husband?"

"Unchanged."

"Do you feel he may be a candidate for recruitment?"

"Not at this time. He is still a political innocent. However, he may be making secret gifts to the Jewish Defense League. He is much concerned over the situation of Jews in our country."

"What is his father's attitude in the matter?"

"It is a subject I have never heard discussed."

184

"What is your husband's general attitude toward our country?"

"With the exception of the Jewish problems, not unfavorable."

"What can be done to hasten his political awakening?"

"It is a problem of which I am constantly aware. He read widely in college, studied Marx, Engels and Lenin, but he leads a very comfortable life. He is happy in his profession and in our marriage. He feels no well-defined sense of social outrage, and his character is unadventurous."

"Under what circumstances might he become a collaborator?"

Having considered the eventuality, Irene said, "To save his father's name."

"Or his life?"

"They would amount to the same." She hesitated before saying, "Are you—"

"We will ask the questions," the voice said curtly. "Your duty is to answer."

"Even so, I must say this: I know my husband as no one else does. If he were forced to collaborate, he could become dangerous. To all of us."

"How, please?"

"He is an attorney. He knows the law. Some of his classmates joined American security agencies—the FBI and CIA. If Maurice were to become desperate, he might be driven to consult them."

"Would you have no influence over his actions?"

"Not unless he confided in me before the act."

"You do not think he would?"

"In the theoretical situation described, it is my opinion that he would probably not consult me."

A longer silence before. Then: "Continue evaluating your husband as a candidate, but make no overt move."

185

With silent relief she said, "I understand."

"Now what of the Senator, your brother-in-law?"

"As you know, I see him only rarely. He lives in Washington and comes to Manhattan once or twice a month for political discussions."

"What are their nature?"

"Financing for his next campaign. Patronage. Problems with the governor."

"You have never attended such a meeting?"

"No."

"Would it be possible?"

"Impossible," she said flatly.

"Even so, ignore no opportunity to be present."

"Understood."

"Now you may list your recent contacts."

In a clear voice she began: "Charles Joplin is in the Foreign Department of the Chase Manhattan Bank. He has close ties in the departments of Treasury and Commerce dating from the period when he worked in both places. His wife, Cecily, is extravagant. She is also having an affair with one of her husband's associates, a bank vice-president named Warren Lukins. The two of them plan to rendezvous secretly in Mexico when her husband next travels to Europe."

"You will provide us further details."

"I will try. The next is George Volk. He is a wealthy stockbroker whose parents were members of the American Communist Party. He is a widower whose only daughter is confined to a sanatorium."

"Why?"

"Brain damage from LSD. Volk blames the current social imbalance for his tragedy. His mental outlook is morose."

"Have you considered the nature of an approach to him?"

"Yes. A young woman could bring light into his life."

"Volk," the voice repeated thoughtfully. "We have

186

an aspirant who might be successful with him. Next?"

"A woman of fifty-seven named Lynch. Marjorie Lynch. Through her late father and husband she controls the firm of Union Industrials. Her firm is heavily involved in defense contracts and manufactures essential components for the propulsion systems of nuclear submarines."

"What is your opinion of her?"

"I think she would accept an invitation to tour industrial plants in our country. Her interpreter should be a man in his late thirties or early forties. I believe that after being compromised, she would cooperate."

"Next?"

"One of my husband's clients. The man is named Dr. Ernest Lonergan. He is a psychiatrist who treats many prominent people, including certain members of the U.S. delegation to the United Nations. . . ."

Finally, her contact report completed, Irene was allowed to leave the telephone. She fitted the scarf around her hair once more and walked out to Fifth Avenue, where the doorman was trying to whistle down cabs for a queue of people from the hotel. With her weekly duty accomplished, Irene Cerf turned her mind to other things. The mist had become light drizzle, and the prospect of a taxi was slim. The time was nearly six thirty, but by walking across Central Park South, she decided, she could reach the apartment in time to undo the damage to her hair, slip into lounging slacks and mix a beaker of vodka martinis before the arrival of Maurice, whose fondness for vodka was a holdover from their Moscow courting days.

She waited for traffic to halt, crossed Fifth Avenue and started south toward the Plaza Hotel. As far as possible she wanted to please her husband, and Maurice expected her to greet him every evening when he returned from his Broad Street office. After lunch

187

he had telephoned to tell her he was bringing color photographs of a possible winter home in Bal Harbour, and so tonight, in particular, she was not going to deprive him of the evening ritual he so enjoyed.

Irene brushed moisture from her cheeks, turned her face from the breeze and allowed herself the anticipatory hope that the Florida home would have, among other features, a play garden for the children and a heated swimming pool.

20

KLAUS JOHANN WERBER, Foreign Minister of West Germany, finished shaving, patted *Kölnisch Wasser* on his face and entered his dressing room, where the valet had laid out his evening clothes. White tie and shirt were freshly laundered and starched, and patent-leather oxfords glistened at the end of the bureau. He noticed with satisfaction that the shirt was already set with pearl studs and cuff links, eliminating what was always a small annoyance when he dressed for a formal affair.

Tonight there was a reception at the Hammerschmidt Villa, tendered jointly in his honor by President von Breuning and Chancellor Staufen, and marking his return from the journey in quest of peace in the Middle East. All officials of Cabinet and sub-Cabinet rank would attend, as would the diplomatic corps, and note would be taken that President and Chancellor had set aside political and personal hostilities in paying tribute to the Foreign Minister. The event would be reported back to the chancelleries of every important nation, and Werber reflected that its significance could not but enhance the reputation he already enjoyed.

The door separating his dressing room from his wife's opened, and he heard Freda come in.

"Klaus? Would you help with my necklace?"

"Certainly, my dear." Turning, he saw her walking toward him, diamond necklace in one hand. "What seems to be the difficulty?"

"The guard chain's come off, so be sure the catch is properly set." Handing him the necklace, she turned around.

Werber circled Freda's throat with the necklace, opened the platinum catch with his thumbnail and locked it through the end link. "There, all done!"

Her hand touched the necklace, testing it lightly, and she murmured, "I was so hoping Annalise would be here tonight. I was planning to have her wear the necklace. It would look so much prettier on her young skin. On mine, well, it's just wasted."

"Don't say that," he chided. "You're more beautiful than Anna will ever be."

Her face glowed. "You really think so?"

"Absolutely."

She stood on tiptoe to kiss his cheek. "My gallant Foreign Minister and husband."

Smiling, he returned the kiss. "I'm still the same shabby Klaus. Inside I've never changed."

"Well, you're very elegant now." Stepping back, she eyed him head to toe. "What a *handsome* Secretary-General you will be!" Her expression changed. "Dear—will I like living in New York?"

"Many people do—and I'm sure you will. You know, we'll be even more active there than we've ever been."

"I suppose so. And it will be good to have Anna with us. She can do so many useful things in our place—things we'd have otherwise to do."

189

"She'll be a superb substitute." He drew the piqué tie around his collar and began tying it.

"Dear, I can't help wondering where she is—if she's all right."

"Of course she's all right, wherever she is. Freda, to you your daughter may still be a little girl, but the fact is she's a grown woman. We both knew the situation that caused her to leave London, and we understand it. Surely she's allowed to find solace, readjustment her own way."

Frau Werber nodded slowly. "Still, it's so unlike her to keep me in the dark so long. Surely, she would have found time to send a postcard."

"I'm sure there's no need to worry."

"And you've heard nothing from our embassies?"

He shook his head, turned and picked up his tail-coat. Automatically his wife held it for him, noticing the spread of his broad shoulders, the smooth fit of the formal coat across them. He exuded power, she reflected pridefully, charisma. If he had begun life as a common man, he had become an uncommon one long, long ago. Otherwise, she would never have been attracted to him.

Or he to her, she thought as he turned, pulling down his cuffs.

"Perhaps tonight," she said hesitantly, "you could make inquiries about Annalise."

"Inquiries?" His forehead wrinkled.

"I was thinking of the foreign diplomats. Surely they would be glad to help. And of course, the Papal Nuncio."

He chuckled. "What about the Nuncio?"

"Well, I've always heard the Vatican has the best intelligence service in the world. And I'm sure Monsieur Berelli wouldn't in the least mind asking around about our daughter. And the Papal Secretary of State . . . he's promised to attend. Everyone knows Cardinal

190

Rossinol has a great deal of influence at the Vatican."

Werber shrugged. "Do you want everyone to know what's happened?"

"It's nothing disgraceful, surely—not nowadays. At least she isn't living in some Chelsea commune with a dozen pimple-faced Cockneys. It just seems to me that considering all the people we know, with all our power and influence, we should be able to find out *something* about her."

He bent over to brush powder from the tip of one shoe.

"Klaus, isn't it reasonable?"

He took a deep breath and straightened his lapels. "It isn't easy to find someone who doesn't want to be found. After all, Anna went away to escape associations that troubled her. In her own good time she'll reappear. More than likely right here in Bad Godesberg."

"Oh, I wish I were that certain." Freda bit her lip, and Werber could see tears glisten in her eyes.

"Now, now," he consoled, "there's not the slightest thing to worry about."

"But I've been worrying for *days*. You were away, traveling, seeing different cities, different people, but I was right here—thinking about her." Tears welled over and spilled down her cheeks.

"Freda, dear, please—you mustn't cry."

"Every night I've been crying myself to sleep. This just isn't like Anna . . . it isn't like her at *all*." Her shoulders shook, and sobbing tore at her throat.

He put his arm around her shoulders comfortingly, but she moved away. Eyes tear-reddened, she said, "Is it possible she's gone because of something *I've* done?"

"Of course not." He felt his patience becoming strained. "What could you possibly have done? You haven't seen her in months."

"I mean just before she left. When she was here those few hours that last weekend."

191

His jaw set. "What did the two of you talk about?"

"Her painting, the love affair. . . ." Shrugging, she began to dry her eyes. "You saw her, Klaus. I heard you talking to her in the library. Now, I beg you to tell me—was there a quarrel between you? I know you didn't approve of her fiancé, but did you make an issue of it?"

"How make it an issue?"

"By for-forbidding her to marry?"

"Of course not!"

"Then why was your voice so angry?"

"It was politics. She had the gall to tell me she favored the British Tories over the Labour Party! Suppose *that* were made public? Wouldn't the CD's gloat? Our daughter, a Tory at heart." He shook his head. "Yes, I'll admit I was annoyed. But we've had disagreements before. Until you asked me, I'd even forgotten the incident—it was that trivial."

"Oh, Klaus, she was only baiting you. Suppose she had proclaimed herself a Communist, God forbid, would you have believed her? Of course not. Tory sympathies? Surely not. Let her say what she wants, dear. You're not to take seriously everything she says."

He sighed. "I'm afraid young people these days have a quite different concept of obligation to their parents from what we had in our day. Times have changed, Freda, they'll change even more. Now let us suppose Annalise decided to fly around the world? Well, why not? She has plenty of money to indulge her whims."

"But without telling me?"

"Young people are different now, I tell you. She may have decided to travel incognito, adopt a different name for a while. Why shouldn't she? She's a young person, my dear, bored with the formalities that surround our official life. Tonight, for instance—do you think she would really *enjoy* the reception?"

"Anna would be very proud to be there, proud of

192

you, Klaus, and the honor of the occasion. I'm desolate she isn't here."

He placed his hands on her shoulders affectionately. "If we don't leave, *Liebchen*, we will assuredly be late. And we don't want those two old men to be angry, do we? They might start quarreling with each other—in public!"

"No—no, you're right. I'll just touch up my face, and then I'll be ready." She hurried from the room, the door closed, and Werber's face relaxed into a scowl. The little bitch, Anna, he thought: the little bitch, stirring things up like this!

He wanted the girl found, but not brought home. If she were to confide in Freda, that would be the end of everything. Tonight, perhaps, the Soviet minister might have news for him. Perhaps Anna was in their hands already. Or even dead.

A lump formed in his throat. He was deeply, foolishly in love with the girl, but nothing as intangible as love—or was it infatuation?—could stand in his way. Foolish, yes—he had been insane to blurt out the truth to her, the truth she had already grasped by overhearing part of his conversation with the courier that afternoon.

He had thought himself alone in the residence, but no, Anna had come unexpectedly from London, kicked off her shoes and padded inaudibly past the partly open door. Luckily for him, the courier did not realize she was there. Unluckily, the courier began giving instructions concerning the peace-seeking trip, the "Werber Initiative," as it had come to be known worldwide, and after the courier was gone, he had taken a few drinks to steady himself, decide what to say to Annalise. And the rest of the afternoon became a nightmare.

Though he tried to dismiss the importance of what she overheard, Anna knew he was lying. *Knew*. And

193

then he had made the mistake of declaring his love for her, his near-incestuous desire, hoping to sway her. That failing, he had shared his vision with her, the vision of the future in which he believed, for which he had trained, sacrificed and dared so much, so many years. With words he took her to the top of the mountain and showed her the world below at their feet.

And what had been the result? Disgust, rejection, panic, and flight, for half-drunk, he had tried to force her, mount the pullet as he had the hen. . . .

Instead, he told himself, I should have killed her then.

"Klaus? *Klaus?*" Freda's voice interrupted from below.

"Coming, Freda," he called. Then with a final glance at his profile, the Foreign Minister left the mirror and joined his wife in the hall of their official residence. Freda was wearing a satin cloak, but Werber, mindful of his robust international image, disdained Chesterfield and topper despite the coolness of the night. Saluting, the chauffeur opened the door of the Mercedes saloon, and Werber helped his wife into it, seating himself at her side.

Preceded by a motorcycle escort, the black official limousine swung smoothly from the drive and drove through the quiet residential streets of Bad Godesberg before turning onto the Autobahn to Bonn.

In the police commissariat on rue Achille-Martinet Detective Pierre Sorel waited in the office of his commissaire, a thin dossier in his hands. The commissaire was occupied with the telephone which seemed to ring anew almost as soon as it was cradled. Detective Sorel was twenty-nine years old, a graduate of Lyons, and nervous in the presence of superiors. He would have liked a cigarette, but smoking in the commissaire's office was forbidden and so he sat in his chair and

194

waited. Presently Commissaire Duclos barked a final *"Non!"* into the telephone, pressed a button and spoke to the switchboard operator. "No more calls, *hein?* Officially I am not even here." Then he replaced the telephone and pressed his palms together. Turning to his young subordinate, he said, "Sorel?"

The detective rose and approached the desk. "It concerns the young woman whose body was found in the Cemetery of St.-Vincent."

"Well?"

"She was strangled." He opened the dossier. "Well dressed, age about twenty-five. Dead perhaps eleven hours before the body was discovered. Bruises on the jaw."

Duclos shrugged. "Another *poule* murdered by her *maquereau?* Is that it?"

"Killed certainly by a man, Commissaire, but there is no indication she was a prostitute."

"How not?"

"No evidence of venereal infections or pregnancies. And she was dressed rather formally, not in the usual apparel of a *fille de joie*. As you know, her purse held nothing to identify her."

"What did the purse contain?"

"A lipstick, a compact . . . some flakes of cigarette tobacco."

"What kind of tobacco?"

"That is being determined, Commissaire. All that is now known is that the tobacco is not a commerical blend—Gauloises, for example, or Players."

"Other means of identification?"

"Her fingerprints are, of course, being checked through our files. But there is no reason to assume she was French, much less Parisienne."

"Her clothing?"

"Of mass manufacture. Both dress and cape were on sale at Bon Marché and Trois Quartiers and at many

195

stores in metropolitan France. Several thousand of each were manufactured, the line being closed down last February."

"Shoes?"

"Also of mass manufacture. However, the shoes give certain evidence that may prove worthwhile. There was no earth or gravel on the soles, indicating the dead woman had not been walking the streets as would a *poule*, and the toes of both shoes were scuffed."

"So she was probably dragged into the cemetery."

"Yes, Commissaire. In addition, the technician found a small quantity of lint between the sole and the last. It is lint from a rug or carpet."

"Then we have a woman killed elsewhere and deposited in the Cemetery of St.-Vincent—in the Eighteenth Arrondissement. *Our* arrondissement," he said with displeasure. "What else is known?"

"For the present, Commissaire, nothing," said Detective Sorel unhappily.

"You have inquired of Missing Persons?"

"Yes, Commissaire. In Paris many young women are missing, but none fits the description of our cadaver."

"Has the press been called in?"

"Not yet, Commissaire. I was waiting your approval."

Duclos sighed. "Very well, let them publish her description, with particular attention to the clothing. Perhaps a friend or relative will come forward." Closing his eyes, he stroked them tiredly. "Thank you, Sorel."

"Thank you, Commissaire." The detective closed the dossier and left the office. He returned to his desk and placed the dossier in a drawer, signed the off-duty roster and left the Commissariat.

Walking south, Pierre Sorel turned onto rue Marcadet and continued west toward the Môquet métro station. Mist dampening his face reminded him of an element so far forgotten in his investigation. In the

196

morning, he would call the weather bureau and determine whether there had been rain in Paris the night his nameless woman had been killed. One way or another, the answer could help determine a little more accurately the time her body had been left in the cemetery's open air. And that small fact might be sufficient to destroy the alibi of her murderer, convict him of what Sorel had already decided was a *crime passionel*.

At a *brasserie* he stopped for *fine café* and stood at the bar, sipping slowly and wondering why he had declined his father's invitation to manage the family *boulangerie* in the little town of Givors.

Like many in Montmartre, the *brasserie* catered to *poules* and their *maquereaux*, to thieves, fences, addicts, heroin pushers and men who lived by violence. In Givors there were none of these, and life as a bakery manager was tranquil and uneventful. Sorel's politics were sufficiently of the left that he felt keenly the injustice of humans exploiting one another, and in his view, murder was the ultimate exploitation, the final expression of personal arrogance: that one must die so another might live.

Over the rim of his demitasse he viewed the smoky barroom, the cheaply dressed prostitutes, young and old, the sleazy men with whom they consorted, and felt a mixture of revulsion and sympathy. They were products, perhaps, of the system, he mused, and although society had to be protected from their depredations, they in turn deserved protection from each other.

Finishing his coffee, Detective Pierre Sorel laid a franc on the saucer and went out onto rue Marcadet. From the Môquet station, the métro would take him in less than ten minutes to the Gare St.-Lazare near which he lived in a one-room, cold-water flat whose rent cost nearly half his monthly salary.

21

FOLLOWING Zarah's instructions, Thorpe and Anna-lise traveled through and around Stockholm for nearly an hour before arriving at the Park Hotel. They entered the lobby, had a drink at the bar and left by the Sturegatan exit. Anna walked up the street while Thorpe rounded the corner and continued along Kar-lavägen past the big garden park. The night air was cool from rain that fell earlier, and streetlights glinted from wet cobblestones and little pools where water gathered near the curbs.

Thorpe paused, apparently to tie a shoelace, and glanced behind, but he could see no surveillant on either side of the street. Straightening, he continued his stroll, occasionally examining a storefront to delay progress until Anna joined him at the rendezvous ahead. Her approach was by a parallel street, and they were to meet at precisely eleven o'clock. He checked his wristwatch and saw with satisfaction that less than five minutes remained. Beyond the park the street angled northward. Another block, and Thorpe could make out an intersection with an open space beyond. On either side of the streets were six-floor apartment buildings that made an unbroken, uniform façade. They were also, he thought, uniformly drab from an architectural point of view, constructed for inner func-tional utility rather than to lend grace to their surroundings.

He could make out the church now, its tall spire and

the clock just under the cupola. Engelbrekt Church, it was called; Victorian in appearance and Lutheran by orientation.

A car passed, splashing the curb lightly, and its headlights showed Thorpe a distant figure beginning to cross the intersection. Anna had walked more rapidly than he thought, and so he lengthened his stride until they joined at the church grounds.

"No lights," Thorpe remarked, looking at the church.

Anna smiled. "I do not think religion does well in Sweden these days."

"The door we're looking for is around the other side." Taking her arm, he walked up the drive, past a stand of cone-shaped pines and into the shadows behind the church.

As Zarah had described, there was a flight of stone steps leading into the church. Another led down toward the basement entrance.

Anna said, "Is it time?"

Thorpe looked at the wristwatch dial and nodded. They stood by the door while Thorpe knocked lightly: four times, pause, then two. From the other side of the door came two sharp knocks. Thorpe knocked twice in answer, and in a moment the door swung open.

From the darkness he heard Zarah say, "Come quickly."

They entered, and the door swung shut behind them. The narrow ray of a penlite illuminated the floor. "Follow me," Zarah told them, and they moved after her until she stopped.

A door opened, and they went into a room lit only by a low-power bulb. Zarah locked the door behind them, crossed the room and knocked on another door.

It opened, and silhouetted against much brighter lighting stood a man.

"Papa," said Zarah Engstrom, "I have brought the friends of Mr. Smith."

"Please come in," he said, and stood aside while they entered. He closed the door, Thorpe blinking at the unaccustomed light, locked it, and motioned at a sofa. "I am Arne Lakka," he said and limped toward a desk. "Please be seated. From what I have heard, you both have a great deal to tell me."

Thorpe said, "You weren't killed in Holland."

"No." He smiled, and his gaze traversed the room. "Now I am caretaker here."

Zarah said, "After the attempt on my father's life he chose this place for safety's sake."

"Security, my dear. There is a difference always between safety and security. Here, as fortune would have it, I am both safe and secure." His eyes found Thorpe's. "So far."

Thorpe said, "We were not followed."

"I would hope not. Will you have coffee? Tea?"

Thorpe shook his head.

"Annalise?"

"No, thank you, Colonel."

Lakka leaned back in his chair. "If you wonder how Smith and I communicate, it is by secret writing. You know something of secret writing, Mr. Thorpe?"

"I was trained in it. I've used it in the field."

"Our system, unfortunately, is low-grade—susceptible of detection if a letter should fall into hostile hands. Security, therefore, depends upon our letters not being intercepted. Because of the rapidity with which you reached Stockholm, my daughter and I were unprepared for you. However, Smith's advice reached us soon after." He lifted the *Herald* Thorpe had given to Zarah at the Tower. "They give you a desperate character, Mr. Thorpe. But then the press always prefers sensationalism. If you are wondering whether the charge bothers me, let me say that it does not. Mr.

200

does not. Mr. Smith and I share a certain world view that permits us a number of presumptions: The first is that the enemy of my enemy is my friend. As friends you are welcome here. But before we discuss broader matters, let me inquire your needs. Is there any way I can serve you?"

"We've changed our hotel," Thorpe replied, "but we have only the identity documents we acquired in New Orleans. We'd feel more secure with others."

Lakka nodded. "Zarah, in your position you might be able to acquire others more suitable?"

"In Stockholm American passports are easy to acquire; the *wandervögel* sell them for money, trade them for narcotics or a night's lodging. I would say that in two or three days I will be able to supply the things you need."

To Thorpe, Lakka said, "Zarah tells me Smith is sending money to you."

"He said he would try."

"Do you need money now?"

"Not urgently. We can last another week."

"By that time Smith's money should arrive. If not, I will provide whatever you may need. Is there anything else? No? Then suppose you, Mr. Thorpe start at the beginning—the beginning of your involvement. After that, perhaps Fräulein Bauer could continue with what will be, to me, the most interesting of your two accounts." As he sat back, the light showed his slanting cheekbones; the pallor of his flesh suggested to Thorpe that Lakka had not escaped unharmed from the car's plunge into the Dutch canal. "I was returning from New York," he began, "when I saw a girl waiting at the Washington airport. . . ."

While he talked, Lakka made an occasional note, and when Thorpe finished, the Finn said, "Perhaps Fräulein Bauer will aid us by revealing the motive for her flight from home."

201

Anna swallowed, glanced at Thorpe, then back to Lakka, who said, "Would you begin with your mother's marriage to Klaus Werber?"

Quietly she said, "There are some things I would prefer Neal not hear. Neal, would you mind terribly?"

"No," he said, went into Lakka's bedroom and closed the door. Stretching out on the bed, he heard Anna begin to speak, but her words were inaudible. His reaction to her request had been brief resentment that he suppressed almost at once, for he had grown to believe that, through no fault of Anna's Werber had tried to press himself on her. And while Anna might be willing to discuss it clinically with Lakka and Zarah, he could understand her reluctance to have him hear details.

It had been a long and tiring day. Thorpe was half-asleep when the door opened and Anna said, "Please join us, Neal. Are you angry with me?"

"Not at all."

Rising, he drew her to his arms and held her while Anna whispered, "There were some things I could not bear that you should hear."

"I know," he said. Then they went back to their hosts.

Lakka appeared deep in thought. Zarah sat silent and tense in her chair. Finally, Lakka said, "I have learned some things that Smith should know, and so I will write him now. Mr. Thorpe, assuming we can provide proper papers, would you be willing to go to Lisbon?"

He looked at Anna. "If Anna will be safe."

"I believe I can arrange that. In Copenhagen I have a small flat not yet discovered by our enemies. She will be safe there until you return." To Zarah, he said, "Let us prepare a letter using the machine with the English keyboard."

His daughter went over to a cabinet and opened it. Inside, Thorpe could see half a dozen manual typewriters, each of a different make. Zarah selected one and brought it over to a table while her father brought out a folder of paper with different letterheads. While he was considering them, Zarah prepared the typewriter. Finally, her father handed her a sheet that Thorpe noticed bore the name of a large jewelry house.

"Zarah, please answer an inquiry from our friend concerning repairs to a watch and brooch."

His daughter fitted the paper behind the roller and began to type. When she finished, she signed a name with a ball-point pen and returned the sheet to her father. He examined it critically, nodded and gave her back the letter with a sheet of wax paper. Turning over the letter, Zarah laid the waxed paper on the unused side and fitted them together into the typewriter.

"My dear friend," Lakka dictated, and Zarah typed the salutation.

With occasional pauses he continued for several minutes, and when he finished, Zarah removed the sheets from the typewriter. Lakka read the typing as it appeared on the waxed paper and nodded approval.

Anna went to the desk and stared at the blank reverse side of the letter. "I don't understand," she said.

Zarah said, "When Smith dusts this with graphite or charcoal powder, he will be able to read the message."

To Thorpe, Lakka said, "As you heard, I asked that he meet you in Guincho five days from now. That will permit the letter to reach him in time to make travel arrangements and fly to Lisbon."

"Why not meet in Lisbon?" Thorpe asked.

"You should know that it has always been an espionage center. Accordingly, I set the rendezvous for a restaurant along the coast, not far from the capital, where you are less likely to be noticed. Before you go, I will provide a further message to take with you." He turned to Anna. "Assuming we can furnish you a passport, would you be willing to travel alone to Copenhagen? If not, Zarah could go with you."

Anna looked at Thorpe. "I will travel alone."

"Good," said Lakka, "because my daughter is being watched. Somehow they were able to insert a transmitter into her telephone. I am afraid that is how my journey to Holland became known."

Thorpe said, "When did you find the transmitter?"

"Not until I returned from the hospital. The device was easy to find—if one knows what to look for. Even so, I searched the flat thoroughly. There was nothing else." He shrugged. "Of course, what I still do not know—and may never know—is whether they identified Zarah—or me. And how it was done. What error was made."

Zarah said, "I told them about the device, Papa."

Anna said, "Could you tell who made it?"

"Probably the East Germans," Lakka said. "For the Soviets. Of course, it bears no trademark." He turned to his daughter. "If you will address and stamp the envelope. . . . "

It was after midnight when Thorpe and Anna left Arne Lakka's sanctuary. They walked through the quiet streets to the Central Station, where Thorpe deposited the letter in a yellow post box painted with a crown surmounting a stylized horn.

Leaving by a different exit, they took a taxi to within two blocks of the hostel where they had moved that afternoon. Each day at six he was to telephone Zarah at her office for word of their passports. Once he had them Thorpe was to leave for Lisbon, and Anna for Copenhagen.

At an intersection, he put his arm around her and thought that after all they had gone through together, he was reluctant for them to be separated for even as little as a week.

Zarah reached her flat, unlocked the door, and roused the girl who had been staying with Rolf. She paid the baby-sitter, thanked her and adjusted the blanket under the chin of her sleeping child. Undressing in the dark, Zarah felt a sense of emptiness. The American, Neal Thorpe, was just the sort of man she had been hoping so long to meet. But it was apparent he and the *Fräulein* shared a sentimental understanding.

It was a trick of fate that left her with a feeling of resentment. Annalise was pretty enough, but she was just a girl, not a *woman*. Zarah pulled on a nightgown and got into bed. But for Klaus Werber's stepdaughter, she thought enviously, Neal Thorpe could be staying in her flat, sharing companionship by day and affection by night.

Nails dug into her palms as she stared at the dark ceiling. Her life, she reflected, was divided among her son and her father and his work, as it had been ever since her divorce.

And, Zarah Engstrom told herself, laudable as it was, it was simply not enough to devote herself to for the remainder of her life.

22

IN the dark bedroom of Edward Cerf a telephone rang. He woke slowly, half-drugged by the lingering effect of the tranquilizers he used in order to sleep. The telephone rang again, stridently it seemed, and as he turned on the reading lamp, he realized the unexpected summons was on his private line. Apprehension stiffened his fingers as he reached for the receiver. In a hoarse voice he said, "Yes?"

"Good morning. There is no need for your investigation to continue."

"No need?" He rose on one elbow, blinking at the light.

"No further need. You may terminate your efforts. Is that understood? Confirm."

"Yes." He licked drug-dry lips. "I understand."

"That is all." A click, and the carrier current cut in.

Slowly Cerf replaced the receiver as his eyes sought the bedside clock. The time was eight thirteen. He poured a glass of ice water and drank it. The water had the sobering effect of black coffee, and his mind began to clear.

The caller's harsh voice he recognized as that of the *rezident* himself, not the usual cut-out with humbler manner. No, the arrogance of the elitist had come through in full measure, Cerf reflected uneasily.

Lying back, he turned off the light in the hope of composing himself for another hour's sleep, but as he lay in the darkness, his mind began filling with questions and fears.

As abruptly as he had been ordered to begin determining the whereabouts of Annalise Bauer, he had been ordered to desist. No explanation had been given him.

Had she been located by other means? If so, why had not the *rezident* informed him?

In the past he had been given an occasional rationale for things he had been required to do, even for their termination. But this . . . this was somehow different.

As in other cases of unexplained phenomena, Cerf personalized their significance in terms of his own life and guilty knowledge. He did so now and felt his heart begin to pound.

Suppose the girl had *not* been located. Removing him from the case carried dangerous implications that could mean the *rezident* was disgusted with his nonperformance despite Cerf's insistence that the task lay far beyond the range of his capability.

Or, Cerf reflected, it could mean they want to remove me from an active operation before I become more deeply involved in it; more knowledgeable and therefore more dangerous to the *apparat*. Again, coincidence could be the explanation: His retirement had been decided upon, and so he was being phased out. One by one they would cut or remove the strings of power from his hands; then, when he was powerless, he would be supplanted by another, a younger man. Was his poor health known? Had his gift to Israel been discovered after all these years? Had—somehow—his responsibility for Rimma's escape been discerned by the KGB? Any of these discoveries would be more than sufficient to seal his doom.

There were other, more recondite possibilities: Conceivably his removal from the urgent search might reflect a new power struggle within the KGB or throughout the Kremlin hierarchy itself. In general, his life remained untouched by recurrent clashes for Soviet power, although he had feared for his life at the time of the so-called Doctors' Plot with its explicit anti-Semitism; again, when Beria was deposed and shot summarily. But he had survived those murderous episodes and remained unaffected by the disgrace of Khrushchev and the ascendancy of sequential replacements.

Nor was it impossible that the *rezident* himself, turned critical, had embarked upon a course of provocation deliberately designed to embarrass and disgrace the Banker. By doing so, the *rezident* could cloak other performance shortcomings for which he might be under fire, failures of which Cerf was ignorant. By making Cerf the scapegoat, the *rezident* could survive.

But all in all, he reflected with growing disquietude, the direct impersonal call was a bad omen.

Very bad.

He groaned aloud and felt the arrhythmic warning of his heart. Rolling on his side Cerf opened a medicine box, extracted a capsule and swallowed it quickly. As it went down his dry throat, he felt momentary nausea and drank a small glass of water.

Nearly eight thirty. Too late for sleep.

He turned on the bedside light, propped pillows behind his shoulders and sat there gazing around the room until his fears became less extravagant.

Now, with his mind fixed on the tangible things of his surroundings, the familiar bureau, the closet doors, the dressing-table mirror, Edward Cerf began slowly to consider what he could do to ensure the survival of himself, his fortune and his children. Always before, when depressed or made uncertain by the implications of some unexpected occurrence, Cerf had stopped short of analyzing the facts of his position. For him, there could be no retirement on the pattern of the bourgeois-capitalist world, no old age secure and free of care. He knew this, had known it all for many years.

But when a man is young, he thought, old age seems distant, impossible. Then one believes that tragedy comes only to the other man, not to oneself.

His chin lowered, and his eyes gazed down over the mound of stored fat, the corpulence of his belly that adhered despite the discipline of diet and self-denial. In it were forty extra pounds of burden on his heart. Like leg irons, it hobbled his activity, menaced his existence. He reflected that whereas he could have felt relieved by the telephoned instructions to disengage, his reaction had been the reverse, and he sensed himself more threatened than ever. Nevertheless, he told himself, now was the time to strip away the trappings

208

of self-deceit and lifelong loyalty and examine every aspect of his quandary in terms of total Socialist realism.

On his side were certain factors that could be marshaled to advantage: his money and his reputation. Just as important was the knowledge, retained over many years, of things that had occurred, events his masters might have expected him either to be unaware of or to have forgotten by now.

His hands opened and closed; opened and closed again. He was nearing a decision that would be irreversible if he were to act upon it. There were broad, formless dangers in consequence of any action he might take, but he was not without defenses. For the sake of his children and grandchildren he should secure his fortune for their benefit, preserve his reputation and save their names. For the first time since young manhood his *muzhik* craftiness, so long veneered, began asserting itself. He was not going to become another *dokhodyaga*—a burned-out husk to be discarded and forgotten by the Soviet bureaucracy. No. Not Lazar Zamoilov.

He repeated his natal name. Half-aloud, it came with difficulty to his tongue, but in its syllables he found a welling of forgotten pride. Lazar, son of Avram, student of the village rabbi, one of the few who had learned to read.

I dedicated my life to the Soviet Union, he told himself with bitterness, and I decline to become another nameless martyr.

His breathing slowed, his hands relaxed and his heart ceased to pound. He felt his pulse, and its pace had slowed. In his mind he could see the safe deposit box he had opened years ago in another name. The bank was only a few blocks from his office, and he could easily review the half-forgotten contents of his box before seeing his son at lunch.

Maurice would understand, he told himself, that this would have to be kept within the family. He would destroy the blank deed of trust he had signed so many years ago before it could be claimed of him by the *rezident* and used to strip him of his holdings to the benefit of his successor. Instead, his son Maurice would become the beneficiary of everything he owned, the administrator of everything the Soviet Union assumed it would one day be able to claim.

Edward Cerf got out of bed, took a warm shower and shaved. At nine thirty he telephoned Maurice at his office and asked him to join him at the bank for lunch.

Then he rang for his valet and dressed for what he planned would be an active day.

Detective Pierre Sorel gazed through the grimed window of his office toward the white cupola of Sacré-Coeur dominating the skyline and the Hill of Montmartre. It was midday, and the skies over Paris had not cleared since morning. Gray clouds threatened rain, but even the prospect of a downpour could not depress Sorel's spirits. The Ministère Aéronautique had identified his cadaver's fingerprints as those of Carlotte Cécile Béranger, employed most recently as a flight stewardess by Charte-Aviation. And laboratory specialists had informed him that the tobacco flakes found in her purse represented a blend sold by only three tobacconists in Paris to a limited number of private customers.

Sorel opened the telephone directory, found the number he sought, and wrote it down. Then he dialed and heard a crisp voice say, "Charte-Aviation. May we serve you?"

"This is an official inquiry. I am Detective Pierre Sorel attached to the commissariat of the Eighteenth

210

Arrondissement. Do you have an employee named Carlotte Cécile Béranger?"

"Carlotte?" A muffled exclamation. "Why do you ask?"

"Just answer the question. Is Carlotte Béranger an employee of yours?"

"Yes."

"Where is she now?"

"*Hélas,* M'sieu Sorel, we do not know. Is she in some sort of difficulty?"

"Permit me to speak with someone in authority."

"Certainly. I will connect you with M'sieu Tardieu, who is in charge of personnel. One moment."

Sorel made a note of his name. When Tardieu came on the line, Sorel identified himself again and repeated his question. Tardieu said, "What is the charge against Carlotte?"

"There is no charge outstanding. When was she last seen?"

"Let me see—yes, three days ago."

"Where?"

"At Le Bourget. She came for a charter flight that did not materialize."

"How did she leave Le Bourget?"

"I will make inquiries and inform you."

"Perhaps you would be good enough to give me her address and telephone number."

"But of course. Here it is: Her flat is on the rue d'Asnières in the Seventeenth Arrondissement. Number four three eight. Her telephone is listed as BA 7-37-08. Could you disclose the reason for your inquiry?"

"Not at present," Sorel replied. "Thank you, m'sieu, and let me ask that you mention this conversation to no one."

"Assuredly not. But one remains curious. . . ."

"I understand. As soon as I have information for you I will telephone."

"Merci, bien."
"Au revoir."

Replacing the receiver, Sorel studied the data he had just acquired, then dialed the telephone number. He let the telephone ring six times before hanging up, went out to a clerk and dictated a memorandum to Commissaire Duclos detailing his request for an official search of Carlotte Béranger's flat.

Surely, he thought, as he signed the memorandum, we will find something there that will be useful. Letters, perhaps, or a list of telephone numbers. Conceivably a diary. Now he would not have to ask the press to publish a photograph of the dead woman's face and so alert the killer, whoever he might be. Sorel believed thoroughly in pursuing an investigation with the least possible amount of publicity. In that way, he had found, it was a great deal easier to locate and arrest the guilty parties.

He went back to his office to wait the Commissaire's decision and received Duclos' permission in less than a quarter of an hour. Sorel walked downstairs and gathered a technical squad to accompany and aid him in the search: two subdetectives, a fingerprint man and a photographer. Tomorrow, he decided, he would visit the Le Bourget offices of Charte-Aviation and interview each person who knew Carlotte Béranger. Aviation personnel were notorious for smuggling activities, and it was not impossible that narcotics were involved in her death.

In any case, he reflected as he got into the official car, it was among Carlotte's fellow employees that he was most likely to find her murderer.

23

AS soon as her children were asleep, Irene Cerf knocked on the maid's door and said, "I have to go out for a prescription. I shouldn't be very long. Answer the telephone, and if one of the children wakes, try to get her to go back to sleep."

"Yes, ma'am," the maid called, and Irene heard the bed creak as it was relieved of heavy weight.

Leaving the apartment, Irene walked west to Columbus Circle and stepped into a telephone booth. She closed the door and dialed a number. An accented female voice answered, and Irene said, "I have an emergency message for Mr. Paul Zweickert. Is Mr. Zweickert there?"

"Who is calling, please?"

"Western Union."

"You have the wrong number. Mr. Zweickert does not live here."

"I'm sorry," Irene said and hung up. She looked at her wristwatch and left the phone booth, walking unhurriedly toward the St. Moritz Hotel. Pacing herself, she went up the stairway to the mezzanine and sat on an upholstered bench. Then, ten minutes after her trigger call, a telephone rang in the booth nearest her bench. She answered on the second ring and said, "Yes?"

"How is Aunt Natasha?" A male voice.

"Aunt Natasha sends greetings."

"Make your report."

She took a deep breath, clenched the receiver and said, "I am concerned about the Banker."

"Give details."

"My husband and I were to lunch together today, but he telephoned to say that his father had summoned him to lunch at the Banker's office."

"Continue."

"At four o'clock my husband telephoned to say that he would not be home for dinner. I asked the reason, and he said that he was involved in a matter of great importance affecting our future. He said his father had forbidden him to speak of it, but he wanted me to know that he was drawing up a series of legal papers which would convey the Banker's estate to him. That he would be both administrator and executor." She swallowed.

"The estate is not the Banker's to dispose of," the voice said harshly.

"That is why I am informing you."

"Do you have further details?"

"Not yet. But my husband never keeps anything from me. In a day or so I am sure he will have told me everything. In the meantime, what am I to do?"

"Nothing. That is not your responsibility. Your responsibility is to keep me informed."

"Of course, and I will do so."

"Is your husband now at home?"

"As yet he has not returned. He said there was a great deal of work to be done, and because it was a family matter, he was obliged to accomplish it alone."

"You were correct in reporting the matter. Can you think of any reason why the Banker would become disloyal?"

"No."

"His health? Some financial reverse? An emotional crisis of some kind?"

"I can think of nothing."

214

"Be sure to ask your husband. Certainly he will know."

"I will ask him."

"Inquire also if the Banker has been in touch with authorities."

"I will inquire."

The line went dead, and Irene replaced the telephone. She left the booth, returned to the bench and lighted a cigarette. Her hand was trembling, she noticed, a reflection of her inner tumult ever since Maurice's second call. And now that she had reported to her superior she found herself wishing she had not. Her reaction to her husband's information had been reflexive: Report it at once. Until now she had not considered the consequences, the implications to herself and her two small children. By reporting she had begun a chain of events whose final episode could end with the liquidation of her father-in-law.

Exhaling distractedly, she wondered how much her husband had learned of his father's background. Edward Cerf could be disguising the conveyance as no more than a legalistic transaction to circumvent death duties and inheritance taxes. Nevertheless, Irene knew that transferring his estate to someone other than the designee of the Soviet Union was fraud on a large scale against the Soviet state.

Against herself, for example as a citizen of the USSR.

But how deeply did she now identify her life and its goals with the Soviet Union? She had given years of service to the USSR, long years that included her youth. And on command she had sacrificed her marriage. What more—really —could the state demand of her?

A wall clock reminded her that she was taking too much time. Reluctantly she rose, stubbed out the cigarette and went down to the hotel pharmacy, where

215

she purchased a bottle of cough medicine and put it in her purse—in case the maid or Maurice became curious over her absence.

She left the hotel and turned back to her apartment house. Already she and Maurice were well-to-do; on his own, her husband had the capacity to become a wealthy corporation lawyer. But as possessor of his father's estate Maurice would be a multimillionaire.

Pausing, she glanced at a shop window to admire a full-length coat of mutation mink. As she moved on, she reflected that ever since arriving in America, she had lived more comfortably—"luxuriously" was really the word—than she could ever hope to aspire to as an honored returnee to the Soviet Union. Tea, black bread and preserved fish, curious tasting coffee and ill-heated, crowded apartments—those were her immediate remembrances of her homeland. In New York City, she mused, even welfare recipients were better off.

On the other hand, if Edward Cerf were to succeed in his design, she would share in Maurice's increased fortune; they could buy the Florida home or one much better. A dozen of them. A hundred if they chose!

She had grown accustomed—easily and without even thinking—to a way of life that was in many respects better than the wives of Kremlin leaders enjoyed. She smoked the best cigarettes, dined in fine restaurants and had charge accounts at twenty shops and stores. Her weekly half days at Gabriel's *salon de beauté* had become *de rigueur*; for years she had not had to set or even wash her own hair. Perhaps by now she would have forgotten how.

Nearing the canopied entrance of her building, Irene's steps slowed. Robotlike she had told the *rezidentura* everything she learned from her husband. Now she was questioning the wisdom of her act.

Instead of letting herself be so preoccupied with the

216

urgency of making her report, she should have weighed the information—and the consequences of reporting it—against the future of her family. If it was noble to hold one's motherland in high affection, was it not even more noble to be loyal to one's husband and children?

Turning in, she nodded to the doorman and walked slowly to the bank of elevators, aware she had been precipitate in making her report. By now the *rezidentura* would be coding a message to Moscow, for the *rezident* would not want to be held remiss in delaying information warning of the Banker's suspected treachery.

As she pressed the elevator button, Irene felt as though she could bite off her tongue, the facile tongue she had let work against her own interests. Her words, the facts she had passed on, were gone now and beyond recall. In the KGB bureaucracy they would form a life of their own. There was no way to cancel her report, no way to nullify what she had done.

In fact, she told herself heavily, there was no one she could turn to. If she confessed her role to Maurice, he would despise her, divorce her and keep the children. That would be her payment for candor. If she told her father-in-law what she had done, Edward Cerf would be shocked, frightened and resentful. She could not beseech the *rezidentura* to "correct" her report; that would reflect dangerously on herself, worsen her difficult situation.

She left the elevator and began walking down the corridor, thinking that one alternative remained: She could make a subsequent report stating that her husband had greatly overestimated the significance of his father's wish; that upon examining the matter, Maurice determined he would not gain control of his father's holdings. She could embroider this assertion by fabricating Maurice's disgust with his father—how

217

Maurice kicked a table and broke an expensive lamp while reciting his disillusion.

A second report was expected of her, then others bearing on the same subject. Now, having considered her position, defined the interests and welfare of her family, Irene was nearing a decision. She got out her door key and went into her apartment. The maid was nodding on a sofa, the television loudly on. Irene Cerf hung her coat in the closet, turned off the television and woke the maid.

Alone in the living room, she mixed a beaker of vodka martinis, and when it was well chilled, she poured a drink for herself and sat cross-legged on the window seat, staring out over Central Park.

There was a way to handle all this—this predicament —she reassured herself, but having made a false initial step, she would have to be exquisitely careful from now on. And everything she did would have to be cleverly planned, flawless in design. At stake were her well-being, her happiness and her future—as well as those of Maurice and their children. She drew her knees under her chin and thought how fond she had grown of the view. In Moscow there was nothing comparable to this green and open expanse: nothing but the grim geometry of Red Square, the bizarre old Orthodox churches. Here in this country there was warmth and physical comfort, even social progress if one would only open one's eyes and admit the facts as they were.

Never before had she been willing to concede the falsity of her education, and the fallibility of her homeland's rulers. But, now, exposed to sudden danger, and through it recognizing a desire to remain she had never before acknowledged, Irene Cerf told herself that she could never go back to the life she had known before, never return to Dzherzinskovo Square and its impersonal, crushing discipline.

In time, she reflected, she would be denounced, and it would be said of her—as of so many others—that she had been corrupted by living in the West.

Her fingers opened a fresh package of filter cigarettes. She extracted one and lighted it, hardly aware of what she was doing.

On her shoulders, now, was the burden of rectifying her earlier mistake and saving her husband and his father from its consequences. She believed herself capable of the accomplishment; at the very least she was going to try, even if it came to interrogation by the *rezident* himself. Of him she knew only that his pseudonym was Viktor, and she had been conditioned to fear him, obey his orders unquestioningly.

She would not make the mistake of seeming to disobey. On the contrary, she would exceed instruction, impress him with her industry and provide no basis for suspicion. She, after all, was Viktor's only window on the Banker; without approaching the Banker directly, Viktor would be unable to verify or discredit her information.

Until it was too late for counteraction, she told herself, and that time could be years away.

Tapping ash from her cigarette, she decided to change into something homelike and attractive for Maurice. When her husband returned, he would be tired from the long day spent poring over the complex range of his father's financial interests and affairs. As a loving and devoted wife Irene resolved to do all she could to lighten his many cares, ensure them a long and happy life together.

In turn, Zarah took Polaroid photographs of Neal and Anna against the bare and unrevealing hostel wall. Satisfied the pictures were usable for the passports she would acquire, Zarah posed Anna once more, stepped back and took a full-length photo of her. When it developed, she said, "Anna, you will send this to your mother."

"Then she will know where I am."

From her purse, Zarah extracted two sheets of paper and an envelope. The blank sheet bore a typed message. "Write it in your own words on this stationery," Zarah told her, "address the envelope, and I will see that it is mailed."

Seating herself at the small table, Anna read the typed words, then picked up the stationery, whose letterhead was that of the Hotel Regina in Zürich. With a ball-point pen she began to write in German script: "Dear Mama—I miss you very much and am writing to let you know that I am quite well. I don't want you and Klaus to worry, and will see you before the end of the month. With much love, Anna."

After signing her name, Anna said, "What date shall I put?"

"Tomorrow's."

Anna dated the letter and addressed the envelope. She inserted the letter, enclosed the color photograph of herself, and handed the finished product to Zarah, who said, "A friend of mine will mail this in Zürich tomorrow morning. By the following day it should reach Bad Godesberg." She placed the letter in her purse and stood up.

Thorpe said, "What's the purpose?"

"Reassurance to Frau Werber, of course; but more importantly, to upset her husband and mislead those who search for Anna."

"Will it do any good?" Anna asked.

"It cannot do any harm. Besides, it is always good to keep the enemy confused. There are many of them and only a few of us. So we must use deception when we can." She turned to Thorpe. "If all goes well, I will be able to give you two passports tonight. Come to the Engelbrekt at eleven. Alone."

Anna said, "Can't I come?"

"It will be better if you stay in your room."

Thorpe said, "When do we leave Stockholm?"

"Tomorrow Anna can fly to Copenhagen. You will wait here two more days before going to Lisbon." She looked at Anna. "You do not mind traveling alone?"

"I can travel by myself," Anna said with a trace of irritation. "After all, I am not a child."

After Zarah left, Thorpe said, "I wish I could go with you."

"It is not at all necessary. I have visited Copenhagen many times, and there will be no difficulty."

"No need to be hostile," Thorpe said soothingly. "It's just that, well, after the distance we've gone together, traveling alone will seem strange."

Her face softened. "I know. I feel the same way."

"No problem, then." He kissed her lightly.

Anna returned the kiss and murmured, "Do you like her?"

"Zarah? I'm very grateful to her."

"I mean something beyond gratitude. How do you feel about her as a woman?"

"She's intelligent, attractive. . . ." He shrugged. "What do you want me to say?"

"That you prefer me to Zarah."

"Of course I do." He kissed her again. "What makes you ask?"

"Because I think that—my feminine intuition tells me she finds you very attractive."

"Nonsense."

"Then why must I stay here while you meet her tonight?"

"Because there's no need for both of us to go collect the passports. Besides, Zarah may not even be there, just her father. And I agree that you're safer here. When we went to the church together, there was a reason."

221

She sighed and looked up at Thorpe. "I don't really understand about the letter she had me write. Not entirely."

"Neither do I," Thorpe admitted, "but I'll ask about it tonight. Until then"—his face brightened—"in the words of the fried chicken commerical, we'll have to trust the colonel."

24

BEARING a Canadian passport Neal Thorpe reached Lisbon's Portela Airport on a CPA flight from Amsterdam, passed without challenge through Customs and Immigration and boarded an airlines bus that took him to the center of the city. An ancient taxi carried him up the long slope of Rua Castilho and left him at the Flamingo Hotel within sight of Eduardo VII Park.

His modest-sized room had a single, rather hard bed, but it overlooked a small inner courtyard where dining tables were set among flowers and overhanging palms.

Opening his window, he felt a surge of pleasantly warm air, smelled fragrance from the semitropical blooms below and decided to sleep with the windows open. He took off his clothing and got into bed, tired from the flight that had begun in a Stockholm rainstorm just after dawn. Before closing his eyes, he noticed a miniature bottle on his bureau, got up and found that it was a giveaway sample of sherry. Twisting off the cap, Thorpe drank half of it, decided the quality was inferior and swallowed the balance as a sleeping aid.

He woke in late afternoon, showered, shaved and went down to the small bar for a roast beef sandwich and a bottle of Sagres beer. He bought three cigars, lighted one and left the hotel for a stroll along the well-kept park, as any recently arrived tourist might do. Unlike Stockholm, the sky was blue, the air clear and comfortably warm. From where he walked he could look down over the center of Lisbon, along the broad Avenida da Liberdade with its rows of tall and stately palms, and his surroundings reminded him far more of Rio than Western Europe. By now Anna should be settled safely in Copenhagen, where, he hoped, she was not sought, the covert search for her presumably having focused on Zürich if her letter home were believed by Klaus Werber.

And sometime today, perhaps while Thorpe was resting, Alton Regester had reached Lisbon. There was a message for him hidden inside Thorpe's belt. A message composed by Arne Lakka and passed to Thorpe by Zarah the night before.

Reaching the huge memorial pediment surmounted by an equestrian figure of the Marquês de Pombal, Thorpe rounded the circle and continued down Avenida da Liberdade. Most of the traffic was up the hill and homeward-bound, with only a salting of modern cars among the large majority of well-kept ancients. Like the city itself, whose buildings were mainly old and well used, Lisbon, at least, he reflected, had declined to join the frantic race toward progress.

He walked past beds of geraniums and other flowers, stands of bougainvillea and miniature palms, down into the center of the Old City. Down narrow alleys he could see donkey carts and peddlers, smell sardines frying in olive oil at curbside stands. Cats sprawled on window ledges, and steeples were blanketed with pigeons.

A few more blocks, and the Rua Ouro gave out into a huge colonnaded square, the Praça do Comercio. Beyond it and the quai was the Tagus River. Here, during the war years, refugees had gathered daily to wait for ships or flying boats to take them westward to America. Thorpe walked nearly to the river, then turned west for the final five minutes of his walk that ended in the railway station—the Cais do Sodré.

From there, he knew, trains left on the half hour for his destination. There was time to kill, so he went into the nearest bar and ordered a cold bottle of Agua do Luso to quench his thirst. He drank part of the water and left the bar for a ticket window, bought a second-class ticket for Cascais and found his way to the departure gate.

It was an electric train. From the station it drew smoothly out into the fading sunlight and gathered speed, swaying a little as it sped along the coast. When it stopped at Estoril, he could see the white façade of the casino where so much of former European royalty idled away its time. From Estoril the train rounded the bay and stopped at the Cascais station, where Thorpe got off. An onshore breeze carried the smell of iodine and fish scales, and he could see extravagantly painted fishing boats being pulled onto sand by yoked oxen whose drivers wore long knitted caps.

Signs guided him to the coastal bus stop, where he waited, boarded the next bus and paid for a ticket to Praia do Guincho. Another quarter of an hour, and the bus stopped near a large hotel. As Thorpe got out, he could hear surf pounding along the coast. Spray drifted across the road, and he tasted its salt with the tip of his tongue as he walked toward a long, low-lying building set over the rocks. Above its entrance was a sign, BARRACA MUCHAXO, and in it he was to wait for Alton Regester.

The decor suggested Tahiti more than Portugal, Thorpe noticed as he went to the bar. Supporting columns were covered with dried palm branches; fishing nets with cork floats hung overhead. From his seat at the bar he could look out over the ocean, at the horizon reddened by the last rays of the sun. Below, waves crashed on the rocks and spray coated the viewing windows.

He ordered a bottle of Sagres beer and sipped as he looked around. Only a few tables were occupied, couples for the most part, holding hands or talking earnestly. A middle-aged pair sat silently, watching the turbulent ocean beyond, and Thorpe found himself thinking of Annalise. What was she doing now? Sleeping or getting ready to go out for dinner; window shopping along the Stroget; taking coffee at a sidewalk café?

Over the loudspeakers drifted the melancholy strains of a *fado*, and Thorpe thought of Zarah Engstrom and her infant son. He admired her, admitted that he was attracted to her, but was not quite sure why. She was handsome, rather than beautiful, and self-sufficient. So attraction was based more on female magnetism than any superficial qualities. He sensed an underlying antagonism toward Anna and wondered if Zarah was unconsciously casting herself as a rival for his attentions.

Beyond the windows the sea was dark; relentlessly surf thundered against the shoreline's massive boulders. The time of rendezvous with Regester had been imprecise; if he did not come tonight, Thorpe was to return tomorrow. There were always late planes, other delays to be considered. He finished his beer and noticed that the big restaurant was beginning to fill.

225

He went to the men's room, and when he got back to the bar, two men were sitting there. Thorpe got onto his stool, glanced at the nearest man and saw that it was Regester.

"Hello," said Regester, and for the barman's benefit, "Didn't I see you last night in the casino?"

Thorpe nodded.

"My name is Smith," Regester said and extended his hand.

"Matthew Lemaire." They shook hands, and Thorpe wondered who Regester's companion was.

"Let me introduce an old friend, Joel Levy."

Thorpe acknowledged the introduction. The man was about Regester's age, he thought, but far more powerfully built. He was almost bald and wore thick horn-rimmed glasses. His nose looked as if it had been broken more than once, and there was a small scar on one cheek.

"I've been reading about you," Levy said as the barman moved away, "and Smith has told me a good deal more. He says you didn't kill your friend, and I believe him. Anyway, in our profession people tend to get killed."

"Let's take a table," Regester said, and motioned to the *maître*, who nodded and waited for the three men to reach his station.

"A window table?" he asked.

"That will be fine," Regester said, and followed him. When they were seated, a waiter lighted a candle lamp and went away. Regester said, "Neal, there's no need for you to know my friend's true name, but you should know this: He is an Israeli Intelligence officer, and he's agreed to help us against Klaus Werber. First, how is Anna?"

"The last time I saw her—three days ago—she was fine."

"Where is she?"

"In Copenhagen. Lakka thought she would be safer there—in an apartment of his." Thorpe got out a cigar and lighted it. "Zarah's phone is bugged. Lakka thinks she's being surveilled."

Regester said, "That would explain the attempt on Arne's life—how they knew he was going to Holland."

Dov Apelbaum muttered, "They never rest."

"Never." Regester opened a menu and said, "Gentlemen, will you trust me to order?"

First came a dry pale sherry, then cold fresh mussels and, as the entrée, large clawless lobsters boiled in wine and herbs. They ate with a dry Ermida wine and chunks of rich Portugese bread. Thorpe reached into his belt, removed the narrow folded message and passed it to Regester under the tablecloth. Regester finished his wine, excused himself and went off to the men's room to read it. Dov Apelbaum said, "We've been making some plans, Mr. Thorpe, and we hope you won't mind helping out."

"I'll be glad to—what else can I do?"

Apelbaum smiled briefly. "From here I'm going to our Paris installation for a current reading on Werber—where he is, where he plans to be."

Regester rejoined them, and Apelbaum said, "I hadn't gotten as far as our plan."

Regester said, "For the time being it's a general concept: Trick Werber into going to Berlin. And let the Soviets dispose of him."

Thorpe said, "Why would they do that?"

"Because by then they will believe he's been a double agent working against them."

Apelbaum said, "After all, the Soviets don't want a hostile UN Secretary-General any more than we do."

Regester said, "I'm afraid we'll have to use Anna as the lure."

"I don't like it," Thorpe said sharply. "Send her to Berlin? Why not just deliver her to the Soviets now?"

"That's where Zarah Engstrom comes in."

Thorpe removed his cigar and stared at the glowing end. Surf spattered the window glass. Below, he could see the phosphorescence of the surging waves. "No risk to Anna?" he finally said.

"Very little. And with Werber removed from the scene Anna will be safe."

"How are you going to do it?"

Apelbaum said, "With disinformation, using the Soviets' own vehicle. We know Werber's residence phone is tapped by them; Zarah's phone gives us a second point of entry. The transcript of one can be false confirmation of the other."

Regester said, "Our friend here speaks several useful languages, and from Lakka we learned the authenticating phrase for Werber; 'Uncle Simon sends greetings.' "

"All this," said Apelbaum, "offers interesting possibilities."

But what about Zarah? Thorpe was thinking. Nothing said about the risks to her. And while words like "disinformation" and "false confirmation" had a professional ring, how detailed was the plan? Regester and his friend were in their sixties; how acute were their minds? Or was their scheme some infantile ego trip indulged in by intelligence romantics?

Regester said, "Neal, you look troubled."

He shrugged. "Probably just tired. Where do we go from here?"

"Well, Joel's off to Paris in the morning. I thought I'd go on to Stockholm and Arne, as his message suggested. As for you, I imagine you'd like to go from here to Cope and pick up Anna and bring her back to Stockholm. I've never met the girl, you know, and now that things are coming into focus, I want to determine how far she's willing to go."

Thorpe said, "Have you met Zarah?"

228

"Many years ago. Zarah wouldn't remember me, I'm sure. Arne told me she was divorced. How is she?"

"Seems to know what she's doing."

"How tall is she? Could she pass for Anna from a distance?"

"Height's about the same, figure's more rounded—perhaps fifteen pounds heavier and a fuller bust."

"The height is what is important," Apelbaum observed. "The rest can be concealed by a coat."

Regester nodded. "Neal, I'll need Zarah's phone numbers—home and office. Does Arne have a telephone?"

"Probably, but I don't know the number." Thorpe gave Regester Zarah's two numbers and said, "Lakka's holed up in the Engelbrekt Church—as the caretaker. Room's in the basement level." He sipped syrupy black coffee from its small cup. "The last time you saw him, was he limping?"

"No."

"Well, he's limping now."

"From the canal episode," Register said slowly. "He's got great survival powers."

"I look forward to meeting him," Apelbaum said, and lifted his cup. "*Lehayim.*"

Thorpe liked the way he said it, but could not remember ever having good health drunk in coffee.

"This is a preliminary meeting," Regester said, "to get to know each other a little better—and to introduce you to Joel. I think I'll stay at the Park Hotel, but you can check with Zarah after you arrive."

"The Park's near Engelbrekt Church."

"I know. Long walks are beyond me now."

He should have realized Regester was thoroughly familiar with European cities. "What's happened on the Bitler case—or is it still the Thorpe case?"

"I'm afraid it is. They're combing Canada for you." He looked at Thorpe. "*Were* you in Canada?"

229

"Mexico. Then Honduras."

"Mind telling us your travels?"

Over Constantino brandy, Thorpe covered his route for them and praised Anna as a good traveling companion. Apelbaum said, "Sounds as if she'll do, Alton."

"I'm sure she will. Apparently an unusually sensible girl."

The restaurant was full now. At the far end, spotlighted, were a guitarist and an extravagantly dressed woman singing a *fado*. They listened to her song, applauded and Regester said, "I'm going to pass you an envelope under the table. Swiss francs."

Reaching under, Thorpe drew back a thick envelope that he slid into a trouser pocket. "Thanks for remembering."

"We'll regroup in Stockholm," Regester told him. "No later than day after tomorrow. Oh, when you see Anna, Neal, don't tell her what we have in mind. The concept is still a little loose, and I don't want her losing confidence if we have to make a change."

"Do you think I'll ever be able to go back to the States?"

"You mean the murder charge? I wish I could sound hopeful, but I can't. Let's take care of Werber, and worry about the cops in that order." His eyes fell on Thorpe's paper napkin. "Doodling, Neal?"

Thorpe looked down and saw that while he talked, he had been sketching the face of Max Bloch. "It's the man who placed the ad for Anna," he told them, "but only a rough likeness."

"Could you make a better one?" Apelbaum asked.

"Well, with hard-surface paper. . . ."

Apelbaum handed him a menu. Thorpe turned it over and picked up his pencil. Consciously, this time, and carefully, he sketched the face of the man who had interviewed him at the Statler Hilton. When he

230

finished, he gave the menu to Regester. "Pink coloration," he said. "Reddish hair and mustache."

Regester studied the sketch and shook his head. "I've never seen him." He passed it to Apelbaum, who cleaned his glasses before studying the face in the light of the candle globe.

Presently Apelbaum said, "I may have seen him or his photograph, but his visit to the German embassy suggests a connection." He peered at the sketch again, concentrating. "No, he's not from the diplomatic or consular service. I think he has a Paris background—a bag man." He folded the menu and put it in a pocket. "I'll ask my people in Paris, but for now this face recalls a name—Kurz or Kotz, something like that."

"Who was he working for?" Regester asked.

"The man we were discussing—Hirsch."

"Edward Cerf," Regester echoed. "I'll be damned!" To Thorpe he said, "Our friend here has a camera eye—developed when he was working in Vienna at the Documentation Center."

Apelbaum laughed shortly. "And while I was trying to trace down ex-Nazis, friend Regester was at Pullach putting Gehlen's organization together again. At least now we're after the same man, for the same reasons."

"It could be a worthwhile lead," Regester remarked. "Particularly in the direction of Bitler's killer. That's not much, but it's more than we had before. Don't give up hope, Neal."

When Thorpe left them, he made his way back through the crowded restaurant and out to the entrance by the parking lot.

As he stood waiting for a taxi to take him back to Cascais, he heard the mournful notes of a *fado* threading though the pounding surf below.

Together, the contrasting sounds fitted and complemented his unquiet mood.

25

"AT ease, Sorel," said Commissaire Duclos amiably. "You of all people have nothing to fear from the DST. In Colonel Leroux's opinion, you may have unveiled an affair of far larger dimensions than a merely vulgar crime. Eh, Leroux?"

They were sitting in Duclos' private office where Detective Sorel had been unexpectedly summoned. Colonel Leroux touched his moustache and straightened a lapel of his civilian suit. The same lapel that held a rosette of the Légion d'honneur. "Quite so, my dear Commissaire. Now, Sorel, I understand your investigations into the Béranger murder have led you to the doorstep, as it were, of a person of prominence."

"Yes, Colonel." Detective Sorel shifted uneasily in his chair. Never before in his career had he met an officer of his country's internal security service, the Direction de la Serveillance du Territoire. He swallowed and began. "The woman Béranger was found in our —this—arrondissement, strangled and unusually well dressed for a *poule*."

"Which is what we have mostly to deal with," Duclos remarked.

"Our investigation was routine," Sorel continued. "Identification was accomplished through fingerprints on file with the civil aviation authorities, and her place of employment determined. With that, it was not difficult to ascertain her place of residence which we entered and legally searched."

"Get on with it, man," said Colonel Leroux. "The details implicating our important personality."

"Yes, sir. There were grains of tobacco in her purse. In a bureau drawer were five cigarettes bearing a printed crest, and the *magot* of one such cigarette in an ashtray. These cigarettes were made by a particular tobacconist for one sole client: the Comte de Rochepin."

"So what did you do? I must determine precisely where we are."

"It was necessary to establish a personal connection between Carlotte Béranger and the Comte de Rochepin. This was accomplished by officials of Charte-Aviation S.A. According to their records De Rochepin chartered an aircraft for a private flight to New York on the fifth of last month. Going and coming, he was attended by the late Mademoiselle Béranger."

"I understand," Leroux snapped. "What of the flight itself?"

"Charte-Aviation was reluctant to provide destination details, but I was able to learn them by questioning the co-pilot, who had been carrying on an affair of the heart with Carlotte. When I suggested De Rochepin's culpability, Jacques broke down and informed me of the flight's curious characteristics: a secret landing outside New York, where De Rochepin left the aircraft to board a private helicopter." He placed a dossier on the commissaire's desk. "The precise location and other details are here."

Colonel Leroux turned to Duclos. "And you are planning to arrest the peripatetic count?"

"Only if such action accords with your desires, Colonel."

"I think," said Leroux, "we would like an opportunity to converse with the count, inquire further details of his travels."

"If further evidence were needed," Sorel went on,

233

"there was a telephone conversation between Béranger and De Rochepin on the evening when she was apparently killed. The count's secretary provided the information."

Leroux's eyebrows drew together. "I regret that she was approached. Certainly she will have warned him of the inquiry."

"No, Colonel," said Duclos. "Her husband is an officer of the Police Judiciare. She remains silent."

Leroux sat slightly forward. "Are the count's premises under surveillance?"

"As yet, no," said Sorel. "No further steps have been taken."

Duclos nodded. "That is the situation as it stands." He lighted a cigarette and blew smoke toward the window. "You have had reason to suspect De Rochepin?"

"Much reason," Leroux acknowledged. "Much reason and never tangible proof. Understand"—he turned to Sorel—"I am not interested in him as a murderer—but as a traitor, a member of some espionage apparatus."

"Soviet?" asked Sorel, then wished he had not spoken.

"That will be for the count to reveal, will it not?" Leroux rose, bowed slightly to Duclos and extended his hand to Sorel. "My compliments, young man. Should you ever decide to leave the alleys of the Eighteenth Arrondissement, I am sure the DST would welcome you."

"No recruiting, Colonel," Duclos said. "Sorel can look forward to a fine future where he is. Merely let us know your desires with regard to De Rochepin."

Colonel Leroux picked up the dossier and enclosed it in his leather portfolio. "If you see this again, my dear Duclos, it will be because my organization failed to exploit the situation. As of now, no inquiry exists concerning the Comte de Rochepin. Henceforth, his affairs are in the hands of the DST."

"I understand perfectly." Duclos rose and opened the door for his visitor. Again Leroux accorded them a bow, and then he was gone. Commissaire Duclos returned to his desk. He picked up his cigarette, exhaled and coughed.

Sorel said, "What will happen now?"

"What will happen? Those fools of the DST will attempt to blackmail our murderer into revealing his foreign contacts, his knowledge of espionage, into giving them a full *résumé* of his life. *Merde alors*." He shook his head disgustedly.

"And?"

"De Rochepin will decline, refuse to have anything to do with them. As you know, he has influential friends, important contacts. Why, he is a Compagnon de la Libération! Do you think this government will allow him to be shamed, discredited? Ah, I have seen it happen before: the conclusive case against a suspect highly placed, one who wields leverage within a ministry. *Zut!* Like smoke, the evidence vanishes or is suppressed; the case becomes a memory. It will be so again." He stared morosely out of his window. "This will be the end of it."

Sorel got up. "What are your orders, Commissaire?"

"Find something else to do, Pierre. Another case. Lend help to your colleagues who require it." He turned and his face softened. "Promise me you will not join the DST."

"No, Commissaire. Never," he said dutifully.

"You are a good boy. Take the afternoon off—get drunk if you desire." Thémistocle Duclos eyed his young subordinate fondly.

"*Merci*, Commissaire." Turning, he left the office.

On the street Pierre Sorel walked slowly toward the

brasserie where he habitually lunched. A cognac or a few glasses of beer might cheer him up, he thought moodily. On the bar was a platter of delicately made ham sandwiches, and he was hungry, more so than usual from the tension of his conference. So much work accomplished, he told himself disconsolately, and now to see it wasted—as if the corpse of Carlotte Béranger had ceased to exist.

As Sorel turned the corner, the *brasserie*'s lettered canopy came into view. But as the distance closed, his mind filled with a memory of finger bruises on the pale throat of Carlotte Béranger, and by the time his foot touched the bar's brass rail his appetite was gone.

In the security of his office Colonel Jean-Paul Leroux studied the Béranger file with exceeding care. Finally, he set it aside and opened a much thicker one captioned "De Rochepin, Gilbert Philippe," reflecting that it would be more voluminous still had not all but the most innocuous dossiers been burned after the war by Communist infiltrators in the ministries. This file, then, extended back only as far as 1949 and could in no sense be considered comprehensive. It was composed of police and intelligence reports, gossip, book reviews, newspaper clippings, travel manifests and fragments of intercepted telephone conversations. The dossier provided the name of De Rochepin's concierge, doorman, and housekeeper, the purchase price of his Avenue Kléber flat, the year, make, license number and cost of his Citroën, his salary and associates at ORTF, scrips of sample broadcasts on Vietnam, Algeria and the Mideast War. Colonel Leroux jotted down a reminder that De Rochepin was an addict of opium and a presumed bisexual.

The Americans, he mused, would be interested in the Mystère's illegal landing on Long Island, the waiting helicopter. Surely, with all their deficiencies, their

236

inability to grasp and pursue the obvious, the Americans would nevertheless be able to determine De Rochepin's ultimate destination that morning and its significance.

Leroux twirled a mustache point and smiled briefly. One method of interesting the Americans, of course, was to suggest that De Rochepin had been carrying narcotics; that was the only subject of importance to them for the past two years. To sniff out a narcotics courier and his American contact, they would tear down walls, tap telephones and violate civil liberties to the nth degree. Perhaps that was the ruse he would employ. And why not? he reasoned. The secret flight, the undisclosed rendezvous, suggested a transaction in forbidden drugs. Until he learned differently from De Rochepin, that was as valid a presumption as any.

Except, Leroux told himself, I *know* what he's been up to.

Closing the dossier, he leaned back in his upholstered chair and considered his next, his proximate move. To surveill De Rochepin at this time seemed inadvisable. The absence of quality among the *mouchards* one put on the streets these days was almost a guarantee of their discovery, and Leroux could not risk arousing the count's suspicion.

By now, he thought, De Rochepin encourages himself to think the murderer of Béranger will not be found. He will be living in delusive euphoria, congratulating himself on his cleverness, believing himself secure. A confrontation now, at this very time, when he is unprepared, would shock him to the core. We are beyond some cat-and-mouse charade, he told himself; if frightened and given time, the count assuredly will run.

To rid the nation of him would be an estimable benefit; to arrest him for his crime would cause a certain momentary stir—then nothing more. These are the obvious, the elemental moves; their profit would be small. His fate does not concern me; the knowledge he possesses does.

I am not, after all, reflected Leroux, a *flic* bound by rules and regulations, the rigid core of criminal justice. My calling is a higher one; my goal is not the *corpus* of a man, but the contents of his brain.

A man such as our count, he mused, is not a mercenary agent; he is of a higher plane, the hierarchy of politicians where entire nations are corrupted. Without doubt a son of Lucifer.

As a citizen I am outraged by his crime. As an officer of the DST I am his antagonist, unknown, impersonal, unseen. He has as allies: a noble name, wealth, image, the friendship of influential persons, intellect, the patronage of powerful masters.

When Joyce departed Dublin, Leroux recalled, he granted himself three weapons: silence, exile and cunning. The last of these is mine.

Slowly he sat forward in his chair, pressed a button and presently the door was opened by an aide.

"Yes, my Colonel?"

"The De Rochepin matter, Jules. You will arrange the following: Recruit his doorman, concierge and housemaid; his secretary at the ORTF—her husband is on the police. See to his office and apartment telephones."

"Yes, my Colonel. Is there to be street surveillance?"

"Under no circumstances. All this is to be accomplished by eight o'clock today. No later." He gestured at his aide and handed him the thicker dossier. "Of my arrangements, Jules, nothing to be set on paper. Even among us, as you know, there are spies and informants."

"Understood, my Colonel." A click of his heels, and Jules was gone.

How much like my own classmates at St.-Cyr,

Leroux reflected: dedicated, loyal, discreet and—young.

He got up and walked to a bookshelf, gazed idly at a row of leather volumes and wondered when and where De Rochepin met with his control. In a month of surveilling we might know, he thought, but I will take a shorter route and hear him tell me of his own accord.

The desk clock chimed three times.

Five hours, Leroux said half-aloud. Five hours from now the stage will have been set. The time has come to study for my entrance.

26

NEAL THORPE cleared through Copenhagen's modern airport with minimum formality and boarded a clean, freshly washed SAS bus for downtown Copenhagen, all within twenty minutes of arriving. From Kastrup Airport to the SAS terminal took only another fifteen through late-afternoon traffic. He checked his suitcase in a terminal locker, changed escudos and Swiss francs into Danish kroner and walked to the hotel, where he found a taxi.

He was glad to be in Copenhagen again, not only because he was going to join Anna, but because he had always enjoyed previous visits. It was a clean, attractive city with fine food and efficient services, lovely women and excellent nightclubs. At City Hall Square he got out, paid the driver and oriented himself. From where he stood he could see the beginning of the Strøget, that mile-long pedestrian street where everything from mink and Jensen silver to pornographic booklets were on display. Vesterbrogade was the first street to the left, Lakka had told him, but Thorpe did not go there directly. He entered the Strøget, glancing casually into shopwindows, and turned left at the end of the block to Vesterbrogade. Number 319 was half a block away on his right, its entrance an unobtrusive curtained doorway. The door opened into a shallow vestibule with mailboxes and a staircase leading up. As described, the flat occupied half of the fourth, the top, floor, and he went to it stepping quietly on the stair lifts. The door was identified by the letter "H." Thorpe knocked, waited and knocked again. From below came the rattle of a trash can being dragged along the hall. He knocked a third time and decided Anna must have gone out. Using the key Lakka had given him, Thorpe opened the door and went in.

The living room was cheaply furnished, the carpet showed worn patches, and there was an air of abandonment to the surroundings. He called "Anna," then went into the small bedroom.

The single bed was made, but he pulled back the bedspread and looked at the pillow. Slept on. He replaced the spread and went into the kitchen. Dishes had been washed and stacked on the drainboard. On a counter beside the stove was a cup and saucer. The cup held coffee measured from a Nestlé can. Thorpe moved to the gas stove and saw a kettle on one of the burners. He felt the kettle and found it warm to the touch, the water tepid. A gas cock was open—the one supplying the kettle burner. Kneeling, he turned on the other burners but heard no gas escaping. Obviously, the kettle burner had exhausted the supply of bottled gas.

As he stood up, he felt his throat constrict. With mounting fear he searched the bedroom for Anna's

240

clothing, a purse, anything. He went quickly into the bathroom, saw a toothbrush and a tube of paste on the washbowl ledge. The toothbrush was damp.

He turned on the single bulb and saw its light reflecting from a wall mirror. On the mirror, in what could have been colorless lipstick, were two words: "Sovs came. A."

Unbelievingly he stared at the message while his stomach knotted. Near panic stiffened his arms and legs. Slowly as a sleepwalker he moved back, sat down on the bed. Face covered with his hands, he felt fear and sorrow surge over him as he realized how helpless he was.

Then, gradually, his power of reasoning began to reassert itself. Anna had been here until today, until two or three hours ago; her toothbrush and the still-warm kettle suggested that much. Then she had answered the door, and men had come in. How many? Two, most likely. One would be insufficient to over-power Anna and carry her away. Three men could attract attention from the other residents. Two, then.

Where had she been taken? The Soviet embassy? Not likely—to another safehouse. Or perhaps to Kastrup for a special flight to—where?

Overshadowing everything else was the fact that Anna had come into their hands.

He thought of telephoning Zarah, but what could she do? Besides, her apartment telephone was tapped. Her father was out of reach. The Israeli Intelligence officer was in Paris, and Regester somewhere en route Stockholm.

There was no place he could turn.

Except one.

The station.

Thorpe lay back on the bed and stared up at the ceiling as the knowledge that he had failed stabbed his brain again and again.

Even now, the place could be under surveillance by the Soviets; they could still use it to mousetrap anyone who came to the apartment, leave no loose ends.

He got up, walked to the door and locked it, went to the sofa and sat down. By asking the CIA for help, he would be surrendering himself, risking trial for the murder of Bitler. Even so, Anna's life was more important.

He got up again, went to the window and looked down at the street. Lights had gone on, the stores were closing.

Who was the chief of station? he wondered. He did not know the man's name, but there was a way of picking him out—two ways.

Quietly Thorpe went to the door and put his ear against it. The hall was quiet. Then, below, the street door opened and closed. He tensed as footsteps came up the stairs, relaxed when they rose no higher than the second floor. He went into the kitchen and found a service door that opened into a narrow rear staircase. Closing it behind him, he went down the stairs, remembering how Anna and he had left his apartment that night that seemed so long ago.

In the alley he looked from left to right, followed it to where it met the street and walked quickly toward the City Hall. There were a dozen wayfarers sitting on and around the benches of the open square. Breeze scudded papers across the cobblestones. He noticed their backpacks and bedrolls, their worn, patched clothing, and wondered how many were his countrymen. They were sharing bread and rolls and milk, and Thorpe reflected that at least they were still eating.

Two taxis were at the stand. He got into one and said, "American embassy."

"*Ja.* Dag Hammarskjölds Allé." The flag went down, the little car eased forward, and Thorpe sat back against the seat.

It was a fifteen-minute drive to the open residential section where the embassy stood, set back from the street, its rectangular concrete face contrasting with the old and graceful mansions nearby.

As Thorpe expected, the embassy was closed and locked. He rang the night bell, heard it echo through the entrance hall, and after a while he saw a marine guard walking toward him. The guard unlocked the door, opened it slightly and said, "The embassy is closed for business, sir. Come back in the morning."

"I'm an American," Thorpe said, "and I need help."

The guard eyed him doubtfully. He was a tall, well-built young man, immaculately uniformed in blue trousers, khaki shirt and white service cap. Around his hips was a white holster belt and an issue .45. "Who do you want to talk to?"

"If you'll let me see the personnel roster, I can tell you."

"I don't understand, sir."

"I was given a name, but I've forgotten it."

"I can call the duty officer, sir."

"That won't be good enough. This is urgent, Corporal. Let me see the roster—you've got a gun, and I haven't."

The guard considered his plea, opened the door and stood aside while Thorpe entered.

"Just stay where you are, sir." The guard locked the door, pointed to a lighted desk beside the staircase and followed Thorpe to it. The guard opened a large black notebook and laid it on the desk.

Seeing the list of alphabetical names, Thorpe shook his head. "I need the functional list."

"Which section are you interested in, sir?"

"Political."

Turning over a page, the guard handed the book to Thorpe, who studied it. Not the chief of the Political Section—that function was always reserved for

243

legitimate Foreign Service officers. The deputy chief, then. His finger found the name, and it was one he knew: Rudy Canova.

Canova. I thought he was buried in Italy!

"It's Mr. Canova," he said.

"You can call him on this telephone, sir."

"No, I'll leave a message. Have you got something I can write on?"

The guard opened a drawer and produced paper and a pencil. Thorpe sat down and wrote: *"Rudy, it's urgent that I talk with you. I'll call you at the embassy at eight o'clock.* Alton Regester."

He scratched out the eight and wrote "seven thirty," folded the sheet and stapled it. Then he printed "Mr. Canova" on it.

As he rose, Thorpe said, "I suppose you know who Canova is."

The guard nodded uncomfortably.

"Please telephone him and say there's this urgent message for him. If Canova can't be reached, call his deputy. Okay?"

"Okay, sir. Will do."

When Thorpe made no move to leave, the guard drew over the telephone and dialed Canova's home. He said, "Sir, there's a message here for you. The man who left it said it was very urgent." He glanced up at Thorpe, who turned and began walking toward the door. Unlocking it, Thorpe let himself out and looked at his watch. About six forty. Ample time for Rudy to reach the embassy, he told himself, and turned down the broad, quiet street, thinking that he had done the only thing possible. Canova had no police or arrest powers, but he could bring in the police, have them search for Anna. Canova would have contact with Danish Intelligence, Thorpe knew, and they would probably become involved. For one thing, the Danes would know where the Soviets holed up, be able to watch their safehouses, the airport and border points.

But Anna may already be gone, he thought despondently, and what I'm doing will prove useless.

Turning down Stockholmsgade, he found himself on the border of a tree-filled park that was dark except for an occasional glint of water in the ponds. For a quarter of an hour he walked, his mind filling with alternatives, each in turn quickly discarded. He could offer himself to the Soviets in exchange for Anna, but he knew they were not interested in him. They already had what they wanted.

Somehow, he thought, it had seemed so much simpler last night in Guincho; now reality confronted him, and it was far different from anything he had discussed with Regester and the Israeli. It was hard, bleak and hopeless.

At the end of the park he turned on Sølvgade toward the harbor and remembered the statue of the Little Mermaid. Somewhere near the port, he remembered, was the Danish Resistance Museum with its grim reminders of wartime Danish heroism and Nazi barbarity: the concentration camp replica, the long lists of heroes' names.

Arne Lakka would have known some of them, he told himself, and realized he would have to warn Lakka from the flat at Vesterbrogade 319. It was dangerous now, poisoned. His mind filled with memories of Anna: at National Airport, in New Orleans, sleeping in his arms on their long flights, sharing coffee in a Stockholm café. . . .

He could see the rear of Rosenborg Palace, its towers illuminated above the trees. The breeze had cooled, become almost chill, and he stopped at a café for brandy and coffee. As he sipped, he remembered he had not had any food since luncheon on the plane, but he had no sense of hunger. The drinks warmed him. His watch showed seven twenty-five, and so he left the café for a public phone a block away.

Depositing an øre coin, he dialed the embassy number, heard the guard respond on the first ring and said, "Mr. Canova, please."

"Just a moment, sir."

Another voice spoke. "This is Canova."

"I left a message for you."

"Yes. I've been expecting your call."

"Would you recognize me?"

"No, sir. I'm afraid I never attended—"

"What are you wearing?"

"Blue suit, polka-dot tie. Black shoes."

"Meet me in the D'Angleterre Bar. Fifteen minutes."

"Sorry. Under the circumstances I think you'd better come to the embassy."

Thorpe swore under his breath.

"After all," Canova said, "you wanted to see me, not the other way around. Besides, I wasn't informed you were coming, so I'm on my own time."

"Have it your way," Thorpe told him and hung up.

A cautious man, Thorpe said to himself as he left the kiosk, but as he strode along the sidewalk, he wondered if he would have reacted differently from the chief of station.

A taxi retraced the dark route he had walked and left him at the embassy. Thorpe went up the walk and saw the guard watching television at his desk. He rang the bell, and the guard let him in. "I'll call Mr. Canova," the guard said, went to the telephone and spoke briefly. To Thorpe he said, "He's coming down."

Thorpe heard footsteps on the mezzanine and looked up to see a rather swarthy man coming toward the staircase. The man wore a blue suit and polka-dot

246

tie. As he came down the stairs, Thorpe saw that his shoes were black. The man's eyes narrowed as he strode toward Thorpe, and when he stopped, he said, "You're not Regester. Who are you?"

"A friend of his. Let's go someplace we can talk."

"The consul's office." Canova gestured toward the Visa Section, and followed Thorpe inside the gate. They sat on opposite sides of a desk. Canova tapped on it and said, "All right, you wanted to talk."

"The Soviets have the daughter of the German Foreign Minister."

Canova grunted. "What's that got to do with me?"

"You can tell the police, the Danish Service."

"Why would I want to do that?"

"Listen," Thorpe said, anger rising, "last night I was in Lisbon—with Alton Regester. I came here to meet Werber's stepdaughter, Annalise Bauer, in a safehouse."

"Whose safehouse?"

There was no point trying to tell the station chief about Arne Lakka, explain a hundred other things. Thorpe tried again. "It's an apartment on the fourth floor of the three one nine Vesterbrogade. When I got there, she was gone, but she left a message on the bathroom mirror: 'Sovs came'—and her initial. It's still there." He took out the apartment key and laid it on the desk.

Ignoring it, Canova said, "So far you haven't told me who you are."

"If I tell you, will you do something?"

Canova shrugged.

"You've heard of Don Bitler?"

"Of course." Canova sat forward. "He was killed. You're not Bitler."

"I'm the man they've accused of doing it."

Canova blinked, wet his lips. "Th—" he began, then

finished the name. *"Thorpe! Neal Thorpe."* Canova stared at him. "But, you . . . why . . . I don't understand."

"What's important is finding the girl," Thorpe said in desperation. "I didn't kill Bitler, Regester knows I didn't. I've been trying to protect her from the Soviets, from her stepfather."

Canova's face was frozen. "Easy," he said hoarsely. "Tell me why she had to be protected from Klaus Werber."

"Because she can prove he's an Agent of Influence."

Canova's head moved rigidly. "Sure. Sure. I understand." He moistened his lips again and glanced furtively beyond the railing. Toward where the guard was sitting. "We'll take care of everything." He began to get up. "Just leave it all to me. Wait right here while I—"

"You've got to believe me," Thorpe said in a final effort to convince the man, realizing as he spoke that Canova was only looking for a way to hold him there. Before the station chief could open his mouth to yell, Thorpe jammed one hand into his pocket, extended the forefinger and pointed the pocket at Canova.

"All right," he said as Canova stared in horror at the simulated pistol, "have it your way. I'm a murderer, I've got nothing to lose. Sit down."

As Canova slid down into his chair, Thorpe said, "You can't have it both ways, Rudy. Either I'm a dangerous killer—in which case you're on a spot—or I might be telling the truth. What I want from you is action. And I want it now."

"What do you want me to do?"

"I'll repeat the address: Three one nine Vesterbrogade, fourth floor. Apartment H. Go there—preferably with the police. Get them to shake down every Soviet safehouse in the city. They've had her at least four hours now, maybe longer. By now, she could be in Leningrad. But let's hope she isn't."

Wordlessly the station chief nodded.

"We're going out of here together," Thorpe told him. "You'll walk ahead of me as though you were showing me out."

There were pale spots on the chief of station's cheeks. "What then?" he husked.

"We'll get in your car and go to a telephone. When I hear you make contact with the police, you're on your own. Clear?"

"Yes."

"Any objections?"

"No."

"Get up and start moving." Thorpe walked to the gate and waited. When Canova passed through it, Thorpe stepped behind him.

They were halfway across the hall when the guard called, "Leaving, Mr. Canova?"

"Yes."

"You'll have to sign out, sir." The guard pointed at the clipboard on his desk.

Canova hesitated, turned and began walking toward the guard. When the chief of station was six feet from him, Thorpe realized his bluff had failed. Canova was safe. Quickly he strode toward the entrance door, heard Canova's shout and bolted. He turned the key, shoved open the heavy door and raced down the steps, both men yelling behind him. There was a car at the curb, Canova's perhaps was Thorpe's first thought; then he realized it had not been there when he arrived. Still he ran toward it, thinking it offered a way to escape. A few feet from it he saw two men inside the darkened car, halted and stared at their dim silhouettes. From the embassy behind him came the sound of running feet. Thorpe poised to sprint away,

249

but he had waited too long. From one side, from behind the concealment of a tree, came a flat whispering sound, a sound of rapid motion. Something struck the base of his skull, stung blindingly, and the image of the car faded from his eyes. He felt his knees dissolve, his legs give way.

Then there was nothing else to feel.

27

ANNALISE BAUER looked around the damp basement cubicle. Light from the single bulb showed a pair of wooden chairs and a small table on which her dinner plate was still untouched. There were no windows; air entered the room from a narrow ceiling duct that echoed occasional footsteps from above.

For the hundredth time she blamed herself for having opened the apartment door, but she had not been expecting danger in the middle of the day. Her guard was down because there was sunlight—and because Colonel Lakka had told her the place was unknown and so secure. Two men entered as soundlessly as flowing water; one clamped his hand across her mouth, the other shut the door. Methodically, they bound her hands but let her go to the bathroom before blindfolding and gagging her. Before carrying her struggling down the service stairs.

While she lay on the car floor she could hear them speaking, recognized Russian as their language, but did not know the words. From sounds she realized they were examining the contents of her handbag. A voice syllablized the name on her Belgian passport: Brigitte Daumier. Gradually, the noise of traffic receded; the car was beyond the business district and traveling through a quieter section. From overhead came the breathy whine of a jet, then another, suggesting they were somewhere near the airport.

When the car stopped, she heard the tires skid on gravel. Men prodded her to her feet and guided her up three entrance steps, across a wooden floor, down wooden steps to a concrete floor. A door opened, and she went through. Hands guided her into a chair, and the blindfold was removed. Blinking at the light, she saw two men standing in front of her: both wore hats and the lower parts of their faces were concealed by handkerchiefs. She recognized them as her captors.

A third man entered. He held her passport, and spoke to her in accented French: "Your name?"

"Brigitte Daumier."

"Date and place of birth?"

"Three, September, 1951. At Bruges."

"What were you doing in the flat?"

"Staying there."

"Who told you to go to it?"

"A man I met in a café."

"Which café?"

"The little one at the end of the Strøget."

"Why did you accept his offer?"

"I had no place to go."

"There was money in your purse."

"It is necessary to eat, is it not?"

"Then you are the kind of woman who sleeps where she can."

Anna shrugged, encouraged by the realization that they were uncertain who she was.

"Where did you come from?"

"Brussels."

"What do you do in Brussels?"

251

"I work as a secretary. Why have you brought me here?"

"That is not for you to ask. Answer my questions."

"Let me go!"

One of the masked men stepped forward and slapped her face. The pain was tolerable, but she screamed in anguish.

"Answer my questions! What is your place of employment?"

"Maison Foiret." She remembered having visited it to buy lace with her mother.

"Address?"

"Rue St.-Michel."

Her interrogator spoke to one of her captors in Russian, and Annalise realized that he was both confused and angry. To Anna he said, "What is the name of this man you say let you use his apartment?"

"He said his name was Soderman. Erik Soderman."

"Where is he?"

She shrugged. "He said he would be back from a business trip in a few days."

"Where did he go? What kind of business?"

"Listen—he did not question me, why should I ask him a lot of things? If you're looking for Soderman, I can't help you. Maybe he'll come back, maybe not. Who knows?" She let her mouth twist suspiciously. "If you're police, I don't have any drugs. Is that it? Soderman's in the drug business?"

"Perhaps," her questioner said. "So you think we are the police?"

"You wouldn't go to all this trouble if you were kidnappers—I don't have any money to pay you. I don't know anyone who does."

"What does Soderman look like?"

"He's young—thirty, maybe, not bad-looking. Taller than me, black hair. Wears a goatee."

Another brief discussion in Russian. Anna kept her face sullen, but inwardly she was elated. They were still uncertain who she was.

The French-speaking man said, "Why did you come to Copenhagen?"

"Have you ever been to Brussels?" She laughed shortly. "That's why. I quit my job and took a vacation. Any law against that?"

The French speaker did not reply. Instead, he snapped orders to her two masked captors and said to her, "Perhaps you are telling the truth, perhaps not. Meanwhile you will remain here."

"How long?" she challenged.

"That depends."

One of the men untied her hands and Anna chafed her wrists. "*Salauds!*" she spat. Great pigs!

"Enough of that!"

The three men went out, and Anna heard the door being locked. Almost at once she began to cry. After a while her tension spent itself, and she dried her eyes, got up and began exploring her place of confinement. Finally she realized there was no way to escape except through the door.

At least, she thought, they don't know who I really am. And if they think I believe they are police, they will not have to kill me. She was grateful for her inspiration, for having been able to remember the name of the lace shop in Brussels.

She pulled the second chair in front of her own to rest her legs while sitting. I must try to put myself in their place, she decided. They've been watching the apartment, probably for a long time. Why? Because they know Colonel Lakka stays there. But instead of Lakka, I came along. They may have thought I was his daughter; they may still think so, but there isn't any proof. If they decide I'm only who I say I am, they'll have no reason to keep me. Or they could wait for Soderman to return, thinking *he* can lead them to Lakka.

For now, at least, they don't know who I really am.

Slowly the afternoon passed. She was given water and allowed to visit the WC while her two guards waited. Then back to her cell. Dinner was brought, but her stomach was too tense for eating. She thought of taking off a chair or table leg and striking the guard the next time he came in, discarding the idea finally as a romantic projecting. No, safety lay in continuing to play the role she had created.

Anna wondered how Lakka's flat had been located by the Russians. Perhaps through Zarah's telephone —that was the only vulnerability she could think of.

And what would happen when Neal returned from Lisbon? He should arrive at the flat no later than tomorrow. He would search it, read the message on the mirror and know she was a prisoner. What would he do then?

What *could* he do?

Tears flowed down her cheeks. She closed her eyes and felt a sense of helplessness drain strength from arms and legs. Neal would be taken prisoner, too. They would torture him, kill him in the end.

All because of Klaus, she told herself and began to sob. If only I had given in to him, none of this would have happened. And now they're going to kill Neal.

For the first time in her young life, Annalise Bauer experienced the undeniable fear of death.

Sandor Varga unlocked his front door, entered the vestibule and hung his hat and damp raincoat on a hook. The ride uptown from his store had been crowded, uncomfortable and slower than usual. In New York, he reflected, taxis disappeared at the first

254

drop of rain, and people were left to jam together into buses and the stinking subway.

"Gyula," he called, walked through the living room and found her in the kitchen.

"Chicken paprika," she said proudly, and turned from her preparations to kiss the side of his face.

"Any messages?" he said curtly.

"Nothing." Her face sobered at his preoccupation. "Nothing. And I have no schedule until tonight." She swallowed. "Has something happened?"

"*Nothing* has happened—and that is what concerns me." From the refrigerator he took a bottle of beer, uncapped it and, without pouring it into a glass, stalked into their living room. He turned on the television for early evening news, settled himself into his chair and drank from the cold bottle. On the screen the blurred face and torso of a newscaster appeared, swelled in size and shrank into focus. Varga watched the man's lips move, words issued from the speaker, but the *rezident* was oblivious of them, his mind elsewhere on other problems. Serious problems. All day he had suffered a miserable headache, and the midday message from Rimma Ivanova did nothing to dispel it.

Her words had been soothing, their content reassuring, but Varga was unable to reconcile her recent reports with Rimma's alarmed initial cry. According to her, she had misunderstood her husband's first report, and nothing whatever was changed with regard to the Banker. Unfortunately, Varga thought, he had sent a flash message to Moscow, suggesting the possibility of Cerf's alienation from the cause, hinting at possible defection to safeguard himself against future events. And ever since he had regretted the flash warning, for Rimma had been unable to substantiate it in subsequent reports.

Unable or unwilling, he mused.

255

Assuming the Banker had decided to withdraw from active duty and retire with his fortune intact, what was the principal factor triggering his decision? Reluctantly Varga decided it had been his unembellished order to the Banker to end the search for Annalise Bauer. The Banker's efforts had been unsuccessful; Cerf realized it, and Varga had subjected him to stern criticism. The order to terminate activity, issued flatly and without explanation, could have been interpreted by Cerf as a prelude to action against him.

If this was the sequence of events, Varga mused, the *Sektor* itself will be responsible for Cerf's disloyalty. I was informed the girl had been located in Europe; but I was specifically forbidden to let Cerf know. Why? Because of the information's source. Compromise could not be risked. That was the *Sektor*'s rationale. Instead, withholding explanation from the Banker turned him apprehensive, provoked survival action.

Now, Varga was forced to suspect the complicity of Rimma Ivanovna. She was covering for her father-in-law.

Why? To feather her own nest, prevent—

"How soon will you want dinner?" Gyula called.

"I'm not hungry."

"Not hungry for chicken paprika?" She came in, drying her hands on her apron. "That isn't like you."

"I've got things on my mind." He swallowed more beer, set down the bottle and tried to concentrate on the newscaster.

"Are you going to send a message about the helicopter pilot?"

"Yes, yes!" he said in sudden anger. "What's the hurry? You don't transmit until, when—twelve o'clock?"

"Eleven thirty?" she corrected. "I just thought I could start encoding—if it's to be a long message."

"I'll have everything ready by ten o'clock," he told her irritably. "I'm preparing it in my mind."

Silently, she returned to the kitchen.

Another botched operation, he thought disgustedly. The Pairs *rezidentura* had reported police inquiries at Charte-Aviation, the charter company that flew the Journalist to Long Island. The stewardess who attended the Journalist on both crossings had been murdered—that was the reason given for the investigation. But suppose the police themselves had murdered her to provide a motive for looking into Charte-Aviation's flights? In the capitalist world any intrigue was possible; one had always to be on guard against provocations. Still, Varga had been ordered to inform the helicopter pilot that inquiries might be made. And what had happened? The pilot had come apart, sobbing and cursing into the telephone, threatening to inform federal authorities of his part in the episode.

Finally, Varga's stern reminder that the pilot's mother was hostage of the MFS in Karlshorst stemmed his wild hysteria and brought a reluctant promise to maintain silence.

Sandor Varga tilted the bottle and drank the last of his beer. Rimma, the Banker and the pilot, he thought broodingly, and then a long argument with Rafael Mendoza over returning a three-piece bedroom suite for cash—even though the mattress was foully stained and stank of liquor. All that today, and when I open the door, Gyula greets me with chicken paprika!

Despondently he shook his head. Mendoza had threatened to return tomorrow with a storefront lawyer. To avoid legal complications, Varga reflected, he would probably have to give the Puerto Rican a full refund. In cash; in front of the lawyer. And Mrs. Cherry Washington threatened to denounce him to the health authorities for selling her a sofa stuffed with roaches and other creatures. How detestable these shoddy transactions, and how distrubing! In all they represented another week sans profit for the store. How long could it go on? Everything he touched seemed cursed—as though he bore the Mark of Cain.

Above the voice of the newsman, Varga could hear Gyula humming in the kitchen. My old *babushka*, he thought reflectively; hardly an intellectual, but she does everything well; transmits as well as she cooks; enciphers as well as she keeps house: everything done neatly and with care.

Now that he had had a few minutes to relax, he let his mind turn to the problem of the Journalist. Because of the murder investigation, De Rochepin was sure to be questioned. Why had he chartered a special plane to fly the Atlantic? What was the purpose of his flight? Why had the aircraft landed in Long Island undetected and unannounced? Where had the helicopter taken him? Whom had he seen?

Sandor Varga sighed heavily. I hope he's more of a man than I believe him to be, he thought. The Paris *rezidentura* is responsible for the Journalist, but if he should crack, Cerf will be exposed. Not that Cerf is witting of my name or address, but the affair could count against me if Cerf were publicly involved.

He looked around the comfortable room, acknowledging how fond he had become of it, how accustomed he was to the way of life it symbolized. If only he could sell the store and start another business, he could make some money. Honest money, he thought. Unfortunately, now was not the time to suggest a change of cover employment to the *Sektor*. Without doubt his reasoning would be challenged; one or more of the desk-borne idiots would suggest reviewing *Viktor*'s dossier, imputing bad management to him—or worse. Each officer would consider which protégé he could nominate to replace the suspect *rezident*. And like an avalanche, the affair could develop dimensions of incredible proportions, an uncontrollable velocity of its own.

Unchecked, the affair could result in his being totally discredited. Destroyed.

And how could he defend himself? What advocates could he summon in his behalf? Who, in the last resort, could he turn to?

From the kitchen drifted the cheerful humming of his nominal wife. Varga's head turned so that he could watch her at her work. She was ungraceful, unpretty and unyoung. But she delighted in preparing his favorite dishes, and as he had already considered, Gyula was an excellent housekeeper.

Moreover, her knowledge of electronics was extensive. It was Gyula who repaired their television set, she who knew how and what to do with the innards of their solid-state radio. Someplace outside Manhattan —Kansas City, for example—they could start a radio-TV repair business and give customers good value for money received. With the funds from his dying enterprise, he could finance a shop for the two of them, sell a line of electrical appliances on the side, and they could live out their lives in financial and physical security.

Gyula opened the oven door and drew out a pan. "Fresh bread, Sandor," she called. "The kind you like. Hungarian style. Will you eat some before it cools?"

"In a little while," he said. "Put it aside for the moment and open two bottles of beer. One for you, Gyula."

Her round face beamed. "So long since we shared a drink together." Quickly, she uncapped two bottles and began walking toward him.

It was necessary to give deep consideration to what was embedding itself in his mind. Subtly, he would have to sound her out. But before that step he would have to prepare a fallback position to present to the

259

Sektor in his own defense. To do so, he would have to find some vulnerability, detect some heretofore-unknown infraction that could be used to incriminate "Nell" so she could not denounce him on her own. Or be forced to do so by others envious of his rank and position.

"Sit here, my dear," he said in a kindly voice. "No—here on my knee."

"*Sandor!*" She blushed until her cheeks became small glowing apples. But she adjusted herself in his lap and allowed him to nuzzle the side of her neck.

"We haven't talked in a long time," he said gently. "It's been too long, Gyula, and I've worried we've been growing apart. But you know the strain I've been under. A man can hardly—"

Her fingers closed his lips. "No more," she said huskily. "Let's just enjoy this time together. You have a headache?"

"A bad one."

Soothingly her fingers stroked his temples. "I know how to take care of that. Just leave it to me." She left him long enough to turn off the television, the ceiling light, and returned. Touching her bottle to his, she murmured, "*Nostroviya.*"

"*Nostroviya,*" he said softly, and tightened his arm around her waist. Things would have to be done slowly, by cautious, careful degrees. To survive was the paramount thing, acknowledged by Marxist and capitalist alike. And to survive required devising an alternate plan. One he could employ if he found more things going wrong.

Not, he thought, that they could get much worse.

28

WHEN Neal Thorpe regained consciousness, he was sprawled on a damp floor in a dark cellar room. His arms circled a support stanchion, wrists bound together. As he sat up, his head pained savagely, and he felt nauseated. He tried deep regular breathing, leaned against the pole and began to think. His first thought was that he was in police hands, but he ruled it out as illogical. He would have been arrested, not slugged; he would be in a lighted station house, hand-cuffed, not tied in darkness.

His next thought was that Canova's action squad had taken him, the station chief having prepared in advance for that eventuality. If so, by now Canova had informed Langley and was waiting instructions concerning the fugitive Thorpe.

At least, he thought over a surge of pain, Canova will have included enough of my story to start someone thinking. But who? Regester was out of the country and Bitler dead. Who on the inside beside Bitler knew about Annalise Bauer? No one, he thought bitterly, believed Werber was a Soviet agent, and that was the foundation article of faith.

Turning his head slightly, he saw a thin ray of light; it leaked from beneath a door in the farthest wall. There was no reason to light an empty room, so who was there? From overhead came the slow tread of feet—a man, by the way the flooring creaked.

By slow millimeters the pain seemed to be subsiding,

261

and after a while Thorpe managed to stand, clinging to the pole to rest cramped legs. The pole was round and smooth, he realized; no way to abrade the rope that tied his wrists. Even to try would scrape his flesh raw. Twisting his left arm, Thorpe tried to see his wristwatch, realized it was gone; removed. Uncertainty about the time depressed him. How long had he been there? How long since he had fled the embassy and stopped to appraise the waiting car? An hour? Three? Six?

He pressed his chest against the pole, realized wallet and passport were missing. Well, that was to be expected. And the passport was legitimate enough—with the exception of his photograph. A laboratory could detect the substitution, but even that would take some time.

Above him men were talking, voices muffled by the floor. Listening intently, he tried to determine from word rhythms what their language was. Not English, not French. Danish, perhaps.

Then he heard what sounded like:

"*Kto on takoiy?*"

"*Miy znayim shto on Kanadinits.*"

"*Kanadinits? Ya nichivo ni ponimayu.*"

Then another voice: "*Kotoriy chas?*"

The word *Kanadinits* suggested "Canadian," so it was reasonable to suppose they were discussing him. The language, though, was not Scandinavian—too slurred, the rhythms wrong.

Nichivo was one word Thorpe fully recognized, and it was Russian. It expressed uncertainty, indifference, lack of knowledge.

Into his mind filtered the sound of someone softly sobbing. It came not from above, but from nearer by. Thorpe turned toward the door and identified it as the source. Body tense, he listened, but the sound faded away, replaced by footsteps behind the door. As he

262

watched the crack of light, he saw it shadowed briefly.

Above, a door opened and closed. Outside, an engine started, and a car drove off. Thorpe's attention returned to the closed and lighted room, and he theorized its occupant, like himself, must be a prisoner. But the other person was free to move around the room.

Why?

The pacing resumed. Thorpe waited until footsteps neared the light, and when it was shadowed, he coughed. The shadow stayed.

He was about to call, "*Who are you?*" when he remembered that oldest of interrogators' tricks, the simulated prisoner and the planted mike. So he stayed silent, and the shadow passed; the footsteps moved away.

By now it had occurred to Thorpe that the walker could be Annalise. She had been captured by Russians, and Russian was spoken on the floor above. The person moving behind the door seemed lighter than the average man, and the sobbing he had heard was female.

He considered calling her name and rejected the idea: what good would it do? At worst, their captors could identify them both; at best they would gain the small comfort of knowing they were together.

Anna, though, after leaving her message on the mirror, might still think he could aid her. To realize he was a prisoner like herself would bring her only hopelessness.

The thought tormented him. He strained at his bonds, but the effort tightened them and made his head throb painfully. Slowly, he sat down, back against the stanchion, and tried to think.

Above him, the house seemed quiet. No footsteps; nothing. He wondered if the place was empty. Then, without warning, a stairway door opened. Thorpe slid to the floor and lay there, eyes half-closed, as the beam of a flashlight crossed over him. He heard a grunt, the door closed again.

After a time he sat up, listened and realized the other prisoner—Anna?—was no longer moving around.

Outside, a car—*the* car?—pulled up beside the house, the engine stopped. A car door opened and closed. He heard the doorbell ring. The door was opened. At least two men came in. Footsteps crossed the floor. They stopped. He heard the scrape of chairs.

Time for another council.

He lay on his back, expecting the cellar door to be flung open again. And so long as they believed him still unconscious, he was safe from interrogation.

By now he was sure his captors were Russians. Thorpe wondered what Canova and the marine guard had done after they saw him captured. There was no nearby car the station chief could use to follow them, so what had he done? Returned home and put the incident from his mind?

Why had the Soviets been waiting there? For whom? Was it their usual night surveillance, or had Canova's leaving home occasioned their appearance?

Copenhagen was not the active espionage arena that Paris was, or Rome. So it was probably infrequently that the station chief was called back to the embassy after the close of business. On that theory, Canova's return would interest the Soviets, who would want to follow him in case he continued on to a clandestine meeting.

Instead, Thorpe thought disgustedly, I threw myself into their arms.

One thing they know: There's a connection between Canova and myself. What kind, they can't be sure. But the fact he and a guard were chasing me suggests I might be useful to the Soviets. They might even be considering me as a possible collaborator. But before

264

they go that far, they'll want to learn exactly who I am.

So it could be, he thought as his face turned toward the bar of light, that they haven't yet connected me with Anna. And I'll assume they don't know who she is.

What it does mean is the apartment was blown before she ever got there, linked to Lakka. And to find him, they picked up whoever went in.

Now things were organized in his mind. He had a plan to use against his captors. At least it would buy time.

Above, the cellar door opened. Footsteps began descending. Heavy footsteps. Thorpe forced his body to relax, eyelids almost closed. The footsteps left the stairs, came toward him, scraping across the concrete floor. Thorpe saw the beam of a flashlight, a pair of legs by his knees. Suddenly one of the legs drew back, the point of a shoe kicked viciously into his thigh. He set his teeth against the pain, stayed limp. Then he saw the legs bend. The man was kneeling, flashlight playing over Thorpe's ankles. The man must be deciding whether to bind them, he decided, and while his captor was staring at his ankles, Thorpe opened his eyes, flung up his left leg and hooked it over the head and around the neck of the kneeling man. Thorpe's feet hooked at the ankles around the man's neck, and he sent every ounce of strength into his legs, closing the vise, choking the neck, shutting off the flow of blood and air. The man's body flailed, fingers, hands and arms frantically trying to pry apart the strangling vise, but Thorpe's legs only tightened. Then the man's body went limp.

The fallen flashlight showed the man's face: eyes bulging, face purple, tongue extruded. He could be faking, Thorpe thought, but he did not think so. To make sure, he relaxed his legs slightly, then took up the clenching vise once more, He counted to thirty, to

265

sixty, to one hundred and eighty, and now, when he looked, the eyes were dull with death. Thorpe's legs felt no pulse in the big neck artery. Yes, dead.

Slowly, he disengaged his legs, muscles aching from the strain. His face was wet, his body shaking from exertion.

He tried to toe the flashlight closer, but it was out of reach. He sat up and looked around. He had seen no pistol, but perhaps there was one on the man's body. He ran his feet over it, felt nothing hard or bulky in the man's waist or pockets. No, he had come down unarmed.

So now, thought Thorpe, that I've killed him, what do I do? He stared at the door, thought of Anna, and was about to call out when he heard a sound from a different part of the basement. It seemed like clawing, scratching, then mechanical tension of some sort. Motionless, he decided the sounds came from a basement window—as though a thief were trying to pick or force the lock.

A sharp metallic snap, and cold air came across his face. Bodies were flowing through the window, lowering to the floor.

Flashlights played across the basement, a beam touched his legs and he heard an exclamation. Knees knelt beside his face, his hands were lifted, a knife cut through the rope. Light struck his face. Thorpe shielded his eyes and sat up. A hand pressed over his mouth. The man said, "*SSssss!*" and Thorpe nodded he understood he was to remain silent.

Unaided he got to his feet and pointed at the doorway. "Someone there," he whispered. "Do you understand English?"

"Yes." A hand touched his back. "Is the door locked?"

Quietly, he crossed to the door, counting the figures of three men. "Anna," he called. "Anna, it's Neal."

266

Footsteps approached the door, blotting out the light. *"Neal?"* Her tone was incredulous.

Turning, Thorpe nodded to the men. They were blond, he could see; not large men, but their motions were coordinated like those of athletes. One came to him, knelt and examined the lock with a flashlight. In it was a key.

Thorpe turned it, and Anna rushed into his arms. He kissed her tear-wet cheeks, cautioned her to be quiet and looked around at the men. "What now?" he asked.

"We go," the leader said, glancing at the dead man on the floor.

"Aren't you going to arrest them?" Anna asked.

The man shrugged. "We just go," he said, and gestured toward the window.

"Wait a minute," Thorpe said. "Who are you?"

An identification card appeared. Thorpe picked out the word "police," compared the ID photo with the holder's face. They matched. Arm around Anna, he walked toward the open window. One of the policemen jogged ahead of them and climbed up and out, then extended his arms downward. Thorpe cradled his hands and lifted Anna's feet. With their help she climbed out of the window, Thorpe behind her. They waited until all five were clear, then ran from the house to a stand of birch trees, where a dark car waited.

Thorpe took the leader aside, spoke with him a few moments. Then the engine started, and they all got in. The leader switched on the car's mobile radio set and called in. For a time he spoke rapidly, answered questions and switched off the set.

As the car turned onto a highway, Thorpe said, "Where are we going?"

"Police headquarters."

"Why?"

"We have information you are wanted in your country. For murder."

Thorpe felt Anna's hand tighten on his arm.

"Canova." He shook his head.

"Who is Canova?" Anna asked tightly.

"The local CIA chief." He swallowed. To the policeman in charge he said, "You don't really want to take me in."

"Why not?"

"For the same reason you didn't go upstairs back there at the house; the reason you made no arrests. It would be embarrassing to Denmark. Now, if you think I'll keep quiet about who kidnapped us and where we were taken, forget it. Getting extradition papers for me will take days—weeks, maybe. And while I'm waiting I'll be talking: about Soviet espionage in Denmark. And about the Soviet I killed back there."

The leader said, "But we do not have to permit you to talk."

"What about this young lady? You can't hold her prisoner, silence her. If I can't see the press, she can."

For a few moments there was only the sound of tires racing over damp roadway. The mobile transceiver switched on, and the leader spoke into his mike.

This conversation was longer than the first one. When it ended, the leader replaced the mike, sighed and said, "Very well. Where do you want to go?"

"Kastrup."

"Kastrup," the leader ordered the driver. Then to Thorpe: "It is too late at night for flying."

"I don't mind," Thorpe said. "I don't have my passport anymore, and you'll need time to get us travel papers to Sweden. And money for our fares."

The leader considered. "Travel papers, yes. But who will repay the money?"

"Canova."

Anna laughed—a little wildly, Thorpe thought. "I'm

268

lost," she said. "I haven't the faintest idea what's been going on."

After a while the car turned onto another highway, and Thorpe saw an arrow sign pointing to Kastrup Airport. A few minutes more, and they pulled up before the departures section. Doors opened, and they got out. With a smile the policeman said, "I think there has, somehow, been a mistake. You are too intelligent to kill one of your own countrymen and have it known."

Thorpe began walking into the building, Anna at his side.

The policeman said, "Who killed your friend in America?"

"Who controlled the house where you found us?"

"I see. This way, please." He took them to the SAS ticket counter, rang a desk bell and roused a sleepy clerk.

After a while the clerk asked Thorpe his name.

"Harlan Sanders," he said. "And this is Evelyn Wood."

The policeman motioned them aside while the clerk prepared the tickets. "Are those the names you want?"

"They're as good as any," Thorpe told him.

"Here are your tickets, sir, miss."

Thorpe examined them and saw they were made out in the names he suggested, tourist class to Stockholm. The policeman said, "Is everything in order?"

"I don't see a cost figure."

The policeman smiled. "You entered Denmark illegally via SAS. You are accordingly being deported, and SAS is required to return you whence you came." He paused. "It *was* Stockholm, was it not?"

"For the record," Thorpe told him. "Now, what will you tell Canova?"

"As little as possible."

"Please omit our destination."

269

"Every effort will be made. In return, you will not publicize the incident?"

The two men shook hands. Anna thanked the policeman, who bowed and assured them he would bring papers enabling them to enter Sweden legally. "Before your flight departs," he said, and left them in the all-but-deserted passenger lounge.

"Flight leaves at five forty-five," Thorpe observed. "Do you think you could sleep?"

"I could try."

"And while you're trying, I'll tell you what's been going on." He led her to an upholstered bench, where she stretched out, head pillowed on his lap.

"Comfortable?"

"Very. And *so* glad you found me."

"The message you left convinced the police."

"But how did they find us?"

"Canova saw the license number of the car that took me away. He had sense enough to phone it in. The cops looked it up and staked out the place."

"It sounds so simple," she said drowsily. "Now tell me what happened in Lisbon."

"Well, I met Mr. Smith as planned. With him was an interesting fellow who turned out to be an Israeli, a man who gave his name as Joel Levy. He's in Israeli Intelligence. We brought each other up to date, and Smith is meeting us in Stockholm tomorrow—today. Meanwhile, Levy's gone to Paris, and—"

Her eyes were closed, her breathing slow and shallow. Thorpe lifted her hand, kissed it and sat back closing his eyes. He had always like Danes, he reminded himself, and what they had done for him and Anna was something he could never forget. In a sense even Canova had redeemed himself.

29

FROM a telephone booth at Arlanda Airport, Thorpe dialed the apartment of Zarah Engstrom. The time was seven fifteen.

When she answered, he said, "Good morning, Zarah."

"Oh. Yes—good morning. Where are you?"

"At the airport. I haven't much time, and—"

"Shouldn't I call you on another phone?"

"There isn't time. Besides, I don't believe anyone's listening to us. Why should they?"

"Well," she said doubtfully, "if you say so. What happened in Bonn?"

"Klaus will make a public declaration."

"Where?"

"In Berlin. At a press conference. Tomorrow or the day after."

"And he will tell everything?"

"Everything."

"Anna will go through with it? Keep her part of the bargain?"

"Of course."

"I was afraid she might not." Zarah paused. "You're going to Berlin to help with arrangements?"

"Yes."

"And after that? Back to Washington, I suppose."

"I'm afraid so. Winding this up has taken longer than we planned. When this is over, I'll come back."

"I hope so," she said softly. "Please try."

271

Thorpe hung up and stepped from the booth. To Regester and Anna he said, "It's done. Zarah sounded just right."

"She's intelligent," Regester said. "And dependable." He looked at Thorpe, "When I saw her earlier, I got the distinct impression she's fond of you."

"Well," said Anna, "she can't have him. That's not in the plan."

"You two had better start moving," Regester told them. "Zarah and I will take an afternoon plane. Remember the hotel?"

Anna nodded. "Schlosshotel Gehrhus—in Grunewald."

"Have you heard from Levy?" Thorpe asked.

"He's to join me in Berlin."

Anna said, "They're calling our flight."

"*Auf wiedersehen*," Regester said. "*Nach* Berlin."

They shook hands and Thorpe and Anna left for the departure gate. Berlin-Tempelhof, the gate sign read. They showed their tickets and followed the corridor to the waiting plane.

In their seats, Anna said, "Assuming your phone conversation was recorded, how soon will the Soviets react?"

"Before we reach Berlin. Assuming the conversation was overheard."

The Pan American stewardess came down the aisle, checking seat belts and overhead baggage. The DC-9 began moving toward the flight line, the tractor disengaged, and the jet engines whined into life.

The flight took them south along the Swedish coast, past Gotland Island and over Bornholm, where the plane joined the Hamburg traffic pattern and cleared for entry into the air corridor at Büchen.

Within a few minutes the pilot announced they were nearing Berlin. Anna pointed out Spandau prison, the Olympic stadium and the Funrturm—the tall radio tower—as their plane dropped low over neatly rebuilt blocks of houses and small walled gardens in the Hansa quarter. Still, Thorpe noticed destroyed, still-barren sections of the city.

They left the aircraft and walked into Templehof's massive arc. In an airport shop they bought a suitcase and toiletries, left the building and took a taxi to the Berlin Hilton on Budapesterstrasse. The doorman took their suitcase, and they went into the lobby, but instead of going to the registration desk, they kept on to the telephone area, where Anna gave a Bonn number to the operator and went into booth 16.

Presently the telephone rang, and Anna lifted the receiver, knowing her stepfather would answer in his dressing room.

Her heart was pounding. Through the glass booth she gazed bleakly at Thorpe. Then she heard the hoarse voice of Klaus Werber.

"Klaus," she said huskily. "This is Anna."

"Annalise! I'm so glad you—"

"Klaus—I'm in Berlin. I have much to tell you, and I do not trust the telephone—you understand?"

"Of course. When?"

"Remember the café at the end of the Tiergarten—beside the Wall? The Zell? We will meet there—before you make the announcement. Eight o'clock. I beg you to say nothing to Freda."

"Don't worry. But she will have to be told."

"From a distance?" Anna said tightly. "Until tomorrow night, dear Klaus." She hung up, closed her eyes and felt her hands trembling. Her breath caught, and she forced air into her lungs before opening the door.

"Done?" said Thorpe.

"It is done." She dried her eyes and left the booth. "My emotion was not for myself—or Klaus, but for my mother. I—I—" she faltered and recovered herself. "Can we just go to the hotel?"

273

The listening post technician rewound the reel for his visitor and played Thorpe's conversation with Zarah once again. Boris wrote down the words as they came, and when he finished, he said, "There was nothing more?"

"That is their conversation—all of it."

Boris shook his head. He was a jowly, heavyset man in his mid-thirties. "The Diplomat," he muttered. "Incredible!"

The technician shrugged.

Boris said, "A decision at the highest level will have to be made."

"Suppose it is not the Diplomat they were discussing?"

"The only names mentioned were Klaus and Annalise. It could point to nothing else. " Folding the transcript, he got up.

"What will be done?"

"A further check will be made—in Germany. Without the Diplomat's knowledge."

"But, how?"

"Idiot—do you suppose this is the only telephone line we are tapping?"

The technician placed a fresh reel on the recorder, threaded the tape and ran it ahead. He resented his superior's rebuke. Just because he had not attended the university as Boris had was no reason to—

"Immediately report any further conversations that could bear on this one."

"Yes, comrade."

Boris said, "Cheer up, Fedor. This may turn out to be a most important contribution to the security of the motherland, one justifying all your efforts and long hours."

"Time will tell," the technician said noncommittally, reflecting that if there were any credit to be gained, it would be taken by his superior. He switched on the voice-operated relay and sat down in his chair. When Boris said nothing, Fedor picked up a Swedish magazine whose pages were filled with color photographs of naked females.

"*Dosvidanya, tovarisch.*"

"*Dosvidanya,*" Fedor replied without looking up from his magazine. He heard Boris cross the room, open the door and go out. Turning a page, he wondered how much longer they would expect him to accept this kind of duty without respite. Even life in the New Lands seemed more attractive than these four dark walls. There, despite the permafrost, there were habitations, occasional gaiety and, most importantly, women.

He spat on the floor and continued examining the nude and lifelike photographs.

From the embassy of Israel Dov Apelbaum took the métro to the Madeleine Station, walked up the stairway and exited on the rue Royale. From there he crossed to the rue de L'Arcade, slowing to locate the address he sought.

The building had a gray stone façade, and on it was a small marble plaque with gilt letters and an incised cross. The plaque marked the spot where a resistance fighter had been killed during the liberation of Paris, and Apelbaum reflected that if Israel were to place similar plaques in Jerusalem alone, the cost of marble would be prohibitive.

The door was carved oak lettered in gold leaf with words: "Cerf et Cie." Apelbaum went in and found himself in a large comfortable room gracefully decorated and partitioned unobtrusively. Seated at the nearest table desk was an elderly woman. A small sign bore the word: "Renseignements." Apelbaum removed his hat and said in German, "Is there someone I could speak with?"

"*Allemand?*" she inquired.

"Oui, je suis Allemand. Peut-être—"

But with a gesture she rose and walked to the rear of the office, knocked on a door and entered.

In a few moments she returned, followed by a balding man whose mustache and remaining hair were reddish. Bowing briefly, he said in German, "I am Egon Koch, manager of this office. How may I serve you?"

"Delighted," Apelbaum said warmly, and shook the manager's hand. "My account is with your New York office, under the personal management of Herr Cerf himself. The reason for my visit is to inquire what formalities require to be accomplished should I desire to transfer the bulk, or even the entirety, of my account to this office."

Koch shrugged. "Indeed there would be very little for you, personally, to do, Herr—"

"Schnabel," Apelbaum supplied. "Kurt Schnabel."

"As I was saying, Herr Schnabel, we are able to arrange the transfer in-house, so to speak. Two signatures and it is accomplished. If you would care to—"

Apelbaum waved his hand. "At this point I am only inquiring, you understand. Before I effect such a change, I will want to consult Herr Cerf."

"Of course. Have you seen our founder recently?"

"Unfortunately I have not. My recent travels have taken me through South America. By chance have you seen Edward?"

Koch beamed. "I am happy to say that I have."

"He traveled here?" Apelbaum said in a tone of surprise.

"Oh, no. It was in New York City. A business matter took me there."

"He continues well, I trust?"

"In the best of health," Koch said warmly. "Our doors are ever open to serve you, Herr Schnabel." From his vest pocket he took out a small case and presented an engraved business card to Apelbaum, who took it and slipped it into his pocket. He shook hands with Koch, thanked the manager for his courtesy and left the banking office.

He walked down the rue de l'Arcade without haste, convinced from seeing Koch that he was identical to the Max Bloch whose sketch Neal Thorpe had drawn in Guincho. Identical with the photograph Apelbaum had studied in the Embassy office of his Paris Shin Bet counterpart. Koch had been sent to organize the search in America for Annalise Bauer, ordered into the dirty affair by Edward Cerf.

So once again, Regester is right, he told himself. Like Klaus Werber, Cerf is a creature of the Soviets.

He walked down to the Place de la Concorde and crossed the bridge and continued along the Quai d'Orsay toward the Aérogare. From there he could see the golden dome of Les Invalides, half-shrouded in mist; below, the trees and gardens of the Esplanade seemed washed in a light, uncertain green, a setting from Pissarro or a Delacroix.

Apelbaum entered the Aérogare, claimed his suitcase in the checkroom and walked to the Lufthansa ticket desk. There he turned over his suitcase and reconfirmed his ticket. Paris to Köln; change to Pan American for the flight to Berlin/Tempelhof.

At a fruit stand he bought an apple and munched it as he rode down the moving stairway to the bus departure area. He paid the ticket taker and found a comfortable seat where he finished all of the apple but the core. It was delicious enough, he reflected, to have been exported from the orchards of kibbutz Shamir.

During the flight to Köln, he drank a bottle of Löwenbräu Pilsener, ate a slice of Münster cheese and enjoyed a twenty-minute nap.

Before claiming his suitcase, Apelbaum consulted

277

the departure board and saw that his flight would leave as scheduled in an hour and thirteen minutes. He went to the public telephone area and entered an enclosed booth. Depositing toll coins, he dialed a Bonn number and after several rings heard the gruff, distinctive voice of Klaus Werber reply.

In Russian Apelbaum said, "Uncle Simon sends greetings."

Shocked silence. Then: *"What do you want?"*

"You are considering visiting the girl?"

"Yes—but not without your concurrence. I was going to—"

"Good. You may visit her. You are agreeable?"

"Quite agreeable."

"Travel incognito," Apelbaum warned. "We recommend an official aircraft to Tegel Airport. If the girl is receptive, that will resolve the entire problem."

"I understand."

"No drinking," Apelbaum warned. "It is essential your visit to Berlin not become public knowledge. Be, above everything, discreet."

"You may depend upon it."

"We do," Apelbaum told him. "You have your instructions and authorization to carry them out. Now do so." He rang off and muttered, *"Ben zonah."*

Apelbaum mopped his damp forehead and left the booth. He bought a New York paper at the newstand and read that the search for Thorpe had shifted to southern Mexico, where, it was claimed, the fugitive had been seen in a remote mountain village.

He folded the paper under his arm and checked his suitcase through to Berlin. Then he sat down in the passenger area and unfolded his newspaper.

If everything had gone as planned, Anna's call to Werber had been overheard by the Soviets, whereas his call—on a private ministry number—was not. A great deal depended on that distinction.

Converging actions had been set in motion. The outcome would be decided, finally, by their Berlin ending. Until then, Apelbaum told himself, there was nothing to do but wait.

30

IN Colonel Leroux's office a special telephone rang, one recently installed. Jules answered, made notes and replaced the receiver.

"De Rochepin's secretary," he reported. "The count is taping a program interview with Cardinal Rossinol and expects to leave the studio for his flat by six thirty."

Leroux grunted. "What is the subject of discussion with the holy man?"

"The attitude of the Vatican toward different candidates for the Nobel Peace Prize. Principally the German Foreign Minister, Klaus Werber."

"Doubtless the cardinal gives his endorsement to Werber."

"In a delicate way."

"I can imagine," Leroux said with distaste. "So the Prince of the Church is one of the *copains*, is he? I wonder how they got to him."

Jules' forehead wrinkled. "Who, sir?"

"The Soviets." His fingers drummed irritably on the desk. "The secretary will call again?"

"As soon as the taping ends." Jules answered another ring, listened a few moments, said, "Continue reporting," and hung up. To Leroux he said, "For the last hour De Rochepin's apartment telephone remains inactive."

"Naturally—with the count at ORTF." He shrugged.

Jules said, "If you do not want me to enter the building with you, Colonel, at least let me remain outside."

Leroux shook his head. "I will not risk your being detected by countersurveillance—and that is final. You will remain here." His gaze covered the office. "In your command post."

It was late afternoon, and the sound of traffic filtered thinly into the fourth-floor office where the two men waited. The building was an old one, not far from the Hôtel de Ville, its business disguised by a plaque identifying it as an office subordinate to the Tribunal de Commerce which stood across the Seine on the Ile de la Cité. From his windows, on an occasional clear day, Leroux was able to see the cross-topped spire of Notre Dame, rebuilt a hundred years and two decades ago by Viollet-le-Duc after its destruction by a mob. Gazing at it, Leroux often reflected that a simplistic view would divide the world into the builders and the destroyers; and in his professional work those broad categories were often sufficient to extend to personal characterization. Long ago he had decided which De Rochepin was.

The telephone rang and Jules answered automatically. After ringing off, he said, "De Rochepin's housekeeper. As of now the count has not indicated to her that he plans to do other than spend the evening at his flat."

"After dinner she will absent herself?"

"She will appear to have left, yes. But she will remain in her quarters in order to report anything her employer does following your departure. The doorman will immobilize the count's Citroën in the courtyard."

280

Leroux nodded approval. Jules studied a checklist and sat back, his young face taut.

This profession, Leroux reflected, should be practiced only by us old ones who no longer have nerves or emotions. By antiques like myself who are accustomed to waiting and do so as devoutly as a friar tells his beads.

Again the telephone rang. Jules listened, thanked the caller and turned to his superior. "De Rochepin has seen the cardinal out and entered his office."

"Place the call," Leroux told him, and when Jules finished dialing, he slid the telephone across the desk.

"This is Inspector Delacroix," Leroux said to De Rochepin's secretary, whose information had triggered his call. "May I speak with the Comte de Rochepin?"

"Would you disclose the nature of your business, Inspector?"

"I prefer to speak confidentially with the count."

"Of course, Inspector. One moment, please." Click of a hold button. Leroux drummed his fingers while the charade unrolled. Presently, the slightly nasal voice of the count: "Inspector—ah, what was it?"

"Delacroix."

"Delacroix, to be sure. Names. . . ." His voice trailed away indifferently.

Leroux smiled, declining to be irritated by De Rochepin's hauteur. "My dear Count," he began, "I am calling in the hope of engaging your cooperation in a delicate matter."

"A—police matter?" De Rochepin inquired, a hint of caution in his voice.

"In a sense,—but not insofar as you may be concerned."

"Well, then," De Rochepin said relievedly "I can say only that I am at your disposition."

"How very good of you," Leroux intoned deferentially. "If it should not be to your great inconvenience,

281

I would be grateful if you would permit me to present myself this evening. Eight o'clock?"

The count considered. "Inspector, might I have a hint of the business at hand?"

"Please understand that my hesitation to discuss it now serves our common interests. Believe me, I would not have intruded at all had the matter not been both urgent and—as I said—of the utmost delicacy."

"Then," said De Rochepin with a trace of annoyance, "I will expect you at eight, Inspector."

"You are most gracious," said Leroux, "and for my part the least I can do is to avoid keeping you waiting. *Tout à l'heure.*"

"*A bientôt.*" De Rochepin rang off, and Colonel Leroux replaced the receiver.

Jules turned off the tape recorder and removed his earphones. "So," he said, "the trap is sprung."

"Merely baited." Leroux rose from his desk and walked toward the window. "You note he did not even inquire which branch of the police I represent. What construction, Jules, would you place on that?"

His aide considered. Presently he said, "That the count has been to some extent anticipating a call from the police."

"Precisely." Leroux glanced at his desk clock. "So for the next two hours our count will relate my coming visit to the Béranger woman. He will prepare himself for inquiries concerning violent death. Thus he will be unprepared psychologically for my disclosures."

Jules' face showed open admiration.

"Examine the checklist," Leroux instructed. "What else remains?"

Jules touched a brown envelope. "Exchange your personal identification for the special series."

Leroux extracted a worn black wallet from his breast pocket and placed it on the desk. Jules handed him an equally worn brown wallet and placed the black one

282

in the envelope. Leroux spread saliva around the knuckle of his third finger and worked off his St.-Cyr ring. Jules dropped it into the envelope and gestured at the nearby coatrack. "Your raincoat and hat."

Leroux nodded.

"That completes the list, my Colonel."

"*Merci*, Jules. You may depart."

"Colonel, I would rather stay, and—"

"Nonsense. I am quite capable of managing myself from now on. Drink my health and have a good dinner."

Reluctantly Jules rose. "I will return before eight, my Colonel."

With a wave of his hand, Leroux dismissed his aide. After the door closed, Leroux returned to his desk and opened the Béranger dossier once more, adjusted the reading lamp and read each entry slowly and thoughtfully. When he put it aside he opened the larger dossier—De Rochepin's. Ignoring the count's early years, he turned to a section containing a chronological listing of De Rochepin's contacts with known agents of the Soviet Union.

I should add the name of Cardinal Rossinol, he thought wryly but did not do so. Instead, Leroux decided, after the termination of current business he would invite an Italian colleague to lunch and elicit information on the cardinal with the help of a bottle of vintage Bordeaux. It would be interesting, he mused, if the Italian service had reason to suspect Rossinol of evil-doing.

From a decanter he poured a small glass of Byrrh and sipped the apéritif with appreciation, then studied the charter flight plan reluctantly provided by Charte-Aviation.

By seven thirty Leroux felt he had all the facts at his fingertips. He turned off the reading lamp, stretched and stood up. He went to the coatrack and donned an inexpensive brown raincoat and a brown felt hat whose headband was stained. Now, he felt, his appearance would provoke the count's condescension, encourage De Rochepin to feel he had the advantage in any contest of intelligence. Leroux stroked his mustache and smiled. This was an evening he was going to enjoy.

For years he had detested the sight of De Rochepin on television, loathed the sound of his voice, his venomous political posturings. Now, at long last, he was going to be the instrument of the Red Count's destruction.

Colonel Jean-Paul Leroux of the DST pulled on gloves and left his office for the corridor. He took an ancient elevator down to street level and emerged into mist that covered the windshield of his small official car. Driving from the DST parking lot, he steered into traffic speeding west along the Seine. He passed the Tuileries, the Grand Palais and UNESCO and just short of the Trocadéro turned north to Avenue Kléber. A block from the count's apartment building, Leroux guided his Peugeot to the curb, locked the car and walked the rest of the way. The doorman was sitting inside the portal, but he rose when he recognized Leroux. With a lift of his head he said quietly, "He's up there. His vehicle is disabled."

"*Bon, mon vieux. Bien réussi.*" Leroux patted the doorman's shoulder and walked down the carpet to the open elevator. After stepping inside, he closed the door and pressed the *étage* button. As the elevator slowly rose, Leroux found himself wondering if it was the means whereby De Rochepin had started the dead Carlotte Béranger on her journey to the Cemetery of St.-Vincent.

At his desk the Comte de Rochepin smoked nervously as he attempted to dictate the draft of an article he had agreed to prepare for *L'Express*. He pressed the recorder buttons and replayed his final sentence, hoping it would inspire another paragraph. His theme was *revanchisme* as demonstrated by the malevolent United States American role in Southeast Asia. The theme was one he had covered dozens of times from every conceivable angle, and another ten thousand words should have been *pro forma*. But the anticipated appearance of Inspector Delacroix seemed to have paralyzed his thinking processes, and every sentence was Sisyphean labor.

His thoughts were interrupted by the doorbell. De Rochepin glanced at his desk clock; three after eight. The inspector was reasonably prompt—for a policeman. De Rochepin ground out his cigarette and turned off the dictating machine. He stood up and smoothed the lapels of his silk dressing robe, a present received in Hanoi from NLF interpreters and guides.

It was annoying, he thought, that his *femme de ménage* had absented herself this evening, for he did not want Delacroix to appraise him as servantless, poverty-stricken nobility. He made his way to the vestibule, unchained the door and opened it.

Before him stood a man wearing a grease-stained raincoat and a cheap brown hat. "Delacroix," the man said, and presented an identification *carnet* at which De Rochepin barely glanced.

"Be good enough to enter." Closing the door, De Rochepin offered his hand. "Let me take your coat."

"Oh, I can do that, Count. I'll put it here on the chair." Delacroix rubbed his hands. "Coolish outside," he remarked and followed his host into the sitting room.

De Rochepin indicated a chair and sat on the sofa. Delacroix said, "I beg your indulgence for this intrusion."

"Not at all," De Rochepin said languidly. "I hope I may be of service."

Delacroix seated himself, glanced around admiringly and noticed the count's desk with its dictating machine. "I'm interrupting your work."

De Rochepin dismissed the thought with a wave of his hand. "Now that we are alone," he said, "may I learn the reason for your visit?"

Delacroix nodded. "As you are aware, my dear Count, our country is a veritable cesspool of narcotics."

De Rochepin swallowed. "Narcotics?"

"Surely you are aware of the laboratory network in the south?"

"I am aware of many allegations. . . ."

"Do not discount them, my dear Count. Where the authorities have been unsuccessful, your own journalistic colleagues have investigated and produced many worthwhile disclosures." He gazed blandly at his host. "That, in any case, is the background."

De Rochepin cleared his throat. "How does it concern me?"

Delacroix smiled. "In a way you would perhaps never suspect. But to broaden the perspective, let me add that from French laboratories illegal narcotics are shipped either to South America or directly to the United States. The principal and least vulnerable method has been by air." Without looking at De Rochepin he patted his pocket and glanced around vaguely.

"A cigarette?" De Rochepin said quickly.

"If I may impose further."

Opening a table drawer, De Rochepin extracted a silver box and extended it to Delacroix, who selected a cigarette, looked at its printed crest and murmured his thanks. He lighted the cigarette and sat back. After a few moments he said, "Where was I?"

286

"You were mentioning air shipment of narcotics," De Rochepin said helpfully. "But I don't—"

"Oh, yes." Delacroix nodded. "Well, for some time a certain aviation firm operating out of Paris has been under suspicion, its flights monitored. Even so, tangible evidence remained beyond our grasp."

"Inspector—" De Rochepin tried to interrupt, but Delacroix bore on.

"Then there occurred an incident which served to clinch the case, as it were. But let me go back to a particular flight, Count. It is known that approximately three weeks ago you chartered an aircraft to fly you to New York."

"Is that a crime?" De Rochepin said stiffly.

"By no means," Delacroix reassured him. "But the flight had certain unusual characteristics—an unreported landing on Long Island, for example—all giving rise to our increasing certainty that the aircraft was delivering narcotics to the United States."

De Rochepin moistened his lips with the tip of his tongue. "Surely," he said, "you do not identify me with the commission of such a crime?"

"On the contrary." Delacroix patted the count's silk-covered knee. "Certainly not. Again, permit me to digress. A few days ago there was discovered the murdered body of the stewardess who attended you on that particular flight, one Carlotte Béranger."

De Rochepin forced his face into an expression of horrified shock. "This is *true?*"

"Entirely true. Lamentably, the poor girl seems to have been slain because of her involvement in the illegal traffic. Perhaps she was a courier—or else she possessed knowledge that was dangerous to the flight crew. In any case, she is dead. And we have reason to suspect the co-pilot of her murder."

One of De Rochepin's hands rose to his throat. "How dastardly! How contemptible!"

287

"And how irreversibly mortal." Delacroix inhaled cigarette smoke and let it drift slowly from his nostrils. "The point of my visit, my dear Count, is to solicit your cooperation in trapping this ring of smugglers."

De Rochepin stared at him. "Smugglers," he repeated.

"*And* the girl's murderer."

De Rochepin opened his mouth, but no words formed. His mind was racing: If he "cooperated" against the pilot and co-pilot, details of his secret rendezvous would become vulnerable.

Delacroix said, "It is also known that Carlotte Béranger and the co-pilot shared an intimate understanding. One theory is that, because of the relationship, Carlotte was enticed into the illegal traffic, then killed to silence her."

Hoarsely, De Rochepin said, "It is most difficult to believe. Inspector, are you *certain* of your facts?"

"Entirely certain."

"Then—in what way am I involved?"

"Your testimony will be required to confirm the location at which your craft landed before continuing on to Kennedy International Airport, together with your remembrance of its reception: which members of the crew left the aircraft, for how long, and so on." Delacroix regarded his cigarette. "It is only equable that I mention the following: Charte-Aviation maintains that it was you, rather than they, who scheduled the illegal landing."

"Preposterous!" the count blurted.

Delacroix's eyebrows lifted. "Just so. Your personal testimony, my dear Count, has become essential owing to the unfortunate death of a potential witness—the Béranger woman. Otherwise"—he shrugged—"our opportunity will dematerialize."

But De Rochepin was already aware of his dilemma. One way or another he was going to be dragged into a vulgar narcotics affair—how was he to have known Charte-Aviation trafficked in drugs?—either as a witness against the crewmen or—and he felt his flesh turn cold—as a defendant charged with trafficking in company with the crew.

"You knew the late Mademoiselle Béranger?" Delacroix was saying in an absent way.

"I—I knew her—met her on that flight."

Delacroix tipped ash from his cigarette. "Another fact of interest: in her room were discovered five cigarettes such as these. I assume them to be unique?"

"Yes—the De Rochepin crest. The girl was fascinated by them. For a souvenir I supplied her with a few."

"On which leg of the flight?"

"Here to New York." Desperately, he was trying to foresee the consequences of any reply. "An impressionable young woman—I could hardly refuse her."

Delacroix spread his hands comprehendingly. "But of course you were not aware the aircraft carried heroin."

"Certainly not."

Delacroix rose as though to stretch his legs, strolled over the carpet and stopped in front of a framed Ruiz landscape on the wall. One finger touched its surface in apparent curiosity, then his hand swung the hinged frame outward. Set into the wall was a safe.

"*Alors!*" said Delacroix, turning to his host. "For your valuables, of course?"

De Rochepin had shot to his feet when the picture swung out. "Heirlooms," he said hoarsely. "My mother's jewelry."

Delacroix tapped the smooth steel surface of the safe. "Foresight," he said after a moment. "One is prudent to protect one's valuables these days."

Shocked by fear that his opium cache was to be uncovered, De Rochepin felt relief surge over him in

289

the wake of the policeman's unconcern. He sank back onto the sofa and stared at his visitor while his mind raced. Was the man a fool or genius? His mode of expression transcended his nondescript appearance, yet Delacroix believed profoundly in narcotics as the *raison* behind Carlotte's murder. Obviously the inspector was far more interested in the narcotics ring than in her unsolved death. Would it be wise to testify against the aircraft crew? How much did the two men know concerning Carlotte's off-duty hours? Was the co-pilot a married man? Had she confided to him, or anyone, her rendezvous with the Comte de Rochepin?

The count did not want to appear uncooperative to the inspector; on the contrary, he preferred to cooperate—unless by testifying against the pilots he placed himself in danger of reprisal. For they knew perfectly well that it was on *his* instructions the pre-Kennedy landing had been made. They had seen the waiting helicopter, seen their passenger borne away. . . . To all that they, in turn, could testify.

Where would it end?

The inspector, he noticed, had not replaced the painting against the wall. He stood beside it, gazing thoughtfully at the carpet underfoot.

De Rochepin also looked at the carpet, wondering what attracted the attention of the policeman. The carpet, he knew, was an unusual one, hand-loomed near Peking, and presented to him by a committee of Revolutionary Television and Radio Workers after a month-long documentary filming in the People's Republic. He remembered with professional pride the excellence of his filmed interviews with Chou and Mao and Lin, even though the Lin Piao segment had later to be excised following the marshal's mysterious flight and death.

Delacroix was kneeling. His right thumb touched the

carpet surface, twirled strands of wool between thumb and index finger and lifted a puff of nap. The inspector gazed at it under the lamp, muttered inaudibly and dropped the lint to the floor.

De Rochepin's eyes flashed to the spot where Carlotte died. No trace of that remained. Carefully he had swept and cleansed the area. Surely, nothing visible—

"I suppose," said Delacroix, "there are few carpets of this quality in France."

"In the world." De Rochepin let his slippered foot glide over the surface. "By now, two, perhaps three others may have been loomed, but I do not think they have yet left China. If they ever leave."

"Interesting," the inspector mused. "Most interesting. And disturbing."

"Disturbing?" Again fear tightened his throat. "How so, Inspector?"

Delacroix returned to his chair, seated himself and looked down at the rug. "As you know I did not seek your assistance to determine the solution of a violent crime. Murder is not my *métier*—narcotics constitute my professional interest."

"So you said."

"Yet. . . ." He touched one side of his mustache absently.

"Inspector Delacroix," De Rochepin said sharply, "you may be entirely frank with me."

Delacroix shrugged resignedly. "Very well. You, of course, were unaware of Charte-Aviation's profitable sideline."

"Utterly unaware."

"I believe you. But the death of the stewardess is inextricably involved in the smuggling affair. Man to man, Count—and you may depend upon my discretion—were you Carlotte's lover?"

De Rochepin felt blood drain from his cheeks. "Never. I deny the association."

291

"Then, of course, the little cabbage was never here—" He gestured across the room.

De Rochepin hesitated. "Why do you ask?"

"Count, would you permit a technical examination of your premises?"

"Technical?" De Rochepin husked. "I do not entirely understand your usage of the word."

"Laboratory technicians. Fingerprint types, for example." His gaze lowered to the carpet. "I will again be, perhaps, indiscreet—and permit me to reassert that my interest lies not in the area of violent crime, but in narcotics traffic."

De Rochepin swallowed with difficulty. "Proceed."

"Discovered on the shoes of the dead woman was a quantity of lint from dyed wool. Technical scrutiny showed this wool to be of the sort used in high-grade carpeting and rugs. Chinese wool, to be precise, holding traces of vegetable dye such as is used by Chinese weavers." He smoothed his mustache.

"What are you saying?" De Rochepin cried.

"Let me return to my question."

De Rochepin blinked. "What question?"

"An examination of your apartment—this carpeting, for instance. Would you?"

"*Why*?" De Rochepin nearly sobbed.

"To authenticate, once and for all, that the lint on Béranger's shoes did not come from this room." His voice was patient, but he bore on. "You must understand, my dear Count, that your testimony against the smugglers will hold up only if you are an unimpeachable witness. To put it another way: Should the defense be able to prove Carlotte was ever here, it could allege intimacy between the two of you, contaminate your testimony, cast doubt upon your motives as regards the two accused smugglers."

De Rochepin closed his eyes. How nonsensical it all

292

was; he was being trapped not through his own errors, but through the crimes of others. In a barely audible voice he said, "I cannot permit such an examination."

"What?"

De Rochepin's head moved loosely. "No," he muttered. "Never."

Sitting back in his chair, Delacroix stared at De Rochepin in apparent surprise. One hand lifted and scratched the side of his face. "Count—do you understand the difficult position you place me in?"

"I understand only that I will never permit your *flics* to paw through my possessions. *Jamais!*"

"Then," said Delacroix in tones of regret, "you are as much as admitting your involvement in the young woman's death."

"I admit nothing!" His world was disintegrating into plunging boulders; around him rubble crashed, reverberated. He found that he was utterly unable to think. Where was the clarity of mind that, until now, had always been his strongest point?

Through a haze he saw Delacroix rise and stroll around the room's perimeter. What was the man *doing?*

In the silence De Rochepin decided he would never stand in the box accused of murder. If he could open the wall safe, he would dissolve opium in alcohol, inject the tincture and die without pain. Without disgrace.

Halting, Delacroix turned to him. Until now De Rochepin had not noticed how deep and penetrating were his eyes.

"There may yet be a means of salvation," said Delacroix in a not-unfriendly voice.

"Salvation?" De Rochepin gasped. "How? What can I do, Inspector?"

"You can help me," Delacroix said simply. "In a related matter."

"*What* related matter?"

Delacroix lifted one hand. "My primary interest is not domestic murder, but international affairs."

"How international affairs? You are not going to tell me you come from the Quai d'Orsay?"

"I protect the Foreign Ministry," said Delacroix, "from its own indiscretions." He drew his chair in front of De Rochepin and sat down, leaned forward until their faces were only a foot apart. "I offer you salvation, Comte de Rochepin. I am empowered to overlook your murder of Carlotte Béranger in return for your full and complete cooperation. A great deal is known of you, believe me. For example, the reason you were dismissed from St.-Cyr. Your brother, Gérard, by the way, was a classmate of mine at St.-Cyr. Gérard, a general of the Air Force! As for you, you have been long known in certain official quarters as a conscious agent of the Soviet Union, apologist, propagandist, agent spotter—man-of-all-work. If you think that we cannot convict you as a murderer and send you to the guillotine, then we can certainly convict you for trafficking in drugs."

"You have no witnesses," he said weakly.

"On the contrary. To save their own skins, the pilot and co-pilot are prepared to testify concerning your charter flight. However, you and I know that in actuality you would never be so stupid as to hazard your career in such an undertaking." His eyes lifted to the wall safe. "An addict is never a successful distributor of drugs."

"Then you *know?*" De Rochepin whispered.

"I will tell you this: Your apartment has been legally searched. There is a quantity of opium in your safe. The wool from this carpet matches the lint in Carlotte's shoes. One way or the other, my dear Count, you will be tried, and at the least imprisoned." He saw with satisfaction the count's pallid face.

De Rochepin tried to still his twitching lips. "You are from the DST!" he babbled.

"As you say—of the Direction de la Surveillance du Territoire. As such, I am able to offer you the continuance of your way of life in return for cooperation." His voice hardened. "Full and complete cooperation, Count. Nothing less is acceptable. Anything less from you will terminate our understanding." Rising, he went over to the desk, brought back the dictating machine. He set it beside De Rochepin and turned it on. "My first question," he said, "is the following: Who is your Soviet handler?"

Eyes closed, lips trembling, De Rochepin blurted, "Marcel. He is Russian, but he uses that cover name."

"How often do you have contact?"

"Every Thursday night."

"Where?"

"There is a sequence of eight rendezvous."

"We will return to Marcel. What was the purpose of your charter flight?"

"I was ordered to contact an agent in New York."

"His name?"

"Cerf. Edward Cerf."

"Why?"

"In connection with the disappearance of Klaus Werber's stepdaughter."

"Explain."

"The girl, Annalise Bauer, discovered that Werber—" His mouth opened and closed, opened again, but he seemed to be unable to continue.

"That Werber is also an agent of the Soviet Union," Delacroix supplied.

Dumbly, De Rochepin nodded.

"Confirm."

"Yes."

"Say it," he said relentlessly.

"She discovered that the German Foreign Minister is an agent of the Soviet Union."

"In the same category as yourself."

"Yes. Of the political category."

"And why was this contact with Cerf necessary?"

Dully, De Rochepin said, "The girl fled to America. Cerf's people were supposed to locate her."

"And then?"

"Liquidate her."

"In short, murder her."

"She was to be killed."

"In order to preserve the *persona* of Klaus Werber."

"Yes."

Delacroix grunted, turned off the set and got up. He went to the wall safe, turned the combination and opened it. From the recess he drew out a plastic bag containing a fist-size lump of material, oily black and streaked with whorls of brown. His fingers entered the bag, twisted off a pinch and set it on the desk. He pocketed the bag.

De Rochepin stared at the opium on the desk. It was smaller than a thimble, a few nights' supply. Delacroix picked up the telephone, dialed and spoke. "Jules," he said, "the count agrees to cooperate. I will spend the night here and the next several days. In the morning I will have material to be transcribed. Bring the recorder and tapes when you come." He hung up and sat down behind the desk, helped himself to one of the count's monogrammed cigarettes. Lighting it, he said, "You were always vain, De Rochepin—the monogram of your crest identified you. From that point, inculpating you was routine."

De Rochepin squeezed his eyelids as though he had been struck.

"That," Delacroix remarked, "and the girl's cupidity. Why did you kill her?"

"She would have blackmailed me." Opening his eyes,

De Rochepin gestured at the safe. Delacroix got up and thrust his hand into the tubular recess, drew out something flat that glinted in the light. It was, he saw, a gold cigarette case engraved with De Rochepin's crest. One corner was so badly dented he had to force the sides apart. "No matter," he said and returned to the desk where he placed the case under the lamp. Its glitter seared De Rochepin's eyes until he looked away.

"Let us continue," said Delacroix, extinguishing the cigarette. He took another from his breast pocket and lighted it, "Activate the machine, my dear Count."

Mechanically, De Rochepin complied.

"Now," Delacroix said, "you have identified yourself, Klaus Werber and Edward Cerf as agents of the Soviet Union. Tell me about Eugene Cardinal Rossinol, whom you interviewed this afternoon."

Hopelessly, De Rochepin replied, no longer recognizing his own voice. "The Cardinal is one of us."

"Excellent. Now tell me how the Soviets were able to recruit a Prince of the Church."

"He was a priest at the time," said De Rochepin listlessly. "Captured in the Spanish Civil War."

"You were there?"

"In Spain, yes, but I did not know of Rossinol until much later."

"You have not explained the method of his recruitment."

De Rochepin smiled thinly. "It was that or a bullet in the head. He saved his life—as I am saving mine."

By midnight they had run out of dictating bands. Leroux allowed the Count to take a bead of opium into his bedroom, looked in on him a short while later and saw De Rochepin in drugged sleep, face pale as the pillow on which he lay.

Leroux returned to the desk and telephoned his aide. "Jules," he said, "you had better come over now. The sooner this material is transcribed, the sooner I will be able to decide how to handle it." He muffled a yawn, stroked the side of his face. "Bring my toothbrush and razor."

"Surely," said Jules, "you will inform the minister?"

"The minister," said Jean-Paul Leroux, "has been identified by our canary as a man with certain secrets to hide. So if the transcripts go to anyone, it will be to the President of the Republic alone."

"Yes, my Colonel. I come at once."

Leroux hung up, poured Hine from a decanter and sipped enough to moisten his aching throat. According to De Rochepin, Annalise Bauer had managed to return to Europe. Still in effect were Soviet orders to liquidate her. So the problem, he thought, was to protect her life without alerting the German Service and through the BfV, the German Foreign Minister.

Where had she gone? he wondered as he turned on the dictating machine for replay.

Where could she take refuge?

31

DOV APELBAUM sat in a modern tubular steel chair and slowly ate a tangerine as he looked through the waiting-room window at aircraft landing and taking off from Tegelhof's airstrip. The waiting room was for private aircraft passengers and pilots, and Apelbaum knew that Klaus Werber would have to pass through it when he arrived.

Runway lights glowed through the deepening dusk,

giving an eerie cast to the moving planes. One by one Apelbaum collected seeds in his palm and deposited them in the ashtray beside his chair. He wiped hands and mouth with a handkerchief, and as he was tucking it away, he heard the tower announce arrival of Luftwaffe Martin 109 from Köln.

Removing his glasses, he saw the twin-engined Martin touch the end of the hardtop and speed smoothly along. Its propellers reversed, spraying runway water along the fuselage, momentarily screening the stabilizer's Maltese cross. The aircraft slowed, braked, and turned off the runway toward the private terminal. Apelbaum replaced his glasses and unfolded a copy of the *Berliner-Tageblatt*. He was reading it when a tall man entered through the arrival gate and strode past the lounge to the exit door. The man wore a black felt hat and a black raincoat, but Apelbaum easily recognized his face. From his chair he could see the man get into a taxi and drive away. Apelbaum folded his paper, placed tangerine rind in the ashtray and went to a telephone. He dialed, heard Regester's cautious voice and said, "The merchandise arrived."

"Accompanied?"

"No. A single unit."

"Excellent. Your advice is appreciated."

Apelbaum left the building and walked to his rented BMW. Driving away from Tegelhof, he turned onto Müller Strasse, following it as far as Potsdamer Strasse. Now he headed south beside the Wall toward the Tiergarten. He drove single-mindedly, oblivious of everything but the gray cinderblock wall on his left, topped with barbed-wire rolls and jagged glass embedded in cement. When he drove over the Spree bridge, he noticed the oyster shaped Kongresshalle on his right, then the Brandenburg Gate's Doric columns bathed in pale, thin light.

They won't even pay for proper illumination of their

299

prize, he thought; then it was hidden from sight by trees of the Tiergarten.

Apelbaum drove three blocks farther, and now there was only the open space of the park thinly spotted with trees. Occasional lightoliers spread light over bus stops and waiting benches. On one of them sat a man in a tan trench coat. He wore a hat, and across his thighs lay an umbrella.

Apelbaum steered toward the curb, braked, and the man left the bench to walk slowly toward the car. He placed his hands on the door sill, and Apelbaum said, "Werber arrived on schedule."

"I know," Lakka said. "He passed me not three minutes ago."

"The girl is already there?"

He nodded. "At the Zell. Waiting."

"Get in," Apelbaum told him.

"I was to—" Lakka began.

"Get in," Apelbaum repeated. "Werber's deranged. God knows what he'll do."

Quickly Lakka rounded the car and got in the other side. "The taxi left him off a block ahead," he told Apelbaum.

The BMW's headlights went off. Slowly it crept forward, hugging the curb.

"Any Soviet surveillance?" Apelbaum asked.

"None."

"That's bad, I don't like it."

"Neither do I," said Lakka peering toward a dim light beyond the trees. "We're depending on them."

"Damn it! Where are they?" He felt Lakka grip his arm.

"There's Werber now—over there—walking toward the Zell. Better stop here."

"I see the *ben zonah*," Apelbaum said hoarsely, braked and rolled down his window. From the pocket of his raincoat he drew a Sauer double-action pistol and placed it on his lap.

300

Lakka grunted. "If it comes to that, I'll use the pistol."

Apelbaum licked dry lips. "I don't want her to get hurt. I've been trying to tell myself there was another way—a better way—to get him here, but it always came back to her. Now I'm sick with fear."

Lakka touched the dash clock's dial. "It's almost eight," he said in a tight, strained voice. "God help us all."

Once, during the afternoon, she had driven past the Café Zell, slowed to look it over and continued on as far as the barbed-wire barrier across the street. Beyond stood Brandenburger Tor, gray-black and bullet-pocked, dominating the broad and open *Platz*. Engine running, she had sat in the car awhile, then turned around and driven back to the hotel.

After dark she returned to the Zell and took an outside table twenty yards from the café's entrance lights and shadowed by an overhead umbrella. She sat facing the café, her back toward the sidewalk and the street, ordered *Kaffee mit Kognak* from the waiter and sipped it sparingly when it arrived. It was almost eight o'clock, her wristwatch showed, and she had been in position for nearly twenty minutes. The air was cold, and a breeze moved branches in the trees. She dug her hands into the pockets of her coat to warm them; Levis protected her legs, but her ankles were bare, her feet wore only sandals. Lifting the little cup, she sipped again, feeling warmth flow outward from her throat.

Where was he? she wondered. From sounds inside the Zell she knew it held at least a dozen people. Today the grounds where she waited now alone were filled with tourists, sightseers craning toward the Brandenburger Tor, cameras clicking at the Soviet War Memorial, drinking, laughing. A holiday mood.

The night was different.

Beyond the Wall, a few hundred meters to the right of the Tor's stark façade, unlighted, was the bunker where Hitler died. She must be looking almost toward it, she thought, and shivered.

Would Klaus Werber come?

She had been told not to be nervous, to avoid looking around for surveillants, for that would cause suspicion. She was to stay where she was, immobile. Until Klaus came.

Somewhere in the night there were watchers; of that much she was sure. Her ears strained, expecting the sound of footsteps; but the café door opened, and a couple came out with a burst of music from the record player. The door closed, cutting off the music. Then, in the parking lot beyond the Zell, an engine started. Headlights streaked across the trees as the car turned around. It accelerated forward, took the street in a rocking skid and whined away toward the center of Berlin.

Again, she was alone.

She pulled her hand from its warm pocket and looked at her wristwatch dial. Just eight o'clock. Suddenly she felt weak, her limbs enormously heavy. Fear spread through her body, draining its strength. And then she heard the sound of footsteps coming from behind.

As Klaus Werber strode toward the Zell, he saw a car leave, accelerating rapidly toward him. Before its headlights swept past, he shielded his face with one arm, thankful for the concealment of his unaccustomed hat. He blinked from the sudden light, peered at the café again and found he could not see as distinctly as before. He glanced at the Soviet War Memorial, noticing the honor guard before it, and saw ahead the Brandenburger Tor surmounted by its three red flags. Werber's attention returned to the Café Zell,

302

and he wondered once more why Anna had chosen it for their rendezvous. He had taken her there with Freda a few times on summer afternoons because of the nearness to the Kongresshalle, where the Bundestag was meeting. So perhaps for her the association was a sentimental one. Or it could be a place she remembered as isolated, where crowds would not eye him—and her. She was not, after all, a Berliner and could not be expected to know the city's many quiet and intimate meeting places.

Her life, until London, had been entirely sheltered, Werber mused. She knew nothing of the proletarian struggle, the workers' war against the exploitive classes, the inborn fallacies of capitalism. Why should she? All her life she had been screened from Socialist reality by her father's money, by Freda's obsessive care. The inbred Swiss bourgeoisie.

A man like myself, he thought, is as alien to her as a creature from Mars. Would he tell her the truth of his birth, the names he had used, the places he had fought—and killed?

To what purpose? he wondered. Merely to see the revulsion on her face, the recoil of her body as though he were something unclean, unworthy?

Unworthy? I am more than worthy of her, he told himself. It is she, on balance, who is unworthy of me. She is no more than a pretty face, a boyish figure. Her only charm is youth. Yet I am here because she summoned me. Here because I had to come.

He could see the café door, hear music behind the oaken entrance. At the walk he stopped and gazed the length of the avenue to the barbed-wire fence with its movable section to admit the War Memorial guards. He could see the strands silhouetted against light on the Brandenburger Tor beyond, the only open section in the Wall for hundreds of meters on either side.

Klaus Werber stared at it. His eyes shifted to the

dark wall, the symbol of division between one way of life and another, and then he began to walk toward the café door.

He was halfway to it when he heard a woman's voice. She called one word: *"Hier!"*

Halting, he peered toward the dark tables outside the building. All were empty but one. At it sat a figure.

"Anna!" he called. "Is it you?" He left the walk and began striding toward her table. Nearing it, he saw that her face was hidden in the shadows; no, her back was to him. Reaching the table, he bent to get under the outspread umbrella and sat down. She was wearing a large floppy cap, brim set low on her forehead. He gazed at the side of her face and felt his throat thicken. "Anna," he whispered. "Look at me, *Liebchen*."

Slowly, she turned. Werber stared fixedly, unbelievingly. The face was youthful, framed with hair like Anna's, but the woman was not Anna. Shock froze him. His mouth opened, and he stared. "Who are you?"

"A friend of Anna's," Zarah Engstrom said.

"Where is she? Is this some kind of trick?" He began to rise, but her hand grasped his arm. "Wait," she said, "there is no trick."

Slowly Werber sat down.

"I have a car," Zarah told him. "I will take you to her."

"Why did she send you?"

"She was uncertain of your attitude, Herr Minister. To be blunt, she was afraid."

Werber swallowed. "Afraid? Why should she be afraid?"

Zarah lifted her cup and sipped the dregs of her cold coffee. Her instructions were to keep him there as long as possible, delay until Werber had been seen. "Aren't you being ingenuous, Herr Minister? She fled in fear of her life. For weeks she was hiding from, let

304

us say, certain persons who sought her. Is it so unreasonable that, once back in Germany, she would take precautions?"

His mind was functioning again, recovering from the shock of substitution. Dimly he was aware of danger. But what danger did the woman represent? No, he must regain control of the situation.

"I am to take you to her," Zarah said. "But we must come to an understanding."

"An understanding? In what way?"

"The terms, of course. Anna depends upon me to clarify them."

"Tell me what they are."

"My car is parked beyond the café. I have been sitting here a long time, and I am cold. Let us go to my car."

"Very well. But the terms?"

Zarah rose and began walking toward the parking lot. With a shrug, Werber followed, thinking there was no harm in holding the discussion there, out of the cold.

They walked together across the lawn in front of the café, and Zarah was aware of the entrance door opening. Another couple leaving, she thought briefly, ardent with wine and ready to make love. She crossed the front of the café as the door closed, continued on toward the parking area, Werber a pace or two behind her. She walked into the darkness toward her car, hearing footsteps on the gravel behind her. Reaching the side of her car, she turned to Werber and said, "Get in on the other side, Herr Minister. Then we will talk."

With a shrug, he turned and walked toward the rear.

From behind came a guttural call: *"Klaus!"*

Werber froze. Turning, he saw two familiar figures silhouetted by the lights of the café. "Yakov!" he called, and as Zarah turned, she saw the pair for the first time, a pistol in the hand of one. It was pointing at her. She saw a burst of flame blot out the gun, felt a sharp impact and staggered. Pain radiated outward, and she staggered against the car. Her fading hearing carried the sound of two more shots, but now she was beyond pain. Vision and hearing ended. She died before her body struck the ground.

Werber stared unbelievingly at the fallen body, at the Russians walking toward him. "Come with us, Herr Minister," said Gleb Kalugin as he pocketed the automatic. "You have been less than frank with us in recent days. The girl is dead, so your troubles are over."

Gorytsev took Werber's arm and pulled him away, toward another car. "But"—Werber burbled—"it wasn't—wasn't Annalise."

"No?" said Kalugin blandly. "Then the problem has lesser dimensions. On your own you do not act intelligently, Klaus, so we came to save you from yourself."

"But the girl?" He glanced back, but Yakov Gorytsev forced him into the Soviet's car. Kalugin drove, Werber seated between them, as they left the parking area, headlights dark, and turned onto the street, away from the Brandenburger Tor, the barbed-wire rolls. Kalugin switched on the headlights, and Werber noticed a darkened BMW parked beyond the Café Zell.

Gorytsev said, "You will return to Bonn without delay. You will forget what happened. Do you understand?" he ended harshly.

Rigidly, Werber nodded.

The car neared the lights of Berlin, steering toward Tempelhof.

Seated in the darkness of his rented BMW, Dov Apelbaum said, "I have the feeling something has gone wrong. You saw the car that passed us?"

Lakka nodded.

"It should have been Zarah's, but it was not."

Lakka swallowed. For the first time in weeks he felt the clutch of fear. "All right?" he said hoarsely. "Perhaps they only went into the café to warm themselves while they talked."

Apelbaum started the engine. "That was not the plan," he said shortly, and slid the car into gear.

As he turned into the lot, he saw Zarah's car, her body lying beside it. Lakka saw it, too, and burst from the BMW to race toward his daughter's body. Apelbaum's throat constricted. Braking quickly, he shut off his lights and joined Lakka, who was cradling his daughter's head in his arms, sobbing. Tightly, Apelbaum said, "Perhaps she is not dead?"

"No. Dead. She is dead. Dead, dead, *dead!*" His anguished voice rose, and he stared at Apelbaum, tears streaming from his eyes.

"There may still be time to stop him," Apelbaum said, took Zarah's legs and helped her father lift the dead woman into the back seat. "Take her to a hospital," he said. "I'll go to the Gehrhus and see what we can do about Werber."

"Werber," Lakka said chokingly. "I want only to kill him with my own hands."

Apelbaum left Lakka sobbing behind the wheel of Zarah's car, ran back to his own and backed rapidly out of the lot, wheels tearing up a spray of gravel. Had they gone to Tegel, Gatow or Tempelhof? he wondered. And what could be done now, after the fact?

He drove with controlled fury through central Berlin toward the Grunewald, stopping at a phone kiosk long enough to telephone Regester and tell him briefly what had happened.

As Apelbaum turned through the Gehrhus' gate, he saw the three of them waiting for him on the steps: Regester, Annalise and Neal Thorpe. Quickly they got into the car, and Anna said dully, "They killed her."

"They killed her," Apelbaum grated. "Alton, what can we do?"

Regester turned to Annalise Bauer. "She died in your place, Anna. You know that."

"I know."

"So everything depends on you."

Swallowing, she shook her head. "I don't know what to do. I'm afraid."

Thorpe said sharply, "You've got to tell what you know."

The car was silent but for the smooth running of the engine.

Finally she shook her head, "I don't want to die," she whispered. "I—I can't do it. I just want to see my mother."

Incredulously, Thorpe said, "You mean—just go home—live there with—with Werber?"

Eyes welling with tears, she said, "I'm afraid to do anything else. Even if I told what I know, who would believe me?"

"God damn you!" Thorpe exploded. "Because of you people have been killed, and now—"

Regester gripped his arm. "That's enough, Neal. Anna, if that's the way you feel, you'd better go home."

To Thorpe he said, "It has to be her decision."

Apelbaum grunted. "Should we try to stop Werber?"

"Where?" Regester said. "How? We've lost too much time. He could be driving back or on a plane by now."

Thorpe said, "Then it's hopeless."

No one said anything.

After a while Regester said, "I'll call a taxi for Anna."

Thorpe stared at her with contempt. She avoided his eyes, opened the door and got out. He saw her walk slowly up the steps into the hotel.

Apelbaum said, "Don't blame her too much, Neal.

She's been brought up in a soft life. She isn't like the rest of us."

"What kind of life can she have," he grated, "living there with Werber—knowing what he is, what he's done?"

Regester opened the door. "What can be worse than living always in fear?" He got out of the car and followed Anna into the hotel.

Thorpe looked at the Shin Bet officer. "What now?"

"I suppose," Apelbaum said heavily, "we go our separate ways."

"Having failed."

Apelbaum nodded. "Having failed." His voice was remote.

Thorpe stared at the hotel's lighted entrance. "I don't want to see her," he said. "I'm accused of killing a man because of her. And I killed a man because of her. The whole thing—" His voice choked and he turned away.

"All of us," said Apelbaum, "did what we thought was right. But Werber was always the Soviets' man. And they take care of their own. Believe me, I know."

"Unlike CIA," Thorpe said thinly. "Damn them, too."

"I'll try to find Lakka," Apelbaum said. 'Want to go with me?"

"How the hell can I face him?"

"Someone has to." He put the car in gear, turned around in the drive, and together they drove through the quiet streets of the Grunewald. .

Epilogue

AS dawn touched the gray façade of Vatican City Eugene Cardinal Rossinol donned vestments and chasuble and prepared to celebrate early mass in the Sistine Chapel.

On eastern Long Island, at eight thirty, servants of Edward Cerf found their corpulent master dead in his bed. He had died of heart disease in his sleep.

Toward noon, a middle-aged émigré couple entered New York's Port Authority station and took adjoining seats on a bus whose destination was Kansas City.

In Paris, the Comte de Rochepin woke from his drugged sleep, wondering whether his interrogation was all a dream, heard men talking in his living room, and realized it was not. For him, the count knew, the worst still lay ahead.

And from an Orly taxi two men entered the American embassy's Consular Section, walked across the marble floor and spoke briefly with the receptionist. They had flown in from Tempelhof, and both were haggard from lack of sleep. They joined others waiting on benches and remained silent until the receptionist announced that the legal attaché would see them.

For all of them, Thorpe thought, as he entered the embassy elevator, the ending had come in Berlin.

Except Klaus Werber, who was, as the saying went, home free.